THE CALIFORNIANS

ALSO BY BRIAN CASTLEBERRY

Nine Shiny Objects

THE
CALIFORNIANS

A NOVEL

BRIAN CASTLEBERRY

MARINER BOOKS
New York   Boston

THE CALIFORNIANS. Copyright © 2025 by Brian Castleberry. All rights reserved. Printed in the United States of America. No part of this book may be used or reproduced in any manner whatsoever without written permission except in the case of brief quotations embodied in critical articles and reviews. For information, address HarperCollins Publishers, 195 Broadway, New York, NY 10007.

HarperCollins books may be purchased for educational, business, or sales promotional use. For information, please email the Special Markets Department at SPsales@harpercollins.com.

FIRST EDITION

Designed by Emily Snyder

Library of Congress Cataloging-in-Publication Data has been applied for.

ISBN 978-0-06-321333-3

24 25 26 27 28 LBC 5 4 3 2 1

For Philip Mitchell

And when he asked the angels what these fires were, he learned that these were the fires that would kindle and eventually consume the world: one is the fire of falsehood, when we do not fulfill what we promised in baptism and renounce Satan and all of his works; another is the fire of avarice, when we place our love of worldly riches before our love of the riches of heaven; the third is the fire of discord, when we do not fear to offend the souls of our neighbors even in superficial matters; and the fourth fire is irreverence, when we think it nothing to despoil and defraud those weaker than ourselves. Little by little, the fires merged together and became one immense conflagration.

—THE VENERABLE BEDE, 731 CE

Stiegl & Harlan Family Tree

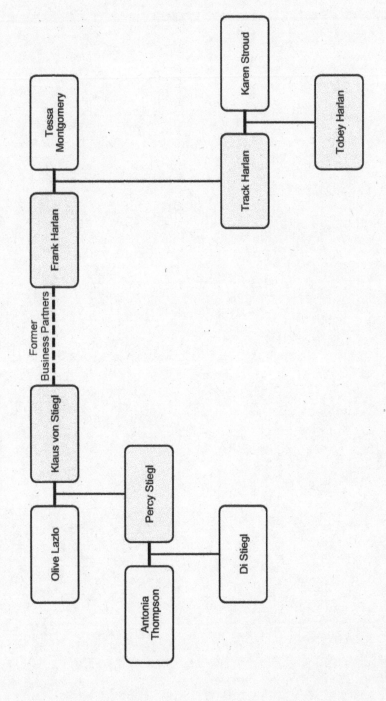

THE CALIFORNIANS

TOBEY HARLAN

2024

I N A COUPLE of days, Tobey Harlan will steal from the walls of his father's home three large paintings by Di Stiegl titled *Brackett #1* and *Dream of Fire A & B*, valued in the tens of millions and assumed by collectors to have been lost or destroyed thirty years prior, when the artist abruptly left Los Angeles for Toronto, where she still resides.

Tobey will be arrested in Eugene, Oregon, with the Brackett painting tacked to the wall of the extended-stay hotel room he will book using his real name after having requested to pay with a cryptocurrency he knows nothing about. The other two paintings, concerned with the climate crisis and so of special interest to those who have followed Ms. Stiegl's work in the twenty-first century, will be tracked to a Luxembourg freeport, where they will have been stored by the billionaire tech investor Osip Yander after a black-market sale facilitated by Mr. Yander's personal assistant, Tobey Harlan's half-brother, James.

But first came the evacuation of Tinsley, California, a town forgotten as soon as the nation heard its name. That day, halfway through lunch, Tobey Harlan rushed with everyone else from the Bad Bean Café, where he waited tables. Out in the apocalyptic parking lot, he watched a massive cloud of smoke turning in the air like new mountains forming from the Earth's crust and wondered what he'd done with his life. Somehow the sun was still overhead doing its regular business, ho-hum, but the particulate-heavy wind was coming right at his eyes and lungs. In an odd way it seemed personal.

Two spaces over, Tobey's fellow server Natalia sat in her car on the phone crying and slamming the butt of her hand on the wheel. The kitchen staff all leaped into the same Corolla and squealed from the parking lot. Vic the Dick, Tobey's boss, locked the steel back door of the restaurant as he shouted into his phone about picking up the kids from school and meeting at a truck stop outside Sacramento. The Bad Bean's towering sign appeared to sway in the wind. And Tobey still stood there like a goon, flipping his keys around on the ring with an index finger, frighteningly at ease. Numb.

Eventually, he dropped into the car, turned over the engine, and stared again at that growing cloud, miles wide, unfathomably high. It had its own peaks and whorls and plumes; it was mesmerizing. His stereo, always with the slow Bluetooth connection, returned to the podcast he'd been listening to that morning: ". . . is really a completely different story than the book. Kubrick left out . . ." Tobey shut off the volume. In the whooshing silence he grabbed the short glass pipe from his glovebox and thumbed his Bic. He took a long drag, held it a moment, and took another without exhaling. To his left, Vic the Dick sat in his shiny SUV, still on the phone, but now glaring down at Tobey in judgment before jerking the SUV back and launching out into the street without pausing to look for oncoming cars. "Okay," Tobey said to himself. "All right."

In college, before everything went south, he'd taken an introductory course on film studies in which the professor devoted the first two weeks to silent films. They watched Chaplin's *Gold Rush*, which Tobey slept through from nearly start to finish, but also the movie *Hans & Greta*, directed by the same guy who would later make Tobey's grandfather's TV show, *Brackett*. Tobey had stayed awake for that one, even brought a cup of coffee, and though parts were a little corny, the big fire scene that decimated the forest where Greta and Hans had built their home had made a big impression. It was gripping, really—as good as anything in a twenty-first century action movie. And Tobey being Tobey, his excitement couldn't help but lead to embarrassment. When the lights went up and the professor asked what the hundred slumped-over students thought of the film, Tobey had raised his hand and said, in his best version of an intellectual, "Feels like a statement about the dangers of climate change."

The professor, a smug, bespectacled, bearded guy with tattoos and a "cool prof" attitude, had leaned against his lectern, cleared his throat, and said, "This picture is from 1928."

Sniggers, whispers. "Well," Tobey said, "I mean it's, like, prescient?"

Well, college. That was a whole other thing . . .

A public relations major in his junior year, cruising a B+ average, he had decided to make a little spending money selling acid. The afternoon the UC police came knocking, he'd grabbed up the Homer Simpson–printed sheets from his mini fridge, leapt out the first-floor window, and run at top speed, first just away and then to a parking lot, where in an inhuman terror he had pushed over a religious studies PhD candidate, grabbed her keys, and shot away in her Jetta, letting sheet after sheet of acid vacate the Ziploc through the half-open driver's-side window. By the time campus police were behind him, by the time he'd wrecked the Jetta into a City of Davis Police vehicle that turned into his path, he had parted ways with the evidence of his first crime and multiplied that of his second. Even with all the force of Track Harlan's money and attorneys, the University of California expelled him and a jury of his peers found him guilty of assault and grand theft and even conspiracy to obstruct justice. He was given three to five and served a little over two of them.

Hence waiting tables in Tinsley, even as the Willows Fire, bigger than Cincinnati, loomed along the ridge outside his apartment window for nearly a week. Hence—*hence*? Why was he thinking like some Shakespearean in tights? He snuffed down the bowl of his pipe with his thumb and—the last to arrive and last to leave—made his escape.

———————

THE HIGHWAY, HE discovered, was at a standstill; the on-ramp traffic stalled a quarter mile down Jacinto. He would have to drive all the way through town, hitting all the stoplights in the world.

He tried calling Sophie but it went straight to voicemail. He tried James and got the same. Of course he'd already missed a call from his father, Track, who had been calling two or three times a day trying to get him to evacuate early, reminding him to, quote, pull his head out of his ass and come down to the house and watch the dogs while they—Track and the fourth wife, Judith—were out of town.

Tobey had tried to explain that if he evacuated early he'd lose his job. But Track likely didn't see his job as an actual job. In a very real way, his father had never worked in his life; money had grown on trees, or at least out of the sand around Palm Springs and Palm Desert, where his own father had purchased acres and acres of property way back in the 1950s and '60s, land that Track came along and cut into pieces for development, using the property to buy more land and commercial real estate, which he would later sell to buy more, etc. It was a widely held belief in the family that Track didn't even know how to balance a checkbook. He could hire accountants and lawyers and contractors for everything—didn't even take a hand in the design of his signature property development, Harlan Estates, had hired some kid still in graduate school to draft the architectural plans, paying him under the table only a fraction of what would have gone to a reputable firm. Susan, James's sister, Tobey's half-sister, believed that little cost-cutting measure was only the tip of the shady iceberg. "He's a criminal, Tobey," she'd said last time she visited, so long ago Tobey himself was still relatively fresh out of prison. "And not just one fuck-up. We're talking a lifetime of socially acceptable white-collar shit that one day is going to catch up to him. Learn from us and keep your distance."

Susan and James didn't really talk to their father anymore. But his business dealings had little to do with that rift. Track had started watching Fox News when no one was paying attention, and suddenly his grown children were receiving long, hyperventilating emails about Benghazi and Long Island drug gangs and "the real agenda of BLM" and finally, somehow the breaking point, "woke fascism." Tobey had gotten the same emails but had only shrugged. "There's no talking to him about this stuff," he'd told Susan. "Better to ignore it." But his half-siblings had known the man far longer, and must have felt more of a betrayal. They had argued with him for a year or two and then finally cut off communication.

Most irritating for Tobey, Track had been won over to the inexplicable position that climate science was a hoax, an idea he'd specifically made fun of when Tobey was still a teenager. Back then they watched Al Gore's movie together like a family—Tobey, Track, and Judith—and all got into recycling and meatless Mondays and fuel-efficient vehicles. In the distant past, the man had called himself an "Obama Republican," whatever that meant. And now, a few weeks ago, when Tobey had tried to connect last year's floods in Palm Springs to an impending climate catastrophe, his father had said two words: "Chinese propaganda." Yeesh.

As always, Track answered as if the phone had awakened him from a deep and foggy sleep: "Hallo?"

"Dad, it's me. They're evacuating us."

"And you're finally coming here?"

"Um, I guess so. I'm picking up Gray."

"Gray?"

Tobey dodged a pickup that lurched over into his lane.

"Oh the cat? You sure you got time for it?"

"I have to. She's Sophie's cat." He cut a left into his neighborhood. "And anyway she's a cat? A living being?"

"Uh-huh. Don't do anything stupid. There are other cats in the world." Track grunted. Tobey was his youngest, by eight years, from the third marriage (James and Susan from the second). Tobey's mother had remarried and moved to Wichita and was the only well-adjusted adult Tobey knew. Well, maybe Susan, an archeologist out in Virginia. "Judith's making tacos," Track added. "I'll be sure there's plenty."

"Uh, okay."

"We'll be out of town this weekend, like I said." A conference in Vegas, he'd explained half a dozen times in the last week. "You'll have the place to yourself."

Even if traffic was light, it took eight hours to drive to Palm Springs. "Cool," Tobey said. "Listen, Dad, I gotta go."

"You know where the extra key is. Don't worry about the dogs. If they wake us it's A-OK."

The dogs. Fuck. All those German shepherds. Judith ran a business literally called Judith's German Shepherds which dealt only with the training of German shepherds. She posted videos of her trained German shepherds on social media, and sixty thousand viewers a week found that content unmissable. Dogs barking and sitting and rolling over and jumping on shit all day long. Judith in the background shouting names like Perseus and Thor and Bludgeon. And of course the four of their own, roaming the house, long-snouted hit men. Tobey couldn't imagine a situation in which Gray shared a roof with four German shepherds. But there really wasn't any choice. Tobey could afford a hotel room like he could afford a rocket to Mars.

Track was already holding the phone away from his ear, telling Judith about the plan, about the need for more tacos. When he was back on he said, "What's that?"

"I said bye. See you tonight."

THE SMOKE THICKENED as he crossed town. Sirens called in the distance. The sky had grown darker and taken on some of that reddish hue. The mountain ridge he'd come to see as part of himself, part of his home, had disappeared behind that swirling continent of brown-gray smoke.

This was it. The thing he'd trained himself to believe wouldn't happen: the end of the world. In the final blocks before his apartment building, every intersection was backed up with cars. One man put his arm out the window and flapped it at Tobey. His face was acne-scarred and wild, his thinning hair fluttering in the choking breeze. "Get out!" he shouted. "Evacuate!"

"I know," Tobey muttered. "Jesus H."

On his own block, he faced a desolate street. Only the old Hispanic guy who always sat on his front porch listening to the radio remained, still listening to the radio. Heavyset, a yellow button-up tucked into his jeans, his hair gray and pulled back to a short ponytail. Maybe sixty, sixty-five. He'd lost that chill, observing quality Tobey associated with him and now hunched over his phone. Two bags of luggage rested at his feet. When Tobey stopped at the curb, the old man stood up. "Hello there!" he yelled across two lawns. "Didn't you hear?"

"Just getting my cat!" Tobey shouted back to him. "You got a way out?"

The old man scuffed toward him, holding out his phone as if Tobey could see the screen from a lawn away. "Uber says no rides. All drivers evacuated."

Shit. Tobey didn't know this man at all, had never spoken to him. All he knew was that he wore faded clothes and a shaggy beard and listened to classic rock music all day long. Up a little closer he didn't look as ancient as Tobey'd thought he was. "You have somewhere to go?"

"My daughter's in Stockton." Tobey could see through the combed-back hair at the front of his head directly to the scalp. "But even a hotel outside town would be more than I could ask."

"I'll take you. Go ahead and get in. I can grab your bags."

He left the old man on the lawn and sprinted to the apartment building. Only last night, Tobey had been down here on the lawn at an ad-hoc party the other tenants had assembled, complete with keg and red plastic cups and smashed potato chips and someone's

iPhone blasting Drake from a portable speaker, toasting the seemingly hilarious and impending end of the world, raising their cups
to the bright line of flame along the distant ridge as if today could
never arrive.

INSIDE, ALL WAS quiet. He could see the mail had come. His box
held envelopes. Bills. Those things wouldn't matter anymore, not
with the whole book of Revelation coming at them. He ran up the
stairs, ran to his door, flung it open. "Here Gray," he called. "Here
Gray-Gray."

He found her half under the bed, her shoulders hunched, her
eyes distrustful. In the first weeks after Sophie left without her, this
is how she always looked, at least when he was around. He imagined what the apartment building must have sounded like half an
hour ago as everyone made their sudden exit. Tobey picked her up,
stroked her a moment, and set her on the kitchenette counter. "You
stay here," he said, though he knew she wouldn't.

In his bedroom he stuffed clothes into his old backpack along
with his laptop and Kindle and all the plugs and wires he could find.
"Okay, Gray, we've gotta go," he said, and grabbed her up to rest on
his arm. At the door he looked back one more time. His apartment.
Their apartment. Sophie.

In the stairwell, Gray wasn't having any of this. She dug her claws
into the soft meat of his forearm and instantly drew blood. "Fuck,"
he said, and scruffed her, tight, the way they tell you to even though it
seems mean. Her eyes bugged out; her ears shot back. Tobey looked
at the gorefest that was his left arm and fled down the stairs.

The world outside had grown worse. The wind had kicked up.
The trees bent. Darkness at noon. Four horsemen riding down from
the heavens and all that.

Getting Gray in the car was another challenge, a minor wrestling
match, and when that round of violence was finished, the old man

cooed at her as if he were part of the family. Tobey dashed to the old man's porch and grabbed his luggage. It was too heavy to run with. During the trudge back to the car, Tobey realized that the fire really was rushing at them, maybe just on the other side of those trees, maybe already a little closer. And that's when he really got scared.

"You're bleeding," the old man gasped.

"I know."

Immediately the old man began rifling through Tobey's glove compartment. "You got any, like, baby wipes or something?"

"Why would I have baby wipes?"

Tobey ran the car up on the curb and scraped some plastic element against the concrete. It didn't matter. Nothing mattered. His bleeding arm stung and burned and staying alive and getting away from here were the only things that mattered.

"People have them," the old man said. "It's a common thing."

Tobey spoke too loudly when he said, "I don't have any."

Now the old man was in the console, poking around, knocking over his pipe and likely spilling the bowl. "Napkins?" he said. "Really anything will do. A handkerchief?"

"It's okay," Tobey said. "I'm fine. Really."

They were driving too fast down the usually quiet street. Tobey didn't look at the speedometer; he didn't stop at the stop signs. Blood dripped onto his good work slacks. His chest felt like it had been filled with bees and pressed into a George Foreman Grill.

"I'm Paul Mercado," the old man said after a few tense blocks. "We never met."

"Tobey Harlan," Tobey said without ungritting his teeth. "The cat's name is Gray. As in 'all cats are gray.'"

The old man looked confused. "But *this cat* is gray."

"She. It's from a song by the Cure. It doesn't matter."

"Okay," said Mr. Mercado. "Whatever."

Tobey parted his teeth. "Really my girlfriend's cat but—"

"That's just fine."

They joined the long snake of cars trying to get on the highway. The silver hatchback ahead held a family with three young children, their hands engaged in a battle of action figures over their heads. On the bumper, a sticker read MY OTHER CAR IS A BIKE. "What do you mean it's fine?" Tobey said, his voice leaning just a little aggressive.

Mr. Mercado turned a full quarter toward Tobey, like a guy in a neck brace. "I think it's good you're saving your girlfriend's cat. So what?"

Tobey shrugged a shoulder. "My girlfriend moved out. So really she's my cat now."

"Okay." Mr. Mercado aimed himself forward again. "She's *your* cat. I'm glad you went in for her."

Tobey decided to let it go. Why was he being so defensive anyway?

"Look," said Mr. Mercado, pointing a thick finger out the passenger window. Orange-red flames skirted the bottom of a rolling smoke cloud only a mile or so north, tracking along the highway. The sight filled Tobey with an unironic sense of doom, like they really weren't going to make it, Tobey and this stranger and Sophie's cat, his cat, scorched and melted like marshmallows at a campfire.

—HONNNNK!!!—

The man in the red minivan behind them was flailing both hands at him, mouthing curse words. It was Tobey's chance to get on the highway: a trucker was flashing his beams at him to wedge in. Tobey waved, nosed the Toyota in front of the truck's shiny metal grille, and tried to shoot the minivan guy an intimidating glare all at once.

Then it was stop-and-go, occasionally cruising at a surreal twenty-five miles an hour, the smoke billowing up between the cars, killing Tobey's depth of vision. Even with the A/C running, the air stank of smoke. They took turns clearing their throats, coughing, outright hacking. In an odd way the situation felt as if it were appropriated from the world of sitcom: they were on a road trip, two fishes out of water and a frightened cat. What kind of silly mix-ups were headed their way? What sort of trouble could finally make them into friends? Unless the fire caught up to the traffic and they and everyone around them got cooked in their cars. Or died of smoke inhalation.

Fuck.

"So your daughter in Stockton," Tobey managed to say. "What's she all about?"

"All about?" Mr. Mercado was leaned up against the window watching the side mirror. "She's a nurse at an old-folks' home. Works the night shift. I tried calling her, but she's likely asleep. Kids at school."

Tobey was really pushing himself to keep up the small talk. "She has kids, huh?"

"Two of them. Joey and Samanta. Joey is a 'they' now. It's pretty new."

"You mean he's—"

"*They*," Mr. Mercado corrected.

"Yes, sorry," Tobey said. Jesus. "You know I fully support the LGBTQ-plus community. I've got a friend from high school who—"

"Their stepfather doesn't care for it. He's a bigot." Mr. Mercado folded his arms on his belly and breathed heavily out his nose. It was a large nose, and yes, from its nearest opening, Tobey could see black hairs spraying out like a tiny armpit. "One of those bigots with the light touch, understand? Sort of nods along. But he stares at the child. Calls them Joseph to their face. He's a teetotaler. The only good thing that can be said about him, and that's not much."

"Sounds, um, awful."

"A royal piece of work." Mr. Mercado held out his hands like he was measuring something's width. "Big white guy. Tattoos. You believe he shaves a little mark in his eyebrow? Like Vanilla Ice."

It pleased Tobey to no end that this old man knew who Vanilla Ice was. His thoughts started running the math, putting old Mr. Mercado in his thirties when "Ice Ice Baby" was a hit and Tobey not yet alive. Good grief. Was this what being in your thirties was like? Everything part of the historical record, lined up on one of those sliding rulers, never just now, never just yesterday, never just a couple of years ago? Is this what getting old was?

Why wasn't he talking?

"But your daughter likes this guy?"

Mr. Mercado laughed. "Indeed," he said. And then, "God, I wish she'd leave him. What did I do wrong? They say if you fuck up raising them . . ." He trailed off.

"Sheesh," Tobey said, hoping to sound noncommittal but vaguely supportive. In the slow quiet, his imagination went to this Mercado daughter, her long dark hair shimmering in the sun as she whipped around to meet his eyes: Tobey Harlan, arriving unannounced, there to rescue her from her teetotalling monster of a, well, husband? Or did Mr. Mercado say fiancé? Just boyfriend? Either way, this man had taken over her life, mistreated her children, driven a wedge between—

—HONK-HONK—

The man in the red minivan pulled alongside them and, cruising no faster than thirty miles per hour, showed them both of his middle fingers and mouthed the words *fuck you*. A whole family was in there with him—a small kid, a teenager, and a wife. All of them glaring hatefully from one fishbowl to another.

Mr. Mercado rolled down his window. The thick stench of smoke immediately overtook them. Gray leapt into the backseat. "Oh yeah?" Mercado shouted, wagging a fist. "Oh yeah, shithead?"

But the minivan's lane moved faster than Tobey's and a moment later they were gone.

"Motherfuckers," said Mr. Mercado. Just as he rolled the window back up, Gray bounded onto the console and then into Mr. Mercado's lap. The man's demeanor and tone changed without missing a beat. "Hello, kitty-witty. You're an itty-bitty kitty, aren't you?"

Tobey began to feel, well, maybe not relief, exactly, but a sense that they may survive. If the basic human experience of hating your fellow drivers held fast in this latest stage of the ever-unfolding disaster called the twenty-first century, then maybe something was okay.

His phone was buzzing. He reached it from his pocket and saw it was James calling. "My brother," he said. "Did I tell you about him?"

Mercado was still petting Gray. "When would you have told me about him?"

Tobey jammed his phone in the space between his seat and the console. Then they drifted back into silence. He guided them with slowly increasing speed away from the Willows Fire; Mercado checked the mirror and petted the cat. Time passed.

Mr. Mercado started to hum. What was that, "American Pie"? Oh sweet Jesus no, it was.

Tobey thought of what his mother had said when he was a kid throwing a fit. "Quiet time." Nothing else, no other instructions. She'd close her eyes, even if they were in a moving car, literally close her eyes behind the wheel, and say, "Quiet time." And it would work. Now, stretching his fingers with his palms on the wheel, exhaling a deep breath, he said it, he said, "Quiet time."

Mercado said, "What?"

"Nothing," Tobey said.

Mom likely didn't know about the evacuation, about the Willows Fire shifting direction, about his current state of flight. How could she? Mom didn't speak to Track at all, not for years, and she'd left when Tobey was still in elementary. There had been all that legal trauma. Somehow—baffling to consider now—he'd elected to stay with his stepsiblings and Track. Of course, Track's lawyers completely massacred her. Occasionally she brought it up. "They said I was abandoning you," she would remind him. "All I wanted was to get away from that cheating asshole." And Track had been cheating, Tobey understood that, a little later, in middle school, when the whole mystery of sex fully absorbed his life. James, by then finishing college, broke it to him softly: "He was screwing the secretary," he'd said by phone. "Classic Dad. Judith worked the front desk at his office. Don't tell me this is a surprise." But it had been a surprise! Yowza. And right after that conversation he'd had to clump downstairs to dinner and watch the two of them eating mashed potatoes and talking about the Iraq War.

Back in those middle-school years, when Tobey first heard the origin story of Dad and Judith's marriage, his disillusionment manifested first as a kind of loneliness and later as a geeky, self-centered quality that now embarrassed him. Maybe it was James and Susan having moved off to college. Maybe it was the cocktail of hormones that kept him in a pubescent inebriation from morning to night. Maybe it was Howard Dean dropping out of the presidential race (James had taken wee Tobey to a chanting/shouting rally for the candidate early in the primary; he'd tacked a blue DEAN FOR AMERICA sign on his bedroom wall). He spent time in his room with the door closed—yes, doing *that*, but not for hours out of the day or anything!—listening to music James recommended to him: gothy, shoegaze, sadsack music. Then he grew suddenly and obsessively interested in the paranormal. He ordered DVD box sets of all the seasons of *The X-Files*, read like 70 percent of Stephen King's books, and checked out from the school library anything he could find about ghosts, aliens, mysterious phenomena, ESP, and telekinesis. He liked to imagine that he had special mental powers, that he could read minds and influence others and even, if he ever were to let down his guard and really focus, he might be able to move objects with his thoughts. Why he believed this, or what evidence he had, was lost to history. In no time, he put away all those ideas. Found ghost-hunting shows offensively stupid, had absolutely no interest in whatever the government was releasing about UFOs, couldn't begin to conceive of brains with superpowers outside the gaspingly tired Marvel Cinematic Universe. But he'd believed firmly at the time. He'd gone all in. For long, tense hours in his bedroom he would put in his "practice": trying to read playing cards facedown on the carpet, attempting to listen in on Track's thoughts from down the hall, willing a cereal spoon he'd pocketed from the kitchen to bend its slender neck without the aid of his hands.

In prison, bored, he thought of trying these little exercises again, but he didn't have the sort of faith required. Instead he'd turned hungrily to books, reading anything that he could get his hands on from the library. The only friend he made during those years was a man named Henry Salazar, in for some white-collar crime he said the government had entrapped him into, and it had been Salazar who had passed along a copy of Pedro Ambrosi's *On Culture & Reality*, a book Tobey had heard about in an environmental studies class and had proceeded to misquote in a paper the year before his arrest. Salazar was a sort of Ambrosi monk—an "Ambrosian," as he called it—a firm believer in Ambrosi's call to tear down all the artifice of human culture, from action movies to classical music to shitty Instagram poetry, so that human beings could live again with the natural world before it was too late. For a while, in his gray-walled cell, in the yard with Salazar and other cushily-housed fraudsters and tax cheats, Tobey had started to become an Ambrosian too.

Now, in a state of old-fashioned end-of-the-world shock, he wondered if "before it was too late" had already passed. They'd just raced from their homes to escape a fire the size of a former Soviet republic. Not a damn thing had been done to stop climate change and there was little hope that anything would be done. He was crammed into a car with a total stranger who seemed a little, well, batty. And—*and*—to get the double-bird from some middle-aged dad in a minivan. You add Sophie and Two Bears to the mix, and well, it was enough to push anyone over the edge.

He closed his eyes. "Quiet time."

"You keep saying that!" Mercado looked at him, owl-eyed, a little shaken. "What is it supposed to mean?"

Rather than explain, Tobey cleared his throat, toyed with the volume on NPR—

—ira glaSS AND ON THis amERICan LIFE!!!—and finally just outright said, "Um Mr. Mercado?"

"What?" the old man said with some alarm.

"You ever hear of Pedro Ambrosi?"

Mercado roused, sat up straight again, checked the mirror. "Some soccer player?"

"No," Tobey said. "What about Henry Salazar?"

"This some kind of Latino bingo you're playing?" Mercado said. And then, when Tobey failed to answer, he lifted Gray up onto his lap. "So what happened with the girlfriend?"

TWO BEARS WAS supposed to have been a last-ditch plan, at least for Tobey. He'd heard about the farm after going to a health-foods store with Judith, maybe three months after his release, where he'd absentmindedly bought a bag of their branded trail mix (bland, altogether too raisiny). In a photo above the ingredients list, dozens of people of all ages—although, uh, pretty *white*—smiled back at him in gleaming sunshine. "Two Bears Farm is an intentional community in southern Oregon," the copy read, "of about a hundred citizens who work, play, and share together. Our products are a reflection of our egalitarian and nature-oriented outlook on the world. Thus they are a gift of our hearts to yours." Ha! Tobey could remember reading it out loud to his stepmom in the car ("And wow, get this, 'a gift of our hearts to yours!'") and then never thinking about the farm or its lame product again, at least not for a few years.

"So not never," Mercado said.

"No." But it was long enough for him to have taken a series of low-end jobs with no future, bouncing from place to place, realizing a little at a time that he really had no prospects. This was a dark time. He was treading water. And then Two Bears appeared to him again like a sign from an almighty power: there on a shelf in a convenience store in San Bernardino were bags of their soy jerky. "No," he said aloud, and grabbed up a bag. On the back: the same photograph and ad copy, complete with "our hearts to yours," as well as a website. He didn't buy the jerky, but in the car a minute later he did pull up the site on his phone, first with some measure of irony, and then again the next day in all seriousness. They weren't just a farm. They also processed and packaged all their soy and trail-mix products, made musical instruments, weaved ponchos, cartoned free-range eggs, shared all their income, took turns teaching at a school for all their children, and ran a popular TikTok account where baby goats frolicked in the Northwest sun and kids ate fruits right off trees without having to wash pesticides from their skins. He read about how to apply and read all the community by-laws. It didn't seem like a scam. They didn't want any money up front, didn't want to take your property or put you in debt. You just had to share anything you made while living there, like everyone else.

"Communism?" Mercado said.

"Peter called it anarcho-syndicalism."

"Who's Peter?"

"A guy there. I don't know. We met him." Anyway, soon an alternate Tobey had emerged in Real Tobey's imagination (sort of like his former telekinetic one), and this Tobey turned away from the modern world, from consumerism and jobs, even as the original—official—Tobey went on sending in résumés and shopping at big-box stores. It was a years-long daydream. A funny thing to bring up, say, on a first date with a girl named Sophie whom he'd met on a dating app and who ran the front desk at a dentist's office across town. "You'd really do that?" she'd said.

And Tobey, more than a little trying to impress her, said, "Oh, absolutely."

It was part of the reason she moved in only six months later—that and the looming feeling that everything in the country had gone mad. They planned to scrap their belongings and go together. They visited Two Bears in January, saw the community pool, the shared dining hall, the schoolroom, the yoga patio. They were shown inside one of the residence buildings and then inside a private room: a twelve-by-twelve square with a window and bed and dresser, a bookshelf and corner desk, a window facing one of the vegetable gardens. "So we're doing this?" he'd said when they left, daring her. "We're really going to do this?"

She was ecstatic. They would throw away all the stuff they didn't need. They would exit the rat race. Together, they would live in a small world apart from all the garbage of modern life. All of a sudden it was a serious relationship, the most serious he'd ever had, the type of relationship where people talk about things deep in the future, getting old and whether or not to have kids and all that business. He had just turned thirty.

In March, they went back to Two Bears for the required two-week visit. Now instead of just an hour guided around, they would be thrown into life as if they were already community members. He'd thought everything had gone perfectly, but a week after they returned home, they got the call: The community would accept Sophie; they wouldn't accept him. "At least not at this time," the caller, a Two Bears citizen named Walt, had said. "But we'd be glad to meet with you again in three months."

"Wait," Mercado said. "When was all this?"

"Three months ago."

Mercado checked the mirror again. "Ouch," he said.

When Sophie said she was going without him, he didn't go out and get drunk or anything cliché like that. No, instead he called James. Tall and thin, tattooed and Twitter-obsessed, his half-brother responded with the usual sensitivity. "A fucking Harlan trying to move to a commune? Dad would have his dogs maul you first, fuckhead."

"James, I'm serious. She's going to live there without me."

"Sounds like it's for the best," James had said. "True colors and all that. By the way, when were you going to tell me about all this? As you churned butter on your little granola porch?"

"I didn't want to say anything until I knew."

"Well, it was a stupid idea. What you need is a J-O-B, Kemosabe. Quit slinging burritos." Then, after a pause, as the foolishness of Tobey's position sank in, James said, "You know you ought to work this into a TV show. Write up an outline and I'll make a few calls."

James had worked in television. Or really he'd been a producer's assistant. He'd brought coffee and taken calls and set up meetings. And that had been years ago, back in the early 2010s, and that producer had never gotten much off the ground. Now James did about the same, this time for Osip Yander, the reclusive founder of something tech-related and investor in many other tech-related things. "He has the mind of a child," James had said. "He knows coding and particle physics and that he has a lot of money. But buying groceries? Getting someone to cut the lawn? He's an idiot, really. He couldn't survive a day without me." On top of his salary, James lived in a house only a mile from Yander's mansion and drove a Tesla, both purchased by Yander with no strings attached. James had hinted once that his salary was something over a hundred thousand a year. With no car payment or rent. Meanwhile, Tobey got laughed at for wanting to ditch a table-waiting job for life on a farm.

"So this brother," said Mr. Mercado, "he's, like, your hero?"

"Half-brother, really. And I wouldn't—"

"But you look up to him?"

"I mean, not exactly."

Did he?

"Then I will tell you this. Based on my life experience. This brother is an asshole."

"Well," Tobey said. "I wouldn't argue with that."

Mercado also had opinions on people like Osip Yander. He'd been a math teacher for two years and then an idealistic computer programmer in the late '80s and '90s. "I couldn't stand the tech gurus. The bigwigs, you know? At some point it became a cult of personality. And what personality? So you wear the same sweater all your fucking life. So you have beady eyes. Is that personality?" He was really getting into it now, going full Live at the Apollo. "They're just rich white guys. Who cares if they were nerds back in the day. Now they're all about power. Algorithms. Data. Controlling people, taking their money. Spouting about freedom. Personality! All of it manufactured." He checked the mirror again. "Anyway, I left. Nobody missed me. I was over the hill by then. That was *my* intentional commune: going back to teaching in my forties. Of course, it meant watching all the kids get absorbed into social media. Proud new members of the Matrix!"

"Oh, I hate social," Tobey managed. "All that preening and complaining—"

"After all that," Mr. Mercado interrupted, "we were going to buy a used RV. Travel the country. But my wife got sick. Cancer. She felt fine, you know? Nothing wrong. Then a spot on her liver. Spots. Eight months later"—he clapped—"and she was gone. I'm not religious. It was a hard time. It's still hard. That's why I'm always out on that porch. It's lonely in the house. And I don't want to go anywhere. You know, the grocery store, that sort of thing. I don't like driving. I've never owned a car."

"Fuck cars," Tobey said.

Mercado laughed. "You don't seem like you worry about money. You come from some rich assholes or what?"

Tobey shrugged. "Sort of. But I'm broke as shit."

"Well, let me tell you—"

Mercado's phone was buzzing. So was Tobey's.

"Hang on," Mercado said, and pressed his screen. A rapid, flowing Spanish filled the car, along with the tinny sound of a woman's voice. The only word Tobey understood was *fuego*. That and *Jesus*. Whatever was being said increased in alarm and volume. Then, suddenly, Mr. Mercado was saying, "Goodbye. Yes, later today. Soon. Goodbye."

Tobey had started leaning forward on the wheel, tense. "Well?"

"The fire," Mr. Mercado said. "Oh God—"

TOBEY DIDN'T WANT to believe that the entire town could have burned to the ground in the time they had been on the road. He couldn't see how such a thing could be possible. "But the firefighters," he said again and again, "the helicopters."

Then he turned on the radio—"when Jane Vernson of Boulder, Colorado, realized there was something wrong with her mortgage statement"—and switched away from NPR, to the nearest channel not playing music. "Tinsley, California," a reporter was saying, "an ideal vacation town, now the site of untold destruction. It appears very little of the town will make it through without severe fire damage. Evacuation orders came at what must have been the last minute for residents of—"

Mercado shut it off. "She says on television the whole town is in flames. Everything. We're never going back."

They sat in silence for at least a minute. Tobey couldn't process the information, couldn't make the words fit together. He felt a squirming discomfort build in his spine and up his neck. Mercado began weeping, a hand over his mouth. All told, they had been on the road for two hours.

"What the fuck," said Tobey. "I mean, what in the living fuck?"

"I can't believe it," Mr. Mercado said. "I didn't want to believe it."

Tobey was still grasping at the concept. He said again, his mouth on autopilot, "What in the fuck?"

"She just got off work," Mercado said. "Came home to the news. She doesn't want me there, either. Oh, she said it was okay. But she didn't seem happy about it. Shouldn't she be happy about it?"

"Um—"

"I'm her father, for God's sake. She should be happy I'm coming. But she said, 'Are you sure?' and then she said, 'How long will you be here?' My home is gone and she's asking how long I'll be there?"

"Well—"

"She lived under my roof for twenty years. Even in nursing school she came back to live with us. Took over Carol's craft room. Put up her stupid NSYNC posters. And now that I'm in need! It's a betrayal. A betrayal!"

Gray hopped to the console and slunk into the back of the car. Even among cats, she was easily alarmed.

Tobey thought about all the belongings he'd left behind. Two boxes and half the closet were Sophie's, the very stuff he thought of as evidence they were still together. If all that junk was gone, would she have any connection to him at all? His own things—records and books, clothes—weren't actually valuable, but having nothing more than an overnight bag to his name wasn't something he'd been prepared for this morning.

"I'm stopping up there," he said, pointing at a big roadside gas station at the oncoming exit. "You want anything?"

Mercado, still weeping, covered his face with both hands, his head nearly touching the dashboard. "No," he grumbled.

It didn't feel good to see an old man in this state.

Tobey eased off the highway. He left Mr. Mercado in the car still sniffling and went inside. The restroom smelled of urine and he tried to not touch anything. Above the toilet someone had written STOP THE STEAL. Someone else had crossed this out and written SUCK MY NUTS NAZI just below.

Out in the store Tobey bought an energy drink and a bag of Doritos, then sat on the hood of the car with them, smelling fire on the air and listening to the highway, letting Mr. Mercado have a little more time to himself. It was already evening. They were just outside Stockton. A sleepy heaviness hit his shoulders and then radiated down through his legs and he stepped down onto the hot asphalt of the parking lot.

"Okay," Tobey said when he sat inside the car again. "Let's get you to your daughter's."

Mr. Mercado's eyes were dry. He held Gray on his lap, petting her. "Thank you," he said. "I'm sorry I lost control there a minute. What a mess all this is."

"You're preaching to the choir," Tobey said.

———

THEIR DESTINATION WASN'T just Stockton but Stockton Street. Mr. Mercado seemed vague on the exact location, watching out the window with a single index finger raised, saying at the end of each block, "The next one."

A blue, Craftsman-style place on a corner with a fat, short palm tree in the front yard made him light up. "This one here."

Two cars sat in the driveway, a bumper hanging out into the street, so Tobey parked at the curb, uncertain if it was a legal space or not. "You sure you got the right place?"

"Yeah," said Mr. Mercado, but his worried expression made it seem like he no longer wanted it to be. Still, when he stepped out of the car, he already had Gray in his arms. The cat didn't scratch at him, didn't seem alarmed about being outside. "My daughter has cats," he said, as if this explained everything. "We'll get Gray here a little food and a trip to the litter box."

It occurred to Tobey for the first time that he really liked this old man. Who would care so much about a stranger's cat? And they had a lot in common. Their homes were likely destroyed, sure, but they'd both been trying to run from things already: Tobey from the world of jobs and materialism, Mr. Mercado from his dead wife. Where one had built a hare-brained scheme to go live on a commune, the other had spent all his time out on that porch so he didn't have be reminded of who wasn't at home. Plus, they both thought Mark Zuckerberg could eat one, and that was a bond worth keeping.

"Dad?" shouted a voice through the closed screen door. When this flew open, a pretty middle-aged woman with short, dark hair and nurse's scrubs ran out and leaped from the brief concrete porch to the lawn like a child. She rushed toward them and shouted, "Oh thank God," her eyes already welling up. "I got worried. You said you'd be here in half an hour."

"This cat will need a waystation, Freddie," said Mr. Mercado.

"It's my cat," Tobey said. "I hope you don't mind." He was thinking with some embarrassment about that dumb fantasy of saving Mercado's daughter. This wasn't a person who needed any saving.

Mercado flashed him a smile. "It's his girlfriend's cat. Very important."

The woman looked at Tobey as if he were a rideshare driver who had mistakenly gotten out of the car instead of driving away. "You must be the boy. Thank you so much for your help." She grabbed at the old man's arm, kissed the top of his round head. "I told him to come and get a hotel days ago. Before all of this. But no, he never listens."

Um . . . *boy*?

"Frederica is too good to me," said Mercado. And then, shrugging Gray toward her to remind her of the cat's presence, "Can we get this kitty-cat inside before we catch up?"

IN THE CARPETED living room with the television replaying video of Tinsley, Mr. Mercado and Tobey watched Gray meet the other cats, two snobbish tabbies, and then show herself to the litterbox just inside the linoleumed kitchen. The two children, Joey and Samanta, elementary-aged, clearly unclear on what was happening, played games on matching tablets. The heavyset white man with tattoos and a goatee whom Mercado had complained about grunted something greeting-oriented in the vague direction of the old man, then gave Tobey only a passing glance. He really did have marks shaved into his eyebrows like Vanilla Ice. When they'd entered, he'd been down the hallway, out of sight. Now he was here with everyone, taking up space that didn't have a lot for the taking. A man on the television said "The body of a male victim found in his home" and then "Firefighters are still trying to control the blaze" and "Search-and-rescue efforts will begin in earnest overnight" and finally "As you can see it is utter destruction."

Tobey recognized the burned-out husk of an old church, that one big house on the corner of Cortazar and Barker, the strip of local shops only a couple of blocks from his and Mr. Mercado's street, but he said nothing, only watched and pretended not to watch. He didn't know what to say anyway. Everything that was left was either a charred frame or still smoldering or an active fire. Here was a truck virtually melted on the street, here a gaggle of struggling prison firefighters soaking a house, here a reporter wearing a blackened mask over her mouth, shouting into a microphone, the fog of gray-brown smoke parting around her almost apologetically.

AFTER HALF AN hour or so of watching the coverage, feeling more and more numb, he went into their kitchen to grab his phone from the outlet kindly offered by Mercado's daughter. As if he'd spent hours out of range, he'd somehow missed a dozen calls and thirty-eight texts. Most of these were from his parents, but a smattering of friends had checked in, along with his half-sister, Susan; his old friend Madeline; Hugo, whom he hadn't really spoken to since college days; his ex-attorney, Will Mitchell; the Ben who used to sell him weed; even Natalia from work. There wasn't a single text or call from Sophie.

Surprise, surprise.

He listened to his brother's message from this afternoon first. "Hey, fuckstick," it began. "A little bird tells me you're on the way to Dad's. Sorry about the fucking fire, dude. That's shitty. Osip's working on something for it. Says he'll be able to put a stop to all fires in, like, ten years. You know he really wants those stupid paintings Dad's got. Maybe you could do me a favor and take them off the wall while you're there? Dad wouldn't miss them. Fucking Dad. What a bitch. You know you should have come up here. Oh well. Drive safe and all that. Later."

Nice. And delivered in James's patented surfer-meets-hip-hop voice, vaguely threatening but also somehow enlightened, sunburned, pot-addled. Tobey needed to smoke a bowl.

"I'm uh—" he said to the backs of the family still watching television, "going to get Mr. Mercado's bags."

"It's Paul," is all Mercado said in response.

NIGHT HAD FALLEN. The faint smell of woodsmoke in the air. Two boys tossing a football in the street, ignoring the voice of a mother calling them in.

Tobey plopped into the passenger seat, dug into the console, and pulled out his short pipe and the Ziploc baggie he had—thank *gawd*—

already had in the car from this morning. He dropped a pinch of weed into the bowl and stuffed it down with his index finger. Then he dug under the seat, bumping his head twice on the steering wheel, trying to reach the lighter, which had somehow worked its way over the little hump in the carpeted floor and into the inky shadow next to the seat's metal base. His fingers were just tickling the lighter's edge, his other hand holding the pipe aloft, when he became aware of a change in the light, a shadow, a form—

"I don't want you bringing that in my house," said the distinctly tough-guy voice of the large tattooed man, what's-his-name, from inside.

Tobey was rubbing the back of his head, bumped now for a third time, as he looked up into the face of this undeniably intimidating douchebag, and said, "Oh sorry."

The man crossed his arms, did a little alpha nod, and said, "This is a sober house. Been that way for two years."

"Okay?"

"So I don't appreciate you getting stoned on my lawn."

Tobey ducked a look over his shoulder. The passenger door was still open behind him and he could see the curb. "I'm not, technically—"

"Look you're basically on my lawn with that shit. I don't like it. There's kids inside."

"Understood."

But neither of them moved.

"Right," said the large tattooed man. "So put it away, say your goodbyes, and get on the road."

"Hold on. I'm a guest of—"

"My fiancée's father? He doesn't live here. And I'll tell you something else," he said, leaning down now, his pasty face and goatee and shaved eyebrows framed inside the driver's-side window, "he's not sticking around either. We don't have room for this shit."

"But I—"

The man stood to his full height. Tobey could only see his belly, stretching the fabric of an L.A. Raiders jersey. Then he turned and walked away, saying, "I said what I said."

Tobey sat there a moment, at a loss. Where the hell was Mr. Mercado going if he wasn't going to his daughter's house? And for that matter—reaching back under the seat—he wasn't going to have some meathead telling him what he could and couldn't smoke in a parked car on his own free time. This was America, after all. Still, to be respectful, he took only a single puff, tamped down the bowl so it wouldn't go on smoking, and exhaled toward the street instead of the house. Then he rolled up the windows, set the A/C, and leaned the seat back. Mr. Mercado's bags could wait. Clearly.

He turned his attention back to his phone, working his way through the missed texts, sending out the same upbeat response to most everyone, messages meant to keep the exchange from turning into a full-blown conversation: All safe here! On the road

Immediately, Susan responded: So you're alive? Still going to dads huh?

Yeah where else

Anywhere else!

LOL

Seriously dads been acting weird. $ troubles I think. And this

She sent a link from the *L.A. Times*: "NFT & Crypto Trades Investigated for Money Laundering, Fraud."

Dad doesn't do NFTs. Doesn't even know what they are

He's literally mentioned in the story!!!

He scrolled through. Yeah, there was Track's name next to a company Tobey had never heard of: Harlan NextGen LLC.

WTF?

For a moment, the speech bubble flashed ". . . " but then it went away.

Tobey had no choice but to read this as aggressive: Susan thought he was too thick-headed to warrant a response.

Naturally, the thing to do would be to text his father and ask him about Harlan NextGen. But that wasn't very Tobey. Confronting things wasn't exactly his speed. So instead he went with: Traffic moving slow. Sleeping over in Stockton. Call you tomorrow.

Track responded: Stars are beautiful tonight. We're floating in the pool. Safe travels.

That didn't sound like him at all. Maybe Susan was right. Or maybe *he* was high? Track Harlan, totally blazed, a Don Cherry tune blasting from the Bluetooth speaker Tobey had shown him how to use last year. The esteemed Track Harlan, of the Harlan Professorship in Classical Studies at the University of California, Davis? Stoned? Nah. It couldn't be.

Tobey couldn't get away with texting his mother, and so after staring at the screen with her number glowing under an old picture of her from the '90s, he finally hit Dial. "My God, Tobe," his mom said before he could squeeze out a word, "I had no idea what was going on. You know I had to call your father to find out you're even alive?"

"Sorry," he said. "It was all a rush. I was at work and then they evacuated us. Then I had this old man in the car with me."

"An old man?"

"Yeah, I'm outside his daughter's house now. In Stockton?"

"Tobe, are you okay? Who's this old man?"

Outside, a woman passed by walking her dog. She didn't seem to notice him reclined on the phone, or the cloud of smoke he exhaled through the cracked-open window. "He's a neighbor. He needed a ride. I'm on my way to Dad's."

"That's so like you," she said. "To help someone."

"Is it?"

His mother sighed. "Of course it is, sweetie. You were always wanting to help people. Remember that family?"

That family was a homeless family panhandling outside a shopping center in Palm Springs, way back in the late '90s, when Tobey was in grade school. He'd demanded that his mother give them money, but the only way she would agree to do it is if Tobey handed the father—a sunburned man with a marker-drawn sign and Nike shoes missing their laces—the five-dollar bill she had on her and ask him if there was anything other than money they could get for them. He'd done this, sure, but the seconds it took seemed as epic as *Lord of the Rings*, which they'd all go to see as a family a couple years later, just before his parents separated. His memory had invested it with minuscule detail: the soft blue of the daughter's eyes, the pleased grimace of the mother, the way the man's hand looked as clean and untroubled as his father's. They had been middle-class, he understood now. People with office jobs. And somehow the system had spat them out. When he'd asked what else they could use, the girl, maybe a year or two older than him, said, "Candy. Please." She was sunburned too, tired-looking, her clothes clean but one of her sandals broken at the strap. Her mother tapped her on the head reprovingly. "We need food, ma'am," she said, addressing her words to Tobey's mom. "Something that doesn't need heating up." Then, looking hard at the asphalt parking lot, "I'm sorry to ask." When Tobey and his mother returned half an hour later with granola bars and crackers and a twenty she got from the ATM, the family was gone. For two weeks he felt too guilty to touch the food until his father peeled open one of the granola bars and ate it in front of the morning news. Tobey had thrown a fit, said that they were for the family, that Track shouldn't have touched them. "Give me a break," Track had said. "I've got to get to work."

"I guess," Tobey said now. "I mean, I couldn't have left him there. And Gray likes him."

"Oh God, your cat," his mother said. "How's she taking all this?"

"Right now she's inside making friends. Eating canned food."

"And you're outside?"

"In the car—I think I'll sleep out here before I hit the road."

There was a pause on the line. He'd expected his mother to buck against the idea of sleeping in his car, to at least tell him to make sure the doors were locked. Instead, when she finally spoke, she said, "If things don't go well with your father. You know. You can come out here."

"Thanks Mom," he said, and then ended the call. He hadn't said a word about that intimidating dude, or how Mr. Mercado may not have a place to stay, or about the news story with Track. And he'd come up with the plan to sleep in the car only in the moment, thinking he should stick around. Mom had softened him up, made him think he should care—or really, admit that he cared. He couldn't actually leave the old man here without a plan. In fact, he needed to get Mercado's bags in the house. But first another puff.

Mom, he thought as smoke filled the car again. How had a person like that ever married Track Harlan?

GEORGE WEST FINE ART

Galleries that Serve the Globe

homepage

about

Seattle	Venice	Paris	Hong Kong	Philadelphia
Los Angeles	SoHo	London	Brooklyn	

Founded by the visionary collector and dealer who put L.A. on the modern-art map, George West Galleries, International, is the premier site—in-person or online, physical or NFT—for the purchase of modern and contemporary art objects, for one-of-a-kind retrospectives and multiplatform auctions, and for the education and development of collectors at all stages of their relationship to high-value visual media. When George West left a promising career in Hollywood after an accident which left him in a wheelchair for the rest of his life, he discovered what he called his true purpose, to "make modern art accessible to anyone who is open to it," and so created the global GWG brand.

His egalitarian philosophy led GWG to host West Coast introductions of artists as varied as Rauschenberg, Stiegl, and Bacon, as well as highly successful showings of already-established figures such as Warhol, Richter, Sherman, and Judd. It also inspired our longtime chief gallery director, Annie Moore, to expand the GWG family to locations in Europe, Asia, across the United States, and—beginning late next year—to our newest location in Dubai.

Contact us today about new and ongoing shows, private sales, auctions, investment opportunities, or with any questions about the artists we represent. Or make an appointment with our valuation services manager, Franklin Brown, to have your collection appraised in part or full.

A member of our aesthetic partner team will be proud to serve you at any stage.

Plans for Our New Dubai Location

Current Gallery Shows

Our Calendar

Valuation Services

Contact an Aesthetic Partner

DI STIEGL

1971

BEFORE ANYTHING, REALLY, was the fire. Well, that's how she would explain it later, to Annie and to Lily and to Nero and to Phil, finally to Michael, to anyone who would listen, to anyone who asked the dreaded questions of where she was from or who her parents were or what made her want to be an artist. To that final question she would always answer that her grandfather—yes that grandfather, the great director—had given her crayons and talked to her about the life of an artist just at the right moment in her childhood, and that later still, when he was sick, had bonded with her in his final days, in Palm Springs, where everything for her would begin again. This was her founding story, her Lexington and Concord, her storming of the Bastille: the fire in the desert the day her grandfather died.

———

PALM SPRINGS, JUST about the worst place to be, and Diane there because of the impending divorce, because her father could only hop from town to town trying to find a job for so long, because there were only so many old college buddies who could give them a room, and more important because he wanted to be there—to put in the time—as his own father's health took an increasingly grim turn. Even at twelve, still enamored with Percy, Diane could see that there was money to be had in this endeavor. Her grandpa was rich, the inheritor of Grandma's estate, which meant the old Lazlo/ Western P&E fortune, and he himself had been a director in TV and the movies. He lived in a big, modernist place that seemed a little rundown, like its golden years were some other decade. But Percy needed money, simple as that. He made no bones about it. Sometimes in the car between towns as they drifted that year, he'd mush the pads of his hands into his eyes and cry or nearly cry, mumbling dark words about ruin and the end of the line and all this woe-is-me stuff that provoked in her an uncomfortable combination of hurt, sympathy, and exhaustion. Why didn't they just settle somewhere? Why didn't he take that job cooking hamburgers in Omaha? Selling cars in Phoenix? How did he manage to get himself canned from that shoe-salesman job in Olympia?

Percy needed money, and for that he would play friends with his own father, or so said Diane's mother on the phone that afternoon, calling from New Jersey of all places, telling Diane again that she would have to stay with Percy at least a couple more months, until everything was settled, though really they both knew everything *was* settled. "I'm thinking of repainting this apartment," she'd said, and Diane knew that this meant one of her upswings was getting a little ragged, a little dangerous. And then, to her surprise, Antonia had said, "Deedee, I love you. I miss you more than anything has ever been missed."

Diane had said the same, had said she couldn't wait to see her again, and after she'd hung up grandpa's kitchen phone she'd taken Peanut Pattie back to her room to sit in the half-dark with the curtains pulled and listen to *Revolver* and try not to feel sorry for herself.

Eventually, she heard her grandpa groan in the near-dark, his bedroom door open down the hall. On the television, *The Beverly Hillbillies* had come on without her noticing. She'd had the sound off. It was evening. Time to take Peanut Pattie on her walk.

"Dad," she called, clicking the leash on her collar. Peanut Pattie ran a wild circle at her feet. "Dad, we're walking. You want to go?"

Percy appeared at the end of the hall, papers in his hands, a pencil tucked into his ear. "Don't be gone long, darling," he said, not really answering her question. "We're going out to dinner."

Ugh. Out to dinner meant another evening with Mrs. Harlan, or Tessa, Percy couldn't figure out what Diane should be calling her. "I want to stay home," she said. Percy's grimace told her this wouldn't be happening. "Then I want pizza."

He looked down at the papers. "I think we can make part of that work, sweetie."

Outside the air was still and dry and she could feel it in her nose, that threat of a nosebleed; she'd already had a dozen nosebleeds since they'd arrived a few weeks ago, had taken to stuffing her back pocket with Kleenex. Everywhere brightness assailed her, even now, with the sun dropping fat and red at the horizon. She had, for reasons she couldn't make sense of to herself unless you counted getting on Percy's nerves, resisted getting sunglasses. She would be the squinting girl, the one with the corgi on the end of a pink leash, at least until Percy decided whether they were staying or going, at least before she was made to go to school here.

She thought about actually living here. Percy had laughed about the idea on their way to Palm Springs but then, about a week ago, he'd come home from the grocery store with frozen dinners and the story of Mrs. Harlan, whom he'd met in the canned-goods section, checking sell-by dates, making what he had called "cute little humming noises" as she turned one can and then another. Mrs. Harlan would be meeting him for dinner across town. He would put Diane's food in the oven but she would be responsible for taking it out, careful not to burn her hands, use both of the pot holders, et cetera, and he would try to be home before her bedtime.

That her father would actually be going out on a date with some woman who wasn't her mother seemed like some kind of joke. Eventually, maybe tonight, they would break into laughter, pointing at her, and after a stumbled explanation of her foolishness, everything would go back to normal, Percy kicking around the house, pining for Antonia, Mrs. Harlan doing whatever it is Mrs. Harlan did, maybe kicking around her own house and pining over her estranged husband, who—Diane shuddered thinking about it—had reportedly lost his mind and shacked up across town with a teenager, a member of the high school pom squad, the girl's parents somehow going along with it. Mr. Harlan had been an actor before all that, star of grandpa's long-canceled cop show *Brackett*, nearly a star in motion pictures in the two decades prior. Percy said Mr. Harlan was in a bunch of films with John Wayne, Kirk Douglas, even Bob Hope. "Always the pal or the extra gun, never the *romantic lead*."

Gross.

So it would be great if Mrs. Harlan could return to tearing up over her wacko husband and Percy could go back to pacing the house trying to figure out just who Antonia could have left him for, though Antonia had told him a hundred times it wasn't anyone, that she only wanted to be alone, out of the marriage, to sort out who she was and what she really wanted and to finally get some help, a set of concepts he couldn't accept. To be honest, Diane couldn't quite accept it either.

Peanut Pattie stopped in a patch of sand to pee. From the door of a nearby house stepped a man in a black suit and narrow tie and a woman in a baby-blue dress and white scarf. They watched Diane with a sleepy look of disappointment in their eyes. She could see herself in her shorts and sneakers, her White Sox T-shirt, her hair cut as short as a boy's, her dog peeing on their lawn. So she waved, friendly, and shouted to them, "Hello Mr. and Mrs. Hilton!"

The man put a hand to his ear. "What's all this now?"

Just then, Peanut Pattie lifted out of her squat and began walking again. "I said you should watch out for the shrimp cocktail, Beauregard!"

Then she set off running. It was something she'd heard on a television show last week, imagining pink-striped shrimp floating lazy circles in a glass of bubbling Champagne, some Englishman in tails just about to take a sip.

Four blocks later, the heat was too much. Diane pulled Peanut Pattie to a stop. "Those Hiltons," Grandpa had said the first night they were in town, his thick German accent made even stranger by his holding his oxygen mask only an inch from his face. "They'll turn this place into a trash heap. You'll see. It'll be Hawaiian shirts and boating shoes by summer. Carbon copies of your dear old dad."

It seemed to Diane everyone who lived in Palm Springs was either an old movie star or someone who had invested in the movies or a penny-pinching shoe salesman living out an impossible dream. The people here already looked like they were on vacation or on their way to some snooty cocktail lounge. Even grandpa, if you went by the photos framed all over his walls, dressed like a celebrity. And the houses! Glass-and-stucco angles in all directions, images of a distant future dreamed up in a goofy science-fiction movie. The glistening pools and alien palm trees and more sunlight than anyone could ever need.

Again she turned, headed back to the house, so lost in her head that she came to a scuffing stop on the dusty sidewalk when she saw the boy, stretched out on the grass of a pristine and glimmering lawn, one leg crossed over the other at the scabby knee, his striped gym socks pulled all the way up his calves. His face was hidden behind a comic book. He'd angled it to catch the final gasp of sunlight.

She looked around. Peanut Pattie pulled at her leash, let out an interested grunt. Then the boy, without moving at all, spoke. "You're that von *Shtiegl* chick, huh?"

"It's just Stiegl," she said.

The boy moved the comic book, resting it in both hands against his crossed leg like it was some kind of heavy burden. His face was freckly, his eyebrows bushy, his pale forehead too big. He wore his red hair shaggy like a Beatle. "Whatever," he said. "I've been hearing about you."

Peanut Pattie lurched for him like he had a treat. "What have you been hearing?" Diane said.

"For starters," he said, sitting up on his elbows, "My mom's got herself all bent-up over your old man."

"You mean Mrs. Harlan?"

The boy laughed. "Yeah, *Mrs.* Harlan. My dumbbell mom."

"And you don't like it?" Diane said. "You don't want them dating?"

He sat all the way up now, crossing his legs Indian-style, looking into the desert. "I mean I don't care who she dates. She can date Barry Goldwater for all I care."

Peanut Pattie was still at the end of her leash, and when the boy smiled down at her, Diane took a couple of steps forward. The dog wiggled and curlicued as the boy scratched under her chin. "We moved in last month," she said, finally. "But I don't think we're staying long."

"Why don't you go to school?"

"Maybe I do."

"You don't," the boy said. By now Peanut Pattie had roamed from his hand to sniff at the end of his sneaker, where a pink wad of bubble gum was stuck in the treads. "My mom's a teacher, dummy. She told me you don't go to school."

It bothered her that this complete stranger knew anything about her. "I'll go back to school when we go home."

The boy stood with a grunt. She'd thought he was taller than her, but when he stood before her, the top of his head hit right at her nose. "Mom says you probably got in some kind of trouble back where you're from. That you're"—he paused, pointing toward her head with the comic—"a delinquent or something."

"What's that supposed to mean?"

He shrugged. "A delinquent? It's like a criminal but, you know, for kids."

"No," she said, and could feel a hot rage at the backs of her arms. "Why'd she say that about me?"

The boy smirked. "Sheesh, I was only kidding." He looked down over his shoulder, dusted sand off his butt, and held out his hand. "I'm Track."

"Track?"

When she didn't take his hand, he stuffed it in a pocket. "Some guy my dad played in a Western."

"So your dad really was in the movies?"

They were walking now, Peanut Pattie leading the way. "He wasn't all that famous or anything. Biggest thing he did was *Brackett*. With your gramps? It's weird 'cause his new girlfriend is, like, nearly our age. But he's a good guy anyway. A good dad."

Her stomach panged thinking about it. To have your family split up in that way, without even the distance of hers, just right across town. But she didn't want to tell him about her own family troubles, so she just said, "I'm sorry."

"It's nothing. He left the house last year without any big fight or anything. I miss him, but like Mom says, his illness doesn't reflect on me." He kicked a pile of rocks on the roadside. "You know he and your gramps are in business together. They sort of own this town. At least a big part of it. Even though Dad hates him now."

"Your dad hates my grandpa?"

"Says he 'murdered' his career in acting. Mom says he's melodramatic."

She wanted to change the subject. "Are you coming to dinner with us tonight?"

"Diane," he said, and for just a moment she wondered how he knew her name, "that's why I was waiting for you. I've been watching you walk by for days."

———

HE WAS ALL right, this Track Harlan. He didn't like Palm Springs, either, though he'd lived here nearly as far back as he could remember. His family used to keep an apartment in Los Angeles, in a stucco, U-shaped apartment building with a single palm tree at its center, with a funny painting of a bird with no feet that his mom left behind when they moved to this desert town, a house that had once been a winter escape from the industry. For some reason his father had hung back at the apartment, and his mother began teaching English to middle schoolers. Of course this meant that Track, this very year, was enrolled in his own mother's class, reading Dickens and Twain, pretending to take notes as Mrs. Harlan stood at the front of the class pushing her glasses up her nose and making a point of not calling on him, even if he raised his hand. In the evenings he spent his time studying or reading comics, listening to the radio, staring up at the ceiling in his bedroom while his mother made plans for the next day's classes. He was lonely, she came to understand. He didn't mention a single friend.

He was, she thought, in many ways her twin.

"You coming in?" she asked outside the house.

But with a shy and confounding laugh, he sprinted away. "See you in half an hour!"

At the sliding-glass door, hazily trapped in the reflection of Grandpa's old movie studio, Percy was tightening his tie at the collar, looking like somebody's bank president. "Who was that?" he said, glaring into the darkness. "Why'd he take off running?"

Diane let go of Peanut Pattie's leash. "That's Mrs. Harlan's son," she said. "I'd think if anyone that you'd know him."

Peanut Pattie had made a beeline for Grandpa's room. Diane heard the old man grumbling good-naturedly as she crossed into the den. "That a girl," he said in his rattling, grumbling German accent. "That a good girl?"

She stopped at the shadowed doorway. "You feeling any better, Pops?"

With her eyes adjusting she could make out Arnetta taking Grandpa's blood pressure, squeezing the black rubber ball in one hand and holding up the meter with the other. Another man, a stranger, sat by Grandpa's bed in a wheelchair, a warm smile taking shape in the dark. This must be "Uncle" George, though he was really her grandfather's cousin. Peanut Pattie lay flat on Grandpa's chest flicking her tail, licking him on his chin. The old man coughed twice, phlegmy and with some force, then said, "Such a sweetums." His accent made phrases like that almost humorous, the *z* and *v* sounds slipped in like a cartoon character. He massaged Peanut Pattie behind the ears, scratched her between the shoulder blades. "Diane."

"Yes?"

"I want to get your *Hans & Greta* pictures. They bring me great joy. Can you remember?"

"Yes," she said. "I'll remember."

The man in the wheelchair, not bothering with introductions, said only, "He's talked about nothing else."

In her own room, she flopped onto the bed and took a deep breath. Everything here was wrong for her. Back in Chicago, just more than a year ago, she and Percy had lived with her mother, Antonia, in a little brown house in Avondale, on Albany Avenue, and in the evenings Diane would take her radio and a book out to the tiny front lawn, leaving her parents to their television, their "discussions," their second and then third after-dinner drinks. In the winter, when nobody was going out to front lawns, she had the attic, half-finished by Percy's handiwork. There, she would sketch the Beatles in their *Sgt. Pepper's* outfits, angular and maybe a little too tall, their eyes a bit more shaded than in reality, maybe looking a little sick you could say, or lacking sleep.

Before this visit she hadn't known Grandpa at all, could only remember meeting him once. From what her father had said about him over the years, she hadn't wanted to know him. A miserly and self-obsessed jerk, according to family lore, who spent most of his spare time watching old movies on a projector, griping about Hollywood, telling his only son that he needed to find a path of his own, or at least not come begging at the door just because his mother inherited some money. Until this trip, in fact, she could only remember Percy on the phone with Grandpa twice, the first when Grandma died six years ago, before they'd all packed up to visit, and the second a year or so later, when whatever was said between them led Percy to stomp around the house cursing and gritting his teeth until long after her bedtime.

Of course, things had gotten worse between her parents after that. And then Diane and Percy had hit the road.

"Deedee," Percy said at the door now. "You getting ready?"

She wasn't, of course. "Yeah," she said. "Just a minute."

She forced herself up off the bed and looked at herself in the mirror: stringy hair, a greasy forehead, her lips fixed in a grimace. Peanut Pattie opened her eyes a moment and then closed them again. From the closet Diane took out a clean shirt, a pair of jeans, her favorite sneakers. In the car drive out here she'd written in ballpoint pen along the white strip of their soles the lyrics to "The Long and Winding Road." Upside down, a little smudged, she could still make out most of the words.

———

"SO LIKE," TRACK said, "are you totally into the Beatles or what?"

"No," she said, and tried to convey her dismissal of his question by gazing pointedly across the room, where a shaggy-haired waiter passed oversized laminated menus to a family that looked like people from television, sharp and pressed and overtanned, the parents with combed white hair, the kids sitting too erect, even the baby looking disdainfully thoughtful, an adult crease across its brow. On the wood-paneled walls, gold starbursts glinted; the wide glass windows faced a parking lot full of long cars. No, she wasn't the one totally into the Beatles. That was her mother. Antonia, who in her more manic moods would put *Abbey Road* on the record player and sing along to every word, strumming the broom handle like a guitar, shaking her long brown hair like tassels to the rhythm. Diane liked them. That was the limit of it. She liked them and liked Antonia liking them too.

"Deedee," her father interrupted, "how's the spaghetti?"

She had been twisting a forkful of it and letting the coils slip back onto the plate for maybe ten minutes. "Good," she said. "Why?"

Her father cleared his throat and gave Mrs. Harlan a tight smile. "The food's delicious here, Tessa. Top-shelf. Really great idea."

Mrs. Harlan squeezed her shoulders and wriggled a bit, pleased with herself. She wore a matching powder-blue pants-and-shirt outfit out of the Sears catalogue with a long necklace of white marbles which she had gathered in her lap beneath her napkin when she sat down. Not a bad-looking woman, though her haircut was a little old-fashioned and her arms, too pudgy for the tight sleeves of that shirt, sported a dark bristle of hair from elbow to wrist that Diane found alarming. As Diane watched, she reached her knuckly hand across the table and took Percy's, and then they both sat there smiling like idiots in a movie about to burst into song.

Later, minutes later, Diane would see the melodrama in her dropping her fork, in its loud clatter on the plate, in the way her jaw fell open though her lips remained closed. She would understand this, later, but in the moment everything was instinct. "What?" she said. "You two are in love I guess?"

Track blew a raspberry so loud, all the other tables turned to gaze at them with a mix of horror and amusement.

"Deedee," Percy whispered, his whole body hunched forward like Quasimodo.

But it got Mrs. Harlan's hand off him. "Diane, dear," she said, but then gazed over Diane's head as if reading fine print at a distance. "Your grandfather has shown me some of your drawings, but your father says you always bring more with you. Can I see them?"

Obviously Percy would go and tell Mrs. Harlan about her sketchbook, her pencils. Diane tried not to feel betrayed. "They're not for showing," she said, and gripped her bag on the floor between her sneakers.

"Deedee," Percy said again, his voice bending lower. She watched his mustache twitch as he looked for words. "Mrs. Harlan has informed me that the middle school offers an array of quality art classes."

"Has she?"

Track sniggered, and now it was his turn in the barrel. "Young man you'll be respectful," said Mrs. Harlan.

Diane gave Track a knowing smile, a faint nod. They were a team.

"Well, Deedee," Percy forced through his clenched jaw. "I'm very proud of your pictures, so I wanted Mrs. Harlan to see them. But I understand."

So they were going to talk to her this way, were they, like she was still a small child, to be poked and cajoled and complimented into doing what they wanted? It didn't matter. Sitting here with her cold spaghetti, she just wanted the whole rigmarole to be over. She reached down for her bag—one of Antonia's old purses, actually—unzipped it, and took out the sketchbook. She flipped the pages to the middle, where she'd drawn Grandpa stretched out in bed with the light of his film projector glowing in his spectacles. Then she handed it over.

Mrs. Harlan gasped, put her hand to her chest, did the whole number adults do when they playact being impressed by a kid. "Oh, it's wonderful," she said. "The shading." She licked the tip of her finger to turn the page at the corner, to one of Diane's *Sgt. Pepper's* drawings, the one where Paul, John, Ringo, and George stood on a tiny, deserted island looking forlorn. Mrs. Harlan laughed at this and turned the picture toward Track. "Look," she said, "it's the Monkees."

Track didn't respond to his mom's mistake, but gave Diane a knowing smirk, nodding slow like he'd caught her with the murder weapon tucked up her sleeve. She wanted to kick him.

"And who is this beautiful woman?" Mrs. Harlan said, showing the sketch of Antonia at the window back in Chicago, tears in her eyes, her high cheekbones and sharp chin caught just right by the winter sun.

Percy looked down at the table.

"That's my mom," Diane said. "That's *Mrs.* Stiegl."

———

WELL, THAT WAS about it. There was more, of course—a little talk and some eating and a little game played with the waiter about whether they would have dessert—but none of that mattered because really the night was over, and in no time she was back in the car with her father opening the door and falling into the driver's seat and sighing. "Deedee, you can't just go hurting Mrs. Harlan's feelings."

Diane thought for a moment of playing dumb, of saying she didn't know what he was talking about. But this would only prolong the conversation, and keep her from saying what she really wanted to say. "I don't like her," she said. "She acts like someone's secretary."

"That's a terrible thing to say."

"Is it?"

"What do you mean by secretary?"

"Mom was always herself, not somebody else's anything."

He seemed to consider this, wrinkling his eyes out at the night. Mrs. Harlan and Track swung past in their long white car, the headlights flashing Diane blind. "Is," he said, and turned over the engine. "Mom *is* herself. But she doesn't want to be with us, Deedee. That's a choice she made."

"I don't like it here," she said.

Her father pulled onto the road. He drove too slow, too thoughtfully. Never before had that fallen quality about him—that sense he'd come from a great position and only lately discovered himself among the rabble—been so apparent to Diane, so palpable. Other cars sped past them. A man in a big truck rode their bumper for half a mile, at least. "Mom told me last time we talked that you may be able to stay with her next year. She's getting her medications sorted out."

She hadn't heard about this, hadn't heard from Antonia in weeks. "You talked to Mom? When did you talk to her?"

"Last weekend. She was in one of her happy moods. I think she thought we were still married."

Diane could see her, hair stringy and uncombed, clothes unmatched, no shoes. Antonia in one of her happy moods meant music playing and all the big plans you knew could never happen. They would all move to Paris. They would get a pony. Why not? A girl deserved a pony and to live in Paris. They should all load up in the car right now and see the Grand Canyon. What colors should we paint these walls? What usually came of it was Percy making them all bologna sandwiches and going out for a box of ice cream and chocolate syrup, a long speech from Antonia about how Diane could be anything, could be the president of the United States, and then something would eventually turn her back from the edge of her optimism. They'd never let her, she would say. Not *them*. Diane you've got to watch out, you've got to always look over your shoulder, Diane they are waiting for you to step out of line, Diane I want you to promise me you'll stay right here with us, Diane it's too dangerous out there, Diane. And then there would be crying, and Percy petting her hair, and the next day she would either be a normal mom again or half-asleep and speechless, sobbing at the kitchen table, muttering in the hall, staring with unfocused disinterest at the nothings that hung in the air.

Antonia had left them both after one of those dark days, first to a hotel, where she called Percy from a payphone to tell him she wouldn't come back, and later to her friend Rona's house all the way up in Evanston. Diane had the feeling she was never supposed to hear the next dozen phone calls, with Percy in the kitchen pacing to the end of the cord and back, shouting and begging and whimpering. Not once did Antonia ask to talk to her, not until it was all final and done with, three whole months later, on Diane's birthday. By that time, Antonia had moved to some seemingly random town in Massachusetts, a circumstance no one had ever explained. "I didn't want to hurt your feelings," she had said, ridiculously. "I didn't want to get you involved."

Then they'd hit the road, Diane and her father.

"Anyway, it's going to be a while," Percy said, without malice but rather with a sense of defeat. "What do you really think of Mrs. Harlan?"

"What do I think of her?"

He needed a minute to build up a response. "Deedee, I only want you to be happy," he said finally. "I know nothing's working out here. Not yet. But it will."

On the radio, the DJ was introducing a John Denver song. Diane hated John Denver, hated the way he made her stomach feel vertiginous and sad. All she wanted to be happy was to have her life make sense again, to feel like it was put together. But she aimed lower. "Dad, will you just change the station?"

———

THE NEXT DAY she met up with Track while walking Peanut Pattie—this time on purpose. He'd called not long after breakfast, asking if she wanted to hang out. No boy had ever asked her to do such a thing. Walking through the neighborhood in the dry, troublingly warm air, her heart fluttered a bit. When she found him on the driveway of Mrs. Harlan's place in a folding chair, sipping from a can of Pepsi, wearing jean shorts and no shoes and no shirt, she thought for a bare second that she might be a little into him.

"Hey," he said.

He left her outside with Peanut Pattie while he went in to get shoes and a shirt—a power move, she would think, years later, to call her over and then leave her waiting. But at the time she watched his bony and brown shoulders, the tan back of his ribs, his scuffed elbows, all the way through the closing storm door. Then she looked down at Peanut Pattie and said, "Don't embarrass me, all right?"

Peanut Pattie only gave her those sad eyes, then sniffed an empty patch in the grass.

"I'm only kidding," she said.

When Track shot back out the door he said, "What's up?" as if they hadn't already greeted each other, and then: "Hey, have you heard Ornette Coleman? I'm getting into Ornette Coleman. Crazy stuff."

She hadn't. But that was fine. They walked around the neighborhood, up and down one block after another, and he told her all about Ornette Coleman, really got animated about the concept of free jazz, listed off a half dozen saxophone and trumpet players she needed to listen to, and finally, when it was likely clear she wasn't all that invested in the subject, he returned to that of his father, that whole embarrassing escapade with the younger woman—the girl, really—and how devastated Mrs. Harlan had remained these last years. "She says she always knew there had been other women. I mean, here's this movie star. Well, TV star at least. Famous and okay-looking and in good shape. And he ran with that crowd, you know, womanizers."

"Womanizer," she repeated—not because she hadn't heard the word before, but because it sounded so strange coming from this fellow kid's lips.

"She's been a wreck all this time and now she sings—literally sings—when she walks in the door after seeing Mr., uh, your dad. You know, I think they're pretty serious? Like we might be brother and sister one day."

Well, that was gross, and in the coming weeks and months, she would feel even grosser about that breathless moment in his driveway, when that flutter of attraction lurched through her blood vessels. Because soon enough—within hours of the fire and then of Grandpa's death—Mrs. Harlan and Track would be over at the house with bags full of clothing, planning to stay the night so that Percy and Diane didn't feel all alone. That sleepover turned into a week, and at the end of the week, it would be Percy and Diane packing bags to go live at the Harlans'. Diane would watch in horror as the threat of her father getting remarried to this English teacher in Palm Springs went from unthinkable to unavoidable.

———

THERE WOULD BE a few good times during this escalating dread: the Polaroid camera Mrs. Harlan got her for Christmas, the few friends she made at junior high once she started classes that January, the art class she took that same semester, her first trip that summer—on Mrs. Harlan's dime because Grandpa's estate had apparently left them nothing but bills—to New Jersey to see Antonia, who of course took her to New York, to the museums, to the galleries, to a show of photorealist painters whose paintings were all in oil so that when Diane returned to Palm Springs in August, she was painting with oils.

And then would come the unbelievable day when Percy set out his plan to return to Olympia without her, only for a while he said, only for a month or two, she'll be with him before Halloween for sure, but also this other woman, Candace or something, a department-store employee, a woman he met trying on pants, was actually going with him, up to Washington. "Don't tell Tessa, okay? She wouldn't understand. Candy's just a friend. And she needs a ride."

All that was ahead of her, ahead of them.

———

TODAY, THIS DAY, the day she'd known Track for exactly one day, was the very day they turned back toward Grandpa's house and saw the smoke, the distant flick of orange-red flame, and took off running, Peanut Pattie panting to keep up. Diane said, disbelieving her own words, "I think it's my grandpa's. I think it's his studio."

And just like that, a fire truck came bounding onto the desert plain, kicking up sand, tearing through brush. When they got to the back fence, Track flung himself over it first, taking Peanut Pattie, helping Diane scale the high planks. "What happened?" she shouted as Peanut Pattie ran irrational circles around her.

Her father stood in the back doorway with his eyes bigger than she'd ever seen them. "Your grandpa had an accident," he stammered. "When he came in he wasn't feeling well."

Track was rubbing at his mouth like he didn't want to say something. But then he blurted out, "Did he start the fire? Like, is he crazy or something?"

"Don't say that!" Diane shouted at Track, and Peanut Pattie, taking sides, sent him a rapid fire of raspy barks. The firemen, too, were shouting. A cone of black smoke tornadoed from the studio's open skylight. In the side doorway, fire swept out like a single fat tongue, lolling to one side and then another, mixed gusts of black and white smoke pumping out all around. Diane's heart seemed choked in her larynx. Peanut Pattie went on barking. Then the firemen had their hose aimed at the studio's front door, steadied their legs in the sand like grown men playing tug-of-war, and the water came. "All his things," she said. And then, to her father, "Is he okay?"

ALL THAT AFTERNOON, Percy and Arnetta and the doctor went in and out of Grandpa's closed room. Diane's job was to watch Peanut Pattie and to make sandwiches for everyone, peanut butter and jelly. She watched hours of television and she answered the phone when Mrs. Harlan called and later when Track called and later still when "Uncle" George and then Mr. Welles and then Mr. Ford's assistant called. At eleven o'clock, long past her bedtime, her father called her in. "He's sleeping," he said, and held her from behind by the shoulders as she stood next to Grandpa's bed, whispering that he would feel better soon and that Peanut Pattie missed him.

She hadn't thought she would be able to sleep, but she did, and when she woke something electric hummed in the air. Her bedroom door had been closed when she always left it open, and Peanut Pattie wasn't around. Sitting up, she could hear voices, and imagined all of Grandpa's old friends gathered in the living room sipping coffee and chatting with him. She got out of bed slowly, though her movements came in jerks. At the door she stopped with her hand on the knob and recognized Arnetta's voice and the doctor's.

Diane turned the knob and opened the door just a crack. There, on the green wingback chair in the living room, her father sat with one leg crossed over the other, his chin propped in the palm of one hand. Peanut Pattie was curled in his lap.

"It happened early this morning," Percy told her when she finally worked up the courage to step out. His eyes were red and empty. He moved his free hand through the air as if he were flinging dust from his fingers. "The doctor said he wasn't in pain. Just slipped off."

Arnetta and the doctor stood in the kitchen under harsh light. That's what Diane noticed now: all the lights in the house were on even though it was another sunny morning. Everyone must have been awake for hours, dealing with this new quiet, starting up the machinery of death. Already the doctor had come, the body taken by ambulance, plans made at a funeral home. "The newspapers still need to be called," her father muttered. "And his friends. Mother's friends too."

Diane sat on the arm of his chair for a while, unsure of what to say. Then, after the doctor shouted his goodbye into the room and Arnetta began packing her things, Diane went to her grandfather's room. It was quiet and clean, the curtains drawn. She couldn't recall seeing this room so full of bright daylight before. Diane stretched out on his bed, now made up with a cover and pillowcases she didn't recognize. Peanut Pattie moseyed in, loitered near the bed, then hopped up beside her. "Lie down," she told the dog. "Down." When Peanut Pattie was settled, Diane stared at the bright opposite wall where one of her grandfather's watercolors showed a beach scene with the sun dropping into the horizon, its orange light leaked onto the gentle waves. A woman and young boy walked into the water to meet this light. She closed her eyes tight and tried her best not to cry.

VARIETY

Nov. 1928

SCHLOSSBERG DECLARES SILENTS DEAD
LAST TALKIE HOLDOUT FOLDS
by PETE PEARSON

Mo Schlossberg is back from the desert—Palm Springs, in fact—with a message for stars who fear the microphone: "SILENTS ARE FINISHED." Bankrolling the rebel von Stiegl in his nutty venture, Schlossberg had said this summer that "the American people deserve a choice between the new noisy picture and the kind of artistic excellence we've seen build up over the last decade." But production on von Stiegl's new studio and its one planned film faltered and finally blew out after star George West broke his neck in the director's pool.

Attentive readers will remember that studio chiefs across the board had gasped in horror when radio personality Dwight Squibb reported on his Sunday program that the handsome star's catastrophic accident came at the end of a clandestine motion picture cooked up in a secret desert studio. The German, previously praised for the pansy picture *Bachelor's Wife*, had finagled the movie legend Schlossberg's money as a way to take full control over a fairy-tale no-talkie picture von Stiegl's boss, Irving Thalberg, had given the thumbs-down. Before this act of old-fashioned treason, our boy von Stiegl had been crowned the next big somebody, his pictures celebrated by critics and sometimes even liked by ticket-buying audiences. But his Hansel-and-Gretel goof was no good for MGM, and rather than grow up, he took his children's story into the desert, making use of somebody else's money to attempt one of Hollywood's dumbest grand larcenies.

At the time, Mo Schlossberg—whose investments range from MGM to Universal and Fox and even the newly minted R.K.O.—had defended his hare-brained prince. Now Schlossberg sings a different tune. "Some actors and actresses just aren't made for sound pictures. Voice, personality, skill, whatever it may be. We wanted to give these talents a place to keep working. But at some point you've got to know when to walk away. That time is now."

Among the stars in question is undoubtably Kay Stone, who rode in on von Stiegl's coattails two years ago. Now let go by MGM (along with another half dozen players associated with Stiegl's folly), the beauty's Hollywood future looks dim. Even von Stiegl, himself a newly unpopular fellow in the picture colony, echoes Schlossberg's outlook. "All that old time is over," he told Hedda Hopper. The German, visiting Hollywood one last time before returning to his Palm Springs hideout, said, "We'll never again see the art of silent cinema. There won't even be time for mourning."

One studio insider I called last night said, "Von Stiegl is finished. He's a thief and a troublemaker. Nobody like him should ever step foot in this town again." But is the day of the "artistic" director finished too? My insider says no. "We always aim for art, and the best way to ensure good movie art is for the *producer* to have control of a property from start to finish. That doesn't mean directors aren't part of that system." But the highfalutin days of directors trying out big-brained intellectualism on the common American looking for a good time? The end of that European-scented trend couldn't end soon enough!

Hans & Greta, the big picture von Stiegl was making in his secret desert studio, was nearly finished at the time production was stopped. Apparently based on the old tale of kids lost in a forest, this one had lovers hiding out from modern life until a city witch came to burn them out. No wonder MGM stamped the brakes. The sort of children who would line up for such silliness can't afford a ticket to split between a dozen. We'll wait and see if anything (or anyone) von Stiegl touches will be in theaters ever again.

As for "Big Mo," he'll be at his famous Ocean House, washing his hands of the whole mess. "I was hoodwinked," he said. "But now I'm ready to get back to business." Rumor has it the Thalbergs and Mayers will be on the invite list to break bread and smoke the peace pipe this very weekend, along with a parade of Hollywood's biggest stars, paying their birthday respects to Kitty Schlossberg, this writer's favorite kitten.

KLAUS

1925

IN 1909, KLAUS Aaronsohn entered New York Harbor a month shy of four years old. The earliest memory he could recall, however, was a night some months later on the Lower East Side when a man his father knew from the piecework trade walked the family to a dance hall where, for a nickel each, they were shown a series of motion pictures: a cowboy rescuing a woman from a mustached criminal, a man in blackface lighting matches under the toes of his factory boss, a beautiful woman descending a staircase wearing more diamonds than could possibly exist in all the world. So taken by the movies was little Klaus that later in life, true or not he could no longer tell, he would relate the story that the day his parents died in a fire in their tiny one-room tenement he had been at the pictures watching a Charlie Chaplin short.

Though the details of that fateful day may be the product of an imaginative and malleable autobiographical impulse, its product was straightforward: he would be raised into adulthood by his uncle Leopold, proprietor of a successful collar company headquartered in Brooklyn, who had for years been on unspeaking terms with Klaus's father. Klaus was educated with the help of a private tutor, taken under the wing of his older cousin George, and eventually made an executive of the family company at the early age of nineteen. That same year, 1924, he sailed with his cousin and uncle back to Germany, to see Berlin for the first time, to visit his unremembered birthplace of Lüneberg, to make business connections, and—though this part was kept from his uncle—to explore the nightclubs and titillating acts along the Kurfürstendamm. The sex shows were of little interest to him, however. His attention was drawn instead to the Weimar movie palaces, where he saw Murnau's *The Last Laugh* at least half a dozen times, determining before their return to America that he would make of himself a film director. Part of his hubris on this count—this abrupt belief that he could manifest a Hollywood career out of lint and spare coins—must have come from his cousin George's announcement during their travels that he intended to go to California and play in the movies. A talent scout from Metro Pictures had written him with a firm offer, George had explained, with a train ticket across the continent enclosed.

———

IN THE YEAR after George Aaronsohn, now George West, had fled New York to make his name in Hollywood, Klaus rose to his uncle's chief assistant, taking the official title of general manager. Still, he pined for a job in the movies like his cousin. It was the 1920s and it was New York, and so it was exactly as people remembered that place and time. Cash sprouted from the sidewalks. Jazz played from the clouds. The great city lurched with one heave into modernity, and nothing of the past seemed to remain. Klaus took up the hobby of photography, enrolling in a night class where he learned how to process his film in a darkened room of his Flatbush apartment. Thinking this would get him closer to his dream, he wandered the streets in his spare time with a Stiegl-100 Reflex camera, hoping for a miracle to land on his head.

When he wasn't clicking pictures, he spent his time alone at the movie theater, especially the Loews Palace on Strauss Street, where he saw Stroheim's *Greed* and Buster Keaton in *Sherlock, Jr.*, and Colleen Moore in *So Big* and *Beau Brummel* with the great John Barrymore and a western called *The Iron Horse* and *The Enchanted Cottage* with Richard Barthelmess and Valentino in *The Eagle* and

the Mary Pickford picture *Little Annie Rooney*. He imagined himself running a film camera as Richard Barthelmess rushed out onto
breaking ice to save Mary Pickford from certain death.

He wrote often to George, and his cousin wrote back with tales
of Hollywood parties and wild movie sets. George West had been
added late to the production of *Ben-Hur*, where he rode alongside
the lead in a grand chariot race; he had been fitted for a tuxedo to
make eyes at Rosemary Treet in something called *The Little Angel*,
a role that sparked the ridiculous rumor he and Treet were lovers;
he had even worn chaps, boots, and hat in a picture called *Prairie
Justice*, in which he'd played the gunslinger's best friend, cut down
by a bandit's bullet early in the third act. His star, George said, was
rising. Soon he would be in the firmament.

Klaus vented his frustrations about sharing an office with the
dull Sid Povich, kept his cousin up to date on all the movies he'd
seen and how Uncle Leopold had come to call his almost-famous
son "The Disappointment," a moniker George would use as his signature in letters for years to come. Klaus had made the mistake of
mentioning in the office that he'd seen *The Little Angel* and thought
George rather good in it, and Uncle Leopold had left early for the
day and avoided speaking to him for a week. Poor Uncle Leopold.
He had come to the conclusion that the entire Aaronsohn family
should never have left Lüneberg, the medieval German town Klaus
had seen only once on a single day's visit with his uncle and George.
The man was depressed. "He'll come around," George wrote back.
"His pride's hurt. Wait'll he sees me in this new William Haines
picture!" Klaus didn't have the moxie to tell him the old man had
taken to badmouthing motion pictures in general and sworn at Sunday dinner that he would never step into a movie theater again as
long as he lived.

Then Artie Banyan, a boisterous and massive scenario writer
with Famous Players–Lasky, drunkenly ran into Klaus outside the
Rialto Theatre, where he had just seen the Eleanor Boardman picture *The Circle*. Klaus had been aiming his camera down the street at

the exiting crowd and instantly Artie wanted to know all about him. "After all we're in the same business," he said. And, making a grand and inebriate gesture with his arm, "Part of the great Edisonian experiment, my friend."

"You would see my photographs?" Klaus said.

"Oh, I'll see," said the giant. "Let's on to the photo-graphs!"

Half an hour later, in the Flatbush apartment, Klaus showed this stranger his pictures and, after watching him down the remainder of the flask he kept pulling from his jacket pocket, asked what he thought. "Talent," said Artie. "Real talent, if you ask me."

"What I want to do is the motion pictures," Klaus ventured.

"Me too, buddy. Me too." And though Klaus wanted to ask him exactly what this meant, the man's wavering form called instead for letting him sleep on his sofa.

The next morning they were fast friends, talking about movies over breakfast at a nearby diner, Klaus increasingly impressed with himself for keeping up with an actual employee of a motion-picture studio. And of course—how could he avoid it?—he pressed this new acquaintance for a way into the movie business. "Well," Artie had said, "it's not as easy as all that. But I could make some introductions."

That very evening he met Artie at a Greenwich Village teahouse called Madame Rovenskaya's Cosmopolitan Samovar, a deep and low-ceilinged space, dimly lit, full of cigarette smoke and the warm damp of boiled water. Its tables were blocky and roughhewn, as if they'd been shaped by a dull ax, and its clientele was a crowded hodgepodge of bohemian types, all of whom looked up at Klaus as he entered with a vague expression of disappointment. Artie was seated at a small table with two attractive young women with bobbed hair wearing frilly, puffy-armed dresses of the type common at the turn of the century. On the table between them was a pair of blond wigs curled with tight locks.

The young women were soused, and like others in the establishment, made no secret of the flask they passed between them as Klaus approached. The redhead looked up at him first. "Who's this?" she said. "Looks like your doctor's here, Kate."

The other, Kate, leveled her blue eyes at him and said, "No, ma'am. This is the fellow I hired to take you to the loony bin."

Artie stood and gestured to Klaus with an open hand. "Ladies, this is the eminent photographer you may have heard of, a Mr. Klaus Aaronsohn?"

The two young women wobbled their heads by way of response.

"And this here is Marge," said Artie, "and Kate. Two actresses just off the clock from our dear Famous Players–Lasky studio out in the boonies of Astoria."

"We had a little on the bus," said Marge apologetically. "And then a little more on the train."

"I'm pleased to meet you," Klaus managed. He took the camera from around his neck and set it on the table as he dropped into a chair. Then, meeting eyes with the woman called Kate, he said, "Just what kind of picture are you—"

But Artie had apparently been in the middle of something. "You see when you take Picasso and the so-called *cubists*—"

The two women seemed only half-interested in hearing about this, and Klaus himself quickly lost track of anything his new friend was saying. Between these cross-purposes, the women would occasionally and without notice begin laughing, and then exchange a portion of conversation Klaus couldn't follow, and then Artie would begin again, reiterating some phrase he'd just said. All of this proved almost unbearable to Klaus, whose cup of tea kept getting refilled by Marge with something from a flask that smelled vaguely of pine needles.

After what felt like an hour of this, Kate interrupted one of Artie's diatribes to say, "We think it's time to take this party over to our place."

The notion was shocking to Klaus, at least in its moral implications.

But then again he hadn't spent any time in such artistic circles. And before he could air any of his trepidation, Artie came out with, "Yeah let's on to the place!"

Let's on. It seemed to be something of a phrase with him.

"The place" stood only a block away, up two narrow flights of stairs, with a single window looking down on Charles Street. On the walls hung more ashcan-style paintings than any single domicile should ever hold, at least to Klaus's taste, and before he had his bearings, the young women had skittered behind a gold-and-red Chinese screen to change clothes. They complained about their day's work as Artie rifled the discs in a wire frame next to the phonograph. Klaus had the strong impression that he'd wandered into the company of—as his uncle would say—low people.

The girls weren't featured players after all, for instance. They were only extras, hired for pickup work now and again for the Lasky studio. And Artie's position as a scenario writer seemed, in the context of a conversation Klaus could only barely follow, to be threadbare. Just as Klaus tried to formulate a method of escape, Marge said, "All day we been walking back and forth behind a comic bit for that D. W. Griffith. What a waste."

"You worked for Griffith?" Klaus said, bolt upright, the evening now glowing with significance. "What's he like on-set?"

"Oh, he's like anyone else," Marge said, coming out from behind the screen and gesturing Kate to take her place. "Artie, I've been thinking of singing again." She turned to Klaus. "I used to sing; it's why I came to the city. All the way from Pittsburgh three years ago. I tried out for Paul Whiteman but he went with some floozy. So I toured a couple years with this little orchestra, the Kansas City Tots, from New Rochelle."

"It's a fine idea," said Artie.

Kate handed Klaus a glass. "Gin and soda," she said. She nodded at him. "Do you lug that thing around everywhere you go?"

She meant the camera. "Yes," Klaus said. And then, wanting to impress her, "My cousin's in pictures. George West? He played the antagonist in that William Haines picture."

"I love William Haines," said Kate. She looked up at the ceiling with her lips puckered. Her throat, white as ivory, looked like the softest thing in the world. "I'm trying to think," she said. "The one with the slick black hair? The handsome one?"

"That's him."

Artie sat up. "Klaus wants to be in pictures."

"Oh you should go with us to the studio," said Marge, who had joined Artie on the rug. "A German? Like Lubitsch? These days they're all the rage. They'd hire a fish with a name like yours to direct."

IT WAS, AFTER all, a miracle falling on his head that did it.

The next morning Klaus set about creating an alter-ego, himself but then again someone else, the aristocratic *von* attached to the name of his camera: Klaus von Stiegl, a mysterious genius who had worked alongside Murnau and Pabst, whose accent was only a shade or two more crisp and declarative than Klaus's own, a man who wore a monocle and riding pants, who carried a cane, who was given to long silences as he considered the aesthetics of this or that image before him. When he told Artie about this, the giant said that he was crazy. "Crazy," he said, looking over the new garb, "but I like it anyway. I mean, who's to know any different? Once a Hun always a Hun, I say."

Klaus bought his new self an expensive bowler hat, scented pomade, and ordered from a catalogue handkerchiefs embroidered with the letters *KvS*. He wrote his cousin to tell him of these developments but wouldn't receive a response for nearly two years.

A month after the night in Marge and Kate's apartment, Klaus got a call at his office at Aaronsohn Collars. Kate's voice on the line, asking if he could be at the Astoria studios at three o'clock. "A cameraman just got fired," she said. "Nick Abruzzo says they need someone today."

"Who's Nick Abruzzo?"

"Oh, he's Marge's sweetheart. Head of photography. She put in a good word for you."

January 3, 1973

Dear Deedee,

Things have settled in here in Olympia,
though I am afraid that job didn't pan out.
Rest assured I'm still looking. Pounding the
pavement, as they say. Candace has found work at
a dentist's office answering the phone, etc., and
so we are sharing a small place together. Once I
find work of my own everything will be better and
you can come up.

In the meantime I have some good news: Frank
Harlan, your grandpa's business partner (the
guy from Brackett!) has agreed to buy the old
property. Since the house needs work and the old
studio needs tearing down, it's not a fortune,
but it's some money. I'm going to be sure to send
some of that to Tessa to help out, too. Funny it
will be money from her ex-father-in-law! Harlan's
agreed to clean out all that junk in his studio-
old papers and drawings and props, etc. I did
save a few of dad's (grandpa's) watercolors,
though, and I'll give those to you sometime. I
remember you like them.

Cold here. The car has been having trouble
starting. Candace and I went to see The Poseidon
Adventure last night, it was very good. If it's
still playing down there be sure to see it. Miss
you and love you,

                                    Dad

DIANE

1979

S HE WOKE TO the sound of Annie Moore stomping through the room, barefoot, wearing underwear and that ratty gray sweater, her thighs wobbling a little with each step. Diane rolled onto her side, pulled up the bedsheet she'd been given, tried wrenching her eyes closed. "You're awake," Annie announced. "You want coffee?"

Diane carefully extended a fist from the sheet and raised her middle finger.

"That's what makes you such a good guest," Annie said. "You're a charmer."

"My head is broken."

Annie filled the teapot with water, spooned instant coffee into two mugs, and leaned against the counter, waiting on a boil. "You shouldn't have taken ludes at a bar. That's common fucking sense. You know that guy Mercer had to help me drag you upstairs? It took me an hour to get him to leave. He thought we were an item all of a sudden."

"Ugh," Diane said. But what she really meant was that she'd forgotten all about last night, had canceled out the whole day, had actually awoken thinking it was yesterday, Friday. "I need to call my mom."

"Oh she already called. Like an hour ago? What I like most about my best friend blacking out on me is getting a wake-up call at seven Saturday morning from her mom."

Diane looked up at her, standing there cross-armed and smirking, half-naked. "Aren't you cold?"

Annie gave her an exasperated look. Last week, after they had taken turns cutting each other's hair short and punk, a dare they'd been pushing each other toward for at least a month, Diane had told her that they should glue-stick all the hair on the floor to their chins and go out to a disco as Dan and Adam. Annie had given her the same look then: eyebrows popped, blinking, taking a deep breath.

"You're pissed off," Diane said, and hefted herself up to a seated position, wrapping the sheet around her like a swami. "I'm totally freezing."

"It's warm in here," Annie said, pouring hot water over into the mugs. "I don't know what you're talking about."

She brought over both mugs and took a seat on the couch next to Diane, who held her coffee in both palms—she really was intolerably cold. Annie's place was on the Upper East Side, only blocks away from Central Park, in a surprisingly shabby building where the two of them had been held up by a man with a knife in the lobby last semester. He'd been wearing a ski cap with a scarf over his mouth and nose, and a long tan trench coat with mud stains all over. This in early September. He too was cold when everyone else had been warm.

"What did my mom say?"

Annie sipped at her coffee. "A lot. Everything. I was on the phone with her until I came out. Did you know she thinks you aced a philosophy exam this week?"

"I may have told her that." Diane had, in fact, quit going to all her classes but the painting studio with Professor Bartolomos. She had rationalized this decision by taking a job waiting tables at Sargento's three days a week, through the lunch rush, and putting in a few extra hours in the studio before heading back home to New Jersey, or, as was often the case lately, over to Annie's. "What else did you talk about?"

"Let's see. Do you want to hear the plot from *Every Which Way but Loose*? Because she basically read me the script. She's lonely, Diane. Don't take this the wrong way but you really need to go home."

She did need to go home, she knew that. Antonia had been living with a lanky-haired guitar player named Tom whom Diane had met only once, during a visit from Palm Springs a year before she came here for school. He seemed too cool to believe—like he'd been cut out of a picture in *Rolling Stone*. Tom's band had broken up last year, and he'd gone to Detroit to form another one, leaving Antonia with the space to put up her college-bound daughter, but also rudderless and alone and on the downswing.

It came as a surprise to Diane that despite all warning signs, by the time classes started at NYU that fall, Antonia was back on her Lithium and she and Diane had a new relationship as adults. Two women who shared dinner and dishes responsibilities, who took turns carrying the trash bag down the narrow stairwell, who shopped together and watched television together and even talked about old times together, as if everything before had been only a weird dream. Until then, Diane hadn't realized how much she needed her mother—how much of her plan to go to New York for school had been, at least in part, a way to get back to her. And yet she also wanted her freedom, the ability to disappear to the city for nights on end. She resented Antonia's attempt at maternal connection, her bald-faced desire to make up for lost time. Diane had learned to live without a mother, save Mrs. Harlan, years ago, and wasn't ready to go back to childhood.

Only last weekend, Antonia's phone bill arrived with a thirty-eight-dollar long-distance charge for two calls to California, mostly from a single call to Palm Springs, to Mrs. Harlan. "I see you spent a whole evening talking to your other mother?" Antonia had said, pushing the bill across the table as they sat before bowls of soggy Mini-Wheats.

Diane gave her a sharp look. "We mostly talked about Track."

Antonia looked at the ceiling and wagged her head. A manic swing, Diane thought. But with the wrong set of emotions. The wrong mood. "That boy you lived with like he was your actual brother," she said with feigned exhaustion. "It's so unnatural. Your father was an idiot for leaving you with them."

And so Diane had stuffed an extra bra and panties into her purse that morning, had grabbed her toothbrush on the way out the door, had called Annie Moore when she got off the train to see if she could crash. Nearly a week ago.

Mom was getting out of bounds. This business about keeping Annie on the phone for an hour worried her especially. Didn't Diane have any autonomy or privacy at all? Besides that, she actually *did* feel a little guilty for partying all week while her mother sat at home with the television, woke for work every morning to the high-pitched buzz of her new digital alarm clock, and faced the world alone yet again. So what was the use of calling her friend in the hungover morning and talking about trash movies? "I'll call her today," she said, finally, and set her empty mug on the coffee table. "We're going out tonight, right?"

Annie coughed something like a laugh. "I'm not going anywhere," she said. "I've got to study. And sister, last night was enough for me. If I even smell beer again I'm gonna lose my lunch."

"So we don't drink beer."

Annie laughed, putting a friendly face on it. "Lady, you gotta go home."

WELL, THAT WAS the morning. By ten she was walking down Madison Avenue eating Pringles from the can, her red scarf fluttering out at each cross street. "How can you put all that junk in your body?" Antonia would ask her if she were here. Antonia, who had gotten into vegetarianism and then something called macro or micro, eating almost nothing but raw foods, the cupboard overtaken by unsalted nuts, dinners of sprouts and slaw, the crunch of apples and celery following Diane into every room. Diane made no attempt to follow this example, even after Antonia's sad "under my roof" talk a couple of months ago. Instead she brought home McDonald's and potato chips, ordered pizza and Chinese, only occasionally dipping into the vast pile of fruits and vegetables that threatened to roll off the kitchen counter and take up residence on the floor. It was a base disagreement on whether they were roommates or family, really.

And Antonia had started running, too, jogging around the neighborhood waving at anyone she saw like a lunatic. Sometimes she would wake Diane and beg her to go along with her, and sometimes Diane actually did go along, bounding next to her huffing and puffing mother, who complained, once they were home, of aches and pains in her ankles and knees. All of this, of course, since Tom left. She was—though neither of them wanted to face it—trying to prepare herself to reenter the market. "The market, Deedee? Are you under the impression your mother is a slab of meat?"

She couldn't call Antonia right now. Or she could, but she didn't want to, not with her mind so ragged from the previous night. Besides, she would have to weave together some explanation for why she'd stayed in Manhattan for three—or four? No three—days without even calling, and then to top that with why she wouldn't be home today. All of this explaining and permission, all the mother-daughter act, was too absurd to even explain to someone like Annie, whose mother had always been around, had never gone off the rails, had never given up custody of her only child without any real explanation. Sometimes, when Diane was frustrated, she wanted to bring up that very thing with Antonia. But her conscience would get the best of her. Antonia was doing better, she was on her meds, and this room in her apartment came rent-free, and at just the right time. All Diane needed to do was get through school, or whatever she was doing now.

She had taken two years off—had wanted to take one, but one led to another—and stayed with Mrs. Harlan even after getting her acceptance letter from UCLA. By then, Track had started his sophomore year of college up at Davis, having settled for in-state though he'd been aiming for one of the Ivies. She wanted to improve, she'd told Mrs. Harlan, and that's exactly what she did. For eighteen months straight she did almost nothing but draw and paint, and far from telling her to go out and get a job or a man, Mrs. Harlan had supported her. Once, outside on the lawn, as Diane painted a delivery van parked at the curb, a bag of garbage leaned against its back wheel, a Polaroid she had clipped to her easel in case the light changed or the van moved, Mrs. Harlan had brought out fresh orange juice and said, "The secret about life is that none of what we think matters is real. None of what we do and say, none of this money and society and shopping. The only real thing is the earth, the birds and trees and land. This perfect living being and all we do is look at ourselves in the mirror all day."

Diane, shaken and inspired by this unexpected insight, had written it down word for word in her sketchbook. It was, aside from when Percy had sat her down to tell her that Antonia wasn't coming home, the most important thing anyone had yet said to her. But she didn't share it; the sentiment felt too corny to pass off to her friends. Instead it became a sort of guiding light, a way to privately understand the world she found herself in at each successive stage of life.

Her portfolio got her into NYU two years after high school. As a freshman at twenty, feeling older but less cultured than her peers, she met Deondre Bartolomos at a senior art exhibit, dressed in a brown suit with a long white scarf that nearly reached his knees. He was unshaven, sharp-faced, with dark eyes and thick eyebrows and a French cap that concealed his balding, tightly curled black hair. In regular life, she maybe wouldn't have found him attractive—not ugly, but not exactly magnetic. A man on the street. In the right clothes, he could be selling hot dogs from a cart. But as Bartolomos, and set against the backdrop of the seniors' paintings and sculptures, he seemed the most civilized and magical being she'd ever laid eyes on.

He asked her: "What do you think about Titian?"

Of course Diane had no opinion of Titian, couldn't have placed one of his paintings next to Warhol's, just knew that he was old, long dead, and so she said, scratching at the palms of both her hands with her stubby fingernails, "I think we've all had enough of the past."

His thick eyebrows went up, and his smile changed to one less embarrassed for her and more dismissive of her. "That's funny, because the past is all we have," he said. "Even now we're all in the past. As soon as I finish this word —"

He paused like that, like it was really clever, like he was some dude passing a joint in a dorm room, and she suddenly couldn't stand him. So she gave him her own dismissive smile, shook her head, and walked away. For the rest of that evening she stayed away from him, kept her distance, tried to breathe shallowly even though her heart was racing: she had been caught out, ignorant, but he had proved himself an ass. She'd told Annie about the exchange, and Annie said that he was a dirtbag. "But he's a genius," Diane had said.

WEEKS LATER, SHE entered the elevator in the Barney Building and found Bartolomos talking with two students who seemed to be coming from his class. She had turned to face the lighted buttons with a hot sensation on her ears and cheeks. "Stiegl?" he said after a moment. "I hear you're related to the silent filmmaker?"

The other students, both men, both with shaggy hair and wearing loose sweaters, looked at her with interest. One of them even seemed to know who Bartolomos was talking about. Her grandfather had been having a renaissance of sorts. Peter Bogdanovich had written about him, as had Pauline Kael. Someone downtown had arranged a weekend festival of his films. Diane had missed it; all she'd ever seen of his was that cop show, *Brackett*, the one Track's dad had been in.

Diane adjusted the strap on her portfolio bag. "Yes," she said. "But I didn't really know him."

Looking at him then, it seemed to Diane that Bartolomos was not embarrassed for her or dismissive at all, but rather deferential, turning to the other students as if he were delivering a lecture. "Perhaps you have heard of the great von Stiegl? Auteur of American film and television? Here is his very granddaughter among us."

By implication it appeared as if Diane herself were someone of

importance, a person to be taken seriously. And she'd felt validated—
not, as would be rational, for her grandfather's work, but for her own.

This she couldn't explain to Annie later. "He just wants you in
the sack," Annie had said that night. "And he was showing off."

"What does he have to show off for?"

Annie had laughed. "Men are always, always showing off to
other men. It's like half their lives. That's like Testicles 101."

"Annie," Diane had said, "you are exceptionally gross."

Bartolomos had—though she couldn't tell this to Annie after that
initial reaction—invited her to his office a moment later. And she had
gone, had seen the books stacked flat-wise on the shelves, one artist after another, massive retrospective volumes with block-letter surnames
on the spine: PICASSO, DE KOONING, EL GRECO, CASSATT,
and yes, TITIAN. When he asked her about her work, she had shown
him the sketches and unfinished pieces in her portfolio bag, had talked
rapidly and at breathless length about the importance of camera-like
realism to "our contemporary moment." When he touched her forearm and then her elbow and then her shoulder, she had pretended to
ignore what he was doing. "I've got an idea," he'd said.

Well, that's how it had started. His idea was to go get a drink, and
then two more drinks, and to talk about art or rather argue about
art, and to return near midnight to his office on some errand neither
of them believed in, and once there to leave off the light and slam
the door and take off their clothes and fuck on the dusty, rough rug
she'd noticed earlier to be dotted with coffee stains, and she had
done all of this, gone along as her mind split onto two tracks: the excitement that this was really happening, really, and the embarrassed
terror that she was part of it. When Bartolomos told her in the dark
to sign up for the painting studio class she wasn't yet qualified for,
she knew that she would.

Within the first weeks of spring semester, she could see that she
wasn't alone. Looking around the studio one morning, she had the
strong sensation that others had been swept up in his, um, passion—

even the boy Leonard, with his fine, clear face and long, effeminate fingers. Diane grew to understand that nothing else was happening between them, nothing at all, not even some special connection over art or whatever she'd imagined.

And now it was today, and her Pringles can was empty, and her stomach hurt, and she should have brought her warmer coat from her mother's apartment.

———————

AT THE BARNEY Building, she rode up alone, her mind whacking thoughts of Bartolomos away like the paddles of a pinball machine. No one was around. The studio, white and windowed and given order by the poles connecting floor to ceiling, massed each student's materials in roughly vertical clumps: stool, narrow cabinet, easel.

Diane flicked on the light and, leaving her coat on, went to her corner, where her canvas rested as she'd left it yesterday afternoon. She'd been painting from the Polaroid she'd taken of her father driving home from that Christmas party at Mrs. Harlan's in Palm Springs. His hand gripped the top of the wheel, the fists bent forward, wrists making sharp triangles that were mirrored in his dropped elbows. Here, Percy Stiegl wore a white polo shirt with short sleeves, and the intricate forest of hairs and mottled skin of his forearms had taken the better part of a week's work. His face she had sketched again and again in preparation, as she'd done the drape and folds of his shirt and the steeply angled dashboard. She had worked out from the center, from the depth of the glass window, the reflected explosion of light from the Polaroid's flash, and now the remaining work was in the car's interior details: the tennis-shoe-like ceiling, the stitch and pillow of the bench seat, the glimmer of chrome on the handles and wands and knobs. At this stage it was mostly a matter of mixing paints and doing the work a little at a time. Having patience.

The work and the quiet was good for her. On her way downtown she'd started to grow anxious, a little low, and she knew when that happened that her next line of thinking would be that she was like her mother, that it was a matter of time, that she needed to watch herself.

Looking at this painting of her father, she wanted to call him. Out in the white-brick hall she requested from the operator a collect connection. "It's not catching," he assured her. "Things like this don't pass down like hair color."

"How do you know?"

"Well," he said, his usual bluster-and-waffling, "I guess I don't *know* know. It's just that you're nothing like your mom. I always thought you took after—"

"You?" She rolled her eyes at the ceiling. "Sure, Dad."

"I wasn't going to say that. I was going to say your grandpa. Only sweeter. Your grandpa was a sour dude, after all."

"A 'sour dude.' Did you pick that up from a Bob Hope special or what?"

He laughed again. "You're driven like him. You've got this thing you do, this art, and it matters more than other things. Not everybody has that. Some of us just have to sit in front of the television anytime we're not clocked into a job."

It was a compliment in its own way, and Diane accepted it. "Thanks, Dad."

"Listen, baby, you've got to go back home. She needs you. I wish I was there, but she needs you."

"I know," she said. "I'll go."

By that point, hours of work had passed, and when she returned to the studio room and looked, she could see that anyone off the street would think not much had gotten done. But she was pleased. The piece was rounding the corner, nearly finished, and she had captured more than its image, had brought forth a feeling of this closing decade: the pervasive sense that something inexplicable was fast on their tail.

BY EVENING SHE was back in Jersey with her mother, pushing a cart around the grocery store, the Saturday ritual, with Antonia asking

---

the man in the apron when they were going to get yogurt again. Diane watched her mother neatly stack the cans of tuna fish she bought for the cat, watched her squeeze the grapefruit, watched her reach on her toes for the cranberry juice she drank two bottles of every week, ostensibly for "kidney health." A dull trip, but for months now, Diane had usually gone along. It was the only time, oddly, that her mother would ask her about her work, about her painting. And perhaps as a defense against Antonia's maybe not taking it seriously (*she* had been the one to suggest taking a typing class "in case you need a job later on"), Diane would go into great detail about the minutiae of whatever canvas she was working on that week, the hours of labor on the fine shadow beneath a parked car, the gleam of a plate-glass window, the grit of a city sidewalk.

"So you want it to look like the picture?" Antonia asked her in the bread aisle. "I mean, just like a photograph?"

"As exacting as a photograph, I guess," Diane said. "But with something else. With my observation, I guess?"

Antonia held still with her mouth half-open, as if she were just about to ask why she didn't just use a camera and be done with it. Instead, after squeezing past a man with a cart overloaded with canned goods, she said, "And just of anything? Your dad? A can of soup? Nothing special?"

Diane wanted to ask what exactly made a subject "special"—did she need a weeping Dido on a balcony? the Grand Tetons?—but instead she'd shrugged and agreed, nothing special, "Just the real world around us, contemporary life."

"Well," Antonia said. And this next part surprised Diane: "I can't wait to see them."

New York Tribune

July 30th, 1927

THE SCREEN

by NEAL ADDINGTON

HEARTBREAK CITY

That a picture could be made relating in a fictional way the events of Teapot Dome and our former President's romantic dalliances should come as no surprise. Those whizz-bang headlines had all the makings of a movie scenario, so the matter was one more of time than expectation. What came as a surprise at the Rivoli Theatre yesterday evening was that the sordid material in question had been turned into something resembling great art. The young émigré director Klaus von Stiegl (whose first American feature, "The Bachelor's Wife," this reviewer championed in January) has created a picture making use of the cinema's full visual potential: not the sound experiments we've heard rumored out of William J. Fox's studio, but a painterly style novel to American screens. The influence of the expressionists in von Stiegl's native country is obvious, but don't expect Dr. Caligari to come snaking through the window in this grabber. "Heartbreak City" shrinks our recent national shame down to an unnamed western state full of oil wells and farms and occasionally upright Methodist church-goers, while still showing us the underworld of concrete and zip guns illustrated in the crime pages of our major city newspapers. George O'Brien stars as a politician divided between what's right and what lines his pockets. But a new star is lodged in the sky by way of his secretary, played by the twinkling Kay Stone, whose only previous role of remark had been in the above-mentioned "Bachelor's Wife." Here she steals the picture, making every scene without her feel like an absence. Where von Stiegl's interesting direction—including some beautiful shots that seem right out of Rembrandt—keep the eyes appealed, it is the stunning Kay Stone who keeps the emotions gripped. When all the fanciness and at-times-overthinking-ness of this "great director" is removed, the audience is left with a powerful, vibrant testament to what the motion picture can be in the star-bound eyes of the illustrious Ms. Stone, sure to outlast the whims of any filmmaker's style. Don't miss it!

KLAUS

1927

THE TRAIN WEST, having trundled through the bright desert, had grown dark as Klaus paced the carpeted walkway from car to car, tapping his cane with a little bounce on every fourth step. Klaus von Stiegl, recently celebrated director of the motion picture *The Bachelor's Wife*, heralded by one critic as "the finest German film yet made in America," had been called to Hollywood by none other than his dear cousin George. Even on the long journey, he'd lost none of the pep and astonishment that had overtaken him when he'd opened that letter postmarked Culver City, California, only two weeks ago:

> *Pack your bags kid, they're crazy for you here. Got L. B. softened up for you and Thalberg is already gaga (saw the picture last week and said "we need Stiegl," to which I said, ha! "that's von Stiegl, sir." When I told him I knew you his poor weak heart nearly bought the farm. Get here quick. Walter has been good enough to enclose a little $ for the trip.*

Walter, described by George as "everything short of a husband, you could say," would be meeting them at the station. Klaus hadn't asked any questions about that setup. His cousin's wants and needs had been made clear on their trip to Berlin, and Klaus, a Greenwich Village denizen for the past year and a half, whose only friends were in the arts, had long ago come to the conclusion that the activities of another's heart were none of his business. This had been the main theme, one could say, of his single directorial product, *The Bachelor's Wife*.

He had climbed up the ladder at Famous Players–Lasky at a speed even his childhood daydreams wouldn't have allowed. He worked under Nick Abruzzo for twelve months, the lead cameraman on six features, his control of the lens a quality sought out by the stable of directors who came in and out of the Astoria studio. When he took a risk and asked Abruzzo to put in a word for him to direct—and not just any picture but one based on a scandalous novel even Lubitsch would have passed up—the department chief told him he'd known it was just a matter of time. "I'll go to Joey's office right after lunch," Abruzzo had said. And the next morning, Klaus received a type-written memo assigning him the property, outlining a budget and timeline, and naming Nick Abruzzo as producer. Klaus was given absolute freedom by his old boss, and so Artie took on scenario duties and Kate—now Kay—Stone was given a lead role.

To be in total control of a movie set. The feeling that coursed through him each day at the studio. It affected him like a strong drug. It was a seduction, an ecstasy. Of course, he couldn't describe this to anyone, couldn't use such words. But he'd realized it as a total presence, the kind of completion one imagines from the lyrics of tawdry love songs. His every decision and action went into the final product, all of which came from the source of his private imagination. He made a habit of sketching out each scene, trying out multiple camera setups, moving his actors about by their arms like chess pieces, running and rerunning the events until everything was perfect and he could finally signal the cameraman to begin shooting. He had begun thinking of his work as breathing life into pictures, or discovering the breathing life already there, and for this he began us-ing the term *Leben atmen* as shorthand, at least in the copious notes he took during each day of production. These were long days, delib-erate work, one image after another. Then came the editing process, the actual piecing together of the picture, that ultimate stack of reels that would be distributed to theaters, to the audience. At each step, he'd had Kay and Artie with him. Now they had traveled across the continent, new lives opening before them like a desert vista.

If only his parents were still alive. He could see his mother's eyes damp and twinkling as she sang to him alternately in German and Yiddish, songs he no longer recalled with any clarity but which still traveled alongside his thoughts, the melodies of his waking hours. He could see his father, too, unlacing his worn-out shoes at the end of the day, his big mustache curled up in a grand laugh, his hearty voice in the midst of some comical story. They would wonder at his name, his look, at the proper and stiff way he held himself now. And they would wonder at his accomplishment, his daring. At all he had already made in the world. How he wanted them to know and to see all these things. But he was alone.

When he wandered accidentally into the dining car and spotted Artie and Kay seated at a far table with steaming cups of coffee before them, he nearly wheeled around. He wanted to be alone to relish the building excitement. But he was too late.

"Klaus," Artie barked. "Where've you been?"

Kay tipped cream into her coffee. "We're nearly there," she said. "Artie and I have been looking all over."

"Thinking," Klaus said. "I was only thinking."

"I didn't even know it rained here," Kay said. "Did you know it rained here?"

"Doll, it rains everywhere," said Artie.

They were staring out the window as the train rushed into Los Angeles. Klaus hadn't even noticed the rain. But it was dark as sundown only a little after noon.

"I thought it was a desert," Kay said.

———

WHEN THEY STEPPED off under umbrellas, a tall blond man in riding clothes greeted them. "Walter Driscoll," he announced, proffering a hand through the drenching rain. When Klaus didn't reciprocate, the man gestured toward the darkly tan, Asian-looking fellow holding an umbrella over them both. "This is Luwalhati. George sent us?"

"Yes, yes," Klaus said. "So good to meet you both."

"Car's pulled up to the curb," Walter said. "Let my man here take some of your bags."

The man called Luwalhati handed the umbrella to Walter and stepped out into the rain, grabbing a suitcase from each of them, one at a time, without a word. Then they all made their way to the car, only Luwalhati getting wet in the process. The car was a long number, something ostentatious and white with shined chrome and a light-tan interior. Luwalhati drove and Walter held forth on the topic of George's career and the unexpected rain and finally on his own fortune, stemming first from his father's oil leases and now wholly invested in the stock exchange back east. Klaus nodded along to all of this, occasionally meeting eyes with his dazzled friends but always returning to the water still dripping from Luwalhati's slicked black hair.

Walter's home could not be called anything but a mansion, its ivy-covered stone walls and aristocratic garden residing at the outer limits of American decency, the sort of place that bred fantasies of guillotines and pitchforks among the common man. The grand hall, a glistening chandelier, that beautiful oak stairway running up the left wall and then to a landing and then up again in perpendicular fashion to a wide seating area and more doors than he could remember. And all around, the Impressionist paintings George had so loved and could now own, thanks in no small part to a meritocracy meted out at picture-palace ticket booths across the globe. They were shown their room, each with an oversized and ornate bed at its center and more of the Impressionists on the walls, and given time to freshen up after the long journey.

Klaus closed the door, removed his monocle, and dropped on the bed. A minute later, he heard a knock on the adjoining door: Kay. "Bejesus," she said when he opened it a crack. "Did you get a load of this place?"

"It's quite something," he said, and returned to the bed. She joined him, stretched alongside, put a hand on the wool sleeve of his suit jacket. "I don't know if I'll ever belong here," she said. "I could never be class enough for this place."

"Oh, we don't have to stay with my cousin permanently," he said.

"Not the house. I mean Hollywood. It's all happened so fast."

And Klaus, feeling heavy on the feather mattress, said, "Don't worry. I'll be right here with you."

Downstairs, after a dinner of trout and grilled asparagus, Walter set up his projector and put in the first of the six reels of *The Bachelor's Wife*—reels Klaus had had to pay Famous Players for in cash, in spite of being their creator. They watched it from an L-shaped sofa, against a bare wall where a painting of ancient Greek ruins had just been taken down, and though Klaus found the nail at the center of the image troublesome, the others only appeared to see the quality of the work. "Outstanding," Walter said, flicking on the lights overhead, getting up to change out the reel. "I don't know how I hadn't seen it in the theater."

Kay said quietly, "It is pretty up on the wall like that."

"What we need are drinks," George announced from the doorway. "Martinis all around?"

They didn't get back to the picture that night. The first round of martinis was followed by a second and then a third and then it was past midnight and a jazz record played from Walter's phonograph. Upstairs, Kay lingered at Klaus's bedroom door and then came in and then they shared a bed, no hanky-panky really, just next to each other, even with the liquor going to their heads.

A WEEK MAY have passed before suddenly one morning Klaus was awakened by his cousin at the bedroom door, shouting, "Time to go to the studio, Count Klaus! Mr. Mayer is waiting!"

In the car a little later, with Luwalhati driving, George explained the plan he'd crafted. "Mayer wouldn't call you out here unless he wanted to put you under contract. So you're a step ahead." He clapped his hands. "Two steps ahead. But he's a tough nut. Or at least he thinks he is. Anyway the family connection's the thing, Klaus. This guy loves family. We're cousins. We got to play up that angle. Gush about it a little."

Klaus thought of his parents, of that dirty hovel where they'd lived. He gestured at the verdant hills and palm trees, the sharply curving macadam. "What does family matter out here?"

"You don't know what you mean, dummy. So perfectly Klaus." George put a floppy newsboy hat over his head. "Mayer's senti-mental for the stuff. Take it from me. Here's the story you tell him: We're cousins. There you are in Germany, wishing for a better life in the good ol' U S of A, dreaming of seeing your dear cousin George, of being an American." George held up a finger. "Not just another lonely Jew in Europe. He'll love that. The Jew thing, the family thing, et cetera. Got it? You'll have the job."

"What about the movies?"

"Yeah the movies too. That goes without saying. But that'll come natural. He's seen your picture. Now it's the sentiment."

He hadn't liked a bit of it. For one thing, George hadn't said a word about telling the folks at MGM they were related. For another, Klaus hadn't expected Jewishness to be part of the equation. He'd been Klaus von Stiegl, that's who he'd made himself to be, and not a small part of that had been putting the Jewish element behind him once and for all. He felt like his cousin had kicked him back to the ghetto. He'd planned to arrive at the studio a German aristocrat, as white as milk, the man he'd made himself to be.

They arrived in Culver City. At the gate, a man in a black cap waved them inside. Modern white-block buildings loomed up front, but even at a distance Klaus could see the backlot: acres of sets, men already working, actors and actresses riding in costume on the backs of open trucks.

In a shiny Art Deco hallway just outside the office of Louis B. Mayer, George said, "Remember: America, John Philip Sousa, family. And I forgot one thing. Don't mention Walter."

"Why would I—"

And then they were inside a deep, carpeted room with ivory-colored walls and a matching round laminate desk, behind which stood a stout man with his back turned to them, peering out the window, though its blinds were closed to the sun. Everywhere pictures of Mayer's wife and children gazed back at them. A tiny American flag on a pole the size of a pencil stood on a wooden platform on the desk. George wasn't kidding about family and country.

"Please," said Mr. Mayer without turning around. "Have a seat. I've got Irving on the way here now."

"Of course, L. B.," said George. "Here's my cousin—Count Klaus von Stiegl—just as promised."

Mr. Mayer popped up on his toes and parted the blinds with a finger, apparently eyeing someone. "Yes," he said in distraction. "That's what we're here for."

Klaus could feel the thrumming blood behind his ears. This would all fall to pieces, he was sure. His words would come out sounding too American. He would say the wrong thing. Mayer would see right through him.

At the most fearsome point in this line of thinking, a man rushed in behind them. He was very young, probably Klaus's own age, dressed in a pinstripe suit two sizes too big, with a baby face and winning smile, his long dark hair combed tight to his head. "Sorry, L. B.," the young man said. "We've got that short in production and I've been herding talent to get in front of the camera."

George stood as if the president had walked into the room. "Mr. Thalberg," he said almost breathlessly. "I want to thank you again for the swell role."

"Having fun?" said Thalberg. Klaus had made it his business these last weeks to know everything about the Hollywood producers, and Thalberg, the Boy Wonder, was already a legend in his mind. He'd read about him in the fan magazines. The most talented producer in the business. Now here Thalberg was, in the same room, looking Klaus square in the eye. "This must be our Mr. Klaus von Stiegl. What a pleasure."

Our.

They shook hands. Klaus muttered as he'd done in the mirror for a week, "Guten Tag, Herr Thalberg."

"Guten Tag," Thalberg repeated, somewhat hilariously. "Guten *Tag* it is."

Mayer finally turned away from the window. "You'll have to forgive me," he said, offering Klaus a hand. "As Irving said, we've got a short in production celebrating all the great work being done here at Metro-Goldwyn-Mayer. It's a headache, a nightmare, but we want the audience to see just what quality, what craftsmanship, goes into the MGM picture. I think it's the first of its kind."

"It is, L. B."

"He says it, so it must be true," said Mayer, beaming with pride. "The first short picture to show how a movie studio works. How it really works. The art of it. You understand? The people sweating it out every day. The stars. The directors. The writers. All the technicians. Did we get you in front of the camera, George?"

"Yesterday," George said. "Having lunch with a young woman named Norma Shearer?"

Something about this fact was humorous, but Klaus didn't understand. When an instant later eyes returned to him, he felt as if he were sinking into his shoes. Luckily, Mayer snapped his fingers and said, "You know we should get you in with our directors, Mr. Stiegl. We're shooting them all in a row at two thirty, isn't that right, Irving?"

"So you're interested in hiring him?" George said.

"Interested?" said Thalberg. "I thought we already did hire him."

"I hadn't gotten to that," Mayer said. "My apologies. But yes, we looked at the footage. Compelling, artistic work. And the Babelsberg studio? Incredible work going on there. Most important is that you can be with your family, Mr. Stiegl. George here told us how you lost your parents in the Great War, and about your wife living here in the States. A good, solid Jewish boy like yourself? And an artist? She and George are your only living relatives. Mr. Stiegl, that means something around here." He looked at Thalberg. "Doesn't that mean something?"

"It does," said Thalberg.

"I was moved to tears, Mr. Stiegl." Mayer came around the desk and took Klaus's hand in both of his own. He was openly weeping like a man at a funeral "You've got a home here," he said, sniffling. "Here you've got a family."

It was a maudlin, awkward performance, and the first Klaus was hearing about any wife in the States and parents dead in the Great War. The whole story seemed quite out of hand. But the only response was to be stoic and avert his eyes, and mutter the words "Danke, Herr Mayer. Danke, danke."

An hour later, Klaus stood squinting in the California sunshine between King Vidor and Fred Niblo. As the great directors around him engaged in small talk, looking as comfortable as old shoes, he glared back at the camera crew, confused, alarmed, but hoping to appear stern and in control. The whole situation seemed like a dream or a joke; none of these great and accomplished men knew at all who he was. Fearful anyone around him would ask him anything at all, would make him answer for his presence, he met none of their eyes. He put on a show of being unapproachable, holding his cane in a fist, tucked under the other elbow, letting a cigarette burn in his free hand like a shield against conversation. He lowered his chin as the lens panned toward him, setting his shoulders as if he were about to be rushed, hoping to come off as a serious gentleman. And then the lens went on moving, past Niblo to Sternberg and Stroheim, all the way at the far end to the cursing flyboy Wellman. When they were told they could break up, he stalked away, ignoring Vidor's friendly Texas voice calling after him, "Hey, pal. Hey there. We never met."

THALBERG HANDED KLAUS his first project, *Heartbreak City*, without input: the scenario was written, the roles were cast, the set was not only designed but already built. The story was about a titan of industry who falls for the telephone operator in his company's skyscraper and, through a series of events Klaus never really understood motivation-wise, gets swept up in a racket to skim funds off a government oil deal. It had been a bestselling book earlier that same year, rushed into print to cash in on Teapot Dome before the scandal became old news. MGM had bought the rights before a single book had hit the shelves. And Klaus was handed this tortured mess of street hoodlums and corporate executives and government stooges and vast plains peopled by oil derricks as if he were just a man hired to help move a camera. He'd come west dreaming that he was an artist, and immediately been made a cog in someone else's machine.

It had been Kay, over one of George and Walter's dinners, who had come up with the plan to gamble it all, to take control of the production in spite of how Thalberg had arranged things. "Give the script to Artie," she'd said. "You'll do it, right Artie? Make improvements? Then keep the script on set, walk the actors through the scenes each day, and if anyone asks tell them the changes came from upstairs."

The idea wasn't especially complicated. It took a measure of confidence, sure, and some luck, or at least faith in the possibility that the daily rushes would either look enough like what Thalberg had in mind or that they would seem minor enough and overwhelmingly good enough to keep him out of trouble. In the end the goal would be to make a better film than the one he'd been assigned.

Thalberg's one fig leaf had been the casting of Kay Stone in the role of the clumsy sexpot secretary, Dana Quills, and one of the first things Klaus had tasked Artie with was to expand her time onscreen, to put her nearer the center of the picture. If the original scenario had her as a love interest, the new version would make the love angle the most important angle in the story. During production Klaus would deal with this by holding back an entire reel's worth of scenes

where Kay could shine—all scenes lacking from the original scenario. Only when everything went to editing would he let Thalberg
see that material, calling them when he did "ephemera." He would
bend the rules. He would claim a little power from the executives.

Once he began work, what he'd learned on *The Bachelor's Wife*
became not just a one-off success but a kind of personal philosophy.
There would be no program to his art, no following the old ways.
Everything would be new, as it should be, as the century around
them already was. If art couldn't always be showing a new path,
revealing what hadn't yet been revealed, then was it art at all? Klaus
would only make films that had never been seen before—not just
in their storyline, their basics, but in their manner. Each film would
have to show the viewer how to see it and understand it, so much
would it challenge expectations. It would revel in its own newness.
Be an independent work of art. And so he found himself locked forever, he understood immediately, in a battle of wills with the studio,
with Irving Thalberg, with Louis B. Mayer.

———

HEARTBREAK CITY MUST have been halfway through filming when
Klaus emerged from the small, motel-like office he'd been assigned
to discover Luwalhati waiting at the car downstairs. "Mr. Stiegl," he
said. "Mr. West sent me. You're to meet them at the Schlossbergs' in
thirty minutes."

Mo Schlossberg had been one of the founders of Hollywood,
from back when settling movie production in Southern California
was more about getting away from Thomas Edison's bullying trust
than getting to the nice weather. He'd invested in mining and farm-
land and even United Artists, helping to create competition with
the big studios he already had a hand in. "Why are we going there?"

"A party," Luwalhati said. He was waiting at the bottom of the
iron stairs, tapping his brown thumb on the railing. "Mr. West told
me to tell you it's a party in your honor, but between you and me
that's baloney. They just want you to go rub elbows with them."

In the car across town, passing under the electric lights of the expanding city, Klaus watched the back of Luwalhati's neck, the side of his cheek, the edge of his eye, for some giveaway that this was a joke. But nothing gave. Finally Klaus said, "Who else will be there?"

Luwalhati turned for a second and met his eyes. "Oh, the whole gang. Movie stars. Bigwigs. Artist types. Mr. West knows a lot of important people." He cleared his throat. "But Schlossberg, whew, he knows plenty more."

For a moment Klaus thought of asking Luwalhati to pick up Kay. She would enjoy this opportunity. It would give her the chance to see that she belonged as well as anyone else in the film colony. But he pictured having her at his side along every step, the whole night an introduction of them instead of him, whatever elbows he could rub being held at a distance. Next time, he thought. There will surely be a next time. So he remained silent, in a sort of preparatory awe: he would shortly be in the presence of grand and beautiful people, the doors of fate opening before him one by one.

He had never seen a home like the Schlossbergs'—a sprawling property not in Hollywood at all, not even Los Angeles, but on an estate overlooking a beach nearly an hour from the city. Leaning forward, Klaus gazed through the windshield at the gate and private cobbled road, the English garden on one side and rose trellises on the other, the half dozen fountains and innumerable statues, the looming mass of the house itself, something like Versailles, if only a notch or two less ostentatious. The place made of Walter's something like a scale model. Luwalhati told him that friends of the Schlossbergs called it Ocean House, and that if you were invited to visit you were part of a special fraternity of motion-picture and newspaper so-and-sos, people who had the ear and interest of one of the most powerful men in the industry. "Plus the booze runs like a river in there," he said, bringing the car to a stop in the big U-shaped drive, where stone nudes wrestled in a fountain. "They got a whole other house behind for the drivers. Feed us steaks and wine. Don't worry, though. We're only allowed one glass."

Klaus stepped out into the warm night air. So this was *his* life, he thought as he gazed again at the moonlit house. He knew people like this. It hardly seemed possible.

At the door a man in tails and white gloves, with the slit eyes of an iguana, asked his name. When Klaus said it the man said, "I don't believe you've been invited, sir."

"My cousin's inside," he said. "George West?"

"Mr. West doesn't have the power to invite guests, sir."

"Then Walter."

"Walter who, sir?"

Klaus, ridiculously, didn't know. "Can you call for them?" he asked. "I can wait."

Iguana Eyes looked at him a moment and then nodded slowly. He turned back, opened the door, and spoke to someone out of view very briefly. For a moment the noise of fifty partygoers could be heard over a tinkling piano; then Iguana Eyes pulled the door closed again behind him. "You may wait here, sir."

The two of them stood on the slate patio listening to the waves crash and crash against the beach downhill. The moon hung over the water, silver and sickle-shaped, three bright stars arranged in a triangle below. Klaus felt a pinch of melancholy here at the gates of Eden, and raced to fill the silence with conversation. "Have you worked here long?" he asked.

"As long as there's been a house here, sir. And before that at Mr. Schlossberg's Los Angeles home."

"Does the old man still make movies?"

"The old man?" Iguana Eyes asked, his face moving through several emotions all related to disgust. "I believe people like you make movies, sir. Mr. Schlossberg 'makes' capital."

"I see," Klaus said.

"Indeed, sir."

After another long spell of listening to the waves, a tap came at the door. "Mr. S. says send him in," said a man with a thick Queens accent, invisible behind the door. Iguana Eyes tucked his chin and without a word opened the door wide.

The grand white entryway with its pair of stairways spilled forward as Klaus's legs moved numbly over the marble floor. Another man in tails passed by him, holding a tray of Champagne in short bowl glasses, his eye dropping judgmentally to Klaus's face. A man in a tuxedo skipped down the left stairway, his hands behind his back, putting on a little show for two women in ball gowns. Near the right stairwell a group of well-dressed couples chattered, their easy voices filled with a sense of uninhibited success. Among their group, to Klaus's terror, stood the grand German actor Emil Jannings, rumored to have come to Hollywood just that month. It was Jannings who had starred in Murnau's Last Laugh, to Klaus's mind the greatest picture yet made.

Klaus slid through the open double doors of a ballroom fit for a European palace, its walls painted with murals of a hunt. Half a dozen chandeliers hung from the ceiling, and across the marble floor was not only a man at a piano but beside him a string quartet, all of them just now beginning the opening bars of a popular waltz. Here were the majority of Schlossberg's guests—only a bit fewer than fifty, arrayed about round tables loaded down with food and drink, milling in clumps, a few already dancing in the open space of floor in front of the musicians.

From one of these clumps emerged George, his smile wide, his hand extended. "Little Klaus," he said. "Little Klaus, you made it."

"Luwalhati brought me."

"And you didn't chicken out." He embraced Klaus warmly, first by the hand and then, as this appeared to be not enough, around the back of his shoulders. "You see who's over there? Eleanor Boardman and King Vidor. And that fellow over there next to Walter?"

"Richard Barthelmess," Klaus said. The actor was as beautiful in real life as Greta Garbo. Klaus looked around the room, taking in other familiar faces, the room a phantasmagoria of picture stars. "Are those the Talmadge sisters?"

"Yes," George said. "But stay away from them. They're all trouble. Bill Haines is here too. He's got a little thing for Walter. Have to keep my eye on him. Let me introduce you to the bigwig around here."

A massive fellow then parted the crowd, looking for all the world like the newspaper cartoons of Teddy Roosevelt from Klaus's childhood—the tiny, wire-framed glasses and great mustache, the bulldog cheeks and overwhelming teeth, his whole body quaking with energy, ready to explode forth from his tuxedo. This was Mo Schlossberg, in the flesh, rambling already about what a pleasure it was to meet one of the great artistic film directors of Europe and what a coincidence that he'd be a relative of one of his favorite new screen actors. It took Klaus a moment to recognize who Schlossberg was talking about on both counts. "A pleasure," he said nervously. And then, thickening his accent, "I am humbled, Herr Schlossberg."

"No need to be humbled, young man," Schlossberg said. "I don't sign on for humility anyway. Overblown. You think this place was built on humility? Leave it to the saints. George here tells me you're a major director. An *artiste*. I can't wait to see your work. You're at Metro? Is that it?"

Klaus looked to George and back at Schlossberg. "I just started there, yes."

"Everyone here is talking about you," said George. "You can thank me later."

Schlossberg reached in front of George to grab Klaus by the arm. "You know if I hadn't floated L. B. a little green a couple years ago *Ben-Hur* would have capsized the place before they could even get started. But that's ancient history. Ha!"

This was apparently a joke, so Klaus gave a dutiful laugh.

"What do they have you working on over there?"

"A modern picture," Klaus said. "Nothing special."

Schlossberg's presence was like that of a great dynamo or the chugging engine of a train, noisy and violent, filled with a sense of action, drowning out all conscious thought. "You mean to say it's a secret project? Old L. B.'s got something up his sleeve, does he? I'll call him up. That's what I'll do. I'll demand the details!"

"No," Klaus said. "I mean, it's only *Heartbreak City*. It's nothing."

"The count is just being humble again," George explained, looking a little embarrassed.

"Well, don't let them waste your talents," Schlossberg said. "Maybe I'll call L. B. Yes, I think I should." He gazed a moment over the heads of his guests, apparently taken by the music. His hand, finally, released Klaus's shoulder. "Where on earth is my wife? Have either of you chums seen my wife?"

The great man bellowed the name Kitty as he wandered away.

That's when Klaus saw her: Olive Lazlo.

He had gazed at her picture in the *Los Angeles Times* society page only that morning. Now, in the gap made by Schlossberg's exit he saw the actual Olive Lazlo, the beautiful heir to the Western Petroleum & Extraction millions, seated at the table next to George's group of friends, looking relatively bored. At her side, a tall, balding man with a fleshy face ignored her entirely, keeping up an animated conversation with none other than Buster Keaton.

She was prettier, to Klaus's eye, than a newspaper photograph would allow. Her exposed shoulders and collarbones made her seem altogether thin, her short-bobbed hair showing off the length of her neck. Pale and slight, she was something like an orchid. He'd read that in some novel, about a woman, an actress, looking like an orchid, and now he understood.

Her eyes raised to meet his and stayed there for just a moment, long enough for his heart to lurch and squeeze and finally thump back into action.

George appeared to register this, and with the force of a barman removing a rowdy customer from a speakeasy, he ushered Klaus over by the arm. "Olive, I want you to meet the esteemed Count Klaus von Stiegl," he announced, gaining Buster Keaton's attention for a passing second. "Klaus here's my cousin from Europe. Directing at MGM these days."

"A pleasure," Olive Lazlo said, and offered a silk-gloved hand.

Klaus didn't know if he was supposed to kiss it or shake it, and so instead lightly gripped her fingers and performed a weak, embarrassed bow. "Madame," he coughed out.

Olive gave him a pained smile and then, with a butterfly's attention span, turned back to George. "Have you met my dear friend Dwight Squibb?" she said. "From the radio show?" She gestured to the man talking to Buster Keaton. "*Dwight*," she repeated. "Stand up. I want you to meet George West and Klaus, um—"

"Von Stiegl," Klaus said.

Dwight Squibb took a bit longer to do her bidding, and in the interim, Keaton looked up at Klaus, smiled, and slunk away. The fact that such a thing could happen in real life filled Klaus with a glowing happiness. But Squibb stood with a look of disappointment on his face. "Mr. West," he said. "We need to have you on the program."

George was laughing in agreement when Dwight Squibb noticed Keaton's absence. "How do you like that?" he said. "Make a guy's career and he whisks off the minute you look away." He glanced around the room and pointed at a tall, tan gentleman in a white tuxedo. "Look over there. It's that fairy Channing. Hollywood's most confirmed bachelor. Hey, Channing!" he shouted. "I didn't know they'd let you in the front door of a place like this."

The tall man who appeared at Klaus's side was indeed Lou Channing, the biggest star here, looking as radiant and charming in his tuxedo as he was in the movies, though about his eyes rested the faint hash-marks of middle age. "I didn't use the front door, Squibb. I came in under your mother's skirts."

No one introduced Klaus, and a moment later, Channing had swept Olive Lazlo onto the dance floor. George had disappeared without a word. When Channing and the heiress started swaying to the waltz, Dwight Squibb crossed his arms and said to Klaus conspiratorially, "That fairy came on my program six months ago and now I can't shake him off. The deadbeat. You know the boys back east want to make him a regular. The sponsors love our 'repartee.'

You ask me, I should tell the sponsors where the old bitch gets off — and with who."

Klaus looked at the hideous man at his side, then out on the dance floor at the object of Squibb's hatred. "He's a fine actor," he managed.

"They could shave an ape to play his roles. I can't stand him."

It occurred to Klaus he hadn't eaten a thing since his morning grapefruit, in spite of all the food here at the party. He'd been too nervous, too buffeted about, to find a plate. More than anything he wanted to get away from all these people, especially Squibb. "Excuse me," he said. "My cousin is calling me over."

Klaus left the great hall, and through a side door found a kitchen big enough for a hotel. There, a woman wearing a white apron wheeled around on him like a robber. "You need something, sir?"

"Soda water," he said. "And crackers? Anything really."

She returned with these a moment later, still looking alarmed by his presence. Leaning against a copper-topped table, Klaus inhaled the crackers and swallowed the soda as men and women scurried about in white hats and aprons and men in long tails sailed through loading and unloading silver trays. Before he could gather his thoughts, before he could make sense of the strange dream he'd stumbled into, Mo Schlossberg came through the door asking the head chef if everything would be ready in time for a nine-thirty supper and then, ignoring the chef's answer, turned his attention on Klaus.

"Young man, you look as pale as a sheet. I daresay you're green."

"I'm fine," Klaus said.

"You're sick. If I've ever seen a sick man, he's right in front of my eyes. You need to sit down." Schlossberg guided him out the kitchen door and back into the melee of impossible people. "I'm going to find that cousin of yours."

Klaus looked at the roll of fat around Schlossberg's neck. "How is it possible?" he said. "How do you know all these people?"

Schlossberg laughed. "How wouldn't I?" And then, already sinking into the crowd, "Stay off your feet, Stiegl. I can't have a great director croaking in my kitchen. Too much scandal."

BEFORE HE KNEW it, he was in the car home. He'd met half a dozen movie stars and the behemoth Mo Schlossberg. His younger self wouldn't have believed any of it possible. " I'm here," Klaus said softly, testing the words. "I'm me."

"Wha?" George said. The ocean glimmered black and silver out the window. Walter only shook his head and went back to sleep. Luwalhati glanced in the mirror. The radio played the Gordon Sisters. "You're My Only."

And Klaus thought again of Olive Lazlo. A perfect orchid.

Welcome to the Harlan Homes Family. Did you know that your recent purchase rewards you with 50% off virtual real estate when you visit the Harlan Nextgen Store on Roblox or Oculus?

Click here to learn more. Text STOP to quit.

Still looking for that DREAM HOME? Visit the Harlan Nextgen Store to explore our finished and ready-to-build real-world homes in 3-D, make an offer, and apply for financing.

Click here for more. Text STOP to quit.

Why live JUST ANYWHERE on the Metaverse when you could have your very own top-of-the-line Harlan Home built on Roblox, Oculus, and now Decentraland.

Click here for a coupon. Text STOP to quit.

DIANE

1980

PHIL WAS AN actor, five and sometimes six years older than her, at least that's how they joked about it: from October to January he made that extra leap ahead of her. He didn't care that she had dropped out of school or that she needed a room with big windows or that she would fill a whole apartment with turpentine fumes or that she listened to music very loudly as she worked. He loved music, had admittedly better taste than her, had actually seen Lance Loud and the Mumps, the Ramones, Talking Heads—all of the bands still coming up in the years before she'd arrived. And he'd read seemingly everything, could quote from Cervantes and Baldwin and Chekhov as if he were recalling gags from a *Saturday Night Live* skit. He knew French and Italian film, and didn't care for the silents; he'd never heard of her grandfather. "I think you should move in with me," he'd said the first night they met, at the Mudd Club, upstairs where a girl with red hair played records and a handful of people tried dancing. "It's perfect. You'll paint and I'll run my lines and we'll throw the best parties downtown has ever seen."

She didn't have any alternatives. Her mother kept hinting she wanted to move out of New Jersey and Diane couldn't keep showing up on Annie's couch. The last time she had come into town unannounced, Annie had pretended not to be home, not coming to the door even though Diane could hear her feet clunking off to the bedroom after she'd knocked. She'd made other friends, but Lily

Wong had a roommate, and in fact already slept on the couch. Diane had stayed over once, too drunk to navigate back down the stairs, and been offered the rug next to the coffee table, a single round chair cushion under her head, a smelly bathrobe pulled to her chin. The guy Diane had started dating a week before she met Phil, a performance artist and emcee in the neighborhood, went by the ridiculous stage name Nero Divisible and lived in a sort of crash pad with four other dudes, all of them underbathed and stoned, the place a fire hazard of rolled-up band posters and stacked newspapers and tattered and jism-stained *Playboys*. No thanks.

Diane and Phil had watched together on television Ted Kennedy give the baton back to Carter, the hooded and disappointed and angry look on his face. They felt the same, the terrible sense that at the end of his words the whole country would drop through a trapdoor. Carter didn't stand a chance, all that folksy goodness nothing against the B-movie actor barreling toward them all with his promise of something grand and new that was also old and spent, the feeling they were witnessing the failure of what they'd long called a country. That afternoon they'd both called in and stayed home and listened to records: Wire, Eno, Sparks, and later, letting down their guard, Joni Mitchell's *Blue*.

Whereas with Annie Diane thought only of theory and marketing (Annie was always on about what a work meant and how it could be explained), and with Lily she felt a desperate sort of competition (wasn't Lily better, the truer artist, the one who knew what she was doing?), with Phil she connected along the median of the everyday, the subjects of process and of letting ideas set or bake or boil or whatever was the metaphor. He wanted to talk to her about her work only in the material of it: what was she doing today, what had she done, how did she feel. He taught her how to live day in and day out, to listen to good music in the morning and then again at night, to play a game of chess without feeling entirely stupid, to feel confident reading the book you wanted to read even if your friends didn't care for it, to cook a whole bunch of macaroni noodles and leave them in the pot in the fridge with just enough olive oil and salt so they went with everything and you had something to eat all week. They read Judith Krantz books out loud to each other for fun, Wittgenstein's *Tractatus* to see if they could follow even a sentence. Some nights were burnt down until dawn with all their talking. He was hungry for new knowledge around every corner and soon she was too.

Two months into Diane's staying in Phil's "extra room," Phil signaled to her with only a faint nod and a half-suppressed smile that yes, it was fine to throw out the photorealism, or at least explore new ways to use photorealism in her paintings. She had begun turning toward a bastard form of what she'd heard recently called neo-expressionism, shaping something that was really more of a mishmash of styles, paintings that looked as if several artists had come along, one after the next, adding this or that. Sometimes these worked and sometimes they looked horrendous. Either way, Phil cheered her on.

She painted. My God, how she painted. Working the door at the Tyro, she didn't clock in until six or even eight in the evening, and by three or four she would be on the train with a pocket stuffed with shared tips, reading one or another library book: Cather and Didion and Beattie and Borges. She slept until late morning and spent any daylight time she had in her section of the apartment, not really a room but a space separated by curtains on a thick steel cable, her mattress and her easel and a stack of her books taking up nearly every square foot. Her only food was what Phil brought to her, asking her things like "Mustard?" and "Pickle?" and "What about tomato soup?" as if he were a short-order cook residing in the ether. At some point as she worked he would begin testing his lines on her, the same she'd been hearing at a greater distance earlier in the day, and she would give him feedback or say nothing, and he would stomp away or sit on her beanbag to explain some details of the play in question, which she hardly understood. Nearly every week she would complete a canvas, all of them experiments, all of them a standard three by four feet, all of them in oils. But in a very real way she had no idea what she was doing. She was on the loose. She was free.

"Imagine a canvas that can tell a story without leaning entirely on narrative," she said to Phil one night. "What if there were multiple picture planes? Not like Rauschenberg. Like an instruction manual. And here was one style and there another. Hyperrealist here, rough expressionist there. Abstraction over there. But all of it a whole statement, a sentence."

Until this point in the evening, Phil had been reading haphazardly from a thick, hardbound volume of Freud, announcing random lines from *Moses and Monotheism* or *The Interpretation of Dreams* or *Totem and Taboo*. Now he stared across the room, over the top of the fridge, and considered. "I don't know what you mean," he said. "Let me think."

For a moment she felt dejected, as if yet another sign showed her that she didn't belong in this city, in the arts; that she had come here to impress her mother, who hadn't even noticed that she'd come, not really, that maybe she wasn't an artist at all but only a kid who sketched the Beatles in a notepad. "I guess maybe it's collage, you know? Something that's already been—"

"No," Phil said. He kept staring over the fridge. "Stop a minute. You're doing that thing again. Tearing yourself down?"

The record player spun John Cale. *Gideon's Bible*. She would remember the song from then on, always have the same feeling when she heard it. "So I should just go on doing what I've been doing?"

The look on his face said, "Did I say that?" But after a moment, he sat upright with a smile. "No, I think you're on to something here. Anyway it's about the process, right? Discover and make mistakes. That's the only way to find something new."

Well, yeah. He was right. And when she wasn't tearing herself down, to use his term, she knew this was the only way art was ever made. At least, art with any sense of daring to it. "Okay," she said. "I'll be in the other room fucking around."

INTO THIS VERY structured form of chaos, maybe a month later, Track reappeared. First came a phone call from Antonia, telling Diane that she would be getting a call from Mrs. Harlan, "Your other mom," she'd added with a tone that perfectly mixed a corny kind of humor with a terrified need for validation. And then came the call from Mrs. Harlan. Track had finished his degree in business at UC Davis. He wanted to visit New York, wanted to make connections. Surely he could stay with Diane, right? "I mean, it's no trouble is it? A few weeks? A month?"

How could it be trouble? Besides being actual trouble, of course. Besides it sounding like hell. But she owed Mrs. Harlan more than she owed anyone. And she wanted to see Track. Her almost-brother. "Not at all," she said. "Oh my God I can't wait to see him."

Next came a third call, this one without warning, from Track himself. "It's stupid," he said. "But she thinks I should give it a try. I'll stay out of your hair."

"My hair?" she laughed, dragging her fingers through her actual hair, still cut short and now feathered. "I want you to meet everyone up here, man. And I want them to meet you."

For six years, they'd lived one room apart in that house in Palm Springs, ostensibly unrelated and yet presented to the world as something like brother and sister. Teenagers together, they fought and confided and dreamed and bitched about a future that seemed limited and luckily out of reach. She knew about his crush on Karen Carpenter; he knew she had a very uncool respect for Fat Elvis. She bought headphones to drown out the incessant squonking and wailing of all his stupid jazz records. He made a big deal of putting one of her earliest oil paintings in a gilt frame he'd found at a garage sale. They went to movies together as if they were dating. For a single month in the late summer of 1975, she lived in the waking nightmare of having a crush on him. No single person on Earth could have felt a more erasing pang of attraction when Vinnie Barbarino first strutted into class in *Welcome Back, Kotter.*

"Don't sound too excited," Track said. "I don't want to have to live up to anything."

"They know you're like my brother," she lied. "I talk about you all the time."

"Well," he said, and paused. This was long-distance, and though she wasn't paying, it made her nervous to waste time. Finally he said, "How's next Friday for you? Pick me up at the airport?"

IMMEDIATELY THE PROBLEM became where to put him. The couch would have to do, of course, but neither Diane nor Phil had an extra blanket or pillow, and their rooms had no walls or doors, and the bathroom was already a battle zone. Not to mention that they kept very unprofessional hours. A recent business-school graduate adjusting his tie in the morning when they were only then getting to sleep didn't exactly fit their lifestyle. "Who is he again?" Phil asked as they picked through a bin at the secondhand store on Prince Street. "I thought you were an only child."

"My dad's ex-girlfriend's son. It's complicated."

Phil found a pillowcase to match the sheet already stuffed under his arm. He let the look of satisfaction drop from his face before saying, "It does sound complicated. Are we sure he can't go to a hotel? No, forget I said that."

Outside it was raining hard. People rushed by the windows in the dark, grimacing into the storm like ancient stone ruins. From a little radio at the cash register, ELO played. Diane realized that Phil was really stretching himself here, being made to stretch. It wasn't any of his business to be housing Track. He'd never asked for another roommate, especially one who wouldn't be paying rent, even if it was just for a while. And Diane had already been leaning on him. She couldn't cover her end of the electric bill last month and he hadn't yet asked her to pay up. A week ago, knowing she needed more oils, he'd surprised her with a bag from Melnick's Art Supply. Now it was he who would be paying for Track's sheets and pillows—and she had already started to visualize asking him for taxi money to pick Track up at the airport.

"I swear it'll be a short visit. He's very California."

"What's that even mean?" Phil said. "You, my dear, are *very* California."

She squeezed past an old woman to grab a crocheted throw pillow with two horses cantering at sunset on one side and a big plastic button on the other. "He'll hate it here. He runs at a different speed."

This had been a soft spot for her since coming to New York, this need to prove that she really did run at the same speed as the city, that it was hers as much as anyone else's. She'd only come to realize this in the past months, living with Phil, listening to his advice. *You don't have to prove anything to me*, he'd said early on. *Party, don't party, but remember you've got work to do.* This because she'd brought a different guy home with her three Fridays in a row and had the audacity to say to him, shrugging, *What?* over their morning coffee. That minor confrontation had ringed a thoughtful cloud around her head the rest of that day. She'd felt as if Phil had called her bluff. The girl from Palm Springs trying to outdo everyone in the downtown scene, trying to be hard and wild and punk rock, generally *trying*. She'd done everything but needles, and once, though she remembered none of it, she'd taken off her top at Annie's place and danced on the fire escape, putting on a show for the party right inside the window, Annie screaming at her to come back in. Well, that was embarrassing. It occurred to her now, in the musty, damp store, her hair still wet against the back of her neck, that she actually wanted to settle down a little. Maybe seeing Track was what she needed.

They weren't ready to brave the storm again, so they rifled through clothing racks, barely looking at the items screeching on their shitty hangers. "My dad left me behind for a job," she explained. "That's what he said at first. But he'd already started dating this other woman—I think, anyway—and she left town with him. I was supposed to stay with Track's mom for just a while. But then it was junior high. And high school. She's the one who kept me painting. She sent me here to see my mom too. Told me all the museums to go to. I mean really she *was* my mom, Mrs. Harlan. She even got me into college."

Phil shook his head. "Well, be thankful you didn't have both your parents cheering you on at every step. I feel like I'll never live up to their expectations."

Phil had grown up on Long Island, the son of a sports reporter and a city councilwoman, both of them forward-thinking liberal types who shrugged when he'd said that he wanted to devote his life to the theatre and, a week or so later, had only shown a twinge of worry when he told them he was gay. "I'd cut off my right arm to have parents as put-together as yours."

"That's sort of what it's like, actually. They hold on to you so tight they pull your arm off."

"Still," she said.

"You know, Annie's right about you."

"How's that?"

Phil laughed. "You think the rest of us are automatons. Only poor Diane ever had any trouble. Oh, to envy our dull, uneventful lives."

Diane could hardly remember Phil and Annie so much as having a conversation. "She said that?"

"Well," he said, picking through a rack of overstarched shirts, "I'm embellishing a little, but it's what she meant to say."

"I'm not like that at all."

"Did I ever tell you what my so-called friends did to me in high school when they heard I was gay? I'd told only one guy, Mark, a real son of a bitch it turns out. Before this we were always close. But he ran off to the cafeteria and told everyone. Hateful little notes slid into my locker, every bad name in the book whispered at me when I passed people in the hall. Those perfect parents of mine said it would prove I was better than all those bullies if I didn't transfer. Of course it was all hell instead.

"Syracuse was supposed to be better, but the first guy I dated broke up with me because I wasn't political enough. I was in *Troilus and Cressida*; I had a character to learn. I didn't have time to yell about Richard fucking Nixon." And it wasn't that he didn't hate the war and hate Nixon as well. But the war was winding down and Watergate was picking up; a powerlessness had overtaken the decade. But word had gotten out. Other actors gave him the cold shoulder. He never once got a leading role. "Yet again, the folks didn't want me to transfer. 'Stick it out,' they said. And I'm a good boy. I did what they told me and graduated without a hope in the world. If I hadn't landed that part in *Checking Out*, I'd be living in my old bedroom listening to Mom tell me I'll be Paul Newman one day if I just put my nose to the grindstone." He shook his head. "Oh and then I met Scott. Have I mentioned him?"

The rain was still going, but the clerk had started to watch them with interest as they moved around the store. "I don't think so."

"Scott, the Upper West Side bank teller; Scott, the married man with two kids."

"Oh shit."

"I should have known something was wrong," Phil said. "He only wanted me to call him at work, he said he didn't have a home phone. I think he had some kind of *Dog Day Afternoon* fantasy, you know? More than once he said I could pull off wearing women's clothes. I thought it was just a kink. Well. Two and a half years I wasted with him. The headaches. The worrying. All that investment and he was just fucking around. Now any minute I'll be thirty."

"You're not even twenty-seven yet."

"Like I said."

Pulled by the gravity of the clerk's suspicion, they scuffed over to the register. Along the way she spotted an old army jacket, faded green, frayed at the cuffs and hems. She didn't even try it on, just pulled it from the rack and carried it to the register. Phil glanced at it and nodded. She'd had her eyes peeled for one of these and both of them knew it.

"It's all chaos," Phil went on. "You know the human brain is all about patterns? We see patterns in everything. It made us good hunter-gatherers. But really it's all a fucking mess. We're all faking some order to our lives because we're too afraid to face the fact that we have no control at all."

Diane wanted to say that art gave that sort of order, that it was meant to put order to the chaos, but standing next to him at the register this sounded goofy and sophomoric. And maybe it was wrong; maybe art didn't put anything into order. Maybe it reflected back the chaos, the ambiguity, the vertigo of living. She made an affirmative *hmmph* noise that she knew would draw the subject to a close, and then they were back in the rain, huddled under the same umbrella, shivering against each other from the autumn chill.

———

SHE WAS LATE to get Track, but he didn't seem to care. He gave her a long, tight hug and then stuffed the paper he'd been reading into the front pocket of his blazer and picked up his worn leather bag—one she knew once belonged to his father—and followed her to the cab. He was handsome now, his jawline and cheekbones and brow suddenly manifested behind a lost layer of baby fat. And he was losing his hair in a movie-star sort of way, the sharpening peak grown long and feathered back, the receding temples only squaring off his head. In the taxi, he leaned forward to the driver, saying, in a gruff voice unfamiliar to her, "Greetings, sir."

Diane had been proud of herself for pulling an extra shift and not asking Phil for the cab fare after all, but now, in Track's presence, dressed as he was like someone on the cover of a magazine, her hand-to-mouth ways seemed unavoidable. She was poor. The jeans she wore were ripped, not as a fashion statement but because they were the only pair she had and she didn't own an iron for patching them. Or a needle and thread. "Phil's excited to meet you," she said. "We'll all go out tonight."

"Phil?" he said. "The homosexual?"

"Um."

"Mom talks, you know?" he said. "And don't worry. I don't have anything against homosexuals. It's funny you're living with one, though."

"How is it funny?"

"I mean it's surprising." He glanced at his watch and she could see that this was a nervous gesture, a way to change the subject. "Mom sends her best. She's still hoping you're going back to school in the spring?"

"I'm thinking about it."

A few minutes passed. She asked him if he had any cigarettes. He didn't. Then they both went silent. "Look at this place," he said a little later, gazing out the window as they crossed the East River. "So gray. So beat-up. I hear the murder rate is worse than in the Third World. Just crazy you live here."

The sun was setting behind the Twin Towers and she had to hold up a hand to shield her eyes. To her it looked beautiful. "You know you just got here?"

"I'm sorry," he said. "Didn't mean to be offensive. It's just on the news is all."

"Track, I'm not going back to school."

"That's what I told Mom. I said, 'Diane's outgrown all that. She's a starving artist now.' But she still has all that money saved up. She wanted me to convince you to go back." He looked at her and smiled and for just a moment they were old pals again. "Do or don't, it's nothing to me. I'm just glad I could come up and see you."

She touched his shoulder. The blazer was padded. "I'm glad you're here too."

––––––––––

THEY WERE OUT at Danceteria, with Sean Cassette DJing and all of them a little drunk, when Track first brought up Ronald Reagan. The mere mention of his name sent Phil and Annie off to the dance floor, even though the song was that Ian Dury one Phil hated, the one with the rapping. Diane said, "Don't tell me you're voting for him?"

Track looked aghast. "For the governor of the great state of California?"

"You used to hate him," she said. He did. As teens, they took turns throwing darts at a photo of Reagan's face torn from *Life* magazine. "We used to call him a fascist."

"I was a child. I didn't know anything about economics or government. Deedee, we've got to do something about this country. It's failing at every level."

"He wants to hand everything over to the banks and big business. I don't see how that's going to—"

"It's better than a bloated government and everyone living on welfare. Is that what you want? A check in the mail to sit at home and watch TV?"

For a moment she thought of throwing her drink in his face like in the old movies. Instead she said, "If the alternative is to stand here listening to this bullshit, then yeah."

He laughed in a smug way that she hated. "Okay, okay. I'm sorry. That wasn't fair. But stagflation isn't curing itself. You've got to free up money at the top. It's all about letting the market—"

"I've got to go to the ladies'," she said, and walked away before he could finish.

She spent the better part of an hour keeping her distance, and when she next saw Track, he was dancing, or at least gyrating, to a record by Polyrock, his eyes glazed and wild. Where's your blazer?" she shouted over the music.

Lights flashed over his sweating face. "I gave it to some chick. She was cold."

"Where is she?"

"Oh she left."

Diane was the only one on the dance floor not moving. Lights swirled and flashed. The music thrummed and snapped and wailed.

Occasionally an elbow brushed her army jacket. Looking at him, delirious and drugged, his shirt open at the collar, sweat darkening his chest, she felt as if she had failed to watch over a country-rube cousin. They should probably leave.

But then he turned to a girl in a fuzzy pink sweater, her hair a gleaming mohawk, and yelled, "What's your name, honey?"

Diane didn't stick around for any more of that. Later still, in the cab Track insisted he would pay for, he rambled about how he already had a line on work, a job, hell his own company, but he hadn't told his mother yet: "No, Deedee, don't tell Mom."

Annie and Phil took turns rolling their eyes back and forth.

"He calls you Deedee?" said Annie.

"She isn't my mom," Diane said. "My mom lives in Jersey."

"Oh, you know," Track said, making a little circle with his pointing finger, like a child placing blame on someone. "You know what I mean. Mrs. Harlan Mom. You're her favorite child, Deedee. So don't tell her."

"Jesus. Will you shut up? What are you on?"

"Just Jacks and Cokes. And these pills." He pulled three blue pills from his pants pocket. "These li'l buddies."

"I saw him do some powder," said Phil.

"You shut your mouth," Track said. He made a lewd gesture with his hand, his lips forming a perfect circle. "I know where you put that mouth."

"Excuse me?"

Diane couldn't believe what she was hearing. "Track, you're really fucked up," she said. "You need to sit back and relax."

"He needs to fuck right off," Phil said.

Annie said, calmly, "He just took one of the pills."

He clearly had. He put on a whole act of swallowing it: chin up, cartoonish sound. "Jesus Christ, Track," Diane said. She punched him on the arm. "You're out of control."

"Daddy's putting me up with the business," he said. "Real estate.

Property. Safe as fucking houses." He turned toward the window, rested his head against the glass. "Safe as fucking houses."

"Great," she said, because she couldn't think of what else to say.

He lurched forward, his eyes glazed and wandering, as if they were no longer attached to his brain. "Your grandpa really fucked him over, you know? Stupid fuckin' *Brackett*. Guy couldn't get a job after that. Everybody thought he was a fuckin' psycho. Grandpa fucking Stiegl has it comin' to him."

"My grandfather's dead," she said, unexpectedly defensive. "Maybe you should shut up already."

"Disgusting," said Phil.

Within a block, Track had dozed off.

"Fuck," said Annie. "That dude is a wreck."

"I want him out of the apartment," Phil said. "He's a bigot. Did you hear him?"

She didn't have any defense. "I'll talk to him," she said. "Tomorrow. I'll take care of it."

Track whipped his groggy head around and said, in a mincing feminine voice, "You're just the best and I'm so proud of you, Deedee." He coughed out a laugh. In his regular voice he grumbled, "That's Mom."

"Oh, will you shut up?" said Phil.

Track didn't even look in his direction. "Faggot says shut up, Deedee. Should I tell him how we almost kissed that time? Pretty sick when you think about it."

Diane thought for a moment that Phil would hit him. When that didn't happen, she said, "Please, Track. You're being horrible."

"She's really into me," he gloated. "I read her diary. Can you believe that?"

When they stopped outside Annie's building, Track got out, too, and alone under a bare lamp, dropped down on his knees and vomited. The cabbie, through square and greasy spectacles, looked over his shoulder. "Out," he said. "Every fucking one of you, get out."

Then they had to stumble him home, five more blocks. It was Phil who ended up paying the fare.

———

TRACK WOKE EARLY. Diane could hear him on the other side of the curtain, messing around in the kitchenette. Seven o'clock. Her head ached. But she rolled off her mattress and grabbed a sweater and peeked out. He scooped coffee from the tin and dropped it into the basket, filled the carafe with water, pushed it all back in place. A satisfied bleariness overtook his face as he punched the On button.

"Track?" Diane whispered.

He jumped. "Oh, sorry. Did I wake you?"

"It's all right."

"I made a full pot. Is that okay?"

From behind the other curtain, Phil cleared his throat. "Can you two quiet down?"

She waved him over, holding a finger up to her lips.

"Deedee," he whispered when he got near. "What the fuck happened? My jacket's gone. And my head. Fuck."

"You were pretty messed up."

He nodded. "Had a good time, I guess? I remember dancing. That's funny. I never dance. What was that place?"

"Listen, Track. You said a lot of things, rude things."

"Shit."

"Phil wants you to go."

He rubbed hard at his left temple. "I fucked it up, huh? Can I apologize?"

Maybe he could, maybe Phil would give him another chance, but she didn't want to risk it, didn't want to be the person saying Track's behavior was forgivable. In fact, she wasn't sure *she* would ever forgive him. But overnight, she'd determined to put a good face on it, to give him the opportunity to return to his old self, and though she knew it was foolish she also knew that she owed him that much.

"You've got to go," she said. "But we can still hang out. Just get a hotel and I'll still show you around."

He shrugged. "I don't even know why I'm here." He plopped down on her mattress. "Nobody wants me around."

She should have predicted this. Guys had a way of turning their shitty behavior into something Diane was supposed to feel sorry for, as if she or one of her friends were the ones who did something wrong simply by witnessing the offense. "Your mother said you were coming to make business contacts, but last night you said you already have a business with your dad. So I don't know. What are you doing here?"

"Fuck," he said, and she could tell that he needed a pause to soak in the fact that he'd spilled whatever beans he'd brought with him that he hadn't meant to spill. "I guess I thought I was here to see you."

She had to resist this play for her guilt. "We're still going to see each other. I just said—"

"I was a total dick last night, wasn't I?"

She nodded. "I'm not going to lie."

"I'm sorry."

She went out to the kitchenette and poured them coffee, both black, just like they drank in high school. "You know I don't need your mom, right? I mean, I'm not trying to take her from you. I never was."

He squinched his eyes. "What are you even talking about?"

———

HE TOOK A room at the Ellison, a swanky place in Midtown, after calling his dad. The Ellison had a stone fountain in the marble lobby, with ferns and whatnot growing in big terra-cotta planters and music playing from a distant piano—an actual piano, with an actual pianist.

Over the next week she rode the train up to the Herald Square station, before or after her shifts, and met him in the lobby of the Ellison. They wandered around like tourists, chatting about old times, occasionally dropping into the testier subjects of art and politics, two things Track was sure belonged far away from each other. "Art is always political," Diane said as they drank beers in Greenwich Village. "If it's worth a damn it's political."

"Okay, Trotsky," he said. "Give me *Star Wars*. Or Pollock. He's good."

"Political," she said, pointing in the air as if at one of them. "Political."

"Garbage. Art's art. I mean, don't let me be the one to tell you. Ask your dealer."

"I don't have a dealer."

He made a gesture like: *voilà*.

"Go fuck yourself."

But mostly they saw things. At the Museum of Natural History, he seemed like Track again, full of wonder, breathless. "It's like we're in Salinger," he said as they left.

"I never read him."

"Oh, you've got to read Salinger."

"As long as he's not political," she said.

THEN HE WAS gone and the whole thing was over and she stretched out on her mattress and realized she hadn't painted in more than a week. The canvas she'd been working on, one she'd thought of sending home with him, was hardly begun on the easel. She had wanted to paint the two of them that day her grandfather tried to burn down his old movie studio. A pair of old photographs was clipped to the upper-left corner. Otherwise only a pencil sketch announced her intentions. She'd been so busy. Funny thing, too. With Track, she no longer felt that she didn't belong here. She'd spent the week as a New Yorker, showing around an old friend. Of course it had been a headache. Not exactly easy. But she had felt, without putting her finger on it until now, like nobody was checking over her shoulder, no one was waiting for a slip of the tongue that would prove she was only a nobody from Palm Springs.

And then she realized something else: He hadn't once asked to *look* at her paintings. He hadn't shown more than a minute's interest in the work she was really doing here, so far from Palm Springs, the whole purpose of her distance. Some brother. Or half. Or step.

At a gallery show a week later she griped about it to Lily Wong, who said she should never again think about what the people in her hometown thought of her art. "You can't go home again. Right? Isn't that from the Bible?"

"Maybe."

"Anyway I heard that guy was a total dick. And what kind of name is Track?"

"A name for a dick," Diane said, instantly regretting it.

Across the room they spotted Marly Feldberg, one of the leading female abstract painters, friend of Elaine de Kooning and Lee Krasner, dressed in a wide black muumuu with white lace down the front. She was dumpy and happy and wore her hair in a boy's bowl cut. In her hand a cigarette smoldered in a long plastic filter. She smiled widely, laughed with her yellowed teeth out. "That lady doesn't give a fuck about home," Diane said. "I mean, look at her."

Lily nodded. "This is her home. She may as well own this city."

"Not really my kind of work," Diane said. But she was in awe that this legend would be here, a week after the opening, chatting and looking as human as they were. "I respect her use of color, though."

Lily grabbed Diane's arm and whispered, "She sees us."

"What do you—"

"Ladies," Marly Fedlberg shouted over the shoulders of those nearest her.

"She's coming over here," said Lily.

And she was, with her hands out before her as she crossed the room. "Thank you both so much for coming."

"Oh we're not—" Diane began, but she wasn't sure what they

weren't. Collectors? People with money? Random people this old woman thought she'd met somewhere? "We're just looking."

When Marly Feldberg took their hands she looked down at them, held them up to her face: nubbed fingernails, paint stains, blisters. "I know sisters when I see them. You both paint?"

"Well," said Lily.

After a pause, Diane said, "Yes."

"Of course you do," Marly Feldberg said. Her voice was gruff, airy, with a loony quality that reminded Diane of an old Lucille Ball. "You two stick around. We'll talk shop. And business. Two young ladies painting in New York need to know the business. Let's get a glass of wine."

LIFE ON EARTH:
A Lily Wong Retrospective

The Museum of Modern Art, New York, 2006

INTRODUCTORY ESSAY BY:
Di Stiegl

"Like our flesh and our senses, the things among us surely burn with passion and die out, as we do, to become ash." —Emil Göttering

A celebrated artist seems by definition not to be an overlooked artist. But taking in the works of Lily Wong from the last twenty-five years, one is left with a sense that she has been greatly overlooked—not because we hadn't seen her, but because we hadn't been looking closely enough. Perhaps no other artist of the final decades of the twentieth century has explored so relentlessly questions of what is real and what is simulated, the effect of marketing and consumerism on our aesthetic appreciation of the everyday, or the very elemental fact of what it means to be—to exist—in a world populated by the products of what some have started to call "late capitalism."

She needs no champion; the work has spoken for itself. When asked to write an introduction to this catalogue, my first response was to turn down the offer. What could I say that Lily hadn't already said, or done, or forced upon the imagination of gallery and museum visitors in the blazing years of her too-brief career? Before her untimely death from cancer in 2003, she was already a major name in contemporary art.

Wong was her own great explainer. In a series of essays published in the late '80s through the '90s, she showed the roots of her thinking: Heidegger, Debord, Baudrillard. But this thinking was not only in conversation with these great continental minds, but often in opposition to them. She had a natural American optimism and rebelliousness, a need to understand the most critical of critical theory (some of which leads to cynical dead-ends more rewarding in the grad-school classroom than in the practice of real life) and then move beyond it to action, to a space where art can speak to an audience, change that audience, and so change the systems of power we find ourselves trapped within in postmodern society.

This led her to be misunderstood early on as the '80s downtown scene's anti-Warhol (in spite of the fact that she would meet and befriend Andy) and later the anti-Koons and finally the anti-Hirst, though none of these monikers really fit her. They were products of an art scene and art publications which believed that a thoughtful conceptual sculptor working at the spear-edge of the field who also happened to be a woman must necessarily be anti-Something. How could a woman be this talented? How could she know what she was doing? Certainly it had to be a reaction to something else. Add to this the fact that Wong was an Asian American woman—by the late '90s, when she should have been seen as a singular and paramount figure in American art, critics began looking for the Asianness of her work. They asked to discuss identity, ignoring her more radical messages regarding the systems of power at work in everyday objects, the shallow emptiness we have traded our lives for as consumers, the vast depth of the real just on the other side of this commodification smokescreen. They asked questions they answered for themselves, we could say.

Had anyone actually been paying attention to the work and to what Lily said in public about her identity—especially her experience of American society in the body of an Asian woman—they would have seen an artist interested in surfaces and interiors, the liminal spaces of Being within which minorities are categorized by the dominant white culture, and modes of resistance against the prefabricated (and white power–nostalgic) monoculture of Reagan's America. "I was born an outsider," she once told a BBC documentarian. "I didn't have a choice in that. In fact, I'm proud of it. Proud of my family and culture. People often look at me like I'm strange when I say that. As if their expectations of a Chinese girl don't fit my saying it. *Oh, so sorry.*"

Misunderstood, then. Often, by critics and those with power, purposefully so. But this circumstance shouldn't come to define the work of Lily Wong and didn't limit her attitude toward the potential of art in the twenty-first century. In a late-2002 interview in *ARTnews*, the critic Brandon Ondaatje, a great champion of her work, asked her what she expected of the viewer in her impressive multigallery installation, *Things Have Skin Like Me*:

What do I expect of them? To be. To touch and smell. To look and listen. To taste if they must. I feel that even looking at some of these objects brings on other senses like taste. But I wouldn't be offended if a tongue were to make contact with the chicken-flesh I've stretched on a stapler, or a television made of pigskin, or the cutlery and plates covered in fur. Mostly I want them to think, and I believe they will think. What are these things? What is that sound of breathing? Where are those gusts of warm and cold air coming from? Where am I? Why? And I would hope that, going home, this turned-up sense continues. That's what art does, after all. It makes us look. Not at it but at the world. It makes us look at our lives. That's why it's always dangerous, always at the front lines. They burn books. They scream about paintings. They censor films. The fear is always that art will do what it is intended to do: remind us that we are here, that we are not the narratives handed to us by a marketing campaign, that we have much more in common than those in power want us to believe. That's what I expect. Nobody should do art without expecting the absolute possibility from it. We are nearly always wrong on that front, but we must go on expecting it. To do otherwise would mean to stop. (Ondaatje, 126)

"Absolute possibility" wasn't an accidental phrase. Neither was "turned-up sense." Wong had been using these phrases in conversations and interviews and artist statements for decades. She truly did believe that art should be aiming at its highest possible stature in the culture at all times, that it should speak to and from a position of authority—not an elitist one, which has characterized art because of the media fascination with values and auction prices and collectors, but as a source of resistance against its true opposite: the dulled life manufactured by those with economic and systemic power, whose only real goal is to create wealth for themselves and curtail the lives of others. When one sees art as a necessarily radical tool against such forces, then yes, maybe one is anti-Something. And for Wong, leaving an art experience (music, painting film, novel, whatever) with a "turned-up sense" meant leaving with one's knobs out of whack, no longer fitting what those powers expected of you. Feeling, in the words of one of her favorite bands, "out of step." To be out of step meant, for Wong, to be focused on the real.

Lily Wong was born in Omaha, Nebraska, the fourth daughter in a family recently relocated from the Bay Area for her father's job at KDM Chemicals, a manufacturer of popular pesticides and detergents, and in her teenage years the family moved to White Plains, New York, just about in time for her interest in the NYC art scene to blossom. She attended NYU and made her gallery debut at Sex Guide in '81 in the *Do We Have a Sex Guide Gallery Show?* show, where one of her early "sculptural objects" hinted at later, more defining work: a television remote control filled with motor oil, which over time leaked onto the glass pedestal where it was displayed and then onto the newly installed carpet. In '88 she would show the same remote control's casing filled with cow's blood, held in a thin membrane that degraded over time. *Surfing* was a major statement, a work that brought her critical praise and public criticism. In 1993, it was purchased as a permanent exhibit by the Guggenheim.

Looking back on her work since that time, it is a mental challenge to ignore her significance to '90s and early '00s sculpture and conceptual art. But her solo, multigallery show with George West, which ran from late 2002 until February 2003, has had the sort of impact very few gallery shows have had in art history. Suddenly, as if overnight, Lily Wong was seen as—

(page missing)

KLAUS

1928

OLIVE, OLIVE. HIS eyes danced across the glimmer of shoulders and top hats and diamonds and fluttering eyes looking only for her. But she wasn't there. How Klaus longed for her, secretly, quietly, even tonight during this ostensible celebration of his work—his greatest film to date, according to the press, according to the attuned eye of Mr. Irving Thalberg. Flashbulbs, searchlights, Kay's arm pulling his tight. Klaus von Stiegl gave the ever-changing crowd one more look before he said, "What, darling?"

"You're distracted," Kay said. "Mr. Schlossberg asked you a question."

Klaus had nearly forgotten the great man towering at his side. "Ja, ja," he said. "My deepest apologies. Such a strain, these nights."

Schlossberg, as was his habit, responded to this with a big, earthy guffaw. "I was only asking if you thought you could get a big star for your proposed, uh, 'independent production.'"

Under a Cherokee Moon's debut at Grauman's Chinese Theatre, late May 1928. A grand triumph for Klaus and for MGM, for Kay and for George, for the returned-from-retirement Lou Channing. And as if that weren't enough, in the pause after Schlossberg's question, a tuxedoed Louis B. Mayer—wound up by the excitement of the live radio hookup and blasting searchlights outside—announced to the world that the movie was "really a success for all America, because *Cherokee* is a celebration of this country's great past and even greater future." Klaus heard the boss say this, saw his chest puffed out, his eyes squinting back prideful tears. But he stood twenty feet away with Kay and with Schlossberg, to whom he had just broached his big idea: a studio they could run independent of MGM to create a picture with absolute artistic freedom. "We could hire the stars of this very picture," Klaus said.

Schlossberg shrugged. "And who else?"

"I could approach Richard Barthelmess. We're moving into his house in Palm Springs, after all."

"And who *ain't* involved is what matters," added Kay.

"Exactly," Schlossberg had said with a conspiratorial grin. "No Mayer and Thalberg. Let the lunatics run the asylum?"

"If you consider me a lunatic, Mr. Schlossberg."

"They'll crush you if they learn about it. They may do so anyway."

"We'll hand them a finished picture to distribute," Klaus said. "Like giving them free money."

But their designs were cut short there. For it was at that moment when Mayer stepped away from the microphone and, holding out his gregarious hand, shouted, "Gentlemen! Gentlemen!" He shook Schlossberg's hand, slapped Klaus on the shoulder. Finally, with a genteel tip of his hat, he said, "And what a joy to behold the lovely Ms. Stone."

Kay dipped her knees in a gesture something like a curtsy. "Mr. Mayer."

She had become synonymous with Klaus, his star. A Von Stiegl picture meant a Kay Stone picture, and aside from her starring role in a Vidor comedy in February, a Kay Stone picture meant a Von Stiegl. And only Kay had seen the new house in Palm Springs, previously rented by the impossibly handsome Barthelmess, now Klaus's, complete with two acres of scraggly desert behind, just enough space to build a functional studio that could produce a single picture at a time. "For us!" he had told her as the realtor motored off. He'd tossed her the keys. "Ein home away from home."

A WEEK LATER, with the wind at his back, Klaus invited Schlossberg out to the Palm Springs house, to the concrete patio, to the kidney-shaped pool. "And you mean to build this structure over there?" Schlossberg said, pointing into the desert. Then, fingering his collar, "A bit hot out here for pictures, eh?"

"At night it cools," Klaus said. "And there is winter."

Schlossberg laughed his big, rich laugh. "They have winter out here? Could have fooled me."

Just then, Kay came out of the house in her long yellow robe. She walked past them without a word, slid the robe onto the pale concrete, and stepped into the pool. Klaus watched Schlossberg watching her every movement. "The first picture I want to produce," he began, "is something I am calling *Hans & Greta*."

"Like the nursery rhyme," Schlossberg said with vague distraction.

Klaus didn't correct him. "It is about a young couple who discover a magical home in the forest. I have Artie Banyan working on the scenario."

Schlossberg's eyes flicked back to Klaus for a hard moment. "Never heard of him."

"He's quite good."

"You ought to get Cliff Dexter. Or Anita Yastremska. You know — a big talent. Anita wrote that Garbo picture —"

"Artie is very good," Klaus said again.

Schlossberg's face went sullen, but just as quickly stretched back into shape. He wasn't a man used to being interrupted. "It's a big risk, Klaus. Nothing to fool around with. We need professionals, not some Joe from the street."

"I understand."

"Do you? I imagine your girl here will star? And that cousin of yours? Old home week is how you have this imagined. Meanwhile, we're raising the flag of revolution for nursery rhyme movies. I tell you it doesn't sound realistic, Klaus. Not realistic at all."

Now it was Klaus's turn to watch Kay, to meet her eyes across the pool. She had believed in him at every step, from the Village to

Astoria and all the way here, this desert escape from Hollywood. "Mr. Schlossberg," he began, "you and I both know the studios have tipped over to sound production. The motion picture as we know it could die in only a few months. Talkies will be all that is left. That chatter and noise. That artlessness. Without an international audience. Heads talking to one another like one endless phone call. What you and I love about the pictures stopped forever. Here" — and now Klaus himself pointed at the scruff desert beyond the pool — "we could save the picture industry from itself. The two of us could be the final bulwark against a thousand Jolsons pleading to their mammies to kingdom come."

Had that convinced Schlossberg? Klaus would never know. Because his other guests — Olive Lazlo and Dwight Squibb — came bounding around the western side of the house like bottle-wielding invaders, reminding him that if this place were to become anything permanent, he would have to put up a fence to keep strangers from helping themselves to the pool. Of course, now the open lawn was convenient. His adoration for Olive Lazlo knew almost no bounds, after all. For the past year, he had made himself a regular not only at Schlossberg's Ocean House parties, but the soirees held at Olive's apartment in the Gildmere Hotel and even recordings of Dwight Squibb's radio program at the NBC studio on Santa Monica. He had invited her on-set during production of *Under a Cherokee Moon* and suffered silently when she had demurred. He had invited her as well to the debut and been heartbroken by her absence. But now she was here, in Palm Springs, and he stood with a jerk to greet them, nearly toppling the tray of cocktails sitting between himself and Schlossberg. "Olive, Dwight," he called out. "So good of you to come."

"Wouldn't miss it," said Dwight Squibb. "Where is everybody?"

It was Kay, only her head above the water, who said, "This is everybody."

"Thought it was a housewarming," said Dwight.

Schlossberg laughed. "I thought it was a business meeting."

And Olive Lazlo, in a trim white dress and feathered cap, gazed up at Mount San Jacinto. "Why Klaus, it's simply gorgeous out here. I've always loved Palm Springs."

———————

BY EARLY SEPTEMBER, the studio structure had been built, electricians had started wiring the building, and Alfonso Niccolo, on loan from United Artists, had begun painting the Lüneberg backdrop that would bring Klaus's long-lost hometown to the screen. For this, Klaus had paid a German photographer to travel to Lüneberg and express-mail a dozen photographs out to California, where Alfonso arranged the pictures on clothespins in the bare sun and began sketching a version of the town on a rectangle of canvas three feet high and five feet long. Only after the image was approved by Klaus did Alfonso start the more involved, detailed backdrop scrim nearly as wide and tall as the studio itself.

On a Saturday only a few weeks before production was set to begin, Alfonso came to the patio door in his white and paint-smattered coveralls, wiping his hands on a rag. Kay had traveled by train back to New York to do a radio program, and in her absence, Klaus had invited Olive Lazlo to tour the studio, hoping the backdrop would be finished in time. To his surprise, Olive had accepted the invitation. For once, Dwight Squibb hadn't come along.

Alfonso led them past the shimmering pool and through the loose barbed-wire fence and then out into the scrubby acres of desert where some years ago it was said that Richard Barthelmess had planned to build a horse stable. Now the great black studio loomed, a hundred feet wide, seventy-five feet across, and as tall as a three-story building. Within the cool shade inside, Klaus could feel Olive next to him, smell her copper-and-rose-scented perfume. Alfonso gestured vaguely to the dark and unlit canvas in front of them before taking the handle of a great flywheel and cranking it leftward, squeaking open the rooftop windows and sending a flood of desert glow down on that city so confoundingly wedged in Klaus's mind.

He trembled, very nearly lost his balance. "Perfect," he muttered. "No, something better than perfect."

Lüneberg. That's what he needed to see. His forgotten childhood home, hardly a sketch in his mind before that trip with Uncle Leopold and George in '24, the trip by steamer to Hamburg and then by car to Berlin, the single day among their business and socializing that he had requested of them to see the city of his birth. He'd walked the place a stranger, awed by its picturesque beauty, daydreaming of his mother and the tales of the Grimm brothers, imagining the Black Forest perhaps just over that horizon, coming back to reality only when a prim German in a well-fit black suit spit at the feet of Uncle Leopold and said, without even a measure of shame, "Filthy Jew."

To be so mysteriously connected to and repelled by a place.

Olive swayed a little on her toes. "It really is magical," she said. "And this is where you're from?"

"I left as a small child. When I returned I was a young man." He thought then, like a flash bulb, of the picture palaces in Berlin where he'd tied his fate to the movies. A fateful and single trip. He gestured up at the scrim and told her, "But I will live here as we make the picture. Then it will be a kind of home."

She gave him a canted smile. "You're a regular poet, Count von Stiegl."

"Oh, I'm no count. That is Georgie's little fib. Listen," he said, turning to face her. "I have a wonderful idea. Why don't you play in the picture? A small part. Just a moment or two."

"I've never acted," she said, and for an instant he thought she blushed. "Not even in school."

"It takes nothing. You only do what I say. It is that simple."

BUT EVERYONE ON the first day of production knew that the heiress Olive Lazlo really couldn't act, really had no idea what she was doing in front of the camera, and the first to complain wasn't Kay— who spent the better part of an hour glaring accusingly at Klaus as shot after shot was tried again—but Artie Banyan, who put his big hand on Klaus's shoulder, lowered his leonine head, and whispered, "We could go with the other girl."

"Nein," Klaus said, so loud everyone could hear. "Again. This time look here, at my hand, and when I snap my fingers, open them wider, make the shape of an 'o' with your mouth. And then hold. Do you understand?"

She did, or nodded as if she did, and still they had to run the scene four more times before a solid take was dedicated to film. And Klaus knew with each run that he was giving her more patience than he would any other actress, ten times more patience, and that everyone on-set knew it as well. It shouldn't have been a surprise then, that night in bed, when the Barthelmess house was emptied of everyone but himself and his star, that Kay said, "You're in love with her. Anyone with eyes can see it."

Klaus ventured a laugh. "She is only a rich woman with connections."

"She's Dwight Squibb's fiancée," she said. "And you're enamored with her."

He turned to her. "You are imagining things. Don't be silly."

The moment his hand touched her arm, she recoiled, stood from the bed. "My friend Margie is arriving tomorrow. I'm taking the car to pick her up in L.A."

"But where are you going now?"

"I'm sleeping in the extra room." At the door, she stopped and looked back at him, her eyes narrow and sad. "You can lie here by yourself dreaming about Olive Lazlo."

———

THINGS WENT ON like this. Kay's suspicion turned to outright jealousy, sniping words when the cameras weren't running. One day he caught her flirting with one of the guys from the four-piece orchestra who played mood music for the actors during scenes. When Klaus glared at the young man, an unshaved Italian with black curls dangling over his forehead, Kay tousled the man's hair like a child's. Word got around set that Olive Lazlo had paid for the opportunity to be in the film, and when Klaus told Artie about the rumor, his friend said, "Oh yeah, Kay's telling everybody that. Marge told me she's saying you picked up an easy five grand."

At night, Kay stayed in the extra room, or drove to L.A. to spend time with her friends. But in front of the camera, she was only magnificent, a perfect mime, the dynamic beauty at the heart of every frame. She was, again, his stand-in, his other self, the embodiment of his artistic purpose. Even as he betrayed her.

———

PRODUCTION WRAPPED ON October 19, a Friday, and it was Olive's idea to throw a grand party. Though she hadn't been needed on-set for three weeks, she had regularly come to Palm Springs to stand at Klaus's side, enthralled by the work and increasingly attentive to his long and extemporaneous diatribes about the art of cinema and the role of the director in a successful picture. With the reels of unedited film stacked in canisters on the dining table, surrounded by bootleg gin and unlabeled sparkling wine from Canada, Artie gave a speech to the assembled cast and crew on the subject of "Klaus von Stiegl's genius" which ended in a round of "For He's a Jolly Good Fellow." Outside next to the pool, the jazz quartet Olive had hired struck up the Charleston. In the cooling desert air, Klaus felt weightless. Here among his people, his greatest vision yet now dedicated to film, with Olive Lazlo smiling at him from across the patio. He had never been further from the poverty and desperation of the Lower East Side.

Kay had put on a big show of leaving with her friend, saying that she had something to do in Los Angeles nearly half a dozen times as she circled Klaus in the living room, never addressing him directly. But the Schlossbergs were there, and Lou Channing, and of course Walter and George.

———

THE FIRST JUMP had been a surprise. No one had seen George scramble up a ladder he'd taken from the studio, jog up the roof's incline, and then speed back down. Instead, some saw a tanned figure in blue trunks arc into the evening sky, arms wrapping around knees, or simply heard "Geronimo!" shouted from the heavens before a great splash erupted from the pool, drenching those standing alongside.

When his head popped up out of the sloshing water, when he thrust back his hair with both hands, George looked something like a statue dedicated to freedom or the wild heart in all mankind, and a raucous cheer went up from all the guests. It was Klaus who raised his glass of sparkling wine and shouted, "Again!"

A chorus of laughter erupted and George was easily cajoled into giving it another leap so that everyone could see. This time, after stepping out of the pool, he did a little act of doffing his hat and bowing to the audience—here, and then here, and now here—like a celebrated vaudevillian from another time. Cheers went all around for him to do the trick once more. And Klaus, playing again the director, the puppet-master, ordered, "Up, Georgie! Up!"

ARTIE WAS THE first to remark, as a group of them waited to see George at the hospital that night, that it shouldn't have come as a surprise. "Threes," he said. "You got three of anything and you've got yourself a plot."

Klaus shivered, ashed a cigarette. "Enough of that."

In the too-bright waiting room with half a dozen revelers pulling mortified faces, Klaus's tan suit was soaking wet, water still dripping occasionally from his wing-tip shoes. He'd been the one who had instinctually dived into the pool to pull George out before his head went underwater. His cousin had landed on the top of his spine, cracking his head. Now they were waiting to find out if he would make it out of this hospital alive.

Walter, leaning against the wall with his suit jacket bunched in his arms, wept openly.

"And when you think about classic tragedy," Artie went on. "I mean Aristotelian—"

"Will you ever shut up?" Klaus said.

Olive looked up from the floor. "Both of you stop it. Have some respect."

She gestured to the other half of the waiting room: normal, average folk weeping into handkerchiefs or whispering solemnly into their hands. When a doctor entered, these people watched his approach with the same alertness that Klaus and his group did. The doctor looked over the room without emotion. "Mr. Stiegl?"

———

KLAUS WAS HOME from the hospital by dawn. The doctors hadn't allowed anyone in the room with George, had only explained that the injury to his spine was very serious, that he may not again have the use of his arms and legs. In bed, Klaus had tossed and turned. At some point he dozed off and was almost immediately awoken by the phone ringing beside his bed. The man on the line sounded only vaguely familiar. "This Klaus?"

"Speaking."

"Dwight Squibb here." He had never called Klaus before, this ex-boyfriend of Olive's, the man she'd toyed with marrying before she had made herself a regular visitor to Palm Springs. And to hear his voice on the line at this hour was unsettling. "Overnight I've heard a few things," he said, as if he were setting up a joke. "One of these things is that George West busted his head open somewhere out in the desert. Another thing is that this somewhere is your very own home. Any truth to that?"

"Excuse me?"

"Is there any truth to this story George West is in the hospital thanks to pulling stunts in your backyard pool, Mr. Stiegl?"

"I heard you," Klaus said, sitting up. "But I don't understand why you're calling me on this subject."

Squibb laughed. "Would you rather I call Irving Thalberg?"

"It's a free country," Klaus said, but the thought of Thalberg and Mayer being brought into this sent a chill through him. "Just what is it you want?"

"I don't want to keep repeating myself, so let's get to this other thing I heard on the wind. You've been making a picture out there in Palm Springs using talent and crew under contract to MGM and elsewhere. Mr. West was among said talent. As was Mr. Channing, Ms. Stone, maybe eight or ten others I could name. Anything to this, Mr. Stiegl?"

Klaus couldn't later remember how he answered that question, what flimsy subterfuge he'd tossed Squibb, but the ruse fell quickly. Squibb had heard the whole story directly from a panicked Lou Channing, who had driven back to Los Angeles after the accident and for some reason picked Squibb to ramble everything to. "You understand I'll have to talk about this on the program," Squibb told Klaus. "That's just the nature of the business."

Defensive, delusional, Klaus said again, "It's a free country. Say what you want."

"One more thing a birdie sang to me," Squibb said, laughing as if he thought himself clever. "You been spending a lot of time with *my* Olive. How 'bout you lay off there and I find a way to forget all this?"

A great pain swelled in Klaus's chest. Olive. He wouldn't trade her like a horse with this insufferable little man. "You go to hell."

After that time had slowed. The Sunday-night *Squibb Comedy Hour* loomed for a full day and then some like a ticking bomb. Klaus went back and forth to the hospital. One of the doctors said that he felt confident George would have use of his hands and arms, had even started calling such an outcome "your cousin's best possible recovery" with a smile. At the Barthelmess house, guests thinned out. Walter took a hotel room near the hospital. The Schlossbergs stayed on longer than Klaus had expected but finally left for Ocean House on Sunday evening. Even Artie took a bus back to L.A. Klaus had told none of them of the phone call from Dwight Squibb. None of them but Olive, who called Squibb and begged him to hang fire. But she was the last person Squibb wanted to hear from on the subject. When she got off the phone she said, "He says I'll come crawling back to him after the broadcast. But he's an imbecile."

TOBEY'S COUCH POTATOES - SEPTEMBER 2007 BLOG

TV REVIEW: SEASON FOUR, BRACKETT (NOW OUT <u>ON DVD</u> FOR THE FIRST TIME!)

THE TOTALLY BATSHIT TURNS AND BEHIND-THE-SCENES MADNESS THAT ENDED BRACKETT

In the early '60s, a new kind of cop show hit American televsion sets. Brackett (played by the always-grimacing Frank Harlan) appeared in the desert outside Los Angeles, apparently with no first name, dressed in a trim brown suit, his gun holster ever apparent. He smoked cigarettes and flicked them thoughtfully into whatever landscape was nearby (parking lot, grocery store linoleum, once the shag carpet of a brothel) and talked fast, really fast, his signature trick not to stare someone down a-la Clint Eastwood or play dumb like Columbo, but to just talk right over whoever was troubling him, hammering them with questions in a surprisingly reedy voice. Bad guys failed to take him seriously and nearly always perished. His colleagues knew to fear him and revere him. Strangely, he was also a romantic. Every few weeks a subplot would reveal another woman he was dating, like a noir Jerry Seinfeld.

For three seasons running from 1963-65, Brackett followed the serial formula: each week's episode featured a single crime solved by our hero, who often dealt out street justice, and while some of the crimes were more grisly than viewers had scene before on the small screen, its most important aspect was the steady and inventive direction of Klaus von Stiegl. Von Stiegl (1905-1971) had been a major director during the silent era known for his artisits compositions. But he didn't make it in the sound era, and after working for years in Mexico (making mostly forgotten movies he himself couldn't understand, as he never learned Spanish), von Stiegl returned to the states as a director-for-hire in the budding world of television, first in live television in New York and later hired by Desilu. Soon enough, he was running his own production company in LA. His visual style gave the show a Wellesian sort of look: lots of shadows and expressionist angles, a sense of symbolism in nearly every shot. This was black-and-white tv taken to a cinematic level.

Then came the notorious season four.

It's hard to conceive of what a radical departure this season was from anything that had been seen on television before—and for many years since. You could say that a show like The Sopranos wouldn't exist without the final season of Brackett, but then again you could say that about a lot of shows in the decades between. Whatever it's influence (David Simon claims never to have seen it . . . ?), it can only benefit our understanding of television history to look at what happened and what made it so radical for 1966.

First off—this is no serial tv show. The full 1966 season is not only brought together by a single arc, but is completely absorbed by that arc. It's really a single episode stretched over 20 hours, broken up by the famous title sequence (eat my shorts Rockford Files) and of course the blip of commercial breaks. A single mystery opens episode one (originally aired September 8th, 1966) and is not fully solved until the final episode (March 16th, 1967).

And that final episode is a doozy. Throughout the season, we've watched as Brackett behaves with greater and greater violence—and as the stakes around him rise. By the bloody final episode, we learn that Brackett is not the moral force we assumed he was. He's been hiding things (something we learn at different steps along this wild ride of a season) both from his superiors and from himself. And Brackett's own ending would be shocking even today. But I should go back to the beginning.

The season opens with the murder of the mayor of Los Angeles (Burt Neville in a recurring role). Brackett is put in charge of the investigation, and it seems at first that a killer from season one ("The Melrose Case"), recently escaped from prison, is the number one suspect. While the hunt is on for the killer, we learn that Brackett's new date isn't a passing fling. After date scene at a swanky 60s restaurant where all the waiters look like Beatles, he tells the chief of police he plans to marry the girl. Uh-oh. You can see where things are going. By episode two she is dead, a note left at the scene of the crime reading: "I know you." But if that sounds like the clichés of revenge plot, buckle in. The following episode shows Brackett going to a shady nightclub where he bypasses the bartender, walks through the kitchen, and down a long hallway. He then literally goes underground, down three sets of stairs and into one of LA's giant drain tunnels. There he climbs a ladder, opens a hidden door, and enters a room where a bearded man sits reading the newspaper. Brackett, without a word, shoots the man dead.

Halfway through that third episode, we go into flashback, where we'll stay until near the end of episode five, once the identity of the bearded man is understood. This flashback (in the mode of Christmas Carol with present-day Brackett observing a series of tableau) tells us all about Brackett's youth after returning from the War. Turns out Brackett was a hoodlum, under the wing of our bearded man, committing hold-ups and break-ins, trying to forget the traumatic events of Iwo Jima, running from his deadbeat family—all the old baggage stuff. This comes to a shocking twistt in episode five in which he kills a black man whose apartment he's robbing and then, in a gut wrenching scene moments later, kills the man's wife when she innocently walks into the room and discovers him. We're led to understand that this horrible crime scared him straight. At least that's where things are left off when we return to the present. But I don't want to ruin the whole story. Rest assured Brackett is not at all the man you think he is if you've been watching through season three.

The show had by now become a kind of scandal for ABC. Executives were horrified by the direction things had taken, and behind the scene had already threatened to pull the plug. The only thing keeping the show on television in those first weeks were the ratings. Brackett regularly competed with Bonanza as the most popular program of the mid-60s and by '66 virtually owned Thursday nights. It was a cash cow for ABC, and with each season Klaus von Stiegl had taken greater risks, bargaining freedom with his independent production company. But episode five spooked the advertisers and letters started to arrive from viewers who couldn't believe a show could get this dark. The show was at this point almost entirely "in the can," as von Stiegl told Time magazine, as in filmed and ready to broadcast. But it went into a three-week hiatus, and if it hadn't been for the efforts of Frank Harlan (his career was still on the upswing: rumor had it he'd be cast in the next Hitchcock*), who announced that fans deserved to see the remaining episodes and that he wouldn't return to the set under anyone but von Stiegl's direction, the show would have disappeared entirely.

(*Cards on the table: Frank Harlan is my grandfather, though I never knew him all that well. We grew up with a painting of him in our living room, in character, gun drawn! Rumor had it the experience on Season 4 of Brackett drove him into neurosis and stomach ailments. It definitely wrecked his career: no call from Hitch.)

In fact all the actors and crew were in thrall to von Stiegl during this time. A letter was sent to ABC vice president Edgar Scherick demanding the show be reinstated at its regular time. Fans did the same. By now the country had turned its attention to the drama going on over the show. Its ratings had been growing steadily during the strange turn of this daring season of television, and now politicians were comparing the hiatus to the silencing of dissidence in the Eastern Bloc. Surprisingly, even civil rights leaders came out in favor of the show, supporting its realistic depiction of racism and police violence. Everyone wanted to know what would happen next and so the show returned with a baffling 45% audience share. Imagine nearly half of America sitting down to watch the same increasingly surreal cop show. Not until Twin Peaks would we see anything remotely like it.

What drove von Stiegl in this strange and experimental direction? One major factor changed in his life following the end of season 3, and that was the death of his wife of more than thirty years, the Western P&E heiress Olive von Stiegl. Only the spiraling depression of grief can explain what happened to Brackett, and why von Stiegl not only brought his very popular show to a sudden end but also retired from television and film altogether. In his remaining years he sat for intereviews with major magazines and became a north star for a young generation of filmmakers who sought out his guidance (though now folks remember him as a bit of a dirtbag), but he always refused to talk about the death of his wife and, when asked about what happened to Brackett he would say that he'd always planned for the show to end as it did. As for its influence on the television to come a few decades later, one has to quote Bracket himself with his famous catchphrase, "Back up, sonny."

Just watch your step near the pool!

DIANE
1981

THE ODD THING, as she waited for her cue to climb up on the stage at Club 57, was that she thought she'd seen Phil far across the crowd in a beige sweater rolled to his elbows. He was supposed to be at work, had told her for a month that he couldn't make it to whatever they were calling this performance: wearing Reagan masks and flapper dresses in a tap-dancing chorus as Nero Divisible pretended to belt out Sinatra.

Maybe Diane was seeing things. She did already have the heavy rubber mask pulled down over her head, with only curved slits for her eyes. "Nah," said Annie beside her, up on tiptoe. "That's somebody else."

Since a couple of months ago, Annie had been wearing her hair like this, bleached to an unnatural white-blond, alternately crimped and straightened, so that a serrated fringe hung out over her eyes like an awning and sharp flat angles shot down the back of her head toward her spine. High-concept. She waited until the absolute last minute to pull her Ronnie mask over this, just as the music overhead stopped and Nero Divisible shot up on stage holding an old-timey microphone, dressed in an ill-fitting tuxedo, his hair glooped and molded into a great blue wave.

The crowd began cheering before he could even say a word. "Ladies and Gentleweiners," he said, pausing for a few coughs of ironic laughter. "Tonight I'd like to sing you a song from the heart."

And then, as planned, "My Way" blasted from the speakers, and Nero swayed and mouthed the words, and there was her cue, a thumbs-up from across the stage, and she charged up with the other girls as the whole place screamed with laughter. Onstage they shuffled across, jazz-handing it, doing a little Charleston-type thing with their bare legs, all of it very practiced and ridiculous. Then, fanned out behind Nero, they raised their hands to their foreheads, saluting something up near the ceiling. To her left, Annie kept hoofing even though everyone else had stopped. At her right, Lily couldn't stop laughing. "My mask," she was saying. When Diane looked, she saw that Lily's rubber face had fallen to one side, the mask too big for her head, its dead eyes aimed disconcertingly over her shoulder, tufts of black hair sticking out the holes. "I can't see," Lily said, and went on laughing.

Well, it was that sort of show. Nobody bothered fixing Lily's mask, least of all Lily, who during the second chorus added a little hula-hoop move to her upper half, nearly losing her balance, and finally, after wobbling it around and around, sending her mask into the air over Nero's head. Silly, theatrical, downtown Dada. They were all in on it here: the Reagans' full-of-shit Americanism, the cowboy schtick, that cartoon of tradition with an edge of blowing us all to smithereens. Surely the administration wouldn't last long, couldn't, not with an old actor in charge. Someone else would pull the strings, hand him his speeches, and then usher him off toward the horizon in '84, when Ted Kennedy would run again, or someone better, maybe a woman. Annie had joked they should nominate Barbra Streisand or maybe Liz Taylor, anyway someone with more talent in the acting field, and Diane nearly agreed with her. But really she'd take someone less flashy. A pet rock, she'd offered. A pet rock with a mustache painted on it to give it a little gravitas.

They got a laugh, and cheers, and after Nero bowed all the girls bowed, and Lily grabbed Diane's hand as they ran back off the narrow stage and yelled to her over the noise, "Diane, I didn't tell you Valerie Szeslak is getting together a show. Just downtown women artists. I'm showing her my work next week. You should come with me."

"Valerie Szeslak?" Diane said, pretending she didn't know the name, hadn't stared at her in terror at a loft party only last week, trying to work up the courage to introduce herself. Valerie Szeslak had put together that show for Jean-Michel, and for the uptown graffiti artists, with a performance by the Fab Five.

"Just bring a few paintings, will you?" Lily said, holding her lightly by the elbow as the other girls dissipated into the evening crowd. Someone had hung a disco ball, ironically, and as Nero stalked down from the stage it was lit up, giving his lanky frame a Travolta vibe. "I'll be at the Sex Guide Gallery at eleven. Will you be there? Promise?"

Lily had been an NYU studio art student as well, though a couple of years ahead of Diane and now graduated. Despite her degree they both worked at the same restaurant, walking steak tartare out to visiting businessmen during the lunch shift, ignoring their gross flirtations and little "accidental" pats on the ass. Diane had learned from her, painted in the bright, near-empty loft where Lily now lived with three other girls. Aside from Annie she was likely her best friend.

"I'll be there," Diane said. But really she didn't feel at all ready. Valerie Szeslak was the real deal and Diane Stiegl was less than unknown: a dropout with an out-of-style oeuvre and a tremendous sense that she had no idea what she was doing.

Someone had put on *Fear of Music* by Talking Heads, and for a second Diane thought of staying and dancing. But then she saw Phil—it really had been him—and up close he looked sick to his stomach. "Your mother's gone!" he was shouting. "They can't find her."

She laughed, the absurdity of the situation convincing her this was some kind of joke. "What are you talking about?"

———

ANTONIA'S CAR HAD been found outside a McDonald's near Pittsburgh, or rather, it had been parked there for a week before the manager had finally decided to contact the police and have it towed away. The car, a new Mustang Diane had previously heard nothing about, had been purchased with her mother's money and her grandmother's credit, and so Muriel Thompson of Cheyenne, Wyoming, had been called early one morning this past week and informed that her vehicle had been impounded at someplace called K-razy Kent's Auto Salvage, several states away. Since then, dozens of others had been drafted into the search, though no one, it seemed, had heard anything from Antonia in weeks. Phil explained all this on the street as they walked the ten blocks to the apartment. "She called while I was getting ready," he said. "I kept letting it ring and when I finally answered I think I cursed at her."

"It's okay."

"The poor woman was crying, Diane. You've got to apologize for me."

Of course, they couldn't afford a tape machine to record missed calls. They were either home or not, and interested in talking to someone or not, and that had generally been good enough. "It's not your fault," she told him. "It could have been another heavy breather."

On the phone, Grandma Thompson was no longer crying—calm, she said, because at this point she didn't know what else to do but wait. Diane didn't really know the woman. She lived in Wyoming on a small farm and, according to Antonia, thought her own daughter was a hippie, always one step from sliding into poverty or devil worship. "If you haven't seen her," she told Diane, "I really don't know where she could be."

"And Dad? Did you talk to him?"

"He's on the case. He's called all their old friends. A woman named Alice told him she got a letter from her a month ago—she read it to him over the phone. But it was all horoscope nonsense and a recipe for an herbal medicine. I don't know what's become of her. She could be off with some cult or another."

Diane had grabbed her coat and pants from behind the bar before they left and now stood sweating, overdressed after a night of being underdressed. The stickiness of her armpits and belly filled her with disgust. She'd been fucking around for the last two weeks planning this stupid "show" about Reagan—which said what? did what?—and all the while her mother had been off her medication and on one of her misadventures, this time without leaving any clues, without making the manic phone calls about someplace she always wanted to visit or some new friend who wanted her to move in with them and study Buddhism or whatever.

Diane thought hard about sitting right down on the naked wood floor and crying. But she didn't. "She's probably fine," she said. "She'll turn up in a few days with a new friend or two."

Grandma took a long breath. Over the line, Diane imagined she could hear the mountain wind, and wondered if it had even grown dark there yet. Maybe it was dusk. Maybe her grandmother was standing in the kitchen with the phone cord stretched over the countertop, looking out the window as lights twinkled to life down in Cheyenne. "I don't think you understand," she said. "This time is different."

It was; Diane knew it was. The building buzz sound in her ears was guilt. "Don't say that," she said. "I'm sure she's okay."

When she finally got her father on the phone two hours and a dozen calls later, she railed at him that it was his fault, yes his fault. "I mean, you drove her to this. We never should have left her. When was the last time you even spoke to her?"

Percy seemed to take a sharp breath on the line. "When did *you* talk to her, Deedee? When's the last time you took the tunnel over and—"

"Never mind that. You're her husband."

"Not for a long time, Deedee."

"I don't want you to call me that."

"I'm sorry."

"Are you? All you do is abandon everybody, and now she's—"

There was a long silence. They hadn't spoken like this before. As hurt as Percy had left her back in Palm Springs, they had never had it out. On the sofa, Phil stared at Diane, holding his hand aloft as if he'd been frozen mid-movement, instinctively bringing it up to cover his face. That's when she realized she'd lost control of the situation.

"Look," she said, "I didn't mean that. I'm upset."

"I've spoken to everyone she knows," Percy said. "Everyone. I even called her neighbor, long-distance, pretty late at night for your time. He says nobody new had been coming by, no visitors, no love interest. She came over last month with her cat and asked him to watch it for the weekend. The guy's still got her cat."

Phil went to the fridge and extracted two cans of Coors. At first Diane waved him off but then she reached for one, and the chilled foam softened her throat. Instantly, something cooled in her head. "What about the police?" she said. "Are they doing anything?"

"Your grandmother did a missing-persons but nobody's taking it seriously. Grown woman on her own, known for rash decisions, you know the routine." She could see Percy: a couple of days' growth of beard, salt-and-pepper now, that pained expression in his eyes. "Honey, why don't Cindy and I come out? We've been needing to visit. We can put our heads together. Get through this as a family."

———

AT ANTONIA'S APARTMENT they found no clues, no signs of special disturbance, though all the vegetables and fruits were rotten. Phil bagged these as Diane rifled through papers and notebooks, opened and closed drawers, peeked under the couch cushions for reasons she couldn't explain. Her mother's neighbor tried to press the cat on them and they demurred, feigning allergies.

Back in Manhattan, Diane spent the next day or two muttering to herself, imagining out loud or in her head a road trip to Pennsylvania, a detective fantasy, a car full of her art and theatre friends knocking on doors, her mother safe and sound behind the very last one. "I worry you'd get yourself lost out there too," Phil said at last, and that also meant he wasn't interested in going, that she, say, couldn't exactly borrow his car.

Since getting the news she'd told no one, hadn't mentioned it when Lily called to remind her about the meeting with Valerie Szeslak at the Sex Guide, had kept her voice chipper when Annie called to complain for an hour about her girlfriend Reggie, who had nearly OD'd Saturday night and maybe would have if their apartment weren't full of people to help toss her in the shower under cold water and force her to drink a pot of coffee. She'd still passed out, but everyone had stayed awake with all the lights on, checking on her every few minutes, returning again and again to the subject that Diane wasn't there, and wasn't that strange. "And you should have been," she said. "I mean, what's going on?"

Even then, even with a perfect opportunity, she had still resisted. "I'm just busy," she said. "I've got this once-in-a-lifetime thing with Valerie Szeslak, really the only opportunity I've had in my life."

"Oh, let's not get maudlin —"

"Don't you understand that literally everything is on the line here?" Diane said, feeling again that she was losing control. "I can't just drop by to watch Reggie puke her guts out in a bathtub."

"Well!" Annie said, breathless as an offended Southern belle, and soon after, they were off the phone.

The next day, her father and Cindy would be in town to "act like a family" or whatever he'd said, and now, having pissed off one of her closest friends, she had no excuse but to focus on her work, on figuring out what to take to the Sex Guide Gallery in just a few days. That could keep her mind off Antonia, off blaming herself for whatever was going on.

She would take the old painting of Percy in the car and the painting of a shirtless Phil smoking a jay at the window from last winter and the one of Annie posed in her bra and underwear, her hair in curlers, a copy of *Ladies' Home Journal* open in her lap. She'd based that one off a Polaroid from two summers ago, staged of course, but meant to look like a snapshot. *Modern Woman*, she'd initially called it, but lately she'd been calling it, simply, *America*. After a minute she added to those three a single painting without a human subject, the one of the rain-glimmered alleyway near Times Square, a sign reading GIRLS AND MOR GIRLS the only sign of civilization. As cornball as it sounded, she wanted to call it *Making It in NYC.*

She lined these up and knew, positively, that she wasn't ready to show with Valerie Szeslak. She'd have to back out. Something had come up. And really, yes, something had come up. But when she went to the phone to call Lily, she couldn't bring herself to make the call. And back in her room she couldn't fathom picking up a brush.

PERCY CALLED THAT morning from the road to let her know they would be staying at the Windmark Hotel, a tony little place—from what Diane had seen—facing a not-so-tony Bryant Park, where she had nearly stepped on a discarded needle when she crossed through to meet them. Diane hadn't met Cindy in person before. She wasn't Candy, whom her father had taken with him to Olympia when he'd first left Diane behind with Mrs. Harlan, but the two women were joined in her imagination anyway. This newly minted wife, Cindy, was an accountant, but she wanted to be a poet. Percy had explained over the phone a few months back that Cindy had even sent some poems to *The New Yorker.* "Rejected," he'd said, "but the man there said they 'really try to say something,' which I guess means he liked them."

Percy always knew there would be some source of cash in all the women he supposedly fell in love with, and Cindy was no different. It was his nature to behave like a Getty or Rockefeller heir, sitting on his hands as if it were a form of employment when he wasn't forced, against every cell in his body, to take some dead-end job he'd either be fired or walk away from. Now he had plans for a business he thought would one day make him millions, selling personal computers by mail. It didn't matter that he knew even less about computers than Diane did, that his entire knowledge of the business came from a single newspaper story he'd clipped from the *Los Angeles Times.* "They'll be all the rage in the '80s," he said to Diane. "Every suburban household will have one. Think of all the novels regular people will be able to write. Think of how easy it will be to do your taxes if you've got a big, powerful calculator right there at your desk. Think of what it will be like for a regular Joe to start a business when he's got a whole corporation's worth of knowledge at his fingertips." Did they have a computer? Not yet. But that didn't matter.

Diane knew that Percy had come into a little money by selling back Grandpa's half of the real estate company to Track and his father for some unnamed but cut-rate amount. She'd heard all about it from Mrs. Harlan, who'd called to check on her a few weeks earlier and gushed about what a big success Track was going to be "in the land development game."

In truth, Diane didn't want to see either of them. Not now. Not while she was worried about Antonia and barely hanging on money-wise and getting nowhere career-as-an-artist-wise. Besides all that, she feared a repeat of last year, when Track imploded on contact with the city. If things went that way again she'd have no choice but to walk into the sea. What did her father think they were going to accomplish "as a family" anyway? Her mother was somewhere west of here, for sure. He'd have gotten more done driving around Ohio calling Antonia's name out the window.

She arrived at the hotel at the time Percy had told her to—4:30 in the afternoon—and the desk clerk informed her that "Mr. Stiegl hasn't yet checked in." So she went outside, bummed a cigarette from a bellboy, and leaned against the front window, one tennis shoe against the glass, flipping through the pages of a wrinkled *East Village Eye* she'd had rolled in her back pocket. Half an hour trickled by. In that time she walked around the park, finished the cigarette, and asked the same bellboy for another. He thought she was hitting on him, gave her a coy little smile, and introduced himself.

The introduction was cut short by the arrival of a green El Camino blasting an oldies station, Roy Orbison's "In Dreams," with Cindy's tan arm waving naked out the passenger window. The woman's hair was big and curled and bleached like it had been taken right off Dolly

Parton's head. Her sunglasses were octagonal mirrors. She shouted Diane's name as Percy bleated the horn. "Jesus," Diane said, and the bellboy laughed, shook his head, and set to work grabbing luggage from the shallow bed of the El Camino.

Percy stepped out shouting about traffic and claiming they'd seen "a living and breathing prostitute" just two blocks from the hotel, whatever that was supposed to mean. When he threw an arm around Diane's shoulders he smelled of sweat and French fries, and as they passed into the lobby Cindy appeared on Diane's other side, grasping her by the elbow with one hand and with the other adjusting an impossible feather boa.

In the hotel room, Percy asked Diane if she had been flirting with—as he called him—the Colored help before producing from one of their bags a roll of paper gathered by rubber bands. "Your granddad's," he said, slipping off the rubber bands with a snap. The roll turned out to be a few sheets of thick drawing paper watercolored with sunburned seascapes featuring tiny sailboats tailed by long shadows, vague images of Venice or something like Venice, a couple versions of a woman swimming at a beach under haunted moonlight. They were the pictures her grandfather had painted, Diane realized, the ones he'd kept on the walls of that extra bedroom where she'd stayed when she was twelve years old. They weren't great. The line work struck her as that of a beginner who had never bothered to develop any sense of clarity or perspective; the blotches of color remained elementary and not complementary. But she felt a melancholy connection to them.

Three sheets slipped loose, fluttered, and slid on the floor. She stretched down to grab them: a few of her old sketches on plain white paper. Two showed the Beatles in their Yellow Submarine outfits, drawn in colored pencil, with that blocky, cartoonish style she favored at twelve. The third she couldn't recall drawing, thought it was unmistakably hers: a boy and girl holding hands, a fire off in the background, an out-of-scale forest and bungalow caught in the flames. In black pencil; no color. The first two had spent time on her grandfather's refrigerator. But this third one, clearly inspired by the fire at the studio and her friendship with Track, confounded her. How could it have found its way into her grandfather's things? And when had she even drawn it? The picture filled her with longing and embarrassment. She had been a child. Just look at that flimsy shading.

Percy was still yammering on about the piles of his father's junk still in their garage. "I left a lot out in that studio, actually. But the next time you're down," he said, "whenever that is, you should pick through it. He's got all these journals. Something he was trying to write about art and film. Old letters too. Your sort of thing, I think."

"It's all very interesting," Cindy said. "One day somebody ought to tell that crazy old man's story."

"Mom would want to see these," Diane said, feeling out of step. "She always liked my Beatles pictures."

The pair went quiet. Cindy fidgeted. "I'm real sorry about your mother. I mean we're both—"

"There's nothing to be sorry about," said Diane. "You don't even know her."

"Deedee," her father said.

"It's Diane. Some people call me Di."

In the elevator back downstairs, Cindy said, without context, "I like that. 'Di.' Can I call you that?"

———

DIANE DIDN'T WANT to have to return to the hotel later, so she kept the watercolors and drawings with her at dinner, first in her hands and then at her feet, occasionally glancing under the table to be sure they hadn't rolled away. Her father and Cindy had insisted on going to either Tavern on the Green—something they'd seen in a movie and didn't know was a sort of local joke—or Mikkelsen's, on Fifth Avenue, where Percy had wasted money back in the 1950s when it had been a classy spot, regulared by well-to-do types and minor celebrities. Diane pressed successfully for the latter.

When the meal was finished and they'd all successfully avoided the topic of Antonia's disappearance, Percy made an uncomfortable moment of asking to be alone with Diane, to talk to her about something, a father-daughter thing Cindy wouldn't understand. When Cindy excused herself to the bathroom, nodding like they had practiced this bit, Diane said, "Weird."

"What?" Percy said. "I just wanted to talk to about your mother. She's sick, you know. This manic-depression thing. We can't blame her."

She found it hard to look at him. Tension had smushed his face down into a mean, nervous expression she didn't like. The tea-light candle on their table flickered against its gold-flake walls. "I know that."

"Well, it's easy to get angry about it. God knows I've been angry about it. The fights we used to have. I wasn't always understanding. I wasn't always the good guy, you know?"

She huffed something like a laugh.

"What you said on the phone—"

"I didn't mean all that," she said. "I was emotional."

"There was so much going on back then, Dee"—he paused, then corrected himself—"Diane. So much to deal with? I was a wreck. And you know, your mom and I had just split. I didn't really want to leave you—"

"But you did leave me," she said. And then, knowing she didn't want to get into it, she added, "Forget it."

He hesitated, looked around the room. "Your grandfather really liked you," he said. "Took a shine to you. You know I really think you're like him?"

"You've already said that."

"Have I?"

She imagined being back at the apartment, all the lamps going, one of Phil's records playing. She'd be working the canvas, blending orange into green, capturing this schizoid little flame before her. "Dad, what's up? I don't know why you're here."

He smiled at her, looked for a second like he might cry. "I'm just sorry is all. I never should have left you. I thought we should be together in this. I love you. You know that, right?"

"I love you too, Dad."

Then Cindy came back and the two of them exchanged looks she couldn't read and there was talk of dessert but Diane pretended that it was late and then plans were made for the morning and by the end of it all, bunching up her grandfather's watercolors in both hands in the back of a cab, with Percy and Cindy still rambling, she realized her father was right: she had nothing in common with either of her parents. Grandpa, that old man she mostly remembered in a supine position, groaning and holding his belly, was far closer to her in temperament and purpose. He, too, had been an artist, maybe not with these flimsy paintings of his, but in film. For the first time she wanted to see one of his movies. But how?

———————

IT HAD ACTUALLY been Nero who knew the answer to this short-lived mystery. "I didn't know you were really related to him," he said upstairs at the Mudd Club that night. Said, but really shouted, because David Azarch was spinning records with the amplifier all the way up, a small crowd gyrating to Devo and Bowie and Tom Petty. "I thought Lily was joking about that."

"No, he's really my grandpa," she yelled. "But I've never seen his films."

Nero was a dropout just like her, a film student until last fall, when he just started walking around downtown with a 35mm camera his parents had bought him with their millions in mall-arcade money. In this he may have been influenced by Diane, though Nero would never admit to having gotten an idea from a girl, especially one he used to date. "I know a guy who can get us into the screening room and pull the reels—at least for *The Bachelor's Wife*. I don't know if they have any of the others."

"Tonight?" she said.

He gazed around the club a minute, grimacing. "Yeah, let's go tonight."

She stood next to him downstairs at the payphone as he made the arrangements, cupping his hand over the receiver to soften the noise, stuffing a finger in his ear. Then they were off on foot up Broadway a dozen or so blocks, Nero in his tight jeans and leather jacket, his head awkwardly big for his tall, narrow frame. He walked with a kind of bluster, even out on the street at night, like he belonged to some old motorcycle gang. She'd fallen for that side of him before she knew it was all an act, a game of easy masculinity meant to disguise his fears.

They got to campus after midnight. Diane had grown tired, the slight uplift of a few drinks now crashing into the hours she'd spent entertaining her father and Cindy. They waited next to a nondescript back door in the shadow of a potted tree for a man named Harry, the "mechanical custodian." Finally the door they'd been occasionally glancing toward squeaked open, and a short, plump man with a brown mustache poked his head out of the darkness within. As if they both weren't looking at him, he put a hand to his mouth and whispered, "Psssst. Andy!"

Diane had never heard anyone call Nero by his real name to his face. It was one of those things people said when they mentioned him if he wasn't around: "You know Nero Divisible? Really Andy-something, from Ohio?"

Harry let them in and thumbed on his flashlight, pointing its beam down a hallway toward a set of stairs. Eventually they got to a low-ceilinged room full of what appeared at first to be bookcases, but which on closer view held round, gray cans displayed on their sides. Nero flicked the beam here and there, mumbling as he went, and when he found what he was looking for had her hold the light. "Yep," he said, pulling down one can and then another. "*Bachelor's Wife* right here. Five reels."

She had expected the canisters to be dusty. Maybe she'd seen something like that in a movie. Instead they were shiny and pea-green, clearly labeled with clean tape VON STIEGL: BACHELOR'S WIFE FP/LASKY, and followed, in smaller print, with the reel number. Diane studied them in the screening room, where the heist silliness of Harry's flashlight was set aside for regular overhead bulbs as Nero reeled film into the projector. Then a screen was pulled down, the lights were shut off, and a new beam flickered across the room.

"The film was controversial as fuck when it came out," Nero said in the tentative light. He sat down next to her. "This gay guy is into this newlywed dude and they fall in love, leaving the girl behind. Pretty wild stuff for back then. But that's your grandpa's thing. He was always making controversy, you know? Stirring up trouble."

"Huh," she managed.

"I mean, that's what art is, right? Making trouble. Fucking shit up. Oh wait—"

In typescript between the elaborate playfulness of a children's fairy-tale book and the throat-clearing conservative serif of a newspaper, her grandfather's name had suddenly appeared above the film's title, the words surrounded on all sides by a thick laurel wreath. The image jumped to a low-angle shot of a long, narrow hallway half in shadow, a man in a white suit walking briskly forward and then past the camera, his face out of focus the whole time. Then came a woman in a sequin gown stretched across a round bed that turned a slow circle, clearly shot from the ceiling. Her eyes sparkled in the overbright light. And then they were back to the man walking in a dark hallway.

The movie was a vivid dream, a poem she couldn't understand. "Is this what it's like?" Diane said.

Even in the near-dark, she could see Nero shrug. "Sort of. I mean, it's silent film. Just pictures."

"Not even any music?"

"They added music later." Onscreen, the man from the hallway entered the room where the beautiful woman lay on the revolving bed. Suddenly the camera focused on the man's eyes—violent with rage, but then, after lingering a little longer than Diane could stand, they softened to something like love. Just as this change registered, the shot went to a hazy field of flowers, the beautiful woman prancing like a child in a simple white dress. The corners of the frame were rounded. It was a corny scene, really, expressing a little more than it needed to, yet it was still beautiful: a shining image of innocent longing. When the film cut back to the man's eyes, now sultry, his dark eyeliner and sharp features shading the border between man and woman, Nero said, "No dialogue cards either. That's what he's known for. Cinema as strictly pictorial. A language of images."

She knew he relished these phrases, these words he'd learned in some textbook or other. "Who's the chick?" she said.

"That's Kay Stone."

The couple were together now onscreen, his hands gripping her shoulders, her neck exposed to the blinding light as if to a vampire's teeth. "Damn," she said. "Kiss her already."

"She's a tragic figure," said Nero. "Never made it in sound films. Ended up jumping off the Hollywood sign, if you can believe that."

Diane watched the woman's eyes grow smoky and then lock on her man. Her chin tucked back into a natural position. Her lips puckered only slightly. She was striking, otherworldly. Then, contrary to Diane's expectations, the woman forced the man off her, sending him reeling back on his heels, his hands held out in supplication.

Just then, Harry opened the screening-room door and cleared his throat. "Somebody's inside," he said. "You gotta go."

There wasn't time to put away the reels or even remove the one in the projector. Nero shut it off and swept Diane out of the room, holding her awkwardly by the forearm, as if they were escaping fascists in a night raid. But not before she'd done something even she hadn't expected—she grabbed the second reel of her grandfather's film and stuffed it inside her army jacket. Nero flashed her a glance and looked as if he might say something, but before this could happen Harry was directing them with his beam to the back stairwell they'd come up only half an hour before. They rushed down, in silence but for their clanging feet, Nero looking surprisingly terrified.

"Let's get two different cabs," he said. "I can't afford to be picked up as a thief, man."

"Don't be chicken," she said, though her heart raced and her eyes jumped from shadow to shadow. "Hey, it's not like they need it."

"Whatever," said Nero, and skulked away into the city night.

———

THE FOLLOWING MORNING Diane was up early to continue the so-called "family visit," and this time it would be bagels in sunglasses in Central Park, Diane half-asleep searching the rocks above Wollman Rink for these two people she'd already grown tired of seeing. When she found them, they had already finished eating, were lazed in the sun sipping coffee, their shoes off, socks off, looking like a pair of hippies who had only recently been introduced to the concept of a shower. "Ah, there's my girl," Percy said as she approached.

"I'm not late," Diane said, defensively.

Cindy did her little laugh. "We were early. It's so nice here. Do you often come?"

Diane squatted next to them. Her stomach was churning. In fact, she felt like shit. When she'd woken up, the sight of the metal can of film next to her in bed had sent the memory of the night rushing through her, filling her with that shame she associated with hangovers. Now, blinking in the overbright light, really in need of a Tylenol, she dug to the bottom of the paper bag and pulled out the bagel and cream cheese she'd asked Percy to get her. "The park? Not really. It's uh—" She was going to say dangerous, but that wasn't exactly true, especially on a Saturday morning. But it was filthy. An actual condom, still glistening, lay in the grass only a few yards away. She hoped it wasn't theirs. "It's kind of far from the East Village."

It struck her that she was talking like someone in a bad movie. The snob. But really she didn't know what to say to them. They were a different generation, from a different world. As if on cue, Cindy said, "The city seems so dangerous. We were watching the evening news last night and—"

"It's a complete shitshow," Percy said, flicking his cigarette butt off into the grass. "It's a wonder you haven't been raped and murdered right on Park Avenue."

Cindy gasped. "God forbid."

"It's not like that," Diane began, though only a month before, she and Phil had been held up at gunpoint in broad daylight for all the cash they had on hand. They'd been walking not far from here, on their way up to the Guggenheim on a bright Sunday afternoon. The man hadn't even bothered to mask his face: just a nondescript white dude with a few days' beard. "Anyway, I'm careful. And most of the time I'm downtown. With friends."

Percy laughed at this. He stood up shaking his head. "Your friends," he said, and then, starting down the side of a short hill in the direction of the closed skating rink, muttered a string of curses and epithets.

"Don't listen to him," said Cindy. "I like your friends."

"You don't even know my friends." But that wasn't what she'd wanted to say or how she'd wanted to say anything. She'd wanted a truce. "Look, it doesn't matter. I live here and it's safe enough."

Percy wandered farther away. Something, apparently, was bugging him.

Cindy pushed the grass around with her bare toes. "You've got to understand," she said. "He always thought he would get more of his father's estate, not just that failing business with Harlan." She looked over at him nervously, as if he would hear what she had to say. "I just think it would be nice if you could do something to help when you can. To even it out. To be fair."

Diane's mouth was full of bagel and cream cheese. She had no idea what Cindy was talking about. "You think I've got some kind of money?"

Percy may have been some distance away, but he had the hearing of a bat when the word "money" was involved. His head jerked toward them. "We haven't talked about that yet," he shouted at Cindy. "Why are you talking about it?"

"I thought you—"

"I didn't get to it," he said, stomping back up the rock.

"But you said last night—"

"I didn't get to it." And then, to Diane, "Forget it. Cindy's lost her head. Just a miscommunication, you know? What are we doing today?"

Cindy pursed her lips, breathed hard out her nose. "My word, Percy. Why are you like this?"

"What are we talking about?" Diane nearly shouted. "You guys sound insane."

There was a pause, a series of faces pulled, an aversion of eyes. Diane began wrapping her bagel back in the paper. At last Cindy touched her on the arm and said, "Deedee you ought to know. You're supposed to know. Your grandpa gave away most of his money—really your grandmother's money, Western P&E money. Half of it went into Reagan's reelection campaign for governor. A bunch more toward some woman back in California, a mystery woman. Then there were investments in his cousin George, money for that nurse who took care of him, some other things. But all the rest he put in a trust for you at the age of twenty-two. Usually it's twenty-one, but he said something about when he made it in Hollywood. It was in the will."

Diane glanced at her father. He glared off at the buildings with his fists on his hips like some great man of action, surveying a place to dynamite. "You said he didn't have anything left," Diane said, standing. "You said you had to sell his house to pay off bills."

"That's all true, Deedee. Listen, I—"

"Grandpa died ten years ago. You've known about this for ten years and didn't tell me? You thought you had a way to get it, didn't you? To take it away." She felt something like terror, something like not being able to breathe. He'd known about this money when he left her behind with Mrs. Harlan. "I wouldn't have kept it all," she said. "I would have shared it. Why would you lie to me?"

"Deedee," he said, and by the way he held his forehead with

his fingertips, there was no doubt she'd cut almost instantly to the truth. "You don't know what it was like with him. Doing nothing to help us. Always on my back about your mother. And at the end he was so hateful, digging up things from the past he didn't know anything about. Deedee you've got to—"

She turned away. There was some shouting of her name. Cindy tried following her a little way, apologizing. But all the noise turned to a sharp buzz in Diane's mind, and soon she was on Fifth Avenue with the hansom cabs, a homeless man stretched on the sidewalk pulling his beard and gazing up at the blue morning sky. She couldn't look back, couldn't allow herself to be pulled back into the orbit of her family's immense wreckage.

———

WHEN SHE CAME out of the room with her canvases the following morning, Phil was in his robe spooning Suisse Mocha into cups of hot water, the radio softly playing an old Stevie Wonder song. "You're up," he said. "I thought I heard you shuffling around."

"I haven't slept."

"It's a big day," he said, handing her a cup. "Hey, remember my friend Eric?"

"Thanks," she said. "Sort of?"

"He's in the hospital, dropping weight, something really serious. They're not allowing visitors, even. All very scary. Only his sister had been to see him. I was just on the phone with her."

"Jesus."

"Likely some kind of infection they're saying. I mean, a month ago he was playing tennis and now from what they tell me he's on death's door. But something's going around."

With the word "tennis" she could see Eric vividly: a tanned, curly-haired man with a dimpled chin, pretty enough to be in the movies. He'd spent a lot of time over here last fall, always in tennis gear, sweaty, occasionally changing his shirt out in the open, revealing the dark, curled hair of his chest. The ape-man, she'd called him when he wasn't around, and Phil would shake his head, laughing, saying he really is a man Diane what do you want me to do? He and Phil had drifted apart and then at some point they'd become actual friends, meeting for tennis and occasionally lunch. "God, I'm sorry," she said. "I hope he's okay."

"Well, that's what I'm saying," he said, setting down his cup. "It's like he's got some kind of cancer but it's not cancer. Something about pneumonia now? Even the doctors are confused. All I know is that it's bad."

She wasn't sure how to respond, and though she was trying, she had a hard time making any of this matter. Her mother, her father, the gallery today: her mind had been running on overdrive all night. The fact that Phil's ex was in the hospital seemed like distant news, like someone on television talking about a bank robbery in Santiago. "I'm sorry," she said again. "But I better get going. We'll talk tonight, okay?"

Tonight they'd planned to go out, to celebrate if things went well, to forget if they didn't. "Okay," he said. "Good luck." And then: "Wait. I'm going with."

———

"I'M NOT REALLY moved by any of them," Valerie Szeslak said. Then, pointing at GIRLS AND MOR GIRLS, said, "This one has some edge to it. I like the tone."

Diane stood with Lily and Phil, feeling hollowed-out and also unbearably heavy, as if she were no longer flesh and bones but a diving bell, sinking into the blue carpet of the Sex Guide Gallery. She had worn the army jacket Phil had bought her, on the back of which she had stenciled, mysteriously even to her, the name EE CUMMINGS. Her plan had been to look tough and unintimidated, but now she felt like a child in grown-up clothing, posing before a mirror, a comical fake.

"The technicals are amazing. I mean, you're a very good painter, Di. But the subjects are a little done. And all this mastery business, it's so, well, male. You know? The photorealism thing. We're look-ing for cutting-edge work that really says something about now."

Diane wanted to mount some kind of defense, but what use would that be? "Yeah," she said. "I understand."

The Sex Guide Gallery was in the basement of a church on Fourth Street. They were still installing the lights; a man in jeans and a Blue Öyster Cult T-shirt was up on a ladder screwing in bulbs as they talked. The place smelled like mildew, like the old carpeted rec room of a church no one had attended in three decades. It had been the brainchild of Valerie, formerly a Mudd Club regular, and its focus was irony, consumerism, and women artists.

"But you want the Girls one," Lily said, Lily who at that very mo-ment was holding Diane by the arm, maybe holding her up, "right?"

Valerie Szeslak looked again. "Yes, the Girls and I guess that one over there," she said, pointing at the one of Percy shocked by the Polaroid flash way back in Palm Springs. Then she looked Diane in the eye. "You've really got something. Don't think I'm saying you don't. But you need vision. Purpose." She looked again at the paint-ings, back and forth. "You'll need to find yourself. But you've got something. That's why I want you in the show."

Out on the sidewalk, they were all jubilation. Diane tried to ig-nore the fact that Valerie Szeslak had called Lily's sculptures and poster "shattering, essential material."

"Our first real show," Lily said, grabbing her hand. "They'll have to write about this in the history books. 'Wong and Stiegl debuted together in 1981 . . .' Like Johns and Rauschenberg but for the Rea-gan years."

Phil grimaced and shook his head like he'd just tasted something bitter. "Reagan years," he said. "Oh God."

Diane couldn't bring herself to talk. She had her first show and her mother was gone and her father had turned out to be his own brand of creep.

She went out. She danced. She whiffed amyl nitrate on the floor and took a hit of acid that a shaggy-faced hippie set in her palm without introducing himself and then lost Phil somewhere upstairs and danced and laughed a while with Lily and then left the Mudd Club with a tall broad-shouldered woman who in a strange apartment made her smoke weed from a blue water-pipe as they listened to Christopher Cross and then Led Zeppelin and then the woman began taking off her clothes and telling Diane to do the same but then Diane left, wandered farther downtown, and then a little farther, and finally to the Battery, where dawn came at her like the screech of a million blackboards, its light the most blinding shit she had ever seen. She couldn't move, couldn't get up from the bench where she'd planted herself, and a cold terror ran through and stuck with her, and then, after closing her eyes hard and taking a deep breath, she wandered back up into the daylight city, lost but heading north, knowing she would find some familiar street, that the city would absorb her all over again, and that then she would paint.

ART THEATRE ON THE HIGHWAY
Just What Does Di Stiegl's Latest Stunt Mean?
Wednesday, 28 June 2023
Harriet Bassani

Drivers on the eastbound 401 coming into Toronto Tuesday afternoon may have had trouble keeping their eyes on the road. If you passed the Hornby exit near the outlets around three o'clock, you likely saw something that looked like a ritual taking place in the open field next to the southbound off-ramp: about a dozen men and women wearing white lab coats and gas masks, handing a swaddled doll back and forth. Above them: an array of cheap box fans going full-blast at the type of air filters one replaces in a home air conditioner.

The message seemed clear, or at least partially so. For the last several weeks, wildfires have raged in every province, billowing smoke that has spread southeast into the major cities of our neighbours to the south. Apparently, the people in lab coats wanted to draw our attention to the unhealthy particulates in the air. "But who wasn't already paying attention to that?" said Mark Dickey, curator at the edgy Coronto Tontemporary gallery. "There's no missing the smoke."

U.S. appeals court says Trump's NY trial should proceed
Ford to lay off 1,000 employees

What this outdoor theatre by the highway meant—and whether it was saying anything new—instantly became of importance when the news got out that the celebrated eco-artist Di Stiegl was behind one of those gas masks and lab coats. What drivers had witnessed, in fact, was her latest work, 'Nearby Laboratory 12: Infant.' The title was announced on the artist's website, along with several black-and-white photographs of the event, staged to appear like newspaper images from the previous century.

Guests at the Museum of Contemporary Art, Toronto, were shown some of the images on the website to get their take. Tabitha from Brampton said, "I've never been one for the conceptual art. It all looks like some high school play to me." A retired couple from Hamilton echoed the opinion of Dickey. "There's nothing to see there," said the husband, a retired schoolteacher. His wife, herself a painter in her spare time, said, "Gosh, the smoke is everywhere. We don't need rich intellectuals telling us so. I'd say do something good for the environment instead of making a mess by the side of the highway." "Or do something for the firefighters," said the husband.

"So the baby is, like, our future?" said Harold, a tax analyst visiting from Saratoga Springs, New York. "That's sort of hitting us over the head with a hammer, no?" But his teenage daughter found the drama more compelling. "It's like a dystopia thing. She's the last baby on earth and all these scientists are trying to save her by filtering the air. I like it." Di Stiegl did not respond to a request for more information about the event's meaning.

The 64-year-old Stiegl has led a charmed career as one of the most successful visual artists of her generation. In recent decades, her work has gravitated away from the paintings that made her name in the 1980s and '90s, and toward conceptual and team-built happenings that the critic Bill Delozier has complained to be "warmed-over sixties idealism wrapped in climate apocalypse." Still, her recent work has remained significant. "There was always something new and something brave about Stiegl, even with these forays into her 'New Earth Art,'" says Mark Dickey. "But this one is hackneyed. Forgettable. I hope she takes a hard look in the mirror and gets back on track."

Fitness expert claims this trick is best for a flat tummy
Aykroyd says blackface in 'Trading Places' a mistake

Prime Minister Trudeau was less concerned with aesthetics. "Di Stiegl is a national treasure and an important voice in the environmental movement," read a statement from his office. "But with visibility low on our highways at this time, I urge all citizens to avoid acts that could disrupt drivers' concentration."

KLAUS

1933

H^{E WAS DRUNK.} That satisfying feeling of numbness and power and being above it all, like he'd cheated some unfair game, like he had an answer for someone who'd thought they were more intelligent than him. Drunk and pacing from room to room alone while Olive and Percy were out of the house, yet again.

Today the reason for their absence hadn't even been discussed. An outing somewhere. They would be home in the afternoon. Over toast and coffee in the morning, Olive had only made vague reference to the fact that they'd be going, and Klaus, hungover, his stomach a fiery knot, had nodded along as if he knew what she was talking about. Now with his head on straight, with that light and confident feeling he'd been waiting to overtake him—first with the martini when they had left, then with the two others after he'd been out to water the plants—he wanted to know where they'd got off to.

He opened the kitchen drawer beneath the phone, took out the spiral notebook where Olive kept their numbers. Then he began dialing: Ellen, Penelope, Nancy, Alice, Elizabeth. Most of them didn't answer. Those who did seemed honestly to know nothing. "Okay," he responded in a jovial tone. "I'm sure she just forgot to leave a note."

He stirred a fourth martini and put Verdi on the gramophone.

"Moping again," Olive would say if she were here. She'd taken to saying something to that effect nearly every day, even when he'd tried to keep up appearances, tried to put a good face on it all. Hollywood had shown him the door. MGM had been punishing him with lousy scripts and third-tier stars since that business with *Hans & Greta*. The studio had sent Eddie Mannix out to confiscate the unedited reels from him as MGM property, being the product of a director under contract to them, and had reportedly tossed the canisters in a furnace. But their vengeance didn't stop there. Mayer and Thalberg had ever since been loaning him out to Poverty Row studios in trade for one of their actors or actresses. In the past year, the only work he'd gotten was two six-reel westerns with Republic and a shoddy crime picture at Columbia. They were trying to shame him out of the industry.

Sipping his current drink, he thought maybe he should call George. His cousin spent his days claiming that one day when Walter's finances finally bounced back from the Great Crash, he'd open his own home decorating company. George and Olive had remained close, though George hardly had a word for Klaus these days. No, no. He couldn't call George. It would mean dredging up whatever had calcified between them. Besides, his cousin would tell him directly that he'd been too drunk to remember where his wife had gone. That wasn't a position Klaus wanted to find himself in.

He rinsed out the martini glass, dried it, placed it back on the shelf as if it had never been touched. Then he made coffee. He would sober up. He would take the car out and see if Olive was shopping somewhere on Palm Canyon Drive. Run into her as if by accident. Lift Percy in his arms. Play at being a husband and father.

When Olive's car pulled up, he was in the shower, trying to regain some balance of sobriety. He slid open the high window, steam flowing out into the dry desert air, his head still foamed with shampoo. Olive was rounding the car with shopping bags, dressed in a long blue skirt and a sleeveless beige sweater. She had on her white driving gloves. Percy hopped out in shorts and striped shirt, one of his socks fallen down to a ball at his ankle. Klaus's heart felt so big it could choke him, and when he called to them Olive looked around for a moment, trying to place the voice, but she didn't see him there, nearly right before her eyes.

When he came out in his robe, she was hanging her purse on the hook next to the kitchen door. Her eyes fell on the gin and vermouth bottles he had stupidly left on the counter. Percy ran past Klaus with a new red toy fire engine held aloft in both of his small hands. "Sweetheart," Klaus said. "I thought we could go to the club this evening for cocktails."

But Olive was distracted by something out the window. "There's a woman in the lawn," she said. "Look."

Klaus crossed the living room, smelling Olive's perfume as he approached her. The presence of this bright and uncannily beautiful wife of his sometimes crushed him; he felt the familiar shame for his unworthy behavior, his inebriate failures. But this passed in an instant. There really was a woman in the lawn, staggering, wild-eyed, and she was Kay Stone. "Mein Gott. It is her."

As if she had heard his voice, Kay turned her head to the kitchen window and marked their presence. Then, suddenly upright and stiff-legged, she started to the left, toward the front door. "What is she doing here?" Olive said.

A knock at the door. "Ignore her," Klaus said.

"Why?" Olive screwed up her eyes. "She looks like she's in trouble."

"Go down the hall," Klaus said. "Close the door."

"Klaus, what are you talking about?"

The knocking turned into pounding. "Klaus!" Kay yelled. "Open up already."

Percy had returned from his room, the fire engine still in his hands. He was already crying. "Take the boy to his room and close the door," Klaus said. "It will only be a minute. She looks drunk. I'll take care of it."

Olive gave him a doubtful and somewhat hurt look. But their son's needs superseded Klaus's uncharacteristic attitude, his sudden pose as master of the house. "Come here, Percy," she said, holding out her hands. "Let's go and play."

Kay banged her fist on the door again. "I can hear you in there," she shouted, her voice horse, rising to high notes that crumpled into breathy silence. That Brooklyn accent the sound engineers had said sounded like an illiterate dockworker's. "Klaus, we gotta talk."

When he opened the door he found a thin woman in a tattered and stained dress, white shoes so scuffed they might as well be brown. Her hair and face were clean, though. Red lipstick. Eyes of a night animal. "Kay, what's all this about?"

She was in trouble, in bad health, at the end of her rope. But what she said to him first was, "You're looking good, Klaus. Just come from the pool?"

He glanced down at his pinstriped robe. "The shower."

"Listen, I need your help," she said in a rush. "You got a part for me in something, right? You can smooth it with Thalberg and those other thugs, can't you?"

"I'm not exactly popular over there," he said, though really, he doubted he would help anyone in her condition, not if it meant a role in a picture. Her ragged New York accent didn't fit her genteel good looks, at least not in the age of the microphone. *No more than a sight gag*, is how Artie had so callously described her prospects. "I don't have any say at all, actually. Last picture I made was on loan to Columbia and—"

"Klaus you've got to put in a word."

They were standing in the doorway, or at least Klaus was. She was on the porch, half in sunlight and half in shade, looking like she would any second dash past him into the house. "I'm telling you my word doesn't go for much around there anymore."

"I need work. Can't you see? After all we've been through and you won't lift a finger?"

"I did lift a finger, Kay. Remember the whole fiasco? Trying to save silent pictures so you'd all have work, so everything didn't turn out like this?"

She took a step back into the sunlight and looked around, accusatively. "Like this? Klaus, you're living like the Sheik of Araby over here. I guess that woman bought the house, eh? Our place? The Barthelmess house?"

"I mean, I tried to help," he said. And maybe too defensively, "We've been through all this already."

"When, Klaus? When? You never speak to me."

It was true. He'd meant that he'd been through it with the press. "I can't be responsible for everyone's career," he managed. "I'm only one man."

Kay laughed a mad, wild laugh, and for a moment Klaus was afraid of her, imagined her attacking him, some weapon waiting for her in the black Buick parked at the curb. "You put a mark on our backs," she said. "Me and twenty or so others. Remember? You made it easy for the bosses to clean house. 'Dutch' Norgstrom? Patty Brunofsky? Salvatore Creccio hung himself a week after they fired him. He had a wife and kids. And what about George?"

Even if George had been able to walk after his accident, the sound experts hired by MGM had already labeled his charming voice "too cute," a label the trades had viciously turned into "a little girlish." But not one of the actors Kay was referring to would ever work in Hollywood again. He'd done that. Had Klaus made that happen? "Listen," he said, "I can try to —"

"I can't even get a meeting," Kay shouted suddenly. She was, he realized then, in tears. "I took elocution lessons and everything. I got nothing to show for it." She leaned into him, sobbing. "Don't you remember?" she said. "Coming out here? New York? Let's go back to New York and start all over, huh?"

He held her out from him by the shoulders, desperate to be away from her quaking body, the feel of her bones through her clothes. "Kay, we can't go back. You need to pull yourself together. It's a different time now and —"

"I'll burn down that damned studio of yours," she yelled, tearing herself away from him. "What do you think of that? Tell me what you think of that!"

Then he said the only thing he could think to say. "They don't want you in pictures anymore. It happens every day. Don't you see? This is nobody's fault. They don't want me either. You've got to look into something else," he said, feeling like he was finally in charge of this situation. "A new line of work. Secretarial school. Hairdressing. But you can't come around here shaking the tin cup and scaring my wife and child."

At this she seemed to shrink, stepping back from him as her eyes widened into an expression of profound recognition. "You," she said. "I can't believe you would—"

And then she turned, sobbing, and ran toward the Buick in a haphazard way, as if her limbs were made of cloth and stuffing, a child's doll scrambling away from a great terror. He closed the door.

Klaus watched from the kitchen window as she dragged her feet to a shabby-looking Ford parked at the curb. His heart thumped and seized. He looked again at the gin and vermouth, heard the door of his son's room open, the determined clack of his wife's heels on the floor. And he wanted to erase everything, to rub it out, to return to some other life he could no longer remember with any clarity at all.

MAYBE SHE HAD known then what she would do, understood the poetic nature of her fall from the sign that had come to stand for the movies themselves. Or maybe it had come to her as she neared the city, maybe it was the first tall thing that had caught her eye. Later, he would try to recall the weather that day, but it was immemorial. Nothing special. Not cold or rainy and not a swelter. A nice day with only a few white clouds and Kay's hair free in the wind.

THE PAPERS CALLED incessantly: reporters from L.A., San Francisco, Denver, Chicago, New York, London, Paris, even Memphis, Tennessee. All of them with the same questions. Did Ms. Stone seem ill? Did she tell him what she was about to do? Did he—and don't take this the wrong way, Mr. von Stiegl—but you didn't tell her to do what she did, did you? Of course, that's the story nearly all of them went with. That the reclusive Svengali had sent his old star up the back of the Hollywood sign to leap to her death, a scenario so far from the realm of possibility that Klaus laughed about it the first time one of his unwanted callers presented it to him. The lone LAPD detective who drove out to Palm Springs a few days after only broached the subject so that Klaus could point out the clear fantasy of its central proposition. Movie directors didn't drive actresses they haven't worked with in five years to suicide. Even so, the detective had asked if there was any reason Klaus would have wanted Ms. Stone to hurt herself. "None at all," Klaus said. "I want everyone to live a happy and productive life."

"Everyone?" the detective said, as if he'd caught Klaus out on a tall tale.

"Maybe not Louis B. Mayer."

The detective turned serious. "You've got a problem with this Mr. Mayer?"

The public took the vague claims about his involvement in Kay's death seriously, however. Hardly a day went by without a letter or postcard arriving, full of language neither he nor Olive would read aloud in the presence of little Percy, whom they kept away from this nonsense as best they could. Even when some angry man stood on the lawn throwing eggs at the front door, Olive had talked Klaus out of calling the police, worried about making any scene that would negatively affect their four-year-old son. And so Klaus had stared out the window at this man, who looked otherwise like a viable member of society, until his energy was spent and he drove away.

And within two weeks of Kay's leap off the Hollywood sign, a boy in a yellow cap appeared at the door to deliver a legal document signed by Louis B. Mayer himself which nulled his contract entirely. He was, for the first time since his childhood, unemployed.

OLIVE THOUGHT THIS shouldn't matter. Why would he want to work when he didn't need to? The Lazlo trust had them living like millionaires and—on paper, at least, when you counted up various properties deeded over to Olive by her father after the wedding— they actually were millionaires. And that was with both of the Lazlos very much alive. When the old man kicked the bucket, oh boy, Klaus would be a kid from the Lower East Side transformed into one of the wealthiest people on the West Coast.

"That doesn't matter," he'd told Olive. "I want to make films again."

"You're not under contract anymore," she'd said, pointing out the window at the old studio building. "Make films. Hire a crew. Daddy will help get them distributed."

"No one will touch me with a ten-foot pole. You don't understand how this industry works. I'm finished."

"Well," she said, "talk like that will make it so."

"It already is so. I'll never be behind the camera again. The only thing that matters to me and it's—"

He saw the arch of Olive's eyebrow and couldn't finish that thought. Instead he bit his tongue and mixed a martini. Drunk again. Getting through the days. Olive shook her head, looked disappointedly at the floor, and left him standing alone in the kitchen, night falling, his whole world smaller with each passing minute.

TOBEY

2024

AT THE START of Tobey's junior year, he moved from the apartment he'd shared with two white clichés who rapped to hip-hop as they downed beers and played Call of Duty every night back into a dormitory room Track had pulled strings to get him. Tobey was in there a week before a guy he met in macroeconomics offered him a tab of acid as they were walking across campus to get lunch. This guy—Tobey will never forget this—insisted everyone call him Fish, even though his real name was William Boughley. Fish was tall and clean-shaven, always in dark clothes, looking nothing like the hippie his chosen moniker would suggest. "It's just the way I move," he said as they walked that day, wiggling and twisting his long body as if he were swimming along with a school of his brethren. "It's the way I look at life."

"Okay," Tobey had said. "Cool?"

"You're going to want to take that tonight. Stay home. Put on some good music. I'd do Joy Division. But whatever."

Tobey put the tiny square of paper in the pocket of his jean shorts.

"Keep it dry, man," Fish warned him. "Like, put it between the pages of your book."

Tobey moved the paper to his macroeconomics textbook. "Do I chew it or what?"

Fish laughed. "Put it on your tongue and just let it soak in. No worries."

But Tobey was worried. He'd never put any thought to using drugs beyond the occasional pot and, well, that time he'd copped some of Judith's ADD meds to focus his way through SAT prep. This Fish character wasn't much more than an acquaintance. After class a week prior, they'd smoked a bowl on Fish's porch and listened to the whole first side of Van Halen's *1984*. The music was meant as irony, but Tobey found himself singing "Panama" for days after.

That evening around six, he'd opened his macro book and found the tiny square, put it on his tongue, and waited. The piece of paper eventually melted down and stuck to the crags of one of his molars. He scratched it out with his pinky fingernail in the bathroom he shared with a study-abroad student from Senegal. Then about forty-five minutes later the borders between objects—lamp, desk, wall, *Life Aquatic* poster—went hazy. His hands glowed and stretched. He rushed to his phone to turn on music. Yes, Joy Division. That sounded good.

Tobey was so taken by that trip (and the dozen that followed before midterms) that he became, like Fish, a proselytizer for the substance, and three or four days after that, a dealer. Fish's guy (a nervous middle-aged seeming dude who adjuncted in the computer science program) offered Tobey a whole sheet for a hundred and twenty-five dollars, which a quick run through the math showed would lead to a profit, at five bucks a hit, of three hundred and seventy-five. Plus, he'd be turning people on to this life-changing little square, bending and opening minds.

It worked pretty well for a time. In his deposition, he'd been coached to focus on this line of thinking. "He's a good kid from a good family," Track's lawyer had said in court. "But he fell under the sway of a powerful drug. And in that sickness he thought he was helping others. In a sense he was doing the right thing. At least, what he thought was the right thing."

During the many months Tobey spent in prison, he came back to those lines again and again. He really was doing the right thing. That's how it had felt. How it still felt. Everyone—even the profit-skimming CEOs and money-laundering accountants at the cushy prison Track's lawyer got Tobey into—knew that the whole war on drugs was a machine of white supremacy, purposefully built to snatch Black and brown men from their lives and paint a whole swath of the citizenry as dangerous and unforgivable criminals, making space for white people to build more wealth, more strip malls, more endowed chairs in classical studies.

And here Tobey was, skiing through life on a white, powdery layer of privilege, still ensnared. He hated that Track had helped him. At least, he hated it once he was convicted, once it dawned on him that his father hadn't spoken to him through the whole thing, didn't write even after he was behind bars, that in all honesty Track had likely put the money behind his defense just to defend himself. Harlan Homes. Harlan/Sunflower Property Development. Track Fucking Harlan, Incorporated. And once Tobey was out, after all that comeuppance, all that thinking alone, all that reading and gazing up through a narrow window with only a view of the sky and clouds, his father still evinced zero interest in him. "Your room is down the hall where it used to be," he'd said, and it was Judith who'd had to order a mattress and box spring, who on that first night had inflated the air mattress and pulled an old TV out of the garage for him. When Tobey said he planned to go back to school, Track had turned the volume up on the bigger set in the living room and said, "That's a good idea. Listen, I'm watching this okay?"

———————

BACK IN MERCADO'S daughter's place, things had grown tense. A drama was playing out between the old man and the teetotaling Jason, who spoke through the saddened, apologetic daughter, informing her elderly climate-refugee father that really, no kidding, there wasn't any room in their house for a guest unless he wanted to sleep on the floor, and even then—a little throat-clearing from Jason—it would be extremely out of the ordinary, because the children slept on the sofa out in the living room and nobody wanted them to wake in the night with a scary man snoring on the floor, without any sort of pad or sleeping blanket, just the single extra sheet they had and maybe a cushion or two from the kitchen chairs, and anyway out in the backyard the hammock would be perfect for him with the fresh air.

"A hammock?" Mercado said, dramatically squishing a finger around in his ear. "Am I hearing you correctly?"

"It's really best," his daughter said. Her searching eyes seemed genuinely troubled by what she was saying. "It's just for one night and after my shift we'll drive back up to Tinsley and see what's there and then get you a hotel."

"Who can afford a hotel?"

At this point, Tobey had felt increasingly uncomfortable. He really shouldn't be here for any of this. He had his own stuff to unpack. Like: what was that story about Track and NFTs and also what was—like actually—an NFT?

"Dad," the daughter went on, "you've got to have a little money. And there will be FEMA, I'm sure. Right?"

Here, she'd looked directly at Tobey. "Um," he said, feeling he had no choice but to answer, "I think so?"

"All right," Mercado said, addressing the back of Jason's head. "The hammock, then. Kindly put my belongings on the back stoop."

Then, taking Tobey by the arm as if they were old compatriots, he led the way back out onto the front lawn. "My cat," Tobey said.

"She'll be fine," Mercado grumbled. "A father gets the hammock but believe me, that cat will be eating canned tuna like feline royalty in the morning."

They were standing at the car when Tobey asked, "What exactly's going on in there?"

"That son of a bitch is what's going on in there. She lets him run all over her. 'He's just like the kids' dad,' she says, like that even means anything. Some guy off the street who moves in for free rent, if you ask me. 'We share things fifty-fifty,' she says. I never should have come here." He raised his hands in the air. "He looks like one of those damn Proud Boys, if you ask me."

"He does have the look, I guess," Tobey agreed.

"The look, the demeanor! A fucking Nazi in my grandchildren's house, stuffing the old man in a hammock. Unbelievable."

"How often do you, um, talk to your daughter?" Tobey ventured. "I mean, about this dude?"

Mercado laughed. "Some things are off-limits, you know? She says, 'Dad, you know I don't want to talk about that,' and then she'll change the subject. We had a fight about the last guy. The husband. He was a criminal! An actual criminal, he's in jail right now. Embezzling from a sporting-goods store! Imagine the kind of idiot—"

He didn't finish his thought because in the quiet out here they both heard the back storm-door squeak open, something heavy be set down, and then the door squeak closed again. Mercado's things were on the back patio.

"I would offer you my car," Tobey said, thumbing at it. "But there's really not room for one of us when it comes down to it."

"Not at all." Mercado waved a hand. "And I'm sorry to chew off your ear. Family! Who cares, right? You get some sleep for your trip."

Mercado had started for the unfenced backyard when Tobey said, "I could take you. To Palm Springs? Spend a couple of days, you know. Then we could go back up to Tinsley together. Survey the damage."

The old man laughed again. "I like you," he said. "You're a living saint. But I couldn't. My daughter and I will go tomorrow. We'll bury the hatchet. Don't you worry."

Tobey watched from the car as Mercado rounded the house, reappeared lugging his bags, and then made his way to the hammock. He thought of watching the old man climb inside, but it all seemed too embarrassing, too private. Instead, Tobey opened the passenger door, pushed up the seat, and ducked into the back. Then he pulled clothes from his bag, wadded them up into something that could serve as a pillow, and put his phone down on the floorboard. He should have called James back, should have texted Sophie. Instead, he stared up at a glowing streetlamp, feeling untethered.

He reached for the pipe from the front console. Took a hit. A second. The whole car held the gray settling cloud of the smoke. He tamped out the bowl. Put his head down. Tried to get comfortable. Took a third and then a fourth hit. Tried again. Eventually just made peace with being folded up in a way the human body wasn't meant to be at rest.

Just as heaviness overtook his eyelids, something hit him like a rock: his home, his apartment, was gone. All his books. His PlayStation. The bits of art he'd amassed, even that painting by Yatika Fields he'd bought online. His stupid dishes. The coffee cup he used every day. That Sonic Youth T-shirt he'd found at a flea market back in high school and kept, even though now it was unwearable for its holes. The socks he didn't like but hadn't gotten around to replacing. His records. Shit, his records. Probably half the value of his life if some insurance agent had come around to add it up. Why had he insisted on spending so much money on those records? Five dollars here, twenty there. The forty-eight he'd spilled on Max Felt's *Death Wish Serenade*, even though it had a scratch through the Moog solo on "You'll Never Make It." This was the sort of thing his father harped on: the proverbial latte keeping a whole generation from buying homes. But who was Tobey without all this junk?

He was so incredibly fucked. They both were: he and Mr. Mercado. What were they supposed to do? He lay back in the dark car with his nearly dead phone and everything he ever learned in that fucking existentialism class he made the mistake of taking freshman year came at him: the vast emptiness, the void where meaning should be, the overwhelming force necessary to live an authentic life. He wasn't going to think about that. No way. Wasn't going to think about how if only he could get Track to let him sell those stupid paintings to Osip Yander like James wanted him to, they could all have all the money in the world and not have to worry about all the garbage they had to worry about (did his father even worry about anything?) and especially not worry about the future, which wasn't a very long-term thing anyway these days, like maybe next week, or next month, another year or so if we're all lucky.

Di Stiegl had called this period of history "a cloud of desperation." That's the phrase she'd used when she came to UC Fresno. She'd said, "As the planet moves ever more rapidly toward destruction and the system of greed and hypocrisy which has led us here is revealed to be nothing more than the wizard behind the curtain, everything will be choked in a cloud of desperation."

She'd been invited to campus after Tobey's environmental studies professor discovered that he knew her—writing on his C+ term paper, "Wait, you mean you actually know Stiegl? Let's talk about this." The night of her presentation, Tobey had snipped a tab of acid in half, diagonally, and so was only half-tripping as she talked through a bunch of slides and gave a somewhat rousing speech that was both extremely depressing and weirdly hopeful, imagining for the audience an alternate dystopia without stupid jobs wasting all our time, when human connection and expression would be at the heart of our days here on a new and more conscientious Earth. Tobey had been impressed, in fact elated by the fact that he nominally knew this incredible person, but when he introduced himself at the book-signing reception that followed, she'd only said, "Oh you're Track's son. You've really grown." As if to remind him that they were strangers after all.

Track had increasingly taken a stand against Di Stiegl, ever since the whole family visited her in Toronto, when Tobey was fourteen. The trip had come suddenly, with little explanation. Tobey could remember with the vividness of a photograph how his father had looked so pleased to introduce them all to the big-name artist whose work they'd been walking past all these years. It was almost convincing, or it would have been to a stranger. Of course, the Harlan clan knew that of all the things Track disliked about this woman number one was the fact that she'd moved to Canada as a form of rebellion, turning her back on her country back in the '90s, and that she only returned to give "talks" on the subject of "New Earth Art," whatever that—Track would always add—was supposed to mean. His final implication always pointed to her hatred of America, a concept that he wouldn't allow anyone to challenge him on, though the paintings remained on the wall.

Tobey had always liked them. Especially the one of Grandpa. He'd even blogged about him a few times back in junior high school, when he imagined himself a future TV critic.

Track hated the paintings, or said that he hated them, but when anyone mentioned the idea of selling them, he would say, "They'll have to break in here and steal them from me."

But what if someone did steal the paintings from Track? What if that person was Tobey? James had mentioned a hundred times that the two of them should nab the paintings and sell them to a museum or a collector just to show their father what-for. "Sometime when he's at one of those stupid dog-training shows," he'd said. "Or a real estate conference."

Tobey would be left alone in the Palm Springs house this weekend.

No.

It was unreal.

Shit, he couldn't do that.

Or maybe it could be pulled off and maybe he would have a good piece of money and maybe he would, hell, why not, send some of it—half of it—to good ol' Mr. Mercado.

He texted James, I want to talk to Osip.

And when he'd waited an eternity for James to respond, he added, I mean I'm taking them and I want to talk to Osip.

And then, Ha! Just fucking around.

And then, Or am I?

About what? his brother typed back.

Huh

What do you want to talk to Osip about MF

$$

You're crazy.

No serious I'm going to get them and Osip wants them, yeah? How about this weekend?

There was a long pause, too long, and Tobey's focus wandered to the yellow porch light out the window at his feet, the half-dead plant drooping in its pot, the black handle of the storm door, completely still.

"A cloud of desperation." More like total system failure, but Tobey wasn't going to split hairs. Things were bad.

With a whiff of reckless abandon, he did what he'd wanted to do and talked himself out of doing all day. He texted Sophie. We're okay, he said. Totally safe! I love you.

A moment later came: Okay

Okay? What the fuck did that mean, Okay? He'd nearly died in a fire, their apartment was leveled, he'd even saved her cat, typed in actual words that he loved her, and this is what he got? Okay?

He started to type but another message came through: This weekend. Expect a call tomorrow at 5, number unknown. Answer it.

He stared at this message until it dawned on him that it was from an unknown number. It was James on a burner phone. James, not Sophie, had sent the Okay.

Tobey thumbed his phone dead and set it facedown on the floorboard, and then he stared at the back of the seat ahead of him, mostly shadow, only the faint shape of an old receipt sticking up out of the magazine holder. Where was that from? For what? How had it come to reside—

_____

BIRDSONG. HE'D DREAMED the large, tattooed man named Jason had terrorized him through the window in the night, shouting threats at him, telling him to leave, but clearly none of that had happened, and now he couldn't recall the details. It was nearly sunrise. Light had begun to creep into the sky, that faint and hopeful blue from the east. By his phone screen it was just after five thirty. And he needed to pee so bad he could barely sit up. When he did—YAARGH!—someone was sitting on his hood. He ducked, and between the headrest and seat he stared at this figure for a solid minute before he understood that it was Mr. Mercado in a purple bathrobe, lifting a steaming cup of coffee to his lips.

"Fuck," Tobey whispered. "Crazy motherfucker."

He rested back and opened his phone. No more messages. The only mention on Twitter of the Willows Fire or what happened in Tinsley were call-outs against climate-change deniers. CNN had moved on almost entirely: they just had a "watch this" video halfway down the scroll. Other sites were in the think-piece stage, with headlines like, "Why Don't We Care About the California Fires?"

So the massive tragedy had already been processed, packaged, and forgotten. Jesus. Maybe it was as hopeless as he'd been thinking; maybe there was no excuse for not stealing the paintings. But that was ridiculous. Sober, pulled back into reality, there was no way he'd be doing any of that.

He tried to move lightly, keeping the car from moving with him, and managed to pull on one and nearly two of his shoes before Mr. Mercado turned and smiled over his shoulder. "Hola," he said, his voice muffled through glass. Tobey pushed open the door, uncertain why he'd been sneaking. Mr. Mercado sounded like a new man. "Beautiful morning, isn't it?"

Tobey tried to wrench his back straight. "How long have you been there?"

Mr. Mercado looked across the street, still smiling. "Oh, just a few minutes."

"I need the bathroom."

"Ooh. That will be a while. Freddie's in the shower. Try the backyard, next to the aluminum shed."

Tobey made quick time of getting to the shed, without saying another word. But once there, he saw that the next-door neighbor's kitchen light was on, that a man with a mustache stood at the window, maybe making toast. This was turning very suddenly into an emergency.

Back at the car he told Mr. Mercado to keep a lookout. Then, close to the back fender, he unzipped. He pissed a hot, tight stream against the tire, splashing on his shoes, the lower half of his pants. The air, it hardly needed remarking upon, smelled of fire.

Finished and zipped up, he accepted the pink thermos Mr. Mercado offered him and joined him on the bumper. The neighborhood grew brighter. A group of joggers, already sweaty, plodded by on Stockton Street. The one at the end of the train, absurdly, was large, tattooed Jason. He gave only a nod to them as he passed. Tobey said, "That was fucking weird."

"Jason's trying to lose weight," said Mr. Mercado. "Runs every morning before work apparently. The rat bastard."

"You sure you want to stay?"

"Yes," Mr. Mercado said. In the morning light, the bags under his eyes seemed like slightly damp paper sacks, like they could burst. "I need to sort this out with her and I really do need to get back for the insurance thing, you know?"

Maybe the coffee was strong. Maybe sitting on the hood of a car at dawn after narrowly escaping an apocalyptic fire did something to one's hormonal balance. But suddenly it seemed to Tobey very important that he get Mr. Mercado away from this place and on to some better life. And so he said, "How can I get ahold of you after all this? I want to help. You know? Insurance is only going to do a little."

Mercado looked at him like he was crazy, a waiter who worked in a Tex-Mex place next to the highway, a flimsy socialist whose girlfriend had left him for the commune. Then he stood from the car, slung the remainder of his coffee to the pavement, and said, "Yeah, I'll give you my number."

SUSAN CALLED DURING the drive south to Palm Springs. She wanted to know how Tobey was doing, how he was holding up after watching his whole town burn to the ground on CNN. "I mean, not great," he said. "Pretty fucked, really."

"You sure you want to go to Dad's?"

"I don't have anywhere else."

"Well, if you feel like making the road trip you can come east. Brett and I discussed it last night." With the lilt of someone's mother, she added, "We can set up the extra room. It's just like an exercise bike and a television right now—"

"That's okay. I mean, fuck, maybe? I'll let you know." But really, driving across the country to stay with his nice-but-bougie sister didn't exactly appeal to him.

"Dad's just shady right now. I called last week to ask him about that news story and he gave me this whole speech about privacy and my generation and how nobody has any respect for their elders. Real Boomer-screaming-in-the-night stuff. I'd get out of there as soon as you can."

Well, that part sounded like Track, for sure. "I read that story," Tobey said. "I mean, like, I don't know anything about this block-chain shit. I swear Dad's gotta know less."

"I think he just ran out of land to pilfer, you know? So he went all in on crypto and NFT shit." She sighed. "Like two years too late too."

"When did everything turn into a grift?" Tobey said dreamily, rhetorically.

Susan laughed. "Real estate got messy, so Dad climbed up a pyramid scheme."

"You really think he'd knowingly break the law? You think he's that broke?"

"Dad once told me, 'The market's America, hon. Here and everywhere. If you're not buying and selling, you're no better than Benedict Arnold.' He literally thinks it's his patriotic duty to make money by any means necessary."

It did sound like the sunbaked, in-his-cups sort of thing Track would pronounce when no one had even brought up the subject. "But Harlan NextGen? You even heard of that?"

"That's James's thing. He's the next gen, get it? Hey, call me when you get there, okay?" She paused, and when her voice returned it had a note of worry to it. "Or text? I gotta get back to work."

———

LATER THAT DAY, after he parked and shut off the engine, Tobey waited for the stereo to time out as he took one deep breath and then another. Then one more. Two. He was on the third when the front door opened and Judith popped her head out, her face stretched in a cartoonish look of surprise. She was a strange woman, neurotic in a way that didn't seem to affect her negatively, what James called "cornily weird." Susan had once remarked that Judith had grown up in Minnesota, as if that explained it all. But Tobey wasn't sure what that explained, exactly. He didn't know anyone else from Minnesota to compare her to.

"Hi, sweetie," she said when he stepped out of the car. "What a tragedy. Your dad can't believe it."

He ducked inside for Gray, but the scars on his forearm reminded him that only Mr. Mercado had safely transported the cat to and from the car. "Do you have a box?"

"What kind of box?"

"For Sophie's cat."

Judith had had some work done a few years ago, a little stretching and what Tobey imagined to be buffing: the region between the corners of her lips and the space above her ears seemed always to be pulled back and disturbingly glossy. A blue vein above her left eye had nearly worked itself to the surface. "You need a carrier," she said. "I'll be right back." She walked away, punching the screen of her phone.

The garage door opened and Judith ambled out, carrying a giant plastic dog kennel, big enough for one of her German shepherds.

A very slow-moving and unfunny comedy routine followed, with Gray alternately hissing and purring, and when finally the cat was in the overlarge carrier, Judith held her hands aloft and dusted her palms like they'd been scrambling in the dirt.

"So," Tobey said on the way in. "Where *is* Dad?"

"He got a phone call," Judith said. "Took it right outside and then left. Hours ago now. I've been texting him but he hasn't responded. Must have his ringer off again. Now, mind the dogs. They're not used to seeing a cat in the house."

When she opened the glass storm door, four large brown-and-black dogs bounded over, first with a goofy affability and then, when the foremost caught wind of Gray, with a snarling intensity. Two of them chomped wildly at each other's mouths as if they were testing out how they would soon tear this ball of fur to pieces. Gray let out a growling hiss. "Oh boy," Tobey said. "Can they, like, go somewhere?"

Judith said something like, "Tiberius, Gracchus, Moebius, Balthus, sit," and each of the German shepherds sat immediately on their haunches, ears back, snouts tucked. Together they made a wall of dog, leaving only a narrow route to the hallway and blocking off the sunken living room. On the television behind them, glowing blue with red-and-white highlights: Fox News. A snarky-looking man with a leathery tan was bitching about "the media."

"My room open?" Tobey said, skirting left. Either Gracchus or Moebius sneaked a closer whiff of the carrier as he passed by.

"Well, it's a guest room now," Judith said. "But it's all made up for you."

When he got down the hall, he saw what she meant. His old room looked like it belonged in a bed-and-breakfast in Colonial Williamsburg: an ancient rifle under glass, a framed painting of George Washington, a decorative sewing machine from some distant century. The wallpaper showed little scenes of early Americana, from windmills and cannons to a happy cartoon slave boy with a bag of cotton slung over his shoulder. Yikes. When had all this happened? Best not to mention it. Besides, he needed to get Gray a litterbox and food.

Back in the hall, he stopped at the wide painting by Di Stiegl, one of those she'd titled *Dream of Fire*, a near match to the other hanging in Track and Judith's room, partially hidden by their headboard. In the foreground, a girl and boy dressed in old-fashioned clothes held hands, smiling, while a dark building in the far background burned a cone of orange flame from its roof. In between, desert hills rolled a wasteland that made the kids' facial expressions seem out of place, and superimposed in comic-book frames were close-up images painted in an almost photographic style: a match burning between two wrinkled fingers, an oil rig, a boardroom table full of men in suits (their heads out of view), a chainsaw cutting into a tree, the bloody leg of what appeared to be a dead deer.

Tobey had been looking at this painting (and its sister) as far back as he could remember. It was a strange mix of styles, like a Warner Bros. cartoonist had wandered into the low-oxygen heights of art with a capital *A* and then stumbled back out again, woozy and rambling. He'd assumed since his teen years that the paintings were about global warming, but his father insisted they were about his childhood. "Diane and I saw this fire the day her grandpa died," he'd said, pointing at the upper-right corner. "That was before we all lived together, before she became my sister. Or whatever she is. Back then we were two lonely kids from broken families. Maybe we'd be married now. Who knows."

That was the sort of weird, unexplained connection Track had with Di Stiegl. Once, when Judith said he should hang the Brackett painting of his father in the Harlan Homes main office, he'd grown angry. "I don't want customers thinking I'm into this garbage," he'd said. "Besides, Diane would kill me if I put it in some office. It's a private thing. A family thing." A week later, he'd said, apropos of nothing, "Don't get me started on what her grandpa did to my father. Turned him into a loon. Couldn't find work. Ran off with some chick. He's the reason my parents divorced."

Tobey couldn't make heads or tails of Track's Di Stiegl thing.

Then again, he couldn't really make heads or tails out of his own dumb idea from the night before. Steal the paintings? How? And how incredibly stupid would he have to be? A little flutter of embarrassment slid through his intestines. He'd actually texted James about it. Jesus. What a fucking idiot. Well, James likely thought he was joking. Right?

He ran back over his messages. "Shit," he said.

"What's that?" Judith asked. He hadn't seen her down on the floor, scratching the belly of one of her dogs.

"Nothing."

She pushed herself up using the arm of the couch and gave him a pained smile. They had never, in twenty-plus years of knowing each other, been close. "Everything okay?"

The Brackett painting loomed, and Tobey tried not to look at it. "I've got to run, get some things for the cat," he said. "Be right back."

Outside he texted James so rapidly he had to fix three different autocorrect mistakes before hitting Send. He sat in the car waiting for what he thought would be a quick response to a pretty strong message: HA! Just fucking around last night. FUCKING BLAAAAZED.

But no response came.

BACK IN THE house, with Gray all set up, Tobey began to think that his brother had likely gotten the message and thought it was unnecessary to respond. After all, why would he have been serious? If anyone knew that Tobey Harlan was completely full of shit, it was James.

He'd been relaxed into this line of thought for an hour or so, flipping and flopping between the idea that his brother would see this whole thing as a joke and that his brother was keeping something very significant from him, had smoked a bowl at the open bedroom window, had been watching some horrible reality show about two heavyset men who collected electric guitars owned by famous people, when his phone, plugged into the wall, began vibrating.

The word PRIVATE flashed on the screen. When Tobey put the phone to his ear, the voice on the other end wasn't Sophie or Mom or James or Mr. Mercado. Instead it was a reedy but powerful voice with sharp consonants and a vaguely European way of slowing and speeding up its delivery, making everyday words seem foreign and indecipherable. And even as Tobey tried to catch up with those sounds, he realized who must be talking: Osip Yander.

"—and so I understand that you can guarantee their provenance as well as—"

"What?"

A pause. "Their efficacy. Where they came from."

"The paintings?" Tobey fumbled for the guest room TV's remote, frantically tapped at the power button.

"Yes," said Osip Yander. Tobey had heard his voice on news shows, on podcasts, in a congressional hearing. And he'd seen him too. Who hadn't? That wide, fleshy face, pale and seemingly without eyebrows, his blond hair trimmed short, shaped oddly like the top of a square from temples to brow. The intense black eyes. "That is what we are talking about. That is why your brother asked me to call?"

"Yep," Tobey said, and stood up, aping confidence. And though a conscious part of him wanted to tell this very rich man that he had only been joking, that he'd been stoned and traumatized and oh wasn't it all so funny, he instead found himself following the social cues of the moment and going along. "They're definitely by Di Stiegl. I know her. I met her. I mean, I was a kid but I definitely know they're hers and so I can absolutely without a doubt—"

"Good. I can offer five hundred thousand. Will tomorrow night work?"

"Um. Yeah?" Tobey said, though the concept of so much money seemed as real as a Marvel movie. "Yes, of course, yeah tomorrow's good."

No no no no no no I'm just kidding. Ha!

"Then you will talk to your brother," said Osip Yander. "You will make plans for a basketball game."

"Basketball?"

But the line went dead. For a moment Tobey thought they'd lost connection, so he went to call him back. There was no number. Strike that. There was no call. Nothing appeared on his "recent calls" list from any number—not a private number, not even a blocked number. Osip Yander had somehow commandeered his phone, made it seem like a call, and then instantly wiped his presence. Impossible. Surely.

"Sweetie, the Thai food is here," Judith called from the other side of the door. "Your dad just got home. Come out and eat."

Tobey's stomach had moved down into the region of his knees. His ears burned. "Fuck," he screeched. "I'll be right there."

Judith, sounding worried, disappointed, maybe a little frightened: "All right, sweetie."

He had hurt her feelings. Poor Judith, who never said an unkind word. Tobey lunged into the hallway. "Sorry about that," he said as she disappeared around the corner. "I was asleep."

She laughed the fakest laugh in American history. "It's okay. Didn't mean to wake you."

He stopped by the bathroom, splashed water on his face. *Get yourself together.*

In the living room, a woman with giant, angry eyes was talking about the economy with a mummified old television personality as Track watched the screen with rapt attention. Tobey found Judith in the kitchen, digging out plastic chopsticks from the back of a drawer. "You were saying earlier," Tobey said, trying to rekindle a more friendly banter, "the dogs get fed at eight and then what time in the afternoon?"

"Three," she said in a bright tone, though she didn't look up at him. "Maybe four, if you're out. But they'll let you know if you're home. Ha! They'll let you know at two o'clock."

"Good, good," he said, and they returned together to the sunken living room, where TV trays had been arrayed before the television. On the wall next to the screen hung Di Stiegl's painting of Brackett, of Grandpa, and Tobey couldn't bring himself to even glance at it

this time. He was, he realized, in shock. Only a minute ago he'd
agreed to do something he knew he couldn't do.

For a moment he wanted to reach out and embrace Judith as if he
were her son, as if they had some kind of close connection. Instead
he said, "Thanks again for the place to crash this weekend."

Track pumped up the volume on his TV program without even
saying hello to Tobey. Judith said, "You really need to put something on those scratches. There's antibiotic in your bathroom."

Tobey opened his clamshell of drunken fried rice. He looked to
the row of hulking dogs sharing two large beds on the floor. One of
them pricked up his ears. *Food?* he seemed to be thinking. *Are we
on the same side?*

Tobey gazed at the television, took a deep breath, and tried to
shut out everything.

from: *That Guy in the Credits: My Few Ups & Many Downs in Hollywood*

by Arthur Banyan

Mariner Books, 1976

Now, von Stiegl on the other hand, he couldn't see a good time until it hit him over the head with a steel mallet. By the late '30s, the guy was living like royalty in Palm Springs, married into Western P&E money, his days no more challenging than the walk from his wife's satin-draped bedroom to the kidney-shaped pool in their concrete backyard. They lived in a big, nice house originally built to spec for a major star of the silent years. But if ever there was a movie character who had feeling sorry for himself nailed down, it was Klaus.

He'd hit some hard luck when sound came in (though when you look it square in the eye, nobody was more responsible for that hard luck than Klaus himself) and had taken on the heroic challenge of drinking himself into the grave. Death by martini in the blinding-hot desert. MGM had taken his last great picture from him and punished him for the remainder of his contract with third-string actors and weak scripts, trading him off to Poverty Row studios more often than they kept him in-house. He regarded it a blackballing, and though the whole country was suffering in the Depression (and no small number of movie-colony types suffering after sound), to hear Klaus tell it, no greater crime had ever been committed against a more noble and sensitive soul. Pshaw! I said. Get back on your feet. Kiss some of those dollar bills coming out of your ears.

I'd long soured on this house-shoed tragedy when I got a call (I think it must have been in August of '37) from his wife, Olive, the millionaire daughter of Peter Lazlo, founder of WP&E, who said she'd had it. "I'm taking my son and we're going back to Frisco," she said. "If you want to try saving your friend, then I'd get over here today."

When these two were married—the rich socialite and the black-balled movie director—I was the only person in the industry aside from his wheelchair-bound cousin to attend the wedding. And I'd been at the hospital when their kid, Percy, was born a year later, too, handing out cigars like the boy was my very own.

"My friend?" I said, though I knew who she was talking about.

"Klaus. He's in the bathtub. Drunk. Rambling about Louis B. Mayer. This is no place for a child."

It was no place for a husky scriptwriter from Brooklyn, either, but I had nothing better to do that afternoon, and so I rolled down the desk, locked it up, and jogged down the metal steps to my Olds, shining there in the sun. I was on my way off the lot when Barb Stanwyck passed by dressed in riding clothes. "Artie," she said. "What are you up to?"

Now, when I say I had nothing better to do that afternoon, what I meant to say was that I was supposed to be working on rewrites for a Stanwyck–Herbert Marshall picture called *Breakfast for Two*—an altogether forgettable comedy that could be described as *It Happened One Night* with all the laughs taken out and the main characters traded out for society snobs. "Going to Palm Springs," I said.

And that's how I came to have Barbara Stanwyck with me when I opened the bathroom door at the von Stiegl residence and found this old pal of mine from the Astoria days stretched out in the bathtub in his pajamas, topping off his martini glass from a bottle of gin, singing "Row, Row, Row Your Boat" with the verve of a real Broadway star. "Well, this is a fine picture," said Stanwyck. "You said we were going to meet some great director."

"This is he," I said. "Gone to seed."

"I'll say."

Klaus petered out with the singing and said, "You're Barbara Stanwyck. I liked you in *Banjo on My Knee*. Stinker of a movie, though," before rousing himself with the song of the same name.

Funny thing was he sounded as much like the German artiste, the great cold genius who made *The Bachelor's Wife* and *Heartbreak City*, as I'd come to know him. Something uncanny about hearing a guy talk like an Austrian prince and use the word "stinker."

"Maybe we ought to let him wear himself out," I said.

Stanwyck wasn't having any of that. "Get the bottle away from him and turn on that shower," she said.

An hour later we were all in the dining room, Klaus shivering in a thick pink bathrobe. Barb had made coffee and sandwiches and ordered me around pouring out bottles and hunting up more of them. The souse had hidden them all over. We got him to talk like a sane person, speaking again in the crisp German accent I was familiar with, and we let him know that the wife and kid had gone north to put distance between themselves and his itchy liver. "Olive?" he said. "Percy?"

When he stood up, Stanwyck pushed him back into his chair and said, "You'll eat that sandwich and you'll get a night's sleep before you'll go anywhere."

The next day, maybe inspired by the costume she found herself in, Barb wanted to go riding. So I called a ranch near San Bernardino that handled horses for the studios and a little later the three of us were riding around in the dry scrub, Barb holding forth about personal responsibility and how there's no excuse for laziness in a country as great as ours (I've long believed this was the day the immigrant von Stiegl found his famously conservative politics). After a couple hours of this, Barb's friends picked her up in an open car and Klaus and I loaded back up in my Olds.

Klaus only looked sicker as I drove back to Palm Springs. He was shaking by the time we got to the house and wanted a drink bad. "No going, pal," I told him, and instead we drank Coca-Colas and listened to the radio and talked about old times. He fell asleep on the sofa at some point after two in the morning. Then the next day we drove to San Francisco.

Old man Lazlo was still alive then (and would be a few more

years), but it wasn't the oil baron who answered the door of that massive white and ivy-walled mansion but a square-jawed pool-parlor dude who I thought might bite off my hand when I held it out and introduced myself. "This is Mr. von Stiegl," I said, gesturing at Klaus in his Sunday best when it was clear the man didn't want to shake hands. "We're here to see Olive?"

"I bet you are," he said with a sneer, and closed the door.

When Olive came out she said, "I thought he was joking."

"Look," I said, "here's your beloved. A new man."

Klaus said, "Hi, honey."

Olive said, "We'll see," and then closed the front door in our faces.

We checked into the Palace Hotel and had the man at the front desk call Peter Lazlo to tell him where Klaus would be. A full week passed without word from the Lazlo home, the pair of us living like men waiting for their execution. One morning I started packing up the few things we'd brought along. Klaus had only finished shaving when a quiet tap came at the door. It was Olive, slight and pretty and heartbreaking to the poor man's eyes, with little Percy at her side in short pants and a sweater. I hadn't seen the boy in at least two years and I don't think he recognized me. Klaus fell to one knee at the sight of the kid, and tearful, gathered him up in his arms. Olive hung there in the doorway as if she were waiting for the little drama to clear up so that she could step inside. When Klaus stood, holding Percy up on a hip, strapped in with one arm, I realized that she, too, was crying.

And what did I get in the end? Not even a thanks. Not a word about it again. Just a note from Barbara Stanwyck on my office door asking me why I was holding up production on *Breakfast for Two* with my endless rewrites.

A month or two later the von Stiegls moved to Mexico, to Rancho Lazlo, one of Olive's father's properties, which had up until a year before been lived in year-round by the great man's less-great brother, who had relocated rather suddenly to Florida. Compared to the house in Palm Springs, it must have been a step down, like they were tightening their belts.

I visited once, during the War, and by then Klaus von Stiegl had come to relax into the ease of his life. He'd taken up painting. Stayed sober. He spent long hours on the beach, the siesta broken up by occasional jobs for CLASA Films, a Mexican movie studio on the rise at the time, where he understood nothing of what his coworkers said in Spanish and they understood a little less than half of what came from him. He told me about the string of cheap, slowly produced films he'd made with no artistic expectations, but which he gave a little von Stiegl touch: vaquero romances, a historical throwaway of Spanish court intrigue, a pair of comedies starring a knock-off Tin-Tan, the biographical picture about Porfirio Díaz that he didn't understand and finally handed off to a more able local director.

The day I left he said, "Someday we ought to work together again," and I didn't see him again for another twenty years.

VILLAGE VOICE

February 20th, 1982

ARTTALK

by ARTHUR COCHRANE

THE PRINCESS OF DOWNTOWN: AN AFTERNOON WITH THE OTHER DI

Diane "Di" Stiegl's name was on the lips of everyone I spoke to in late January, when her "Gipper Triptych #2" stole the opening night at Sex Guide's "Six Abnormal Women." Monumental in scale, the set of 8 x 10 canvases narrate one of the final moments in the life of a dying man. In the central panel, this man, bone-thin and sunken-eyed but clearly young, reaches for a cup of water on his bedside table. In the left panel, a nurse exits the hospital room: a hulking white form with no emotion or connection to the patient. The right panel reveals another young man in a denim jacket, his hair curly, flopped to one side, elbows on knees, a pained expression of hope on his face. That these images are painted in a photorealistic style based on Polaroids taken by the artist, and that the dying young man is suffering from the mysterious outbreak of pneumocystis carinii pneumonia which has spread terrifyingly among gay men in the last year makes taking in the image something like a full-body assault. One can hardly stand before these paintings without feeling that one is there and suffering as well, that this dying and the suffering may be what most connects us to others, that something must be done. That the artist (and granddaughter to a legend of Old Hollywood) has chosen to title her work using the B-movie-derived nickname of the sitting president makes the work unabashedly political.

I knew at least as much about the triptych before traveling downtown to see it myself. A friend had described the work to me in tears that morning and, calling ahead, I was given permission to view the full show an hour before the gallery opened to the public. Within moments of stepping to the paintings, which are displayed in a corner of the wide-open, concrete-floored basement gallery beneath a youth center, I realized that going alone, without even the company of strangers, had been a mistake. On one level, nothing could have prepared me for the experience of such realism. It is no secret that I am not a fan of the hyperrealist or photorealist style. It strikes me often as formally redundant, its common subject matter (parked cars, shop windows, aluminum and cellophane ephemera) as overwhelmingly 'done'—already baked in Mr. Warhol's screen-printing oven, let's say. But here I felt none of those qualms. Here was a human subject made more real by the paint. Its effect, like that of the Old Masters (not to inflate the ego of Ms. Stiegl), is multiplied by its physical presence before you. This is no photo rendered onto canvas but a slice cut surgically from the body of the real world around us. Its level of detail is almost prurient. On the sufferer's chest one sees a missed button and so a view to a single rib, pale and meatless, the horror of it there in public no less mortifying than the wounds of Christ. The unshaved face, the dark and skeletal eyes, the terrible and sleepy look of hunger that animates his reach for the plastic cup of water. A perfect head of brown hair, parted to one side, makes the sufferer's youth all the more inescapable and leads the eyes to the comb, on the edge of the table near his visitor in the right panel.

Here we see the full weight of the tragedy depicted in Ms. Stiegl's almost mythic scene: these two are most certainly lovers; as one wastes before the other's eyes, we still see all the attendances of romantic connection. And this is where the left panel adds another layer of meaning: the cold exit, the shrugging disinterest, the still-moving world outside the one inhabited only by our two young men.

An unexpected mix of Francis Bacon and Sherrie Levine, the triptych is part nightmare and part rumination on the nature of images. I walked away from the show with the image haunting me (other works are excellent, especially the mixed-media landscapes of Lily Wong and the video work of Carol Bunting; the show continues through Saturday), and so I asked about Ms. Stiegl's studio. The gallery called ahead. Before noon I stood in the doorway of a shabby red building in SoHo, sharing the steps with a homeless woman examining the sores on her foot. After a minute or two of waiting after the buzzer, and just as I readied my retreat, a stocky young woman with a pleasant face appeared at the door wearing a matching blue sweatsuit which emphasized the sheet-white quality of her skin. This was our Ms. Stiegl.

Shoeless, stepping carefully over random trash in the stairwell, she led me to the fourth-floor apartment she had once shared with the subject of her famous triptych, a place she explained she would likely be vacating at the end of the month. When I asked where she would be going, she said she was still figuring that out. "There's a house upstate," she said. "But I'd do nearly anything not to leave the city."

A regular in the downtown scene, Stiegl's work had featured (to less of a splash) in a wide-ranging show at Sex Guide late last summer called "Flat Commodities," her second group show, and she has taken part in performance work at Club 57 and other venues. A few years ago she had been a student of Bartolomos before leaving NYU for a more bohemian life. The influence shows: in several earlier canvases (including those featured in "Flat Commodities" and more so in a pair featured in the now-legendary "Do We Have a Sex Guide Gallery Show") one can see the shadow of that photorealist chieftain, though at the same time something independent, an interest in narrative and an astonishing gift for shaping the human body and capturing the particularity of gestures. "There's something classical here," I told her. "I can't think of a photorealist who is this good at people."

"My art is about people," she said, with the confidence of a middle-aged standard-bearer.

In fact, it is at about this point in my visit that I come to understand that Ms. Stiegl may be more self-assured and clear-eyed than most of the established artists I've spoken to over the years for this column. I asked her about Levine and Cindy Sherman, about the downtown artists who are her friends and acquaintances, about her famous instructor Bartolomos. She quoted from memory several passages from "Greater Than Seeing," the Greek photorealist's manifesto, and without any help from me, debated its points, dismantled what she called its "ideological weaknesses," and finally—having exhumed canvas after canvas for my perusal as she spoke—declared his work "a failure on its own merits. I learned from him but only technique. There wasn't anything else to learn."

For her contemporaries, however, she has nothing but appreciation. She talked glowingly of street artists and conceptual artists alike, photographers and painters. But then she added, "I've determined in the last year to resist any form of influence. I am open to the world and always want to learn, to develop, but as for style I'm up to my own thing and I plan to keep it that way."

"Does that mean even if the art market turns away from what you're doing?"

"The words art and market are mutually exclusive terms," she says, holding up both of her index fingers and moving them apart to illustrate. "I'm not concerned with markets."

A young radical, then, or a banker's daughter? She only laughed when I asked. She waits tables, she explained. For a time she answered the phone at a dentist's office. At the end of this résumé she repeated her statement about exclusive terms.

An idealist, I determined. Perhaps even a performance. She knew who I was, after all, and I knew that the triptych I'd seen that morning had sold for $35,000—quite a price for an unknown painter who doesn't believe in the art market.

The phone rings, and for a few minutes I am left to mill around the paintings. On an easel, a half-finished painting shows a woman locking the door of her parked car outside a restaurant, the vast Midwestern plains disappearing over her shoulder. Large black clips hold at least a dozen Polaroids of various subjects (including several of who appears to be the woman) to the unpainted edge of the canvas. From what I can see, Stiegl's unshown work is beginning to bridge the wide chasm between neo-expressionism and photorealism, a pastiche of hybrid visual narratives that may yet be art's story in 1983. We'll have to wait and see.

When Stiegl returned from her phone call, together we pulled out and displayed the other two triptychs in the series, "Gipper #1" and "Gipper #3." Together they tell an even more astonishing story and reveal an even greater talent. Formally, in shape and design, each of the panels matches, or at least echoes, its siblings in the other triptychs. The left panel shows a doorway with an exiting figure; the central panel shows the subject in a supine position; the right panel shows a figure seated and leaned forward, elbows on knees. With the same hyperrealist style, Ms. Stiegl has rendered her subject listening to music on headphones, on the floor of a teenager's bedroom, and in the other he is stretched on a couch—the very couch I'd stood next to in the other "room"—in the blue light of late-night television. Here a father turns toward a middle-class suburban hallway, there a hairy-backed man removes his shirt as he ducks through one of the diving curtains; here a hippie-looking teen in untied sneakers appears to look at both the father and young man on the floor with equal terror, there the painter herself stares empty-eyed at the screen, reflected in her glasses, her mouth open wide in laughter. With the meticulous detail one would expect of this artist, it is the face of our current president, holding up his hand at the inauguration, who has captured their attention on the television.

Had these other scenes been staged? How had she matched the layout of these incredibly realistic scenes using photographs? These questions showed my ignorance of her process. Ms. Stiegl doesn't directly copy or trace from a single photographic image, as I'd let myself believe. Instead she uses a series of photographs as research into individual elements within each painting. She dealt a stack of Polaroids out on the floor, assembling as she did the figures that made up the right panel of triptych #3. The panels themselves are not documentary but fictional, assembled by the artist.

"Would you say this is a cubist approach?" I asked.

"It's what has worked for me," she said.

"And overall," I asked, "what would you say the meaning of this series of triptychs to be? Is it a biography of the subject? A narrative? Some kind of moral lesson?"

She laughed and picked up her Polaroids. "I don't do moral lessons," she said. "When you lose a person close to you, when it happens this quickly, with so little warning . . ."

I think for a moment that she is going to continue her sentence, but she doesn't. Instead she finishes clearing up the Polaroids and shows me to the door. I'm walking down the narrow stairwell alone when I understand that I have just met one of the artists who will define this decade.

On the stoop outside, the homeless woman is gone. All that remains of her presence is a paper bag. Inside this I discover not a liquor bottle but rather a plastic Virgin Mary, the sort of thing you'd see in the window of an immigrant shop, her right hand raised in an awkward gesture that is both surrender and revelation. The object is so overdetermined by symbolism that I passingly thought it had been planted for me to discover, and later, when writing this, I was determined not to mention it. I placed it back in the paper bag. Maybe the woman will return for it. But maybe not.

Di Stiegl's "Gipper Triptych #2" can be seen at the Sex Guide Gallery, St. Mark's Place, until March 8.

DIANE

1982

E ARLY IN JANUARY, to help out Annie, she placed a call to the George West Gallery in Los Angeles, explaining that she was Klaus von Stiegl's granddaughter, to three different people who each in turn placed her on hold before eventually a nice-sounding man who introduced himself as Franklin Brown asked for her number and said that Mr. West would call her back in five minutes. When her phone rang twenty minutes later, a gruff but genial voice came on the line. "Little Diane? I can't believe it. My dear cousin spoke very highly of you. And look at you now!"

She had only met the man her father called "Uncle George" once, just before her grandfather died, but after Annie had spent six months casting around trying to find any gallery job at all in New York, Diane thought she could use the family connection. "She has a very good eye," Diane had explained over the phone. "And she's brilliant on art history. She wrote a paper on Lee Krasner that our professor said—"

"Say no more," George West sang into the phone. "Your word is enough."

"You've got a job for her?"

"I've got an interview for her. Let's not put carts ahead of horses here. When can she be out here to chat?"

SHE TOLD ANNIE that the money Diane was spending on her airline tickets came from the sale of a painting she'd posed for, which in some tricky accounting could be partially true. "I'll pay you back," Annie said, elated. "Oh God, I'll owe you everything."

"Never," Diane told her. "Don't think about it."

When Annie got the offer two weeks later, Lily decided that she would go with her, that they would room together. "The city's too much," she said. "I need a break. And sunshine." But then at the last minute she was offered a role in a low-budget movie about the downtown scene, something she couldn't pass up. "Imagine gallery owners seeing me in a film with Richard Hell. It's going to be so cool." The role only took a few days of shooting, looking smoky and mysterious in a trench coat and saying all of one line to the lead actress before getting shot by a sniper. She explained all this during the walk over to a backup dancing tryout—a paid gig, unlike the movie—strutting behind some act that would play at Danceteria in a couple of weeks.

Diane, cold in her army jacket, had for some reason been drafted along on this adventure. "I didn't know you had your eyes set on being an entertainer."

"This is just money," Lily said as they came to the entrance of a shabby-looking apartment building. "If I get this I won't have to call my parents for rent."

Up a freight elevator busy with graffiti, Diane experienced a sensation that had grown familiar over the last few months: a kind of guilt about having all that money from her grandfather and a deep need to give it away to her friends. But she knew if she offered to pay her rent for her, Lily wouldn't see her the same. She wanted to avoid that awkwardness. Still, with Annie gone, Diane worried that her group of friends, her real family, was beginning to fragment. At times she dreamed of bringing them all together in one house, maybe upstate, with a pack of dogs and a great live oak they could all relax under in the afternoons.

The elevator door opened directly into a small loft where a Black man in thick glasses and a trim beard was heating up a kettle just an arm's length away. For a full second, Diane thought they were in the wrong place.

His name was Michael. He was slim and tall and dressed in a worn-out gray T-shirt and checkered slacks and Chuck Taylors, and his turntable played Bowie's *Scary Monsters*, the record sleeve propped against the wall as if it were on display, which it was. "Which one of you is Lily Wong?" he said, and Diane knew that Lily had it for him by the way she raised her hand like a kindergartner, all sheepish and silly. Michael smiled at them both and then gave Diane the up-and-down. "And you are?"

"This is my friend Di," Lily said.

"Di Stiegl? I thought it was you. I read about you in the *Village Voice*." He dropped a teabag into a small white cup with a starburst design on the side. His eyes were radiant. "Wow, this is a real honor."

Diane didn't know how to respond to moments like this. She'd thought for so long that she would handle them with aplomb, that they would feel validating and warm, but instead they only made her nervous. Plus that critic had made a point of calling her a chunk in print. As if she was; as if it would be anyone's business. She'd been wearing baggy clothes specifically so he wouldn't talk about her body.

"Thank you," she said. "It meant a lot for them to print something about the painting." And then, worried she seemed too self-centered, "Lily's here for the tryout and we had plans to get a drink."

That had been the agreement. Because Lily couldn't decide how creepy this would be, she said they should go in saying they were expected somewhere.

"Oh yeah I'd love to go," Michael said, though they hadn't invited him. He poured steaming water into his mug. "This won't take long."

What *this* was quickly proved to be more absurd than Diane had expected. Michael directed Lily to stand in front of the closed elevator door, between a coatrack and the kitchenette, and to dance as she saw fit, keeping in mind that this was for a background position, one of maybe three or four women who would look good onstage during a performance by some new pop singer. He pulled out an extra chair for Diane near the one already set up behind a VHS camcorder on a tripod across the cluttered room. Then he removed the Bowie record, put on Grace Jones's "Warm Leatherette," and sat down next to Diane. "Okay," he said, switching on the camera. "When you feel comfortable you can take off your dress."

Diane turned her head with such a jerk that a pain throbbed up the back of her neck. "What do you mean?"

"Diane," Lily said in a hushing voice.

"Wait, so this is a striptease in front of the camera?"

Michael looked at her without expression, their faces inches apart. "I know it's a little weird. But the promoter wants it on video. I call in the girls and then I hand them all to him on a single tape so he can watch and pick out the ones he wants."

"This isn't just for you to whack off to?"

"Diane!"

She looked at Lily, who was working her dress up over her shoulders. Underneath, she was wearing a silver one-piece swimsuit. "Lily, you don't even know this guy."

Michael had stopped the recording. A quiet zipping sound came from the camera. "Rewinding to tape over that," he explained. "Listen, I know this isn't ideal. But it was all explained—"

"To me, Diane. It was all explained to me." Lily hung her dress on the coatrack and began to dance, slowly and tentatively, turning her elbows and shoulders to the beat, moving her hips only as much as was required to shift her weight from one heeled foot to the other. Diane could see that she was embarrassed, so she put her face in her hands and let her friend dance, and only looked up again as the song neared its end, by which time Lily had really gotten into it, making catty little faces for the camera, looking over her shoulder as her butt swayed suggestively, or not even suggestively, directly and literally, and then it was over, the record fallen in the dead groove between songs, Lily pulling on her dress, Michael standing up from the cam-corder. "How was I?" Lily asked. "Was it the absolute worst?"

"No," Michael said. "You were super."

Diane felt for a moment that she couldn't unclench her teeth. Her face closed in on a flammable state. "You were amazing," she said. And though it made her internal organs cringe to say it, she added, "So sexy. Really sexy."

———

AGAINST ALL ODDS they actually went for a drink with Michael, in a dark cellar of a place with a jukebox playing one Rolling Stones song after another and a shark's jaw hanging above the bar and a clientele with the glaring eyes and hunched shoulders of aged-out street thugs. The bartender's tattoos told a story about badly drawn women and a few years in the navy, and though Michael called him by name (Otto, was it? surely not), he'd only grunted in response. They ordered beers, Lily flirted with Michael, and Diane, her focus drifting, wished she'd brought her Polaroid. The three men seated nearest the jukebox, grimacing at each other in silence and leather jackets, looked like an '80s Cézanne.

"Di, did you hear that?" Lily said. "He makes music videos."

"Well," Michael said. "I've done a few. I'm really more of a video artist."

"Oh, stop it. He's on MTV!"

Michael grinned, embarrassed, and then said, "I mean, they played one of them but that's it."

"What do you mean video artist?" Diane said. "Girls dancing in your entryway?"

He laughed. "Hey, I gotta pay the bills like anybody."

Then his eyes fixed on hers and the evening felt tight and warm and she knew that she was crazy about him and that she would hurt Lily and a deep warmth spread up her belly to her throat and so she took a long drink of her beer and said, "You know I'd better get out of here? Supposed to meet someone in like half an hour. Sorry, guys."

Lily's brow lowered with doubt and then eased back up as she understood. "That's right," she said. "We won't keep you."

Diane fumbled a hug with Lily and shook Michael's hand, and walked alone to her building, where the naked blue windows and the sky fading orange were erased by the flip of a switch, turned to weak mirrors, the ghost of a city sketched behind. Then she painted, all of the day's events closed off from her, everything now between hand and eye and canvas.

———

LILY CALLED THE next afternoon to say that Michael had kept talking about her, about Diane. "I mean, he likes you, Di. He wasn't sticking around for me."

"He doesn't even know me," Diane said, but the rush was there, that pleasant feeling: he likes me. As if she were a girl back in high school; as if he were Track in his blue letter jacket, that summer she'd allowed herself to feel enamored with him. She hadn't been dating much these last couple of years, had gone home with a guy from the Mudd Club maybe six months ago, had been too busy for all that. "Did the whole night go south?"

"He got really drunk. Kind of messy. I gave him your number."

"You gave him my number?"

"He said he'll call you. He said he wants to see all your paintings. I told him about your mom too. Is that a secret?"

Diane hated when people she didn't know talked about Antonia. She didn't like explaining it, didn't like answering for it, didn't like having to put on the proper bereaved attitude. "It's okay," she said. "I mean, whatever."

There was a long pause on the line and Diane wasn't sure what to say, what she was expected to say. Should she be saying she wasn't interested in Michael? Should she ask Lily what to do if he called? Get her permission? "Anyway," Lily said finally, "what I was calling about was yesterday at the tryout. You were really judgmental. You embarrassed me."

"I did?"

"You made me feel like a slut, you know?"

A pigeon strutted back and forth at the window. The light was already fading. Winter. "That whole situation was just creepy. I mean, this guy with a camera in his shitty apartment?"

"But that's why I brought you."

"Look, I'm sorry. I just didn't know you were going to take your dress off is all."

Lily cleared her throat. "As if it's any different from what we've done in Nero's stupid little shows. It's for a backup-dancer job. I need the money."

For some reason Diane thought it would be best to make a joke of it all. "You come over here and dance and I'll pay, okay?"

"You know," Lily said, her voice sharper, "I think you think I just fuck anything that moves because you—"

The pigeon dived for the street. Diane had been working on another painting of Antonia, this time in her car in the exact pose she'd painted Percy in years ago. Her mother shocked by the flash; Diane in the passenger seat with the camera. She'd had to take the train to Long Island to find a Plymouth dealership with the same model of car Antonia had left behind when she disappeared. When she'd snapped the pictures a salesman came by to ask if she was interested in making a purchase. Now her concentration was blown and she wouldn't get any more work done today.

"Because *I* fuck anything that moves?" Diane said. "Is that what you were going to say?"

Lily wasn't taking the bait. "What did you mean when you told Annie 'Chinese girl different' in that fucking ching-chong voice?"

"When did I say that?"

Lily was crying. She was sniffling and crying. "Last summer. I heard you say it. I was kissing that guy Tod from the record shop and Annie said, 'Get a room you two,' and you said, 'Chinese girl different. They do it wherever.' Like you were Charlie fucking Chan."

Diane remembered it suddenly, a bad joke, some stupid shit that had come out of her mouth. She hadn't thought Lily even cared about it. Why had she said such a thing? Where had it come from? "I'm sorry," she said.

"You know you can be a real asshole sometimes? Like you think you're above us all. Do you know how hard it is on like a daily fucking basis to be a Chinese girl in this business?"

"Jesus, Lily, I'm sorry," Diane said. Had she been living a double life as a piece of shit? "Look, why don't we meet up or something?"

"I don't know that I want to see you," Lily said.

"There's a party at Geoff's tonight," Diane said, remembering it only now. "Keith and Jean-Michel are supposed to show. Maybe even Warhol. Why don't you come with me?"

"Oh, Mrs. Famous Artist. Daring to be seen with the Chinese slut."

"Please, Lily." But she knew by Lily's joking that they would remain friends. "I wasn't going to go but if you'll go with me—"

NONE OF THE big names showed up, at least that she recognized, though a large white man in gold silk pajamas and a ponytail was treated by several of the other guests as if he were important. She never caught his name, but did get into a short conversation with him about Lucian Freud, a painter she knew little about but determined to look into more. A friend of this stranger's, wearing S&M leather and ringlets, his hair short and bleached blond, offered Diane "a little bump," and when she looked down at the plateau of skin made by his tucking a thumb into the closed palm of his hand, she saw a neat mound of white powder.

For only an instant the snort tickled her nasal passage and she thought she would sneeze, and then everyone around her took a bump of their own and then nobody sneezed and then she walked away thinking it would have no effect and then it did. Happy talking people everywhere. By the time she found Lily, dancing to Billy Joel in her blue jeans and sleeveless gray T-shirt, she thought her heart would burst with everything she wanted to say about everything ever and she loved and loved her and so she danced close and loose, all the while keeping up a steady stream of banter, making Lily laugh and making her look at her like she was crazy and making her—knowing it was coming and still making her—say, "Di what's got into you?"

They found the S&M guy seated on the arm of a sofa, tapping his hands on his knees and nodding to the beat. He'd cut himself shaving; three red blotches colored his neck. Diane told him she'd buy some if he had any to spare and he led them to a bedroom where he opened the top drawer and reached behind a pile of jockey shorts. "Isn't this Geoff's room?" Diane asked.

"It's okay," he said. "Geoff wants everyone to have a good time. He told me to keep it in here."

Just like that Geoff came in as well, smiling like a gracious host. He brushed his hand over the S&M man's shoulders. "I see I'm just in time."

Diane said, "I want to paint you. The two of you."

"Us?" said Geoff. He was bearded and slim-faced, with square glasses and a lanky body, dressed like someone's accountant but for his white tennis shoes. He and the other two guys in his conceptual art group made a point of looking dull. "We're not even a thing."

"The three of you," Diane said, roping Lily into the game. "Sit here on the floor in front of the bed. Just look casual. Be yourselves."

"Why?" said the S&M guy. He looked at Geoff and gestured to Diane. "I mean, who is this chick?"

"She's a painter, Bradley." He looked at the ceiling. "The one I told you about?"

Lily sat on the floor. She looked confused, maybe a little put out. "Why are we doing a picture right now, Di?"

Diane was already working her Polaroid out of her bag. She'd brought the purple bag with the snaps and she'd had to force the camera in there but thank God she'd brought it. "First let's have just a little of this," she said, pointing at the baggie Bradley held between his knees there on the floor. But really she'd already started snapping photos, one of them spitting out into her hand, tossed to the side to process, here all of them in profile, there looking head-on, a close-up of one, two, three. Then they were all on the floor and Bradley held up a tiny metal spoon for each of them and some of the photos had slid under the bed and she said, "We need music."

Geoff laughed. "There's music out there."

"Wait you're that chick with the gay cancer painting," said Bradley. "Don't you think it's sort of freaky to make all that money off a man's death?"

It took her a moment to realize he was talking about Phil. "I didn't—"

"Don't listen to him," Geoff said. "He's an idiot. Doesn't know anything about art."

"I know about art," Bradley said, offended. "I know everything there is to know about art."

"What you know about is giving me another spoon of sugar, honey."

Back in the party everyone moved too slowly and stood in the way chatting and someone put on that Meat Loaf record for a laugh, or at least some people laughed when it started, "Paradise by the Dashboard Light," the dumbest song on earth, and it was so interminably long that Diane grabbed Lily's elbow and said they should go, this party was lame anyway, they could go to a club and dance. But honestly, she was angry about what that guy said about Phil. She'd fired Valerie Szeslak because Valerie hadn't believed in her enough when she wasn't all that good and when she was good she found a different gallery to represent her and here were these people at this party set against her like a bunch of snobs and Lily, too, wasn't she, saying she was some kind of prick for a lame joke? She wanted to go. Diane wanted everyone to fuck off so that she could go.

But Lily gave her that look again and said, "We just got here."

It didn't matter. She was leaving. It was okay if Lily wanted to stay because anyway maybe she'd just go home and paint, and maybe it was better anyway, she needed to paint, yes that was exactly what she wanted to do. "You stay, really," she said. "Have fun."

Lily followed her to the door. "You sure? Di, you're acting weird."

———

IN THE CAB she chewed a piece of Juicy Fruit, her teeth grinding now and again, the fleshy-faced man at the wheel looking back at her as if she might explode. The city was all lights and noise, streaking past, and it seemed that not only was the cab window made of glass but so were the streets and people and fire hydrants. A dog made of glass on the end of a glass chain led by a Black man in a glass tracksuit. Two glass prostitutes smoking glass cigarettes next to a glass trash can. Sidewalks of glass. Buildings. Loose newspaper pages. She would paint on glass: one side a perfect representation, its glinting backside an abstract imprint, a statement about painting as a form. A dumb idea: She'd never do that. But she did want to do something new, to change her style. After the article she'd been haunted by the feeling that she'd reached the end of something. It was either something new or a lifetime of giant triptychs, maintaining a brand name, fuck brand names, fuck marketing, she didn't want any of that. She couldn't sit still.

She had Grandpa's money in the bank. Six hundred thousand dollars. Six hundred and two thousand, eight hundred and twenty-four dollars. That's what was left. She'd told no one but Phil and then only at the end, not even Lily or Annie, though she'd paid Phil's hospital bills and then for his funeral. She wouldn't have told him at all except at the hospital when no one else would come he demanded to know what was going on, how any of this was getting paid for when he had no insurance, how she would ever live without him. "I won't need to live without you," she'd told him. "You're going to be better soon. Don't be crazy."

He'd looked up at her, trying to smile. "Let's be honest," he said.

So she'd told him the whole thing: Grandpa, her father keeping it from her, turning twenty-two.

"Absolutely fucking Dickensian," he said after some thought, and then he did smile, even coughed a laugh.

They sat a moment, with all the beeps and murmurs of the hospital around them. "I brought my camera like you said," Diane said at last.

"Fix my hair, will you? It gets so sweaty in here sometimes."

After he slipped off into the night a couple of days later, Diane paid rent on their place for five years. She would never have to give it up. Would never have to leave like she'd told that interviewer— that had been a ruse, a way of seeming interesting and hungry.

The cab pulled to a stop at the curb and she peeled off ten more than the cabbie asked for and tossed it up front. "Thanks," she said. "You're a saint."

"That's what my mother thinks."

On the stairs she realized what she needed was not a new style but more ideas. More narrative. More politics. A person can't go around painting her parents in cars all her life.

In the hall outside her door she could already hear the phone ringing and she knew somehow that it would be Michael. She flicked on both the overhead lights, went to the phone, and carried it around by the extra-long cord as she twisted the knobs on all the lamps. "Hope you don't mind," he said when she answered. "I didn't want to be cool and wait a week."

"It's okay," she said. "I never thought you were cool."

Their conversation had none of the stops and starts it should have, just an endless bantering and complaining and philosophizing. He'd thought a lot about art, knew the work of Cindy Sherman and David Salle and had been to that graffiti show uptown everyone was talking about last year. He'd read Franz Fanon and Jacques Derrida, listened to the Clash nearly every morning as he drank coffee and ate oatmeal and showered, had very strong opinions about French cinema and an obsession for Bergman and Fellini. For Americans he only liked Hitchcock and Chaplin and a half dozen B-movie directors she'd never heard of. He'd never been west or south of Philadelphia. "Sheltered life," she said. "I spent a good part of my childhood moving around, really."

"Lily said that." It was nearing midnight. Long ago she'd begun setting up her paints: the dabs of yellow and white and green she needed for a few details on that canvas of her mother. Now that seemed a waste. "Said you're related to some old movie director?"

"Herr Klaus von Shtee-gul," she said. "Ever heard of him?"

"No?" he said, like he was trying to sneak his answer by her. "Guess I shouldn't spout off about film when I don't know everything."

"He's from the silent days," she said. "I think he's more a legend in my family than anywhere else. He made some things in Mexico and then did TV. You ever see *Brackett* on reruns?"

"Shit," he said. "He made *Brackett*? Frank Harlan was my idol when I was a kid. 'Back up, sonny,' he'd always say. Drove my little sister up the wall with that."

They laughed about *Brackett* or both having watched it or something she couldn't define. She was starting to crash—that's what this was, she knew it: a crash—but she still held on to a pinch of elation and nerves. "What are you doing tomorrow?"

———————

HOURS LATER, THEY met for breakfast at a corner diner in the East Village with heavy white coffee cups and water served in tall red glasses with crushed ice and Barbra Streisand playing from a boombox sitting on the metal shelf where the cook set food for the waitress. Diane hadn't slept; she'd come early for the coffee. Her muscles hurt all over like she needed to stretch everything and then sit in a hot bath for the rest of the day. She felt stupid and tongue-tied. Twice the waitress had asked her to speak up. When she arrived she'd been the only customer, and even now, an hour or so later, just a handful of other diners grimaced into their food.

Michael swept through the door in a purple sports coat and black trousers, sharp-toed boots and a black hat with a purple feather that didn't quite match the coat. Sunglasses. He looked like he was out on a date with someone a great deal cooler than her: she was in her army jacket and the paint-stained blue polka-dot dress she never usually wore out of the apartment. He removed the hat just as he approached the table, revealing a newly cut mohawk like the one Jean-Michel wore a year or so ago. "What do you think?" he said. "Did it myself last night."

He looked cute, boyish, his green eyes somehow bigger, but all she said was that it was cool, yes she liked it, very punk rock. "Why the change?"

"That's just it," he said. "Change. It's the only thing I believe in. You've got to change all the time. Never sit still."

She was reminded, again, that this was the guy making videos of girls dancing in their underwear. But also: *change* was exactly what she'd been thinking about last night. "So what is it you do?" she asked, wondering why it hadn't come up already. "I mean, to make a living."

"You're gonna laugh."

"No, I want to know. I wait tables. Or used to. Probably will again."

He ordered his coffee, bacon and eggs. "I wash dishes," he said after the waitress had left, "Three, four nights a week. But I'm hoping to get on a film production, you know? Or have one of these music videos catch someone's attention."

He hadn't studied film like Nero, hadn't even gone to college. But he'd learned how to handle a camera and then gotten into video thanks to a friend's father who ran an electronics shop in the Bronx. He'd had a vague desire to become an artist ever since reading a book of poems by Stanley West, and so he'd moved downtown where he knew things were happening, even back in '78. Ever since, he'd been self-educating, reading two or three books a week, spending all his time with painters and photographers and want-to-be critics. He'd made a short film, all on video, about a glowing alien showing up in an apartment building on the Lower East Side and claiming to be an old woman's long-lost husband. "Silver paint and flashlights," he said. "Real cheap effects. But it was fun and Diego convinced Steve to play it at the Mudd Club on a Saturday night. That got me an offer to do a video for a band, and then another, and so on. But I want to do conceptual stuff, you know? Gallery work."

"I guess I've been wandering, myself," she said. "Trying to find my way." She was jittery, tired, and felt after last night and this morning that she knew him better than she did. That's why she ventured the remark, "I mean, that's why I haven't been all that good at dating."

He raised his eyebrows. "Oh, is this a date?"

"Well, I mean whatever. Talking to the opposite sex."

"Whoa," he said, leaning back in mock surrender. "Now we're talking about sex already. Slow down, lady."

In that perfect way waitresses time everything, theirs stopped to ask if they needed any more coffee. "Yeah," Diane said, and pushed her mug over. "Thanks." When the woman had moved on to the next table, she added, "Michael, I really like you. Is that terrible to say?"

"No," he said. "It's great."

As the day filled up out the window she told him about her grandfather's famous concept of "breathing life" in a picture, *Leben atmen*, how it had become her guiding principle. She'd read the short Bogdanovich book on von Stiegl by then and developed a confidence in talking about his work. Michael told her about ideas he had for new videos, a project he was thinking through, and it seemed to her that in no time they had become something like collaborators. Soon they had paid and were out on the sidewalk. In the natural light, standing next to him, he seemed unreal, dropped down out of the sky to fill an emptiness she'd ignored. She hated the idea of parting ways. "How about tonight?" she said.

"I've got a thing," he said, and by the way he slid his sunglasses on she recalled that he hadn't really said, as she had, that he liked her, that this had been anything special. "But I'm free tomorrow."

She had absolutely nothing to do tomorrow. Nothing. But some mean part of her rose up and said that she did, that tomorrow wouldn't work at all, and even as the words came out she wanted to stop them. "Maybe we can all meet up this weekend."

All, as in she and her friends and he and his friends, at some neutral location, like children, like flirting teenagers. She left wanting to kick herself and as soon as she was back at the apartment, she pulled all the curtains closed and slid under her bedcovers. She hummed that Streisand song "Memory" into her mattress and tried not to think about her disappeared mother or about her own brain doing things she didn't want or about the vast quiet and horror of space or about Phil, who'd gotten sick right here, not twenty feet away, sick until he couldn't stay here, until he had to go to the hospital, and about how quickly he'd gone, erased from the world, taken away with all his dreams and gripes, his little habits, his burned toast with extra butter, his fancy Russian teapot, his *Dynasty* parties, and then she tried not to think of what Bradley had said to her, that she'd used Phil somehow, cashed in, and she hummed the song and when she woke it was dark night and the couple upstairs was arguing and the woman below was listening to "Arthur's Theme," cornball but still able to squeeze Diane's heart, and she called Michael and said that she canceled the thing tomorrow and then that no, she was lying, she had nothing tomorrow, she'd been afraid and now she wasn't and so she wanted to see him, tomorrow, if he was still up for it. And then she said, "I'm free anytime."

Handwritten note, summer of 1949

Klaus—
Dropped by this afternoon and no one was home. Thought we were supposed to swim and get dinner. Walter says maybe you forgot. You're leaving for NYC next week? If we don't see Percy before you drop him at school tell him his uncles miss him and to wire if he needs anything.
Wanted to tell you about the CBS thing we were talking about. Television? Like I said they're looking for people who know where to aim a camera. The man you want to call is Jim Stonefield, vice president of something, MU 5-9975. I already put in a good word. Seems like something better to do than twiddle your thumbs into the grave.
Cheers and hugs and kisses,
George W

KLAUS

1952

VISITING CONGRESS, GOING before the House Un-American Activities Committee, being on live television rather than behind the camera: none of that had been planned. He and Olive had still been in New York, packing for California since the television season ended, when the phone call had rung through, an aide to some congressman from Idaho, asking if Klaus would be a friendly witness or not. A friendly witness to what? Well, the squeaky-voiced aide had explained, a friendly witness on the subject of communist subversion in the TV industry. Did he know communists? Socialists? Working currently on the *CBS Sunday Theatre Program*? Or in any capacity? He couldn't be certain. He'd hung up the phone after telling the aide he would call back, and when he explained the conversation to Olive, who was filling a small trunk with shoes, she had looked up at him from the carpeted floor and said, "If you don't go, they'll smear you. And if you don't talk, they'll burn you at the stake."

Unlikely, he'd wanted to say. He was a Republican. Why, he'd only last week made an example of that Pomeroy fool, so-called playwright and author of the *Sunday Theatre* script "Mercy on 125th Street," a pinko teleplay if he'd ever set eyes on one. Klaus had taken the script right up to Ken Barker, the show's producer. Twelve minutes were cut, replaced by scenes with a new banker character who helped out the old Black woman at the center of the tragedy and showed the commonsense grace of our enlightened business leaders.

Pomeroy had stomped off, announced he quit, that he'd never work for CBS again, et cetera ad infinitum, and that's who Klaus had thought of up on the stand. "There are certain troublemakers," he'd said, leaning a bit too close to the microphone, drawling out his German accent. "Agitators, I would say. Idealists. They believe the function of television is to educate the masses about certain political concepts, viewpoints. They may mean well. They may be patriotic. But it is unnatural in our medium, gentlemen. It doesn't fit. Take this Jimmy Pomeroy—"

———————

THAT'S WHY THE name Marjorie Pomeroy—scrawled in the upper-left corner of an Express Mail envelope in the stack of mail waiting for them in Palm Springs—sent a shock through his nerves, made him slip the letter into his jacket before Olive could see it. Whatever waited inside couldn't be good news, after all.

Marjorie Pomeroy. A wife? Sneaking another glance at it after dropping his bag on the sofa, he saw that this Pomeroy's address was in Bakersfield, California. But Jimmy Pomeroy, unless he'd moved cross-country by jet plane, lived in New York, where the *Sunday Theatre Program* and nearly everything else on TV was shot and broadcast live to the country. In the kitchen, as Olive shouted something about dinner plans down the hall, he tore open the envelope, unfolded the letter in the bright shaft of light at the sink, and read:

Dear Klaus,

You likely don't remember me but I remember you. I know you. And you're lousy through-and-through. A real piece of work. How you could get up there and say those things about Jimmy, well, I don't understand. But when I saw you with your fake monocle and your oiled mustache and your cane (did you ever need a cane?) I knew that whatever came from your mouth would be a lie. I just can't believe it was about poor sweet Jimmy (my brother-in-law if you need to know).

*Anyway you LIED about him. He's a good Christian boy. An
American. Fought in the WAR though you didn't, did you? I
mean whose side were you even on there? Must have been a
tough—*

He paused, gazed out the window at the desert, at the Spanish-
tile roof of the Rubensteins' place, the great palm tree beyond. Who
in the living hell was this, writing to him like he was a well-known
public nuisance? He looked at the name again. Marjorie Pomeroy?
Little Jimmy's sister-in-law, writing to give Klaus a piece of her mind.
He skipped to the next paragraph.

*But what I wanted to tell you, you glorified S.O.B., is that
you have been a backstabber from the beginning. I got you
that job at Astoria and you may as well have spit in my face.
And Kay—what you did to Kay should have put you in jail.*

Kay? Kay Stone? The actress?

*You backstabbed her and me and half a dozen others at
least. I think that's what HUAC needs to hear about. CBS,
too. That Edward R. Murrow could do a whole program on
your sins, you bag of filth. Everything about you is a lie and
you know it and that's why—*

He crumpled the letter in his fist. He wouldn't entertain this sort
of defamation, this hateful invasion of his privacy, this complete nonsense from some aggrieved woman he didn't remember at all. She
likely didn't know Kay Stone from Helen Keller. Maybe she'd seen
one of her old pictures on a Saturday morning. Though that detail
about getting him "that job at Astoria" was maybe a little troubling.
It didn't matter. He tossed the balled-up letter in the trash.
Three days later, another came. This one featured even more
coarse language, the threats about Murrow and CBS and telling the

world "about the real Klaus von Stupid" even more detailed. This letter Klaus folded neatly and placed in his desk drawer. In case he needed to send it to his lawyer, he thought.

Only a day or two later a third one arrived—this one inviting him to Bakersfield to "talk it out."

> *I get the feeling you don't remember me. Kay told me once you don't remember anyone who isn't of use to you. She must have felt that way the day she came to your house.*

That last bit cinched it. No lawyer, no Olive, just Klaus. No need to widen the circle of this defamation. He would listen to what she had to say and he would put a stop to whatever this was meant to be. That afternoon, when Olive was out shopping, he wrote his blackmailer back:

> *Dear Mrs. Pomeroy,*
> *I received your letters of the last week and a half. While I strongly disagree with their tone and intention, I would look forward to discussing their contents in person. I will meet you at your address on the 3rd of this month at 2pm. Please make an effort to be present at that time. If you cannot, then I will plan to turn over your letters to my family lawyer and be done with it.*
>
> > *Sincerely,*
> > *Klaus von Stiegl*

——————

A DAY OR two after sending this missive, Percy called long-distance, the charges reversed. "I'll accept," Klaus told the operator.

The boy immediately started talking. "I gotta talk to you, Dad. Mom wouldn't understand. I mean, this is serious, you know? I'm in trouble here. Real trouble."

Klaus wasn't sure the operator had even rung off. "Slow down," he said. "What's going on?"

"It's a girl," Percy said. "I guess I should say *we're* in trouble."

The boy would finish an English degree at Yale later that year—hopefully, and with grades that foretold a career in janitorial work—and the name of the young woman he'd gotten in this trouble was Sally, whom he had promised to marry before changing his mind, a circumstance that had forced the news of the impending child, which further created a need for this Sally to "go away for a while," at the end of which time the problem had been resolved to no one's satisfaction and then the relationship had fallen back apart again.

"Jesus," Klaus said.

"You're telling me," Percy said, nearly making light of the situation. "For a day or two there I thought it was the end of my life. I'd be married and have another mouth to feed. Scandal. Mom ready to kill me. You're not going to tell Mom, are you?"

"If you want it just between us, then it is."

But really, Klaus could barely follow his son's story. The boy had learned a savvy and oblique way of talking about the products of sexual intercourse and ways certain doctors had of removing those products, which made it sound more like a jazz orchestra or baseball game than anything so sacred and salacious as human procreation. And the coldness, the carelessness—if Klaus really did understand him—seemed like a sort of pose, the kind of act young men put on for each other's benefit, something along the lines of a romantic tall tale in which the teller claims victory by capitalizing on his lover's outright defeat rather than pleasure.

"To be clear," Klaus said, "the child is no longer a consideration here?"

"No longer," Percy said. And then, for added clarity, "Not at all."

"And you don't love her? The girl?"

"I thought I did. Then things went sideways."

Klaus looked out at the pool, where Olive was sunning. "Sideways?"

"I met another girl," said Percy. "And you know the rest. It's been hell, trying to make everybody happy. And Sally needed money for the uh—" There was a pause on the line. "She needed money, so I gave her everything I had. Now I'm broke. I can't ask Mom, you see?"

Klaus had never been trusted in this way by Percy, not since the boy was a child, and though the position his son had put this poor girl in troubled him, he felt also a surge of pride in gaining his trust. Things between them had been cold for years, since an argument over dinner back during the War that had culminated, irrationally, with Percy shouting, "You're certainly not a Lazlo. You're just around so Mother isn't alone at cocktail parties."

Olive had gasped like a woman in regional theatre. "Percy, you be silent this instant," she'd said, and clutched Klaus's forearm as if she were about to fall out of her chair.

"I won't," Percy had said then, imperious and haughty, standing though Klaus couldn't remember him getting up from his chair. "He's only here for your money," he'd added, pointing at Klaus. "For Grandfather's money."

"You apologize, young man!" Olive had shouted.

But Percy had only rolled his eyes to the ceiling, huffed, and disappeared upstairs.

Now, eight years on, Klaus wondered if this wedge between them had been loosed. "How much do you need?" he asked.

"I gave her eight hundred. More than the procedure, but you know, she needed a little something for a vacation, to take it easy?"

"I could imagine so," Klaus said, but trying, he really couldn't. "So eight hundred, then?"

"To tell the truth, a round thousand would be best. I was already pretty tight."

Giving the boy a thousand dollars, on top of Olive's regular monthly allowance, felt both morally repugnant and emotionally necessary. And so Klaus told him he would wire the money by Western Union. "You'll have to come to the studio next time we're in New

York," Klaus told him. "I tell you, I'm enjoying this television business a great deal, whatever the society-types have to say about it."

"That's swell, Dad," Percy said, though it was clear his mind was already elsewhere. "My buddy Richard has a set. Maybe I'll watch the *Sunday Theatre* over there."

KLAUS SAT IN the car watching the white box house for some time, his thoughts wandering from Cottingham and the strife at hand to where he and Olive had gone wrong with Percy. Had they given him too much? Had they led him to believe in his own privilege, that the world was centered on him? If only they had lived a more humble life like the one here, in this cracker box of a house with its untended shrubs and dying rosebush, its two out-of-style Chevrolets parked outside. As a child on the Lower East Side, poor as dirt and hopeless about his way out, Klaus couldn't have imagined a home like this, its promise of quiet and safety, its green expanse of lawn.

He stepped from the car feeling weak and assailed, more tired than he should be at this time of day. The feeling, he realized, was one of guilt, of things catching up to him. He was a man who made television, no one important, having a bad day, a bad week, looking now at a life he hadn't observed from the proper angle, a life he had never seen with clarity. How long had he thought the story of Kay Stone was no longer part of his story? He'd made such a habit of running from things. Even in Washington, he had taken the easiest way out of what could have only been a slight inconvenience. He didn't need the work. CBS could fire him and label him a communist agent, and he would have returned to Palm Springs, put on his swim trunks, and maybe gotten around to reading Proust. His life with Olive had been a reprieve, a vacation; he dangled over no fiery pit.

He'd only reached the short cement porch when the front door opened and a bald man Klaus's age emerged, tall and lanky, his tie loosened, his shirt untucked. Behind him the noise of a television, an old movie, the voice of Myrna Loy. "No solicitors, fella," said the man. "Didn't you read the sign?"

"I'm here to see Marjorie Pomeroy. Does she live here?"

The man troubled his eyebrows. "What's this about?"

"I'm Klaus von Stiegl. She has," he hesitated, "written me letters."

The man's eyes widened. His mouth fell open. "From the television," he said. "My brother. You—"

For a moment Klaus thought the man would strike him. But in the long, glaring pause between them, another voice rose up from inside. "Jack, is that Mr. Stiegl? I thought you were going back to work."

Jack Pomeroy didn't move from the doorway. "I was on my way out, and this," he said, looking with contempt at Klaus, "this *man* was on our porch."

Marjorie Pomeroy appeared at her husband's shoulder. Instantly, Klaus remembered her. Kay's friend from Greenwich Village, from Famous Players–Lasky, a bit actress who had never made it in Hollywood, a face he hadn't seen since sometime in 1928. A quarter of a century ago. Not even when she mentioned Kay in that letter had he thought of her. For a moment he couldn't breathe.

"Jack," she said again, her eyes on Klaus's. "I think you should go."

"I will not."

"If it's not a good time, Mrs. Pom—"

"This is the time we agreed upon, Mr. Stiegl," Marjorie Pomeroy said. Then, pushing past her husband, she added, "Come inside. Please."

It came out that Mr. Pomeroy owned a small hardware store nearby, had left a teenage employee in charge when he'd come home for a late lunch. He would make a call alerting this young man to his continued absence and thus be able to stay and interrogate Klaus with Marjorie. This he put into motion by walking into the kitchen, glaring all the while over his shoulder at Klaus, and picking up the phone.

On the television in the living room, one of the Thin Man movies played. Only a couple of years ago, it would have been exceedingly rare to find a television in any home at all. Now they were everywhere, even in this little matchbox of a house.

When Klaus could hear Jack Pomeroy on the phone, he wasted no time getting down to business. "You wanted to speak to me about something? Well, I'm here."

"Yes," she said. "You're here."

She looked older, yes, her blue dress hardly concealing a filled-out figure, her face a bit careworn by what he imagined would be grown children, her hair styled like Doris Day's. It was all a far stretch from her beanpole flapper look: more attractive, more respectable. She gestured toward the sofa as if he were here to watch a detective comedy. "No, thank you," he said, remaining near the door. "If we could address the topic of your letters?"

She looked at him as if she were reading fine print from across the room. "I really couldn't believe it was you," she said. "I had the television going with the sound up. I was putting a pot roast on in the kitchen. When they announced your name I thought it was some kind of joke. Wasn't that man dead already? But there you were, looking like a cartoon of some European count or other, an aged version of that silly little act you used to put on in the Village."

"That's quite enough," he said.

"Nobody's heard from Jimmy," she said, leveling her gaze at him. "You single-handedly ruined him for nothing. I knew it was you when I saw you. But when you opened your mouth, when you went after Jack's little brother like that, well, I knew it was *really* you. Only Klaus, I thought. Only he could do this. Just like you did with Kay."

"Let's leave that aside. I didn't mean to hurt your brother-in-law. But I don't see the need to work with agitators who want to upend our society. That's not what art is for."

"Art?" She laughed, actually laughed. "That's what you think you're doing? Excuse me, Picasso. Jimmy isn't upending any society.

He wrote a play about Blacks and whites and how to make things better. I read it. It's good. Better than the drivel on your program."

It was at that moment that Jack Pomeroy came from the kitchen. "Where's Jimmy?" he said without segue. "What are you doing in my home without hand-delivering my brother? He's a married man with two kids, you cockeyed bastard. His wife hasn't seen him in a week. I want you to tell us why you lied about Jimmy up there, and then I want you out of my house."

All of it was so absurd: Klaus stooped to this level, this Spam-breathed shop owner threatening him, a forgotten woman from the '20s staring at him as if she were about to spit in his face, the goofy murder mystery about to be solved by a jovial drunk. How he hated the talkies. "Sir, I'm here to respond to your wife's flaccid attempts at blackmail."

"Flaccid?" said Jack Pomeroy.

"Blackmail?" said his wife.

"These threats against my character and livelihood."

Pomeroy looked as if he'd finally readied himself to sock him. "Not another word," he said. But then his whole body went slack. He dropped into a wingback chair at his wife's side and covered his face with his hands. "Why'd it have to be Jimmy? What did he ever—"

Marjorie Pomeroy turned down the television and sat in the remaining wingback. "I want you to understand that you were used, Klaus. You ruined a young man's life to serve an evil man's purpose. Cottingham is an old America-Firster. Hated Roosevelt, called him 'Jewsevelt.' Before he was in Congress he was a dues-paying member of the Klan. Jimmy wants to change the world. To make it a better place. But he's not a communist.

"When I saw you on television telling your lies, saving your own pampered skin, I knew it was you not just because of the name and voice and the look of you. I knew it was you because this is who you've always been. After that picture of yours was shut down, you gave the same performance to the Hollywood press. You wrecked everyone but yourself. Even badmouthing your cousin's acting. And him in a wheelchair. But worst of all what you did to Kay." She stared at the television a moment. The credits had rolled on the Thin Man movie and now a man in a lab coat was extolling the cleaning power of some product called Glee, to the astonishment of an overdressed housewife. "I don't know how you live with yourself after Kay."

He thought of Kay at the door almost twenty years ago. The strain in her voice. "But I didn't do anything to Kay," he said, though he knew this to be false. "I didn't have any way to help her."

"She called me that day," she said, ignoring him. "Called me from a pay phone in Palm Springs. Said that if you wouldn't help her, she had no more reason to live. I tried to talk her down but she just hung up. I had the operator return the call and it just rang and rang. I spent the whole day waiting to hear from her, driving around Los Angeles anywhere she usually went, dropping by our little cottage every hour thinking she could be there now, she could be there now. But she wasn't there and she didn't turn up the next day and you know what happened, 'Mr. von Stiegl,' you know some sightseers found her body crumpled under the sign on the third day, already stinking, flies all over her. Dead, Klaus. Now, that's someone *you* killed. How about that?"

"I didn't have any pull with the studios," he began. "A man doesn't have to open his pockets to just anyone—"

She turned dramatically as if she were going to show him some evidence, but only shut off the television. Suddenly the room felt even more tense, the air even harder to breathe. "Remember how I got you your first job? Called up my boyfriend and told him to hire you. And never a word of thanks. Not one. You left me behind when you all went west. Like you never met me."

She spoke of this as if it were calculated, as if he weren't focused on his career, as if she had been the center of the story all along. And looking around this meek house he knew she was right. He'd done anything and everything for his own sake and no one else. He threw up his hands, doing his best to mount a defense. "What am I supposed to do?"

The woman was in tears. "All you ever do," she said, "is tank everyone's life and fall back on your wife's money. Just go. Go back to your ivory tower. Your—what's it called?—your Xanadu."

Even here, this seemed like a low blow. "I don't know what you people want from me."

Klaus sat there on the sofa, completely immobile, feeling cold all over. There was nothing he could say and nothing he would say. He couldn't answer to these things. The room radiated the kind of silence where new religions are formed, where men go raving mad, where visions overtake the sensible world.

She wiped her eyes, cleared her throat. "I want you to take back what you said about Jimmy. I want you to find him."

Then another long silence followed.

Jack Pomeroy broke through this as he gathered his wife in his long arms. "I think that's enough, sweetie. I think Mr. von Stiegl is going to leave now."

"Yes," Klaus said, but for a moment he couldn't push his body up off the sofa. The husband glared at the wall across the room with his eyes electrified, rocking his wife very softly back and forth. Klaus listened to her sniffling and to Jack Pomeroy's comforting mumble, and when he saw on the starburst clock over the television that three o'clock neared, he stood as if it were nothing at all, no special feat against gravity or sentiment, and said, "I should be going."

His legs moved under him like the Mummy's, or Frankenstein's monster, and his mind went absurdly over to Artie, who he'd thought must have worked on those monster-movie scripts at Universal. But likely he hadn't. Likely, Artie's career had been in tatters during those early sound years. Klaus hadn't bothered calling, hadn't checked on him. He'd betrayed him, betrayed Kay, betrayed Marjorie. Even betrayed George. And he'd gone along, just as Marjorie said, drinking in the wealth and ease of life with Olive.

At the door, Jack Pomeroy surprised him, reaching past Klaus, grabbing the knob, uttering some instantly forgotten pleasantry. He'd left Marjorie seated, facing the empty television screen.

"Thank you," Klaus discovered himself saying. "I'll find Jimmy for you."

Jack Pomeroy said, "You promise?"

ONLY A FEW months ago, the last time he and Olive had been home in Palm Springs, he'd met an up-and-coming actor, a handsome-enough fellow to ride a horse next to a picture's star or play someone's husband in a comedy, a local guy who because of his handful of Hollywood roles had become a kind of celebrity at the golf club, a favorite son. He owned property and was looking to buy more, over shrimp cocktails in the clubhouse had given Klaus a whole spiel about becoming "an investor in the most beautiful city in America," had given him his card. Frank Harlan was his name. A friend of a husband of one of Olive's friends. Olive had liked the idea. "He seems pretty straight-and-narrow," she'd said that evening on the ride home. "And Lord knows people want to get out of L.A. Everywhere's growing these days, you know."

Klaus had thought a dozen times of calling him. As manager of Olive's money—she always claimed to have no interest in it "as long as it draws interest"—the scheme had actually sounded like a solid one, and Klaus had figured that a sizable investment, a partnership with this rather shallow-seeming actor, would bring a substantial return. But now, making his slow exit, Klaus envisioned another plan—one not altogether honest but one that would at least solve the dilemma before him: he would write in the ledger that he'd invested two hundred thousand in the Harlan scheme but give Harlan only one hundred thousand. The other half would go to the Pomeroys: to help Jimmy and his family, as well as Marjorie and hers. Split however they chose, it would mean a fortune. A windfall. He would change all their lives for the better. He would clean up the mess he'd caused in Washington and, so many years before, in Palm Springs. He could do that. He was Klaus von Stiegl. He still had the power to do almost anything.

THE VERY NEXT day Klaus learned that Percy had also touched Olive for a large sum of money, not to pay for an abortion but to make an investment in his friend's "new idea for a competitive checkers league" that he'd assured his mother could make them all rich.

"Doubtless the entire concept is nonsense," Olive told Klaus over dinner. "I'm positive he had some other use for the money. He's alone out there with all these new friends."

"Indeed," Klaus said, feeling suddenly quite weak. "Likely wanted a new suit or something."

"Not that I appreciate being lied to, but competitive checkers was a comical enough idea. You have to give him that." She laughed. "But beyond this I really think he needs to make his own way. The allowance is enough, don't you think?"

She stood in a bright shaft of light at their bedroom window, her eyes squinted, peeling silk gloves from her hands: his glowing and all-too-patient wife. "Yes," he told her. He was sure then, without doubt, that Percy had lied to him; there had been no Sally, no unwanted pregnancy, no secret bond. He'd been duped. "It's quite enough for any man his age."

Then his thoughts traveled to Jimmy Pomeroy, a misguided young man, certainly, but a driven one like Klaus had been, the type who grabs the world by the lapels, demands his opportunity to succeed, doesn't stalk about with his hat in his hand expecting a free lunch. Percy would never sacrifice anything for gain, would perhaps never work a day in his life. Somewhere along the line Klaus had failed with the boy. A heavy tiredness fell over him.

"Imagine," Olive said with a bright and hilarious voice, as if telling a joke at a cocktail party. "Competitive checkers! It's almost insulting."

"Yes," he said again. And then he tried his best to execute a convincing laugh.

Oct. 13, 1958

Mother dearest,

I write with splendid news about the girl
of my dreams. Her name is Antonia and we're
going to marry. I've asked for her hand and she
accepted. I wanted to write or call to tell you
about her earlier this summer when we first met
but life has been so busy, spending every hour
away from this dull job (I am writing on one
of Mr. Smithson's typewriters now) with her,
my Antonia—hehe! just like the book—and when I
realized that I wanted to spend the rest of my
life with her I couldn't wait to ask after your
opinion before making it concrete between us.
She will be my wife and I her husband in little
over two weeks.

There's no need to come to Chicago. Our
ceremony will be the simplest imaginable: a
justice of the peace, whatever papers need to
be signed, my pal Nick as the witness. But we
would like to go on a honeymoon and I hoped
that you could help. In fact, I would greatly
look forward to a part of that honeymoon
including a visit to P.S., to see you and
father, to present to you this most wonderful
of all women, my princess, my only love. I had
hoped to show her more of California as well
(she is from a middling family in the mountain
west, daughter of a schoolteacher and small
bank executive), perhaps San Francisco and the
old family property (from afar of course) and
down through L.A. and then over to P.S. and
finally to Rancho Lazlo, where spending a week
or two would mean the world.

Of course we will be ready to set up
our lives soon after. I would be endlessly
appreciative if some of Grandfather's funds
could aid in our relocation and homebuying, as
it has long been time to quit this busywork and

return to the life of a proper Lazlo, and more
than that to be nearby, perhaps even in P.S.,
or really wherever you would want us.

I have included a photograph I'm sure you
have already gazed upon: she is a beauty beyond
words as you can see. Somehow her glow nearly
makes this haggard loan officer's assistant
look nearly handsome.

                              With all my love,
                                        Percy

                                   Oct. 22, 1958
Dear Percy,

Imagine my dismay at receiving your letter
of a little over a week ago. If you cannot
imagine, I will explain the various aspects
of that dismay so that it will be understood.
First, my son, my only child, informs me of a
marriage so impending in its nature that he may
not receive my response before the ink is dry
on its license. Second, this message—already
such a shock as to send any woman of lesser
fortitude to the hospital or an early grave—
moves on swiftly to shaking the tin cup, begging
again for unearned money so that a celebratory
vacation may be paid for by parents who are
absolute strangers to this mysteriously-named
Antonia, who may as well be a Mexican housemaid
as a schoolteacher's daughter. Third—when the
shock of your letter up to this point hasn't
fully resonated—a further request is made for
untold sums of money from "Grandfather's funds,"
a term unfamiliar to me in both family life and
business, and certainly not an account easily
drawn from to begin a life of ease and plenty
without consequence or labor, as your letter
implies.

In answer, no. Your father and I will not be
funding any such "honeymoon" or relocation or

whatever you believe yourself to be asking for.
You may speak to us as an adult—a man of nearly
thirty years, after all—or keep to yourself.
I look forward to hearing from you in a more
respectful tone.

                                    Your mother,
                                 Olive von Stiegl

                                    Oct. 29, 1958
Mother,
     You and I both know the last thing I would
want to do is to cause family strife or to
offend you, specifically, as no other person on
earth has done more to ensure my success in life
and prepare me for this momentous situation.
But I, too, am aghast—not only at your refusal
to help us with money you most certainly have
at your fingertips (the inheritance from
Grandfather, as well as the value of PG&E stock,
are public knowledge), but at your disappointing
and judgmental remarks about my character. To
tell the truth I'm appalled.
     You and I both know that "Father" was never
and could never be a Lazlo. Grandfather said as
much twenty years ago. Or don't you remember
those weeks in San Francisco, when we ran
to the open arms of the family who has made
"Father's" life such a cushion all these years?
You had sobbed in the car all the way up the
coast and told Grandmother and Grandfather
that you intended to leave him and they had—
remember this?—said that he'd been nothing but
a freeloader, too lazy to hold a job, a failure
at the one thing he ever put any work into,
and they had never wanted you to marry him.
And he has proved their theory of him, doing
very little for most of my life, living in a
cushioned state unworthy of the money you have
so liberally fed him.

As a youth during our time in Mexico,
I watched that man leech off of you, only
occasionally working, never once a credit
to his race, with only this late dallying in
television to show for himself in spite of all
that you've given him. While I've taken common
jobs and waited, lest the rent check bounce,
for your "allowance." It should be me taking it
easy, Mother. In the last five years I've done
more work than "von" Stiegl has done in his
lifetime . . .
   Antonia and I will be married, we will start
our family, and maybe someday in the near
future we will all speak again. For now I have
no interest in doing so. My soul aches that
you could treat me in this way, as if I meant
nothing at all to you. I wish you both the
best. Goodbye,

                                        —Percy

                                   Nov. 5, 1958
Percy,
   "His race?" Exactly how dare you communicate
in such a way to me? I would greatly suggest
letting your bruised feelings heal before
writing again.
   Your father is a man you may never
understand, not really, not with your current
outlook. The artist seeks and risks everything
for a dream that is both unattainable and the
most necessary product of our time here on
Earth. That he has been given space and time to
do this work should be seen as a plus and not a
minus. He is a man of great vision and insight.
It would behoove you to attempt some of either
of these qualities. That he is your father,
that he is my husband, should be seen as all
that is necessary to know about the economics
of "Grandfather's funds."

Forgive my meanness on this subject, Pers. But you are tracking the wrong rabbit if you believe this is the moral and decent way to achieve your goals.

                                                   —Mother

                                              Dec. 20, 1958

Mother,

I have considered your last letter for some weeks now and I have no response but to again emphasize the great feeling of betrayal which now defines my everyday experience. Happiest of holidays in spite of what has transpired between us. I hope that you will eventually see the light when it comes to the support of your son, his wife, and the grandchildren soon to come.

                                                   —Percy

DIANE

1983

THEY WERE GOING to stop, my God. They were absolutely
going to stop. Here they were, rattled, actually shaking, on the
side of the highway with Diane's new car—why the hell did she
ever buy a car?—flipped in the grass, the hood sticking through a
barbed-wire fence, a weak curl of smoke seeping from the engine.
Cars racing past.

It was the middle of the day. They'd been on the way to Martha's Vineyard, invited by Leon Daphine, the collector, whom Diane
had met at her show at Leo Castelli's gallery last month. Leon had
bought three large paintings and one she hadn't finished, which he'd
come to inspect at the apartment, and that day he'd offered to help
get Michael's video work, *Black Material*, into a gallery and also offered as a sort of artist's residency an off-season stay at his summer
home on Martha's Vineyard.

Diane couldn't get her breathing under control. She tried sucking
and punching air between her cupped hands. Michael held her by
the shoulders, looking like someone out of a Jason movie waiting
for a machete to split his skull. He was bleeding, a dark gloss on his
forehead, dribbling past his eye, streaking his shirt. After a moment
he said, "Dump it out. Throw it in the grass."

He meant the coke. Some of it in her pocket. In a baggie. Because
of course the cops would come. The cops would come and see this

Black guy and his white girlfriend and the New York plates and they better not find the coke.

Diane took the baggie out of her pocket and disseminated the white powder into the green blades and dirt. As she kicked at the ground with the toe of her shoe she said, "We've got to stop. This is fucking serious. We've got to stop."

Michael loosened his hands from her shoulders and said, "Shit, there's more in our luggage."

He was right. In another baggie containing two baggies, tucked in a pair of white athletic socks with red stripes—Michael's—were two ounces, more than enough, certainly, to send them to jail. They hobbled over, holding hands in a vague way, as if neither of them had any grip, and crouched together at the driver's-side window, busted out, its frame smushed. The keys were still in the ignition. Michael reached a long arm in and pulled them out.

As soon as Michael turned the key in the trunk everything fell out in a huff. "It's in the big bag," Diane said, finding that she was freezing up, that she couldn't move at all. "In your socks with the red stripe."

Michael let go of her hand and shot her a perturbed look, with eyes that said she could pitch in. Then he knelt down and unzipped the beige leather bag (worn nearly white in spots; purchased at a used-goods shop) and dug around, coming out with every pair of socks but the right one. "I don't see them."

"Green," she said. "I mean the green ones."

He'd already tossed those in the grass, on that part of the grass with a bed of pebbles, the not-road not-grass that separated the highway from the chaos of nature. He grabbed up the socks, un-rolled them, and shook out the baggies of powder. She instinctively looked over her shoulder. Just cars. Faces forward. Hands knuckled over wheels. "Come on," he said.

———

AT FIRST THEY had kept separate apartments, had put on airs that they were so independent they needed their own space, that it was a decision adults made, civilized people made, intellectuals. But by January they were on the phone with each other for sometimes hours at a time and by February he was bringing over his editing equipment to work while she painted. By the end of that month, with Michael traveling to record music videos and Diane working nonstop on what would become the Castelli show, her big one-woman debut, her life-changer, it seemed irrational to live apart.

The coke, of course, was everywhere. Everyone had it. Well, not everyone. But enough people had it and Diane had money. Everyone called her Di by then, like the princess. At galleries and parties she moved in a new circle, hardly saw Lily, forgot to call Annie in California (even after her big promotion at the George West Gallery—"basically second in command," she'd said, "just behind Franklin"), almost never made it to Club 57 and failed to show when the Mudd Club closed. But she met Sherrie Levine and Julian Schnabel and Eric Fischl and the dealer Larry Gagosian. And mostly she'd worked. The year had been her year of work, a conscious decision, a New Year's resolution even. Everything had focused down to painting. To painting and meeting people and selling works. The coke was really the only way to socialize, the only way she could wind down, or wind up. That's how she and Michael talked about it. They weren't druggies; nothing was out of control.

In March she finished ten large paintings, an unheard-of number for her, each of them a mix of the techniques of photorealism and expressionism, a pastiche of images examining issues of power and gender and capital. Housewives stalked by their murderous husbands, dead-faced shoppers in a grocery store, AIDS patients posed like a class photo. Formally, she was unsure at times if her mix of styles came across as purposeful or indecisive—or even just messy, ugly, inarticulate: though collectors loved them. It was political art, that's what she'd told Mary Boone, who helped to sell three of the March paintings to collectors who came by while Diane was painting. Political art because the vast middle America had declared war on them, on her kind, on those she loved.

Michael had pushed her there, or rather, given her permission to go there. "This fucking cowboy is going to blow us all to hell anyway," he'd said when Diane told him she was worried about being seen as a 'message' painter. "If you can't say what you want to say then what's the point of any of it?" In April, ever more sure of herself, she painted twelve.

THE PAIN SET in soon after they turned from the car. Michael noticed it first, pointing his elbow around in a circle, stretching his neck from side to side. "Fuck," he said. And then his knees buckled a little. "Fuck my back is killing me."

As if waking from a numb dream, Diane realized pain was surging through her body in all directions. Her left knee barely functioned. A burning, heavy sensation resonated out from her right shoulder blade to her neck and spine. Her head felt like it had been hit with a brick. She stumbled to catch up to Michael, who was already at the fence peeling those socks apart, letting them fall into the rugged green field over the fence. When she reached him he tore open one of the baggies and snorted up a pinky-nail full. She did the same. Then they each wetted an index finger, dived it into the powder, and rubbed it into their upper and lower gums.

Michael reared back and launched the baggies deep into the field. They watched them arc, flash in the sun, and drop into anonymity. Only the faint rustle of grass could be heard. "Okay," he said. "That's it."

SHE HAD PAINTED Phil again in April, constructing a series of long, rectangular panels with a single black dividing line off-center and fencing the left from the right image: Phil shirtless on the fire escape in sunglasses next to a close-up of his arm attached to an IV drip; Phil making toast in his robe trying to ignore her camera next to the blotches on his sunken neck in the hospital; Phil reading Ezra

Pound on the sofa next to his thin, sick form at Rockaway Beach, where they'd gone as his last wish a week before he went into the hospital. But she also painted from the Polaroid of Lily, Geoff, and Bradley, blurring their faces by turning a sponge in the wet oil, creating Bacon-like masks. The uncanny faces in the low-lit room with all its close detail, its shadows, its half-unmade bed, looked like the scene of a nightmare. Michael was astounded, said it was like nothing else, said she wasn't allowed to sell it. So she began painting more of the same type of figures. She bought more sponges.

The Castelli show formed around three sets of works: the smushed faces, the Phil paintings, and the political allegories she'd worked on at the beginning of the year. It was that last group that gave the show its name, *Di Stiegl: Allegories of War*. By opening night nearly half the pieces were sold. Warhol came. Jean-Michel. Lily and Nero, too, and in her nervousness Diane found that she couldn't get too far from them. They hung out that evening as if they'd never drifted apart. Michael, who hardly knew them, clammed up as the others talked over one another. She lost track of him.

The remaining paintings sold. Collectors pressed their business cards and phone numbers upon her. Lily looked stunning in a shimmery black outfit, her hair cut short with a corner bleached blonde, a red sweatband above her brow. Nero wore a gray sports coat with the sleeves rolled up and leather pants, his hair combed and sprayed. They looked like adults with money, or kids playing at adulthood, as she felt herself to be. They sat together and talked about old times at Club 57 as if it weren't only last year, or was it two years ago, and only after the gallery cleared out did she see Michael talking animatedly to an attractive brunette in shoulder pads and a short skirt, offering her a little of the coke Diane could see, even across the room, in his pinky fingernail. The brunette wasn't interested; she laughed and sashayed out of the gallery. Diane didn't meet his gaze when he turned back in her direction.

They splurged on a cab. "Who was that girl?" she said. "The one you were talking to?"

"Elizabeth something," he said. And then, as she stared out the window, "I'm not going to sleep with her, if that's what you're thinking."

"I didn't say you were."

Blocks went by. A summer night in the city full of people in short clothes. She longed to open the window but the cabbie was running the air conditioner. "What kind of dude do you think I am?" Michael said. "Besides, your friends were ignoring me. That Nero guy thought I was a graffiti artist."

"He's an idiot."

"He's your ex." Michael huffed. "Surprised he didn't ask me if I knew Sidney Poitier."

"He's not that bad."

"Dude literally said 'Oh, like Michael Jackson' when I shook his hand."

They were laughing now, a team again. "Okay, he's pretty bad."

Upstairs they did a few lines and listened to the Chameleons and fucked on the sofa and when Michael came back from the bathroom, naked and holding his boxer shorts over his dick like he was trying to muffle it during a kidnapping, she had already cut two more lines and wrapped herself in a blanket. Looking at his trim form she said, "We should get married."

His mouth opened; his pace slowed. "You're kidding?"

"Maybe," she said, and really she hadn't given it much thought until this moment, the idea taking form in a rapid montage of images: a white dress, a home, kids in the yard. But they wouldn't do it that way. They wouldn't turn into suburban parents. They would stay in the city; the only thing that would change would be the commitment. "Maybe not."

He pulled on his boxers and dropped in next to her, reached for the framed picture of John Lennon they used to make lines. She watched him snort one up with half an ink pen's tube. "Yeah," he said. "I'd do it. Not now. But in a little while. Soon."

She took the picture and tube from him. "Me too," she said.

TWO OFFICERS ARRIVED at once, a car from either direction. They wore reflective sunglasses and literally sauntered across the grass to Diane and Michael. One had the face of a fat man with a regular-sized body. The other had the build of a professional wrestler. The latter asked, "Let me guess. Bear in the road?"

Michael said, "Going too fast, officer. That curve was sharper than we thought."

"Uh-huh," said the fat-faced cop.

"You got a driver's license, fella?" asked the wrestler.

They both stared at Michael like they were squaring up with a loose tiger, only occasionally shooting Diane a glance. Time filled with an understood threat. After squinting at Michael's license for a long minute, the wrestler said, "And you were driving, Mr. French?"

"That's right," Michael said, though it wasn't true. Diane had no idea why he said it.

The officer fiddled with his pen. "Distracted?"

"Messing with the tape deck," Michael offered. "Didn't get enough sleep last night."

It went like that, a whole story of the event that had nothing to do with reality. She'd been at the wheel, wide-awake, "Total Eclipse of the Heart" playing on the stereo, and they'd been arguing about Elizabeth, the brunette he'd said months ago meant nothing to him, but with whom he'd started working on a mock music video project. Elizabeth had connections at a TV studio where they could produce cheap video effects like rolling Texas hills behind them or the canals of Venice or, for reasons Diane couldn't understand, a doctor's office. The mock music video would star Michael's alter-ego, Clay Cassius, who'd appeared in his video *Black Material* as a sort of bumbling nerd, tape on his glasses and all, walking into rooms full of white people to impress them by talking about "white" things: opera, golf, Wall Street. Michael had played it at a house party of mostly white guests and it had gotten a lot of laughs, but afterward no one seemed to want to talk about what it meant. They were, Michael said later, "too uncomfortable in their own skin, too chicken."

Diane made no excuses for them: they were chicken. A part of being white was finding ways to never have to talk about it. A knowing laugh, sure, a pose of hipness. But more than that would be too much.

Michael hadn't lost a beat, though. Went right into conceiving the next adventure of Clay Cassius. At some point, without his even telling Diane, this Elizabeth something had become a central part of it, his partner. That's why they were arguing. That's why she had been driving too fast. That's why she was looking at him instead of the curving road. "Just tell me you're fucking her!" she had yelled. "Just have the guts to—"

And now he was making up this story about him driving and she couldn't understand why. "This is all about your parents," he'd said when the argument began. "They abandoned you and you think I'll abandon you. It's not like that. I'm not going anywhere."

Now, here, the fat-faced cop said, "We'll give you a ride in to the service station. They can send a tow truck in the meantime."

There would be a citation, of course. "Nothing too heavy," said the wrestler. "And Jim at the service station rents a few cars if you want to finish your trip."

In the back of the cop car, with their bags wedged in the trunk between a spare tire and a shotgun, Diane kept thinking about Michael saying her parents had abandoned her. They'd done no such thing. Antonia was sick. Percy was a grifter. Any feelings bound up with who they were were *her* feelings. Nobody else got to call it abandonment. Crossing through an unfamiliar intersection, knowing they looked like a pair of criminals on the way to lockup, she said to him, "I'm mad at you."

"Surprise, surprise," he said.

———

SHE HAD GONE out to the Bronx with him in July to meet his family. His father greeted them at the door of their walk-up, a white-haired, white-mustached man with a stoop dressed in slacks and a thin button-up with no undershirt. He appeared to already be smiling before the door even opened. Diane got the feeling he wasn't comfortable. Michael's mother came from the hallway stretching her face, doing her best. "Our Mickey's said so much about you."

"It's Michael, Mom."

A look at him that seemed more tired than anything. "Forgive me," she said to Diane, reaching out for both her hands. "I mean Michael of course."

"We called him that when he was a boy, you see," said Mr. French. He shook his head to gather a little comedy. "His mother's just over-excited."

Dinner was served in a dining room not much bigger than a roadside diner's booth. Closed in by flowery-wallpapered walls, Diane had made the mistake of shoveling her fork into mashed potatoes before Michael's sister came clumping down the stairs, singsonging his name like something out of an old horror movie. Both parents glanced up, brows wrinkled, measuring something Diane couldn't discern.

The sister, Nina, was heavyset and pretty, with a smart look in her eye that said she already had Diane's number. Diane felt herself wilt in Nina's presence, the tight knowingness of her smile too much for her to bear. "This the artiste?" she said as she pulled back a chair.

Michael cleared his throat. "This is Di. Di, this is Nina."

"Michael's said a lot about you," Diane said, though that wasn't altogether true.

Nina raised an eyebrow. "Di? So you're like the princess?"

"Don't listen to her," Michael said. "She's just like that."

"Like what?" Nina said.

"You two," warned Mrs. French.

"No, I want to know," said Nina. "What am I like, Mickey?"

"Always making trouble when you're not getting all the attention."

Nina laughed theatrically, clapped her hands once, and left them together like she was about to pray. "You bringing a princess in here and saying I want attention. I've got news for you — "

"No, you don't," said Mrs. French. "Now, that's enough."

Mr. French speared a green bean with his fork and pointed it at Diane. "What sort of things do you paint, Ms. Stiegl?"

Somehow things didn't completely unravel. Everyone was uncomfortable, sure, and Nina kept trying to stir the pot, but they got through it, even had cake in the living room as Mr. French messed with the rabbit ears, trying to clean up the signal from a UHF channel playing an old John Wayne movie. It struck Diane at some point just as everything eased into congeniality that she had never been in a room where she was the only white person, had never spent time with a Black family at all. Everything she and Michael had talked about regarding race and segregation and the power afforded those whites who ignored and upheld the social structure seemed like just a warm-up act. The discomfort she'd felt, the disagreeable pressure they could all wander back to at any moment here, despite their cake and friendly conversation, seemed to her suddenly *political*. This was being done to them. To everyone. Later, on the train back to Manhattan, she explained this to Michael like she'd come down the mountain with the word of God on a stone tablet, but he just nodded, and she realized he'd been reading that tablet all his life.

Before they left, Nina invited Diane upstairs to see her room. "Don't worry," she said. "I ain't going to kill you."

Diane had trudged up the carpeted stairs just behind Michael's sister, watching below as Mrs. French and Michael quietly conferred out of her hearing, a worried look in Mrs. French's eye.

In Nina's room, Diane couldn't miss why she'd been brought up here. One of her paintings, of Michael standing in sweatpants, no shoes or shirt, his face smushed and twisted, but everything else as photographic as possible, hung over Nina's bed. Diane hadn't even noticed it missing, and for an instant she was angry that Michael had taken it, nearly said something she would have regretted, but for Nina saying with all the pride in the world, "I love it. I just wanted you to see where I put it. Sorry about the mess in here. Mom and Dad don't know it's yours yet. This is just the best birthday present of all time."

"You told me I could give it to her," Michael said on the train when Diane asked about it. "Two weeks ago. I said, 'My sis would love this one Di,' and you said, 'Give it to her.'"

She vaguely recalled a conversation like that, but as with a lot of inconsequential things lately, the memory lay out of her grasp. Anyway, she said, she was happy one of her paintings would stay in the family. "I'll paint another," she said. And later, after the Castelli show, she said, "When we go to Martha's Vineyard you'll be my only subject."

WITHIN A COUPLE of hours they were on the road again, Diane's car behind them at an auto-body shop in Groton. They had no tapes and didn't want to fool with the radio, so they listened to the noise of the highway. Diane felt hard and cold, and later, realized she desperately needed to sleep; she was coming down, getting that itchy feeling for more, and her earlier anger weakened into something closer to depression. Only when she saw the sign for the Martha's Vineyard ferry did she work up the will to talk. "I'm sorry," she said. "I don't know what's got into me."

"Same here," he said, and reached for her leg, squeezing it reassuringly. "I don't want to fuck this up.".

"We'll relax here," she said. "Start everything over. And when we get back we'll stay off the powder."

THAT FIRST NIGHT, on the island, was sleepless pain, sweating together in the dark, their legs shaking, finally laughing at themselves for the wreck of their bodies, chemically a shambles, so grumpy and bone-ridden that it hurt to hold each other. They went out on Leon's porch to watch the sun rise in a yellow whisper. "Why did you say you were driving?" she asked.

"Because you already have tickets."

"I do?"

He reminded her: speeding, bumping a light pole with her fender, two parking violations. She really was forgetting things, or determining they didn't matter. But he didn't judge her. "I'm doing the same," he said. "Forgetting things. Elizabeth just the other day—"

"I don't want to talk about her," she said. "Not here."

"Di, it's nothing. You've got it all wrong."

She squeezed his shoulder and it was like her hand had been possessed by a one-hundred year-old woman. "I know," she said. "But let's not talk about her."

He shrugged, looked out at the sun. "Anyway we stopped the coke. That was it. I'm sick of it."

"Me too," she said. "I feel the worst I've ever felt in my life."

After a few minutes she said, "I'm jealous of your family. They're all well-adjusted people, you know?"

Michael laughed and squeezed her hand. "If you say so."

"I ever tell you how my grandpa tried to set fire to his studio before he died?"

"Nah," Michael said. "He had cancer?"

She wasn't sure why she was on the subject. "It's like he wanted to erase himself before he went. Get rid of whatever he could. At least, that's how I understood it."

Michael considered this a while before offering, "That's fucked up."

"I think I want to talk to my dad again," she said. "Sometime."

That evening was a little less painful and sweaty, and they slept, and woke only with headaches, and dressed for the beach and went swimming until they had to come in to eat something. They napped on the porch. She painted. They talked into the night over a bottle of red wine Michael walked to the store to get. He told her about a woman he'd dated just before they'd met and how he'd been thinking about calling that woman up the night she and Lily had come to his apartment, how she'd left him a note under the door that morning, how really they would have eased back together, and then Diane had walked in the door and he'd seen her wide brown eyes and recognized her from that article and it had been like a sign from above, and now here they were. "Look at that," he said. "I mean, just look at that."

"It's something," she said.

The whole rest of the trip was ideal, full of sun and breeze and the tragic scent of fall sweeping in, and they talked again about getting married, the kind of couple they would be, each supporting the other, an art power couple, really, the kind of thing magazines and dealers would salivate over. They would never let it go to their heads. And they wouldn't be in it for the money. Just the art, the play of life, together.

But the story of that earlier woman prickled her, it dug in. If Michael could throw her aside just because Diane showed up, couldn't the same happen again—another woman walking in Michael's door? Their door? And if she woke up too early one morning and watched him from across the room, if she drew him from across the room, if she thought a little about her parents, if she thought of Phil, if she thought of leaving before he could leave her, if she thought she was losing her mind, if she thought everything in the world was perfect and beautiful, if she thought they were made to be together, then he would wake and they would swim again and nothing would ever change.

––––––––––

THE NIGHT THEY got back to New York, they had to go to Palladium. One of Michael's videos would be on display upstairs—not a Clay Cassius but an abstract music video made to the beat of one of Steve Reich's drum pieces. Diane called Lily and Nero and a bunch of others to meet them out there. They danced. They went upstairs and watched Michael's video as a group. Someone had coke. Diane saw it first. It would be fun, she thought. One last time. She did a bump and then thought she shouldn't tell Michael but then she did, and so he did one too. A little later a friend of Nero's said he could get them a few grams to take home and so they took him up on it and at the end of the night went back to the apartment with eight or nine others and they all stayed up, partying, listening to music, talking quick and loud and emotionally over one another until the night had wizened out entirely and a few left and then a few more and Diane tore open the baggie and rubbed her damp fingertip along the dusty plastic to catch whatever was left and rub it into her gums. She showed them all the charcoals she'd done on the island, sketches of Michael wading in the water, stirring a pot in the kitchen, lounging on the front porch. After sunrise they slept with pillows over their faces, Lily and Nero in the other room stretched together on a couch like they were at camp, foot to face, and when they all woke it was afternoon, New York City, 1983, nearly October, a minute or two closer to doomsday.

Harriman & Bialofsky Detective Agency
New York, NY

                              January 8th, 1953
Mr. Von Stiegl,
   On the 7th of January, approximately 10pm,
the individual (Mr. James Pomeroy) whom you
requested our agency locate and physically
return to his spouse was tracked to a one-
room apartment on West 57th near the corner
of 10th Avenue. The individual was found
to be inebriated and combative. A modicum
of force was used to remove him from the
premises. This force left some bruising around
the face and arms, and a fall was taken on
the stairs which left the individual with a
slight limp. After this latter mishap, the
individual did not resist my guidance to the
vehicle. The individual then slept off some
of his excitement as we traveled to the Bronx
location you gave us as the individual's
family home.
   Approximately at 11:30 on the 7th, the
individual was walked to the doorstep of
that location and the bell was rung. A woman
answering to the name of Mrs. Pomeroy then took
the individual into custody. She showed some
pleasure at the individual's return but did
not appreciate my presence. This woman also
became combative and insulting with my person
upon further examination of the inebriated
individual. By approximately 11:40 I had
left that location, considering my enterprise
complete.
   You will find attached a summation of payment
due which includes tailoring expenses produced

by the ripping of my overcoat by the woman who
answered to the name of Mrs. Pomeroy.
    Thank you and let me know if you are ever in
need of our services again.

Sincerely,
Stan Bialofsky

KLAUS

1965

CHROME GLINTED IN the Palm Springs sun. Percy, braking, tapped the horn in two quick beeps, as if Klaus weren't already standing on the patio in suit and tie, turning his hat over in his hands. The wife stared rigidly ahead through dark glasses, in the direction of the empty scrub desert, but the girl, Diane, pressed her face to the backseat window, her breath fogging the glass. Klaus walked around the back of the car—a long, brown box with a white top—and when he reached the other back door, the girl had followed him over to smash her face against its glass, to fog its window.

He wasn't in the mood for this sort of humor, but he leaned down anyway, gave her a knowing wink, and smiled what he hoped to be a grandfatherly smile. It wasn't a role he was used to. Percy lived in Chicago, and the only other time Klaus met his granddaughter she was two years old, a hellish child who seemed to run her parents' lives, crying and screaming for this or that, almost always getting it. The more pressing discovery during that visit had been Percy's wife, who had been exhibiting strange behavior, what had been described as "moodiness," something that had drawn more of Olive's concern than Klaus's own. *Why should they butt into the private lives of a married couple? Let her be moody. Let them raise their child like a cave-child.* But Olive had been worried, had given advice, had mentioned doctors, and over dinner the second night they were in town, the wife had told her all of a sudden to mind her own business.

"About what, my dear?" Olive had asked. "About me," the wife had said, and then dug into her mashed potatoes.

They didn't get along, Olive and Klaus and Percy and the wife. He knew her name: Antonia. A favorite book of the woman's mother. But around the house, Olive and Klaus only called her "the wife," and so even in her presence he had to work to call forward her name, and out of fear he would accidentally call her "the wife," in person he avoided trying to name her at all. Atop his worry of offending the wife by calling her such was mounted another worry: that Percy would see his mother's funeral as yet another opportunity to beg for money. And so Klaus had set himself that morning on refusing to entertain the subject when it inevitably came up.

Such is life, perhaps. One picks at one's scabs until one's injuries become a central feature. Who said that? He couldn't recall. Percy had been born with his hand out, waiting for what he believed himself entitled to: namely the old Lazlo fortune. Communication with him had grown disparate and tense, and recently there had been more silence than anything. The wife, her troubles, they frightened Klaus and Olive; endless and repeated arguments about money, about helping them out, had thickened the scab into a leathern mass.

"Let me in," he said to the girl, still trying to sound like he was having a good time. But Diane stuck out her tongue and shook her head. He tried again with the smile, but when this didn't work, he was out of patience. He tapped his knuckles on Percy's window. "It's locked," he shouted at the glass, and pointed back at the door.

Percy looked into his rearview mirror and said something muffled to the girl. With dramatic resignation, she reached over, unlocked the door where Klaus was waiting, and flopped back in the seat, farthest away from him, tightly crossing her arms. "Well," he said, sliding in. "How is everyone?"

He was surprised to realize the radio was playing. Rock-and-roll music. Neither of the adults reached to turn it down. "Doing better today," said Percy. "How's Chinese?"

Klaus nodded. "There's a new place on—"

"We saw it last night," said Antonia.

He felt as if he'd said something he shouldn't. Apparently, no one was going to make this experience any more pleasant than it had to be. Still, he turned his attention to the child. "I have something for you."

Diane lowered her brow, playing at not trusting him.

He had purchased her a box of crayons and a pad of paper, nothing that special, just something that had caught his eye at the grocery store last night, awkwardly placed next to the canned cat food. He produced these from his jacket and offered them to her, and she continued her little pantomime, leaning toward him, stretching out her fingers, and finally grabbing the gift hungrily.

"Now, Deedee, what do we say?" said Percy.

But Klaus drifted away from this exchange. Yesterday at the funeral, the Harlans had come with their son, about Diane's age and ridiculously named Track, after that cigar-store Indian Frank had played in a John Ford picture. Between seasons, Frank grew a mustache that Olive had always hated, its edges bent down the sides of his mouth like a staple. The *Brackett* star had mingled and signed autographs while Klaus watched men in coveralls tamp down the final shovelfuls of dirt above Olive's casket.

———————

CATHAY GARDEN WAS unusually busy, and for a moment as they waited at the front podium, Klaus wondered if they would even be seated. He weaved his fingers together tightly, pressing the knobby knuckles against one another. An old habit from movie sets, what he did with his hands as the actors took control of the moment, pulling their faces, reading their lines. Across the dining room, in the corner: the table where he and Olive had sat only a week or so ago. He avoided looking in its direction. Instead, he lit a cigarette and watched Antonia, who had taken off her dark glasses and was smiling, apparently not in the bad mood he'd imagined her in. He tried to think of something to say to her, some way to strike up a conversation. Olive had mentioned that she'd started a new job at a law office. Filing papers and answering the phone. He was about to ask her about this when the manager appeared, waving plastic-covered menus in the air, asking them to follow him.

Over food they made small talk about television programs, some of which Klaus had worked on, more of which he hadn't, and then suddenly Antonia looked him in the eye across the table and said, "I read an article only last week about *Hans & Greta*. It's supposed to be a masterpiece but it was never finished?"

Percy, apparently taken aback by this subject, cleared his throat.

But Klaus was unperturbed. In fact, he was flattered to know that his daughter-in-law, who he'd long assumed an enemy of one sort or another, had done her homework. And that she believed him capable of a masterpiece. "I was quite fond of the picture," he said. "I can say that for certain."

"It was about Hansel and Gretel?" Antonia said. Turning to her daughter, she added, "Did you know your grandpa made a famous movie about Hansel and Gretel? It has a clockwork man and a mean witch and a great big dog and a great big fire."

"No," Diane said, as if she honestly believed none of it could be true.

"I did," Klaus said. "I made it in that big black building behind my house. Can you believe that?"

"No," Diane said again.

Percy cleared his throat for a second time. "Dad," he said in the high voice meant for the child. "Er, I mean Grandpa. He built his very own movie studio, Deedee."

"Maybe if you ask very nicely," Antonia said, "Grandpa will let you see the movie on his projector."

"They . . ." Percy said. And then, after glancing at Klaus, "MGM took away the picture. It's a sore thing with Dad, see."

The wife, Antonia, looked at the table. "I'm sorry."

Klaus laughed. "It's nothing. A lifetime ago, really." He felt out of place even discussing his emotional attachment to an old film a day after watching his wife's casket lower into the grass, listening through closed eyes to the *shhfft, shhfft* noise of shovelfuls of dirt dropping onto her permanent home. But the subject of Olive remained avoided.

But still, the girl, half-distracted with her drawing, wanted to hear the story of *Hans & Greta*, and so he described it to her, leaving out all of the mess that would follow him around for a decade or more, just the straight story. "I came from the German town of Lüneberg as a small child, too young to remember it. But as a young man I visited again. It became the model for the town where Hans and Greta live." The painted scrim of his birthplace still hung in the studio behind the house, but he didn't bother telling her that. Nor did he tell her that, when Eddie Mannix and a pair of goons came to collect the reels of film, he'd had to threaten them with the prospect of a nonexistent shotgun to convince them to leave the sets and props behind. "These two, Hans and Greta, go to live in a magical forest where they can talk to all the trees and animals." He leaned forward, putting on his best Vincent Price. "And there they meet an evil witch who is busy sawing down all the trees."

"Why?" Diane said, pretending to be only half-interested.

"Because the magic is good and she's jealous that Hans and Greta are so happy there. Then one day she starts a terrible fire and all the trees and animals try to run away. And Hans and Greta are led by a dog—a talking dog, remember—all the way back to Lüneberg, where no one believes them about the witch and a mean old man tells everyone that they started the fire."

Diane looked up at him and said, "That all sounds real scary." She nodded thoughtfully and added, "Daddy says we can get a dog when we get home."

"Is that right?" said Klaus.

BACK AT THE house they all sat together at the dining table drinking iced tea and Klaus listened to Percy and Antonia talk about their jobs, about people they knew, and finally about Olive. Percy was brought to tears talking about his mother.

Klaus could never have imagined a truck in the wrong lane on a California highway could sweep away all that seemed permanent, could leave him here, watching his and Olive's son wipe tears from his face with the sleeve of his shirt like a child. She had been going to San Francisco that day to see her mother in the nursing home. But the call from highway patrol had made no sense. The wreck had taken place outside Gorman, far off her normal route. He hadn't told Percy about this; he wouldn't. The boy should be allowed to mourn without any further confusion.

After everything that had come between them, Klaus had to put in effort to unbury the sympathy he knew resided in his heart for Percy, who had squandered so much of Olive's love and, yes, her money as well. Klaus's own childhood had been defined by poverty and the unconquerable tragedy of his parents' death. For whatever his son thought of him, Klaus really had built his own career. He knew, too, how hurt Olive was by Percy's begging and lying and name-calling. But this wasn't the place for any of that sort of talk. So instead he reached across the table and put his hand on the boy's shoulder. "She loved you dearly," he said.

Percy then told Antonia and Diane about Rancho Lazlo outside Puerto Vallarta, those grand and miraculous years in Mexico, where the three of them had passed the end of the Depression and the War. "We were all so happy then," he said. "I'd do anything to get that back."

Klaus pictured his son's tirade against him that night he said that he was no Lazlo. That had been during those grand and miraculous years. Still, he said, "Those were fine times. Your mother—"

"She was always on my side," Percy said. Wiping away his tears, he held up his chin and met eyes with Antonia. "That's how I'll remember her."

It was a silly and rather pointed thing to say. But Klaus, still eager to keep everything on an even keel, said, "You're absolutely right. She was a very good mother."

Minutes passed. The child grew restless. The wife, Antonia (he must remember to *think* her name), announced to him that they had had a great time today, that she only wished it had been under better circumstances, that he should come out to Chicago soon. "I will," he said. And then, soon after, they were gone.

———————

WHEN NOTHING ON the television was worth watching, when the silence of the house became too much for him, Klaus gave George a call. His cousin answered in a chirpy salesman's voice, "George West Art and Design?"

"It's Klaus," he said, and set his coffee on the counter.

George lowered his voice. "Klaus? I've been meaning to call since the funeral. How are you?"

Klaus looked at the clock, a starburst of gold Olive had brought back in layers of paper from New York only last year. "Bored," he said. "Depressed?"

"Come to L.A.," George said. "We can catch up and then go to dinner after I close up shop."

"Do you have any idea what I've been through this week?"

"You just said you're bored and depressed. I am too."

"But the drive."

"I'll see you at five," George said, supercilious as ever, his voice now high and light, as if a customer had just walked in his door. "Sooner if you're ready to go now."

———————

THE GEORGE WEST Art & Design Gallery took the corner shopfront of a modern development of glass and stucco and blinding aluminum only blocks away from the hip contemporary galleries farther up La Cienega. Along either side of the shopping center ran two competing hair salons, a bookstore specializing in European literature in and out of translation, a pharmacy, and a kitchen-supply store that wasn't open to the public and which, because of this fact, Klaus assumed to be a front for organized crime. His cousin had moved into the space five or so years before, after the previous tenant, a branch of a leather-goods company that had overextended itself in the previous decade, had folded. Its chief benefit as a location, more than location itself, was that no curb lay between the parking area and the covered walkway of the development and that the previous tenant, concerned with the entry and exit of wheeled racks full of heavy bags and coats and jackets, had installed a wide ramp into the space, making it easy for George's wheelchair to get in and out.

Klaus left his car in a spot three from the door. He could already see George through the wide plate-glass window at his special desk, running an adding machine, fingering over the tape, holding a pencil in his other hand. His wheelchair glinted in the evening light.

At the front door, Klaus tried the handle to no effect and then tapped on the glass. George looked up from his work first with an expression of sleepy annoyance and then with what appeared to be a relieved smile. He wheeled back from the desk and started forward, pumping with both arms, the thickened muscles flexing and loosening, flexing and loosening, his legs skinny and awkward. With a quick grace, he swung open the door and caught it with one of the chair's shining metal stirrups, wheeling himself forward to make space for Klaus to pass behind him. "You really took your time. Couldn't pick out a shirt?"

This was an old joke. Klaus only wore a white button-up shirt, sometimes with a jacket and sometimes not. "I wasn't sure I would come," he said.

"It's a good thing *I* was sure, then." His cousin's satisfied smile faded. "Anyway, I should be the one saying 'I'm sorry.' I know you've been going through hell these past days."

The door clanged to a close and George clicked the lock. Inside, lighting fixtures glowed at eye level between the separate "suites," as George and Walter called them, really just the furniture of half a dozen rooms: two dining sets complete with sideboards and dishes and cutlery, an office/library, two living rooms in both the classic and more modern styles, and a single bath with a claw-foot tub and his-and-her sinks. In the back corner hulked two desks piled with interior design books and binders of George's work in the homes of stars and magnates throughout California and even Las Vegas. On all the walls, with more in a separate back room, Impressionist and abstract paintings were displayed, their prices kept in a catalogue in George's desk.

Years ago and with the patronage of Olive, his cousin had branched out from interior design to selling paintings, even these childlike blobs now found in banks and doctors' offices. Klaus never recognized the artists' names. He imagined this to mean they weren't all that significant. Still, George appeared to be doing a swift business with them. He'd said recently that they could soon be only selling art. Last year, Walter had a catalogue printed in full color of all the works that would go up for sale in a special autumn gallery event.

"You changed the leather sofa," Klaus said in order to have something to say. "I always liked that one."

George wheeled past him down the ramp to the wingback chairs that stood in place of the sofa. "So did Dolores," he said.

His cousin had never tired of name-dropping. Klaus wasn't about to ask which Dolores. He'd fallen for that trap before.

George reached under the desk and produced a bottle of whiskey. He nodded toward one of the dining tables. "Can you hand me a glass?"

Klaus picked a tumbler from the head of the table, clean as the Queen's silverware, and set it on the desk in front of his cousin. He sat in the chair facing him as George poured two fingers of whiskey, humming an old Bing Crosby tune.

"So how's business?" Klaus said.

"Walter has left me."

Klaus leaned forward sharply. "What?"

"I know, he was with me at the funeral and everything. That was for show. To be kind, really. We've known each other so long. But it ended weeks ago." George belted the whiskey. "We're old men. It's only fair for him to go and live his life. Lord knows he's had to take care of me all these years."

"I don't understand," Klaus said. "I thought you were happy."

"Well," his cousin said, but didn't elaborate. "There's something else too. I wanted to tell you the other day but, you know, we were mourning a great woman and I didn't want to confuse things. I didn't want to make trouble."

All of this was too much. "George, what are you talking about?"

"I saw Olive last week," George said. "The day of the accident. She was right here."

Klaus felt the stabbing pain in his chest and eyes that had come for days now at the mention of his wife's name. "She was going to see her mother. Why would she come here?"

"That's just it." George took another sip of his whiskey, held it in his mouth for a moment, and gulped it back. "She wasn't going to her mother's."

A bereaved man shouldn't have to play games like this. "What are you talking about? Jesus, George."

George smiled and looked up at the ceiling. "It's a little about Kay Stone. My God, remember her? Such a beauty. And talent. Imagine if she were still around. I bet she'd have her own television show playing someone's mother. Maybe even grandmother."

Klaus put a hand to his head. "You're talking about Marjorie Pomeroy. She was writing to Olive?"

George looked away, as if registering his surprise with some ghost seated across the room. "You knew about this?"

"I know about Marjorie," Klaus said. "But nothing about her and Olive. What's all this about, already?"

His cousin took a long, deep breath. "Well," he said, "Kay and Marjorie, um, had been living together off Sunset before the leap, before she died, you know?" He paused, waiting for something Klaus didn't have.

"Go on," Klaus said.

"Marjorie's last name was something else back then, unmarried, a Jewish name. I'm talking about the '30s. Early '30s. They'd been living together all along of course, but by then it was in a cruddy little place off Sunset and Kay couldn't get a job in pictures and occasionally they touched me for a little money, you know, a little of Walter's money, but mostly Kay talked about getting back into pictures, that Mayer would get over it or someone at Columbia or Republic or even Fox would give her another shot, and Marjorie was only getting bit parts, even Central Casting jobs—you know, "lady with dog," "lady at the bar," that sort of thing—and all the while you weren't talking to them, you weren't talking to anybody. You were off in the desert with your new wife and your little boy and over time they got the feeling—no, it wasn't just them, it was everyone, it was all of us—that you didn't want them around, that maybe you were part of why their careers, or really Kay's career, had stalled out, had dried up."

This again. "You're forgetting I couldn't get a job myself—"

"I know all that, Klaus. My God. I've heard it for what?" George looked at his watch as if it revealed to him a calendar that went back decades. "Probably thirty-five years. It's the von Stiegl legacy. It'll be on your tombstone. 'Born 1905, blackballed 1929.'"

Klaus stood up. "I didn't come here to be insulted. Can you get to the point?"

"Let's not get into the Bette Davis routine," George said. "Sit down and listen to me for once. You know, you're always like this. You were like this with Olive as well. Never listening."

The very idea that such a thing would be said to him only a day after burying his wife. And yet it struck home. Klaus dropped back into the desk chair. Olive had spoken to Marjorie Pomeroy. The thought was only catching up to him and it emptied him out onto the floor; his nerves were as jangled as if a gun had just gone off. He averted his eyes to a bookcase filled with the fine, leatherbound volumes of an encyclopedia and muttered, nearly under his breath, "How dare you."

"How dare I?" said George. He pointed at the wheelchair beneath him. "I've lived a lifetime like this because of your inconsiderate, stupid—"

"I didn't make you jump off a roof. Why, that's fantastical."

"You did, though, Klaus. You actually did."

"Absolute insanity. I've never heard such garbage. I saved you from drowning."

"And then told the world I was afraid of the microphone." George's face had grown intense, his words sharp blades clearly delineated one from the next. He seemed violently sober. "The word around Hollywood was that I couldn't handle the failure and tried to kill myself. Did you hear that? Did any of that get around to you? To this day I have clients, Klaus, people who are in every other way decent and upstanding people, who get to know me and one day they can't help it, they have to ask: 'So sound pictures, huh? That had to be rough.' Looking down at my legs and all. Can you believe that?"

"I never said anything about suicide. Jesus, George, I never said a word against you."

"It all ties together in a neat bow. Kay leapt from the sign and I leapt into a pool. Two sad and useless people whose only purpose in life had been to make movies, who couldn't be saved by the brave and genius film director Klaus von Stiegl." He wheeled back a bit, toward the bottle on the table. "You made us out to be losers who got what they deserved. Meanwhile, we were all supposed to be heartbroken for you."

"I never," Klaus said again. "You can talk to me like this after everything we've done for you? For this shop of yours? Just who floated Walter after the Crash?"

"Olive," George said. And then, pointing in the air at each of Klaus's questions, "Olive, Olive. *She* did all that."

A vile anger burned through Klaus. For a moment he imagined striking his cousin across the face. Instead he closed his eyes, breathed deeply.

"Anyway, it's where she was going," George went on. "She was driving to Bakersfield, you idiot. That's the whole reason she was on the road that day. And there wasn't any blackmail. The two of them had become friends. She was going because the woman's brother-in-law had died. I believe you had some run-in with him?"

The highway just outside Gorman, headed north, far out of the way if she were really going to San Francisco, the truck turning onto the highway, the blast of the horn, the screech and crumple of it all. When the police arrived both Olive and the truck's driver were dead, the latter almost unrecognizable to his family, the story front-page news: HOLLYWOOD LEGEND'S WIFE, ONE OTHER, DIE IN FIERY CRASH. Jesus.

She'd said she was going to see her mother at the nursing home, something she did at least once a month, though the woman didn't remember her, though she often mistook her for a long-dead sister. Sometimes Klaus would go with her, for the travel more than any family attachment, for the open road, for dinner at one or another beachside diner on the way back, that feeling of being part of the world still, not entirely gripped by their social set. But this time she hadn't even asked him. And he hadn't offered to go.

"The junior communist," Klaus said. "I did all I could for him."

George laughed and shook his head. "The ego on you, Klaus."

"I pulled him up out of the gutter. I stuffed his pockets with money."

"They found his body in a parked car down by some pier in Manhattan, loaded up with alcohol and heroin. Frozen."

His throat clenched. "Well, I didn't—"

"It doesn't matter. As far as she was concerned, you killed him. And she told Olive as much. She told her everything she could ever tell her, I guess you could say. And Olive listened."

The image formed in his mind: Olive hearing this woman out,

letting Marjorie's version of Klaus replace her own, returning home to him as if nothing had happened. Until she didn't return home.

"It's defamation," Klaus managed, though he was only speaking to get away from what he was beginning to understand. Pressing forward as a way of changing the subject. "What was she getting from Olive?"

"Nothing, from what I can tell. Just friendship."

George wheeled over to his desk, pulled open one of the drawers on the right, flicked through it, and produced a torn envelope with rounded cursive lettering in black ink. He showed this to Klaus from a distance, then folded it in half and tucked it under his hip, adjusting the blanket there as if he were trying to maintain some kind of social nicety. "Olive said that at first she didn't remember this woman at all. They bumped into one another in Oxnard, of all places, at a grocery store on Wooley Road. Olive had been there because you were scouting locations nearby. Staying at some shabby hotel. Marjorie was there with her daughter and grandkids. That's where her daughter lives."

"Why are you telling me all this?"

George looked at him with strained patience. "They half-recognized one another. Probably strangers. But then in the next aisle they passed again. Then the next. Finally at the mayo Olive said to her, 'Don't I know you?' But even then she didn't remember her from '28, that she'd been around during *Hans & Greta*. They knew some of the same people, though. And finally she—I mean Olive here—said her last name. 'As in Klaus von Stiegl?' Marjorie said. 'I knew him long ago.' That's when they made friends, when Olive began to fill in the blanks, to recall a woman she knew to be attached in some way to that silent film star, herself in some way attached to you. They had tea together, cocktails, something every couple of weeks."

The level of secrecy involved, the silent betrayal: it felt to Klaus something like what being cuckolded must feel like. Then again, he'd kept secrets from Olive. Why hadn't she ever confronted him about all this? That she had failed to do so made the whole thing worse.

And then something else occurred to him. Marjorie must have told Olive about their arrangement, about the money, Olive's money. The payoff he'd masked as just another brilliant business investment. "Did she say anything about the money? What I gave the Pomeroys? Did Olive know about that?"

George shrugged in a way that counted as either an affirmative response or an admission he was completely ignorant of the subject.

Klaus was getting a headache. His blood pressure was up. Dr. Cantor had asked him to reduce his salt, to avoid red meat, to get a little exercise, and he'd tried all those things a little before losing interest. Then in the last week he'd lost Olive and gotten little sleep and now this. He thought for a moment that his heart would seize up here in his cousin's gallery, that he would go into cardiac arrest in front of one of these stupid blob paintings.

George rocked his chair back and forth, his eyes turned toward the locked door. In a film, or in a scene from *Brackett*, this was where the scene would go dark. But the moment lingered on until finally, weighed down by more than he could ever have conceived, Klaus said, "I'm sorry for what I said earlier."

"I am too," George said.

"And I'm sorry about Walter."

George just shook his head.

"I wish I had some excuse for leaving but I don't," said Klaus. "I only have to go now."

"It's okay."

And still another minute went by before he dragged himself back into the drenching sunlight, the sprawling city, the highway back to the relentless desert.

———

AT HOME IT was dark, and for a few minutes he stood in the kitchen and then the dining room and then the living room without turning on a single light. He had left here a different man. That was okay. He was here and he belonged here and so did Olive, whom he could

feel in the walls and the floors, in the closet where clothes she'd
hung only a week ago still hung, in all the drawers both bedroom
and kitchen, in the screen of the television and across the top of its
cabinet, in the curtains, in all the knobs and rails and handles one
could grasp.

In their room he found the drawer in her dressing table and the
thick envelope and inside it more envelopes and all the letters that
told the story of Olive's communications with Marjorie, all the way
down to the first, which began, "Dear Mrs. Von Stiegl, I got to say
I was surprised to hear from you this week. Your inquiry about
Kay touches my heart. I hadn't thought much about my dear friend
in years, and hardly thought anyone remembered her. Those years
and what happened with your husband are painful ones to consider
and I'm not sure I feel good doing it, especially since I told him I
wouldn't . . ."

Another began: "As far back as my husband can remember,
Jimmy wanted to be a writer. That job with the Playhouse on television was the biggest thing to ever happen in his . . ."

He didn't need to read them all; he knew what they would say.
And besides, it felt like a second betrayal to go snooping on his
wife's private letters, even if they were about him.

So he gathered it all, this evidence against him, dug the flashlight from the kitchen drawer, and stepped out onto the patio. Dawn
would come soon. Off to the east, the sky already showed its pale
approach. The desert stars glimmered in their last brilliance before
daylight. He rounded the pool and went through the gate and out
into the field of sand and scrub. At the studio fence he used his key
in the padlock and squeaked open the mesh gate; farther on, another
key unlatched the studio's great south door.

Inside were his old sets, looking in the yellow search of the flashlight's beam like artifacts from long before his own birth. He passed
the interior set of the little house in the woods, the clearing set with
its deer and flowers and trees, the grand painting of his dear Lüneberg. They were all covered in dust, bleached from the sun. He'd

been painting out here for years, nothing more than a pastime, never really getting all that good, but still aping William Turner, horizontals troubled by ships and seaside towns, evaporated by the glare of an overpowering moon or sun. He didn't mind the repetition, found it meditative. Most of his watercolors were still out here, hung on a line in front of the Lüneberg scrim or stacked in the old editing and processing room. This tiny chamber is where he was bound, scuffling along with his load.

The electricity had been cut off decades ago. No reason for power. He painted in midday with the sun beating down through the opened roof, shirtless as on the beach, in linen pants, the bald top of his head getting sunburned. But he knew his way around in the dark. Even if he hadn't brought the flashlight he would have found the room, its loose knob, the metal shelves where film would have long ago burst into flames from the heat, filled now with paper, his watercolors, all the works too messy and juvenile to show to others, a bank that stored the signs of his folly and iniquity.

This is where he placed Marjorie's letters to Olive, out of reach, out of sight, most of them unread. Who had he been to her near the end? She must have seen him as little more than a fiction. And who had she been? A woman living another life beside him, hiding her secrets and his, betraying him as he had betrayed her. Or no. It was that he had seen himself all these years as the protagonist of his story and seen Olive as his second. That she could have a private life of her own, with purposes and interests and even friendships that were secret to him would have seemed before today impossible. What she learned from Marjorie had exposed his own shortcomings, his failures and lies, the parts of him *he* had kept private from *her*. She had seen him in full light. And still she would have returned home to him that day outside Gorman. She had still wanted to be with him, to be his wife.

He lit a cigarette in the dark desert night and returned home, tired beyond measure, to fall onto the sofa, where he sank and sank, and knew he wouldn't reach the bottom.

C+

What If Art Were Society:
On Di Stiegl's "New Earth Art"
Tobey Harlan

→ why start w/this wide frame?

      For centuries, art has been a way for people to com-
municate about the values of their society. Painters like Rembrandt and Leonardo de Vinci made Christian art that upholded
the Christian values of their times. At the same time, more
modernist painters tried to start making paintings that challenged their society by being more complex and sometimes
even shocking to the audience. Cubism is a good example of
this but also Futurism and Fauvism. By the 21st century, those
concerns were old ones and society turned its attention to the
climate crisis. One of the most important artists to address this *how?*
is Di Stiegl. This paper will argue that Di Stiegl's work in the
twenty-first century is actually more important than what she
did in the years before and also that it shows a way forward
for art and for society in a way that other artists ignore at their
peril.
      Di Stiegl was born in Chicago and lived as a teenager
in California, where she first became an artist. For college she
started at NYU but decided not to finish so that she could focus

→ necessary?

*does the paper
do this?*

on her paintings which were then in the "photorealist" style
which attempts to make paintings that look just like photographs.
This style grew out of an era of "pop" art, "minimalist" art, and
"postmodern" art but can also be traced back to the goals of Renaissance artists and others. In the 1980s she began to develop a
more distinct style of her own which mixes "photorealism" with
"expressionism" sytles and may be best compared to a painting
by Peter Blume called "The Eternal City" or other, more contemporary painters like David Salle and Julian Schnabel, but
true. | also Cindy Sherman, who made photos that were posed like she
was in the movies. By the early 2000s, after 9/11, she announced
that she was finished painting and that she would be devoted to
an "aesthetic philosophy" she called "New Earth Art."

    This art "melds conceptual art and land art to climate
change activism" (1). But it also "points back to Cristo and   *more*
Jean-Claude by centering public art that is physically created   *clarity /*
by a team of non-artist professionals, hired contractors" (2). A   *description?*
good example of this late style by Stiegl is "Forest in Target
Parking Lot (2008)", created outside a Minneapolis Target
store by hired workers and designed with the input of the
members of the local homeless population. Featuring a small
cliffside, a running waterfall, dozens of trees, and a small lake,   *more?*
this man-made greenspace was made available to the public
for a two-week period, becoming both a public park and a
shady area for the homeless to cool off during the day, get
fresh water, and sleep at night. A study group from the University of Minnesota's Environmental Studies program were also
employed to measure surface temperatures and other scientific
data, finding the site of the faked forest to not only reduce
temperature but to show promising results for reducing green-
good house gases (3). Several onlookers also remarked that it was a
beautiful work that reminded them of nature and what really
mattered to them as people (4). — *vague*

In class we discussed the Ambrozi (sp) chapter about art after "art," and Prof. Ambrozi famously said that "once the business of art is over we will all become artists," which I think fits well with another work by Di Stiegl called "Forest Happening (2009)." This one takes an even more radical approach, creating a participatory event where with little direction from the artist, non-professional "artisans" roamed about a forest watching plants, animals, and insects while wearing brightly colored clothes and Stiegl photographed them. This work was meant to show the beauty of everyday nature and reconnect the artisans with that aesthetic experience (5).

is this right?

more?

I have been lucky to know Di Stiegl as a friend of the family. I can say without doubt that she cares deeply about climate change, as do I. I'm excited to see what she does next with "New Earth Art" and how art will help to shape a better future for us all in spite of everything we face. With temperatures rising exponentially in the coming decades (Dessler), I think art like Stiegl's could change peoples' minds and behaviors for the better.

really? let's talk about this

Works Cited:

1. Prof. Heinen, lecture, Nov. 20th.
2. Prof. Heinen, lecture, Nov. 20th.

not a source for citation

3. "U. of M. Students Study Art & Sustainability in Target Parking Lot," *St. Paul Bugle*, May 3rd, 2018, author unnamed.
4. Prof. Heinen, lecture, Nov. 20th.
5. Prof. Henine, lecture, Nov. 20th.

same

6. Andrew E. Dessler, *Introduction to Modern Climate Change*, Cambridge, 2012.

—needs more research and analysis of art (see assignment instructions)

DIANE
1985

S HE ARRIVED LATE in the afternoon, and since she had no plans of staying long, she'd brought only a small carry-on with a few changes of clothing and pajamas, her makeup and hairspray, and all the magazine stories about her work over the last four years. Antonia had written her six months ago, sealing an envelope within another envelope addressed to Cindy, who had called her and read its contents to Diane over the phone. The gist was that Antonia was alive and living in Oklahoma City, had remarried, had gotten back on her meds. She was Antonia Nelson now, and she worked as a teller at a gold-domed bank at the center of town. Her husband, Bruce, ran a drive-through carwash installation and maintenance company. They were happy. And there was something about Bruce's sons from a previous marriage. There was no apology, no clear interest in what Diane had done with her life since 1981, no concern that her letter would be greeted with anything less than delight.

"There's another thing," Cindy had said when it was clear all Diane could muster up were grumbled curse words. "Have you ever heard of a woman named Marjorie Pomeroy?"

"Who?"

Cindy had said something with her hand over the phone, likely to Percy. "Well, it was worth a shot. I've been trying to track her down. She knew your grandfather."

"Okay, well, I don't know her. You do know I was a kid when Grandpa died, right?"

Diane had finally started to communicate with her father, mostly through Cindy, and often with an unspoken tension between them all. Diane had come to see it as her prerogative to be spiky with them both anytime they talked. After letting the heat on the line cool, Cindy had said, "Do you want the return address?"

"Not really."

Diane had thought for a while she wouldn't respond at all. Knowing her mother was safe and remarried to some doofus named Bruce in Oklahoma City actually felt like Antonia *had* abandoned her, that Michael had been right. But after a couple of months with her presence known to her, out there haunting the plains, she called Cindy back and asked for the address.

In her letter she left out the breakup with Michael, the drugs and going clean, finally—left out anything that seemed as if any part of her life were imperfect. She was a successful painter. That was all she wanted to project to her mother, the only thing she really had to say. A little over a week after she mailed it, she received a response. Antonia said almost nothing about Diane's career, only that she'd always known she was a great artist, and continued to describe her life in Oklahoma City, as if her garden and the boys' Atari and her husband's new truck would matter to Diane at all.

Diane didn't write again for several weeks, and when she did, a little tipsy after the big George West SoHo opening party, she demanded an explanation. "I deserve to know what happened," she'd written. "A woman can't just walk away from her family like this and not explain anything. We thought you were dead." Writing that last sentence, she realized it was a sentiment she'd never allowed before to be put into words.

Instead of any real explanation, Antonia had written back that those had been rough months, that she didn't like to think about it all, but that now she was happy, and had been for years, that she would truly love it if Diane would visit for Christmas.

She'd had no one to consult. Or no, that's wrong. On the flight to Dallas—where she'd had three hours of layover time to acclimate herself to the occasional sight of cowboy hats and boots and the wistful, contemplative way people spoke—it occurred to her that she should have called Mrs. Harlan. From her she'd heard of Track's success in his father's real estate company, his housing developments and his strip malls and his first and second marriages. Mrs. Harlan would have talked Diane out of it in that nice Mrs. Harlan way, reminding her that she didn't have to go, that no one would blame her if she didn't follow her mother's whims, that maybe the experience would be, well, dear, unsatisfying. But Diane hadn't called Mrs. Harlan, and in the months since she and Michael split up, in the months since she'd gone to a rehab spa upstate for three weeks, she hadn't been in contact with any of her old friends either. She had the work and she had gallery managers and she had collectors. She had that cover story in *Art in America* that she had—it all seemed so silly now, so childish—packed in her bag to show to Antonia like straight A's on a report card.

And now she was here and she wished someone had been around to tell her not to go through with it. She herself, walking too fast in the small and slow-moving modernity of Will Rogers International, was telling her to not go through with it. Instead she sailed forth into the bright winter afternoon, the apocalyptic flatness.

Her hotel room at the Holiday Inn offered another view of the limitless expanse. This place made her think she could grow to understand Rothko and Newman, those abstract painters whose work others stared at but had always left her cold. She sketched the view—bare but for a highway and two billboards and the hint of trees—and thought of composing a series of paintings. But would they really say anything? Did she care?

Evening had flashed into night and she had to call to let her mother know she had arrived. A man picked up after two rings. "She's out at Wal-Mart," he said. His voice had an accent she couldn't place, flat along the vowels with a nasal lift to it. "Is this Diane?"

"It's pretty late," she said. "Why don't I come by in the morning."

"Oh no. She said if you called to tell you to come on over."

She was tired from the flights, this bad decision, spacing out at that window. "Okay, I'll be right there."

The man at the front desk called her a cab and then she had to wait twenty minutes, part of it listening to him whistle a butchered tune as she flipped the pages of magazines in the lobby. When the cab arrived it was, impossibly, the same driver who had brought her from the airport. Neither of them spoke of this. She stared out the window as they flew up a busy highway, past a clutch of small towers that appeared to be the downtown, and up a residential street that passed by a giant indoor mall.

Before she'd left she'd called Track, but he'd wasted half an hour of long-distance bitching and moaning about regulations and unions, about how rich he and everyone around him would be if everyone would just get out of the way and let them build. "A rising tide," he'd said. And then, a little later, "Hey you know a thing or two about money now don't you? More of a pain in the neck than they tell you—all the responsibility. Saw in the newspaper you had a big show?"

"It went well," she said. "But I try not to pay attention to that part."

"Okay, okay," he had said, doing his best Joe Piscopo. And a minute later she'd been back to packing her bag.

The cute brick house stood in the middle of a block of cute brick houses, vaguely alike in shape and style, their lawns dead and yellowed, Christmas lights blinking to life. Night had settled in. Diane pressed the ringer and heard heels nearing the door. Then it opened.

Antonia had grown out her hair and gathered it into a loose ponytail, its wild strands haloing her tall forehead, her eyes expectant, almost fearful. "Deedee," she said, and reached out her arms. They hugged, though Diane felt completely outside of it, like those stories you hear of people floating above their beds and looking down at their sleeping bodies. "Come in," Antonia said. "Come in."

The boys weren't necessarily boys but actual teenagers, both in V-neck sweaters and collared shirts, their faces so similar in their snottiness that Diane thought for a moment they were twins. Brad and Dan, preppies right out of the Sears catalogue, standing alert to shake her hand as the fireplace raged behind them. A Bing Crosby rendition of "It's Beginning to Look a Lot Like Christmas" played from the tape deck next to the tree. From the decor—an expensive nativity on the mantel, a needlepoint Christ across from the bathroom door, a literal Bible on the coffee table—Diane got the impression her mother, or at least her new family, was religious, maybe even born-again.

The new husband, Bruce, came out of the kitchen with a tray of eggnog and cookies. He was round and short, his beard neatly trimmed, his sweater a garish thing with a decorated tree on the chest and a giant moth hole on one arm. He laughed too much for Diane's taste, and near bedtime broke out an actual trumpet with a mute stuffed in its bell so that he could play along, melancholically, to "White Christmas." After "White Christmas," Antonia—who seemed to Diane as if she were an actress playing either her mom or theirs—announced that Santa would be here soon, and with the same horrible joviality that had colored the evening, everyone gathered themselves for bed.

"You'll stay, won't you?" Antonia asked her. "We can make up the office. There's a fold-out."

"I'd better go," Diane said.

Bruce said, "You won't get a taxi this late. This isn't New York City."

"I'll take her," Antonia said. "Let me get my coat."

Her mom shuffled a little. Her gait was shorter than it had been. She had, perhaps following Bruce's lead, put on a little weight. Either way, she was less and less recognizable the longer Diane was around her.

Diane said her goodbyes, first to the snotty boys and then to their father, who insisted that she call him Dad.

"Well, thank you for having me, *Dad*," she said, laughing—though really, saying it creeped her out. Then she waited in the shadowed entryway looking out at the yellow bug light and the orb of dark beyond as Antonia and Bruce whispered to each other like characters in a British television drama. When Antonia appeared in the hall, she wore a puffy red coat with a fur ring on the hood and held a brass-handled purse big enough to serve an old-time doctor.

In a powder-blue station wagon on the highway Antonia said, "Mother tells me you came into some money. I guess she spoke to Percy—sorry, your father. That's good. What a relief to know you're okay." She glanced at Diane and back to the road. "I mean, as far as jobs go. I know it's got to be hard with the art."

Just then, Diane remembered the magazine and news stories she'd brought to show her. But before she could mention them, Antonia said, "That man always hated me. Your grandfather. He was a bigot. Afraid of, you know"—she pointed to her head—"something about a woman from his films who killed herself. He thought I was dangerous. He wanted your father to commit me. But more than anything he wanted him to leave."

"Jesus—"

"Deedee, don't say the Lord's name in vain."

Now her initial impression was made concrete. Her old mom, the one she'd grown up with, the one she'd lived with when she started college, would never have even used the phrase "the Lord's name."

"I've never heard that," Diane stumbled. "I mean about Grandpa. Why would he do that?"

"He said if your father wanted money I needed to go in a hospital. He thought I was a danger to you and your father. That's why Percy wanted a divorce."

"I thought you wanted the divorce. You moved out."

"Nothing's that simple," Antonia said.

"You literally moved out. To Massachusetts. I was present for all this."

"I mean, your dad was always fighting near the end, always saying I needed help. I couldn't take any more."

Diane didn't know what to believe. "Dad isn't perfect," she managed.

"We were young and stupid."

"I'd agree with that."

Her mother tried a laugh. "For a long time he *was* perfect, more than perfect. At the start he had all these dreams — said that with his family's money we would be traveling the world and living the high life and all that. But it always had to do with catching a windfall from his parents. He never got over your grandmother's telling him that wasn't going to happen. Sure, he did his best. We were happy, normal people with jobs, with a kid. But then, you know — " Here, Antonia circled a finger next to her ear, *crazy*. "I was sick, on and off. I couldn't always work. It put pressure on everything."

"That's not your fault," Diane said.

"Oh I know, I know. But it's what happened. And your father's whole self-image was made of that Lazlo fortune. He really thought it was his." Her mother squinted into the dark distance. "Who knows? Old Klaus may have meant well. But he beat a dead horse with not wanting to help your father. There was something mean in there. Maybe on both sides."

They were exiting the highway now, the dark plain south of the city stretching into faint and distant points of light. "He lied to me. Dad. He had a lawyer trying to get the money left to me. I would have given him half or more if I'd ever known."

"Percy did that? My goodness."

"I only learned about it when you disappeared. He came to New York to ask me for some of it, I guess. I'm not sure. When I understood I sort of stopped talking to him for a while."

"Deedee, you poor girl," Antonia said, shaking her head in disbelief. "Your father is his own head case. He's one who could use a therapist. You know?"

They were pulling into the Holiday Inn parking lot now. A single tree near the entrance glowed with green and red lights. At its top was a bright white star. "What happened to you?" Diane asked. "Why did you disappear, for what, *four* years?"

Antonia shook her head. "I don't want to talk about that right now," she said. "It was a difficult time. Very difficult. I made mistakes. I got lost and in trouble but then I found Jesus and he led me to Bruce. I'm on my meds. I'm seeing a therapist. I'm doing really well. Your father was right that I needed help. Even if he didn't know what he was saying."

Diane thought for a moment she'd cry. Her eyes watered; her nasal passage pinched. An old anger she'd never confronted built in the silence between them and welled in her throat. She had to take one slow, long breath to control it. "You should have called me or Grandma or someone. It's not fair to do this. To just say you're doing well. It's not fair."

"Deedee, I'm sorry. I made mistakes. I've always made mistakes."

Diane opened the car door. Earlier in the evening she'd said that she would return for Christmas Day, presents, a late breakfast, the whole family thing. Suddenly she couldn't imagine participating. To be around this stranger who'd gone on an adventure and remade herself as a born-again bank teller in Oklahoma City who hadn't asked Diane anything about her life back in New York. She stood up with a jerk, and, grabbing up her bag, she remembered again the magazines. She pulled them out and slapped them on the passenger seat. "Here," she said. "Here's what I've been up to while you were making your mistakes."

She slammed the door, righteous in her hatred, fire running up her neck and out her ears. In the lobby she turned back, her jaw tight, expecting to see the station wagon pulling away. Instead, there was her mother, unfolding the pages of the *Village Voice*, bathed in the weak blue of a dome light.

———————

WHEN DIANE HAD returned from rehab and didn't know to whom else to turn, she had called Mrs. Harlan, to whom she'd barely spoken in years. Mrs. Harlan flew out later the same night, arriving in New York early in the morning, when Diane was still awake, drinking coffee, listening to records. Over the phone, Mrs. Harlan had wept and asked why Diane hadn't told her about all of this sooner, why she hadn't come home to Palm Springs instead of going off to some rehab facility full of strangers. In all honesty, Diane couldn't imagine being able to call her before rehab, this woman who'd already done too much for her over the years. It had all been too humiliating. So she had told her, "My phone was disconnected."

In person, Mrs. Harlan's hurt feelings were behind them. In jeans and a faded California Raisins sweatshirt, looking thinner and younger than Diane had remembered her, Mrs. Harlan came in rattling off her plans. They had to go the Museum of Modern Art and maybe the Guggenheim and maybe the Met, too, and shouldn't they go to a show, something silly like *Cats*? Was Diane hungry? Where was good for breakfast? "I'll have to leave Friday," she had said, the only time she let a note of sadness into her voice. "I could only get someone to come by to check on the cats until the weekend."

That visit had been a lifesaver. Diane had no idea how badly she needed someone, needed something like family, to anchor her back to her own life. They really did go to all the museums; at MoMA Mrs. Harlan insisted on buying her a framed print of *Guernica*, which they hung behind the sofa when they got back to the apartment. The next night they bought scalped tickets for *Cats*, a baffling experience, nothing close to enjoyable for Diane but somehow eliciting grand, broad laughter from Mrs. Harlan. She wanted to see all of Diane's paintings, all her sketches, even the charcoals from that trip to Martha's Vineyard. When Diane mentioned that a handful of paintings were at the George West SoHo Gallery, Mrs. Harlan immediately wanted to go there. "You mean *the* George West? I met him at least a half dozen times over at your grandfather's. During *Brackett*? Still handsome as the devil."

At the gallery, she was breathless with elation. "And they're all sold?" she said, gazing bright-eyed at the three canvases. "My dear, you're such a success."

Before she left, they talked about Diane's time at the rehab center, how she was getting along, why she was keeping her distance from her friends for a while, and what had happened with Michael. "I liked him," Mrs. Harlan said, though she'd never met him. "He was good to you. I hope you can find a way back together."

Diane had her doubts about that. She showed Mrs. Harlan the reel she'd stolen from NYU's film library. "I can't even look at it. I don't have a projector. But that's what I've been like. Trouble, you know?"

Mrs. Harlan found this endlessly funny, even quoted her the next morning as she waited on the cab that would take her to the airport. They stood in the stiff, cold air like two junkies, clasping their elbows with gloved hands and bouncing their knees. "That's what you've been like," Mrs. Harlan said. "Trouble, you know?"

Two weeks later a package arrived from something called the American Video Library. Inside were three VHS tapes from their Silent Classics Collection: *The Bachelor's Wife*, *Heartbreak City*, and *Under a Cherokee Moon*. Diane watched them in order, one after another, that very night. They had been a solace to her, an inspiration. Now, in Oklahoma City, alone in the cigarette-scented hotel room with a television bolted to the dresser, she decided that she didn't want to believe what her mother had said about "old Klaus" trying to usher her into an asylum. Neither of these parents of hers had ever shown any allegiance. But Grandpa had been different.

————

THE FILMS SET her back to work when the idea seemed impossible, gave her a purpose outside survival. Although on that front she certainly had to start painting again: she'd ransacked her bank account over the last couple of years, spending and spending. She and Michael never went back for her car in Connecticut; she'd bought a new Volvo, right off the lot, when they had returned from Martha's Vineyard. She'd bought painting supplies and electronics for Michael, had bought them both drugs, had bought extravagant gifts and shipped them to Lily, who was teaching now in Providence, and Annie, still out in L.A. She'd bought the apartment outright too. Even before the expenses of rehab and falling behind on her painting, she had been losing more than she was taking in. And that had been with multiple shows, her work fetching higher and higher prices, her name mentioned alongside Koons and Sherman and Basquiat. Annie—now the manager at the George West gallery in Los Angeles, Franklin Brown having moved up to an executive position—had called her rich over the phone a few weeks after the rehab trip. "Rich?" Diane had said. "We're practically broke."

Annie had laughed. "Uh-huh. I'm sure you're just pinching pennies."

"It's not that bad yet. Anyway, I need to get out there."

"I told you we're almost exclusively abstract," Annie said, knowing that she'd meant a show and not just a visit. "It's Mr. West's specialty."

Diane had seen pictures of George West but only met him once, sort of, when her grandfather was dying. Silver hair, big sunglasses, velvet jacket, a wheelchair with zircon gems on its wheels: no other dealer had such a flashy public persona. He'd been a guest on *Lifestyles* only a couple of months ago. But he was old, in his eighties, and Annie was supposed to have given his galleries a connection to the present. "What about all this talk of new blood?" Diane said. "Don't tell me he's just a vampire."

"Only a little," Annie said. "I'll keep up the pressure. But I'll also call around. I know some people now."

"Actual people?" Diane said. It was a running joke between them that Californians weren't even real, that they'd been manufactured in a tanning salon on the Nevada border.

"Yes, actual people. You know Gagosian did a whole retrospective of your old friend Bartolomos. I'm pretty sure he was in town."

"Gagosian? I know Gagosian. Or I met him. Once."

But the name Bartolomos had set her off, and right there on the phone with Annie she imagined cutting up a line and snorting it and cutting up another, and when she thought she would make this happen, she told Annie that she'd better get off the line, long-distance bills and all that, talk to you soon, kisses, et cetera—and called the hotline number the recovery center had given her.

AT THE HOTEL in Oklahoma City, she paced. Then she tried reading the book she'd bought at the Waldenbooks in the airport, *White Noise*, but every sentence seemed bent on being funny and impressive and smart and so she couldn't even make sense of it, and eventually she grabbed her room key and put on her shoes over bare feet and went downstairs, out into the cold blow of winter, and gazed into that long dark, feeling herself dissipate into the vastness of the west. She was used to loneliness—it came with the job of making art, however miserable it made you—but this place was something else entirely. She smoked another cigarette.

A few minutes later a young man with long, stringy hair and a Walkman joined her, about twenty feet away, to smoke his own cigarette. The volume on his headphones was turned up so high that she could make out the words to Van Halen's "Jamie's Cryin'." She thought that he would say something creepy to her, but long after she'd finished her cigarette, he tossed his on the tan lawn and disappeared inside. An employee. The laundry guy or something.

Upstairs she took a second shower, dug out the peanuts they'd given her on the plane, and tried the television. The only channel still on air was playing *Brackett*. At first this seemed natural—the show was often aired late on the UHF dial, its aging fans a little more nostalgic for *Dukes of Hazzard* and *Perry Mason* during daylight hours—but at the first commercial break she twisted the volume knob all the way down, annoyed by the coincidence of seeing *Brackett* on air only minutes after Antonia had been talking about Klaus. What was this about him pushing Dad to put her in an asylum? Was that a thing people even still did back then? The notion seemed intensely Victorian, like fainting ladies and bicycles with one big wheel. And the grandfather she remembered would never do that. A furniture ad with two men in tan suits who looked like characters from *Dallas* lit up the otherwise dark room. She closed her eyes.

When she opened them, Brackett was floating in a swimming pool, a red cloud of blood growing around him like billowing smoke. The camera rose, turned, and faced the woman in the wheelchair. Somebody famous, though Diane couldn't recall her name. It was the end of the series. Outside, dawn neared. Birds made noise in the short trees. She missed Michael; maybe she'd been dreaming about him.

A LITTLE LATER, delirious and itchy-eyed, gazing at the romantic emptiness out the window, Diane called Nina, Michael's sister, on an impulse. After Diane had returned from rehab, Nina had come to visit her, to talk about Michael's ongoing problem, to assure Diane she wasn't trying to get them back together. At the time, Diane pretended she didn't want any updates. Now she hoped for them. When Nina answered after several rings, she told her the whole story: her mother's manic depression, her disappearance, and her reappearance. "And I'm here in fucking Oklahoma trying to be a daughter or something. I don't know what to do."

"It's Christmas," Nina said. "Just go do Christmas. It can't be any worse than what we've got going here."

Diane inferred what that meant, that Michael was there, that maybe he still wasn't cleaned up. But she didn't ask, couldn't. "Okay," she said. "I'll go back."

"And Di?"

"Yeah?"

"You know what time it is?"

Light was just starting to brighten the horizon. "Early?"

"Fucking early," Nina said. "On Christmas. Goodbye."

SHE HADN'T ACTUALLY told Antonia that she wasn't going to show up that morning, but everyone was surprised when she arrived anyway. Diane pretended not to notice how they looked into each other's eyes and moved slowly to set the table. All the gifts had been opened. A single garbage bag stuffed with wrapping stood next to a recliner like a rotund and silent guest. "All the gifts but one," said Antonia as Bruce poured pancake batter over a griddle. The family had just been finishing breakfast. Antonia went down the hall and returned with a small package wrapped in Rudolph the Red-Nosed Reindeer paper. "For you," she said. "I remember you liking them."

It was a cassette of *Sgt. Pepper's*, the soundtrack that that was as much Antonia's as Diane's. Diane squeezed the cellophane wrapper with the pads of her fingers, trying to get a hold to tear it open. She was crying. The boys sniggered. Antonia put her hand lightly on Diane's shoulder. "It's okay," she said. "Deedee, I'm so glad you're here."

A minute later Bruce cleared his throat as he crossed the room with pancakes. "Would you like coffee," he said, "or juice?" When Diane didn't answer he cleared his throat again. "Boys, go to your rooms. Let's leave the ladies here to catch up."

After he'd left, as Diane poured syrup on the pancakes she had no appetite for, Antonia said, "Bruce has been joking for a week that Gorbachev and Reagan met this year so that we could meet. Me and you. Can you believe that? Can you believe how afraid I've been?"

"I don't know," Diane said. "I don't know anything." She felt crumpled and sick.

Antonia poured them both coffee with sugar and cream. "The paintings of the young people with wiped-off faces were interesting," she ventured. "The ones in that *Art in America* story? What are they supposed to mean?"

Diane could never answer these sorts of questions. She wasn't like Lily or Annie. "It's like a mask," she said. "Or like a masked identity. How we don't know each other."

"Is that me in one of them? In the orange dress? To fit into that thing these days! I'd be a scandal."

Diane talked for a while about her paintings, how one image led to the next, how it was about exploring a visual idea rather than explaining things. But then drifted to Michael, to New York, to her loneliness. She spilled everything but the addiction, which felt like too much to give her mother just yet, too much to trust her with. "Sometimes I don't even want to be there," she said. "I mean, I love it but I'm so tired."

"Then don't go back," Antonia said.

"Mom, I couldn't—"

"I don't mean stay here, dummy. Go somewhere you want to go."

It was one of those magical little things her mom said now and again. A quality of hers that Diane had nearly forgotten. Once, in grade school, when she'd come home hurt that Tina Montgomery didn't want to be her friend, Antonia had made her write a list of every other kid in her class. Then she said, "I don't even see Tina what's-her-name on this list," and walked away.

Eventually Bruce and his sons returned. The boys wanted everyone to watch them play a new Atari game, and they all did, chatting

amiably about weather and movies for half an hour before Diane
went to the kitchen and called a taxi. She pushed the *Sgt. Pepper's*
cassette tape into her coat pocket. Everyone hugged. Then she was
gone and the sky was too big and blue and then she was on a plane
again, back to New York, to pack everything she needed, to make a
few phone calls, to go to California. She needed space. She needed
something like home.

To: DiSt187
From: TessaFab   [Reply]
Subj: Your Kind Gesture

That was very nice of you to offer to send money but really
you do not owe me anything. Your years living with me and
Track were more than I could have deserved. And it has been
wonderful to watch you grow as an artist—I always knew that
you would succeed and find your way. It is like watching my
own daughter become a famous painter! Besides your father
helped with money a little after he sold that old house and your
grandfather was such a help to us in the years before (I think
he may have been setting up me & your dad, actually—but a
story for another time!). You're right that your dad hurt me a
great deal. I won't hide that fact. I don't feel great about that
experience—even after 25 years! But you owe me nothing.
Please do not be offended that I have torn up that very kind
and very generous check. Track has done very well taking
over his father's business and has been very helpful to me in
retirement, building me a house and covering my healthcare
and other expenses. Only last summer he took me on a cruise
to the Bahamas with his family! Imagine me in the Bahamas! I
have to look at the photographs on my wall to believe it really
happened. His youngest son, Tobey, is a real heartbreaker. And
a talker! Susan and James are in junior high now. Looking like
grownups. I hope you're staying warm. Toronto must be awful
cold in Christmastime. Happiest of holidays to you, Michael,
and little Turner.

(PS: Track showed me the paintings you shipped to him a few
years ago. They are beautiful! What a talent you are, my dear.

And you won't believe who sent me a Christmas card this week:
your mother! Somehow we have never met. I can see now
where you get your natural sense of graciousness and joy.)

Yours, Tessa Harlan

[Delete]   [Help]

THE SACRAMENTO BEE

"I WON'T BE A PARTY TO IT" - PALM SPRINGS REAL ESTATE DEVELOPER REMOVES NAME FROM UC DAVIS ENDOWED CHAIR

by <u>MOLLY KREBST</u>

Updated August 17, 2022, 6:22 p.m.

Last spring, Dr. Saanvi Bajwa was elated to learn that she had been selected as the Track Harlan Chair of Classical Studies at UC Davis. "It was such an honor," she said. "It felt like the culmination of my academic career. I personally wrote Mr. Harlan to thank him for endowing this position two decades ago and so elevating classical studies at Davis."

But that honor rapidly soured. Professor Bajwa's work on gender and sexuality drew the attention of Doug Smith, then a longshot candidate for Sacramento City Council. In a Twitter post, Smith accused Bajwa of "spreading transgender indoctrination and using the college classroom to convert students into gay activists." The false accusation was quickly taken up by right-wing social media users who flooded Prof. Bajwa's university email with hate messages and dogged her Instagram account with threats. "It was a nightmare," she said. "One minute I am quietly doing my work and the next I am getting all this abuse from total strangers. My family felt as if we were in real danger."

Then the issue came to the attention of Track Harlan, the Palm Springs real estate developer who funded the endowed chair in 1999. A UC Davis alum, Harlan wrote the school's president this summer, saying in part that "this is not what I wanted this money to do. The chair of classic (sic) studies was meant to hold up our shared Western heritage and to celebrate the foundational cultures that created democracy, poetry, and the European Judeo-Christian traditions which have long made America the greatest country in the world. The sort of false indoctrination peddled by Bajwa is an insult to my family's name. I won't be a party to it." He demanded that Prof. Bajwa be "stripped" of the title immediately.

In the past two weeks, right-leaning media has turned the issue into a national cause, posing Prof. Bajwa and her academic work as another sign that universities have grown dangerously out of touch with American society. Her book, "Queering Ancient Greece: Three Studies of Sexual Expression," has been the target of negative online reviews. Memes featuring Prof. Bajwa's face have proliferated on social media. One cable news pundit even called for Prof. Bajwa to be deported "back to Pakistan, where she can spread her hate and see where it gets her." Prof. Bajwa was born in Dearborn, Mich., to American citizens.

Students and faculty have rallied around Prof. Bajwa. On Sunday, one day before fall classes were to begin, a protest consisting of well over a thousand concerned members of the UC Davis community held signs calling out Mr. Harlan—including those accusing him of holding anti-LGBTQ+ and racist views. Prof. Bajwa—currently on leave due to the stress caused by this situation—called in to thank the protestors. "We must believe in free speech," she said, her voice amplified to the crowd by a megaphone. "We must believe in academic freedom and in the defense of minority groups from a majority who wants to deny their existence and their history. Thank you for standing with me."

Harlan has now asked the university to remove his name from the endowed chair. "All this is out of hand," he said in a written statement. "I don't want this poor woman vilified. I just want my name off this title. As far as I'm concerned, I'm not even an alum of Davis anymore. It's a different place now." It is unclear what university administration will do to solve the problem at this time.

(This story has been updated to include Mr. Harlan's request that his name be removed from the endowed chair's title.)

KLAUS

1966

GEORGE HAD COME out from L.A. for the holidays and continued to stay on a while at the Ocotillo Lodge, putting his assistant, Franklin, up in the room next to him. Since Walter had split, George had needed someone to help him help run the gallery—now almost exclusively dealing in art—and been lucky enough to find a man who had, in George's words, "memorized the details of every auction and private sale in the last thirty years, God bless him." But with this professional work came the personal: helping George in and out of his chair at times, or up flights of stairs, and of course to answer the phone and write letters when he was busy.

So when Klaus met him for dinner in the Candlewood Room—a vast open space with windows looking out on the pool and the mountains beyond—Franklin Brown, a prim Black fellow with a narrow mustache, sat with them, occasionally jotting down notes when he received the signal from his employer: a single raised index finger.

It was all very strange to Klaus, who knew his cousin fully capable of taking his own notes. But in this swanky modernist clubhouse, with a short man tinkling at a piano next to the round metal fireplace, the process became part of the general dream. "You said on the phone you were at an impasse," George said when their steaks arrived. "But here you are, looking like an aging society type out on the prowl."

Klaus had recently shaved his own mustache, had—on the sugges-tion of his barber—darkened his hair, which he now wore combed back in an old-fashioned way. "To be honest I'm thinking of quit-ting television, returning to feature films," he said. "I mean, what am I doing here? Making a cop show nobody needs, that says nothing, adds nothing to world."

"And what if it did?" George had asked.

Klaus had been complaining, unfocused, and his cousin's words hadn't really registered. "I ought to just hand it over to Frank Harlan, let him produce his own show. Hire his own writers and director."

George lifted that meaningful index finger of his. "I'm saying what if *Brackett* made a turn? What if it became something new and interesting, something you actually want to do? Something you want to say?"

His cousin had never been a practical man. "George, it's a detec-tive show. He knocks on doors. He interrogates a bunch of guest stars. At the end he solves the crime, usually a murder, and then it's credits."

"I think what Mr. West is saying is that if it were no longer a de-tective show but something else entirely, you'd have the freedom to do what you want."

This, from the assistant Franklin.

Klaus said, "That's not really how television works."

"Klaus, you own your own production company. Which re-minds me: any movement on my little idea?" George had proposed Klaus a sitcom about a woman artist in a wheelchair who spends each episode working on a painting as her wacky neighbors come in and out of her rooftop apartment. He'd wanted to call it *Getting Around*. He also thought a beautiful celebrity would snatch up the role. "I'm thinking an Angie Dickinson type?"

"Angie Dickinson in a wheelchair every Thursday night is not something the American public is going to go for."

"Franklin loves the idea," George said, to which Franklin shrugged.

"Anyway," Klaus said, "I'm thinking of retiring. Since Olive—"

He let the name hang there, let noise of the other diners and the piano fill in the gap. "It's hard to see a purpose at this age. Maybe it will pass."

"You shouldn't say that, sir," said Franklin. "An older gentleman like yourself has a great deal of wisdom to impart. Look at Mr. West here—"

"Yes, look at Mr. West," said George.

Franklin laughed. "We're expanding the business. A gallery in San Francisco and one to come soon in New York. One hundred percent contemporary paintings."

"He's a visionary," Klaus said.

"Klaus knows all this," George said. Which was true: he had become a kind of silent partner, bankrolling his cousin's gallery since the pair of them became bachelors again. But where Klaus's own widowerhood had felt like a slow decline, George's loneliness had elevated him into a new focus and almost obsessive activity. Even now, he was being called to the phone. Franklin would have to go with him in case any notes needed to be taken.

As he wheeled back from the table, George said with grinning irony, "He can finally do anything he wants and it looks like he wants to do nothing at all." Putting a melodramatic hand to his forehead, he added "Tragic, really."

Klaus shook his head. "Go take your call already."

Alone, surrounded by dining strangers, he gazed at the mountains, the peak of San Jacinto pale and shadowed in the full moonlight, and returned to a familiar theme from these last months: how he had only lately discovered that he wasn't the man he'd long thought himself to be. He'd never purposefully hurt anyone. But at nearly every key point in his life, when he'd had the opportunity to make a decision of consequence, someone around him had been hurt, while Klaus himself had sailed forth, unaware, insensitive. This understanding had been a final gift from Olive—a painful one, a complex one—and he had learned to examine it without letting it devastate him as it had in the early weeks after her death. "A great deal of wisdom," Franklin had said. He was right—even if some of that wisdom was unsightly.

He was in this state of pondering himself when he heard Frank Harlan's deep voice repeating the phrase "Good evening" to one table of fans after another. He was crossing the Candlewood Room with his wife, Tessa, just behind the hostess. When Harlan spotted Klaus, he stopped in his tracks, grinning. "Looky here," he bellowed. "If it ain't *mein Liebling* himself. Klaus, you old dog!"

"Frank," Klaus said. "Tessa."

The couple hovered at the table, dressed for a grand ball. Tessa Harlan pointed a thumb at her husband. "This one's had a few already."

"Celebratin' the anniversary," Harlan explained.

"Many congratulations."

From across the room, Klaus saw George and Franklin making their way back from the phone call. For a moment he worried about having to introduce Frank and Franklin to each other, the tedious jokes and pretend confusions, but before such a boorish circumstance could come about, Harlan said, "We gotta eat, buddy. But let's talk *Brackett* soon, eh?"

AT HOME THAT night everything clicked into place: *Brackett* would be about guilt, about looking at it without rose-colored glasses, about trying to exorcize it through violence, about coming up short. It would be about a guilt that can't be outraced. It would be a single case explored over the duration of the entire season. A case *about* Brackett. Something shocking and dark and expressionist, a real throwback to the early days, that gilded time of German cinema between the wars. A single man taking on the world with violence, trying to right some old wrong, but paying for it in the end.

Around midnight he called the Ocotillo Lodge and asked for Mr. West's room.

"You know, maybe it works," George said when he explained it. "Any way to get my Angie Dickinson character in there?"

"I'll take it under consideration," Klaus said. "I'm going to bring on Artie Banyan."

"Banyan? Is that guy still alive?"

"The last of the great silent scenarists. He's been working on *Rawhide*, I think."

"Oh, that horrible song. Klaus, let me sleep!"

"I think this will end my career in television," Klaus said.

"Well, that's a very optimistic attitude to start with, Klaus. I'm ringing off."

———

A LITTLE OVER a year ago, before Olive's accident, Klaus had run into Artie Banyan on the set of *Brackett*. Artie had been visiting a nephew cast in the role of a two-bit car thief. The screenwriter lumbered over, a little waddle to his step these days, Wellesian in shape and size, still sporting a Vandyke, now splotched with gray like his receding hair. "The great artist," he'd announced as he approached Klaus's chair. "Brought low by the cathode-ray tube."

Klaus had stood and smiled, but really he was surprised at what a bellowing and cursing cartoon of his former self Artie had become. They shook hands, Artie's like a mechanic's, Klaus's like a gentleman's. "I believe you, too, have been brought low, then?"

Artie parried a finger at him. "Touché."

They made plans for lunch. Vague plans. Klaus made a point of forgetting to follow up. Then in the doldrums of summer, Artie had rung him at home in Palm Springs: He was in town, how about that lunch? They met at the country club, where Klaus put their Cobb salads and pork chops on his bill, and then they played nine holes. Artie talked about his kids, his grandkid, the time he met Frank Sinatra and Nelson Riddle at a bar near Capitol Studios on Melrose and told them, "Frank should really cut it with the upbeat stuff. Sad tunes. Heartbreakers. That's what people want to hear."

The story was beyond unlikely, but of a piece with Artie's hyperbolic character. The man had always projected a personality twice the size of his true potential, and he took glee in cornering even the smallest audience with one of his fish tales. "That's something," Klaus had said. "I really like those records."

"Brilliant," Artie said. "I can only take a scintilla of responsibility."

What they didn't talk about was the old days of New York, of Kay Stone, of *Hans & Greta*. But when Klaus invited him out to Palm Springs for a meeting about what Klaus only called "a television project I want your help on," the subject came up in almost no time.

Artie Banyan, rotund and tall and as hirsute as a bear, in his baggy gray swimming trunks, a thin yellow robe hanging from his thick shoulders, had plodded out to the pool with Klaus and said, without any warning, "Look I'm happy to partake of your hospitality, to catch up and all, but you and me aren't working together again. Nothing personal—" He squinted down at the glinting water, stirring the ice in his gin and tonic. "Actually, it is personal."

Klaus slid into the pool. This had become his life as a widower: in and out of the pool, talking to his fellow old men. "Hear me out," he said. "I've got an idea with *Brackett* and I think you're the only man for the job."

"Hey, I already saved your ass once and I barely got a thanks."

"Things are different now. I've had time to think about life. About my friends."

"We're friends now?" Artie said, shrugging. "That's something."

Klaus gave him the rundown: a dark new *Brackett*, the story spread over the whole season, an expressionist style with minimal dialogue. "Imagine if Murnau were still with us and could make a television show."

Artie's gaze had landed on the hulking black studio building. Standing armpit-deep in the pool, he gestured at it now with his drink. "That what I think it is?"

Klaus nodded. "I've kept it exactly as it was in '28. The sets and bulbs and backgrounds and everything. Olive's idea at first. But at this point it's a kind of monument. A younger part of myself is still there. Part of all of us."

Artie pretended to shiver. "Spooky stuff, Klaus. Say, remember that broad who lived with Kay back in New York? Thought we had something going there but she never returned my phone calls."

"It was a long time ago."

"Yeah," Artie said. He set his glass on the lip of the pool and dunked his head underwater. After he'd rubbed his face clear, he said, "So you got a first draft of this script, or what?"

"I don't have anything," Klaus said. "That why I called you."

FRANK HARLAN, JUST over the line of middle age, tanned and wrinkled and silver-haired, dressed in the loose silk shirt and blue jeans of a younger man, leaned his ass on the corner of Klaus's desk, his arms crossed, his eyes squinted at the wall. "So you're telling me," he said, "Brackett goes off the fucking reservation here? And the network boys are on board?"

"As I said," Klaus explained, "he's the lone hero, the last American. Look at this country. The crime. The marching. He is a man who will do what it takes."

"Like John Wayne," said Harlan, the name uttered with the slow reverence usually reserved for great holy men. But Harlan knew Wayne, or at least had been in a few of his pictures back when he had a film career, before he'd been relegated to television, before this, the biggest role of his lifetime, Detective John Brackett, the gruff cop who carried a healthy second place in the Nielsen ratings every Wednesday night for ABC.

Klaus knew the power Wayne's name held in his star's mind. "Just like the Duke, Frank. Like in *The Searchers*."

Harlan stood upright and began pacing the office. "Hell of a movie. So give it to me again. Brackett has to go on this killing spree? Where's it end?"

"It ends," Klaus said. "That's why I asked you in. Where the show is going, where the script is taking us, we'll be ending *Brackett* with season four."

A flinty rage pulsed through Harlan's whole body, though only his fingers moved, clutching at the air next to his hips as if he were searching for something to throttle. "You son of a bitch."

Klaus had known this would be a blow, had prepared a little speech to bolster his star, to ready him for what was ahead. But that was before Harlan had marched in with his playboy swagger, assuming he had some control over a show completely in Klaus's hands, daring to sit on the corner of his desk like a schoolyard bully, like a showoff.

"There has already been talk of replacing the lead," Klaus said. "To make it easier on the audience. Make the change more obvious."

Harlan narrowed him eyes. "A new Brackett? My fans would revolt."

"A brother," Klaus thought up in the moment. "The sponsors said to me, 'Herr von Stiegl, let's kill off Bracket and introduce a brother bent on revenge.' They think it would sell the idea, you understand, make it more palatable to a general audience."

"And nobody called Murray? I want Murray in here this minute."

Klaus adjusted his monocle, gestured at the chairs provided for guests. "Frank, have a seat."

"No," Harlan said, backpedaling toward the door. "You call me in on July Fourth weekend. I got my wife and kid out in the car in the sun. On the way to the fucking beach, Klaus. You call me in here and give me your stilted Kraut monologue about my character—*my* character, Klaus—going apeshit and scaring the bejesus out of half of America and now the show's going to end and now you want to replace me altogether and nobody had the decency to call my fucking agent? Get Murray in here or I'm not saying another word."

Klaus didn't get up. He glanced out the window at the parked convertible, Tessa Harlan checking her makeup, their boy, Track, picking his nose. "There's a phone at the front desk. Tell them I said you could use it. But nobody will be replacing you, so you should sit down."

Harlan paused at the door, his hairy and tanned hand gripping the knob. "You were bullshitting me?"

"I'm looking out for you. That's what I've always done. Remember how long we've been in business? The housing development? The shopping center? When this show started, how I came to you first in Palm Springs? You said you'd retired, and now you're a household name. The new season is going to be risky. But the risk will mean big ratings. Front-page news. Movie studios giving you another look. You don't want to peter out your life on the boob tube, do you? I tell you: when *Brackett* ends, your real career—the career everybody will remember—begins."

Harlan stood there like a chump for all of this. The longer his hand rested on the doorknob, the surer Klaus became that he would, eventually, come to his senses and sit down. Still, he put up another "I want Murray in here."

"We'll call Murray," Klaus said. "We'll get him in here after the holiday. Hell, we'll work up a new contract. A ten-percent raise. Or more. We can negotiate that. Now, sit down already. You believe in the individual, don't you? That a single great man is better than a rabble of beatniks marching in the streets? That's something me and you have in common, isn't it?"

The actor crossed his arms and moped his way back over toward the desk. He reminded Klaus of a guilty child, finished with his tantrum and ready to return to the loving arms of his father. Reminded him of Percy at the age of nine or ten, during that year the boy was always threatening, emptily, to run away. "Well," Harlan said, "yeah?"

"Do you like what happened in Watts? That mess at Berkeley?"

"Next you'll be asking me if Pat Brown deserves a third term as governor, Klaus." Harlan sat down. "You see that ad where he's calling our man Reagan John Wilkes Booth for crying out loud?"

"I did," Klaus said. "And that's just the sort of thing Brackett is against. Name-calling, bureaucratic inaction, fear of the mob. He's a lone gun."

Harlan's eyebrows popped up. "I like that. *A lone gun.* That's good."

THAT'S HOW IT started, his fourth and final season of *Brackett*, the first episode of which wouldn't air on television before Klaus announced his imminent retirement. Announced isn't the correct term. More like alluded to, let slip. As part of a fluff piece on the new season of ABC television for *TV Guide*, in response to the finely shaved face of a horn-rimmed Yale graduate who had rattled off some vapid question about what to expect from the legendary Klaus von Stiegl now that his films were shown in museums and his signature detective show was nearly the most popular thing on Wednesday nights: "Well, I plan to do nothing," Klaus had muttered. "I have completed the goals of my career."

This youngster—Clive something—had come alive with the sudden realization that he'd caught a scoop. "You mean to say you're finished with *Brackett*?"

"*Brackett* is finished," Klaus said without considering the words to have any special weight. "Or will be soon. And then I am done. As a director and producer. Time to work on my golf game, as they say."

The kid wasn't interested in that part. An old man saying he would bow out at the unexpected second pinnacle of his career was not news. Not compared to saying *Brackett* would end, not from cancellation, not from the whims of some executive boardroom, but because its creator said so. "Can you do that? End the program, I mean."

"I own the program," Klaus said. "That little insignia at the end? When the music is playing? That's my company."

Within a week the fluff piece became a page-long story in the magazine, headlined, I OWN THE PROGRAM: STIEGL KILLS "BRACKETT," and Klaus had to answer for all of it, nearly losing the show, or at least its potential to be broadcast, thanks to the apocalyptic nervousness of that same executive board. In the end it was all okay. ABC was in the business of selling ads, and thanks to Klaus's radical idea, his decision to turn the season into a single artistic statement, to make a show like no one had ever seen, the Madison Avenue boys started knocking down the door. Soon enough that same board had Klaus on the morning talk shows harping about "this rare opportunity, a crime show as important to everyday people as the World Series, a reason for every American to tune in each week," and always adding, with a leering adjustment of his monocle, "Of course, it will not be for the weak of stomach or the children."

BY LATE SUMMER, he had Artie out to Palm Springs again to hash out the ending. Again there was gin and tonic, again the pool. Work on the show had been for the first time fully rewarding, something akin to that initial sensation way back at the Astoria studio, before either of them had headed west. He'd come to understand that television had unforeseen potential, that a visual story could work on an epic scale, even if it would only be seen on tiny screens in the suburbs. He'd even managed to get Angie Dickinson signed on for a cameo in the last episode, wheelchair and all.

What they needed now was that last episode, an end to the program that would stick in the audience's mind. A final image. They had already discounted a shootout as too easy. Dying in the line of duty seemed redeeming, and Klaus had determined that Brackett would not be redeemed.

After an hour or so in the heat, just as Klaus was ready to go inside to the air conditioning, Artie swam up to the pool's edge, wiped his face with both hands, and bobbed there, still underwater but for his shoulders and head. "I got it," he said. "Brackett drowns, like in *Sunset Boulevard.* He solves everything and gets his revenge and clears his name, and then in a stupor he goes over into the pool, hits his head, nobody's there to save him. Just this guy alone without a friend, dead."

Artie, too, had been there the night George cannonballed off this very roof, into this very pool. They let that connection hang between them a moment.

"The audience will be unable to save him," said Klaus.

"Or unwilling."

"We'll turn our backs on him. The whole country. Like shrugging off an old skin."

Artie puffed the water off his lips and pushed off, backstroking toward the other side of the pool. Water splashed up onto the patio, wetting Klaus's sandaled feet, his cane, the cuffs of his white trousers. They had been around the block: Klaus nearing sixty-one, Artie some unnamed set of years his elder, both of them born near the opening of the century. They could remember the first and second World Wars, Korea, the Great Depression, the Jazz Age. Radio had been a new thing when they were young, television a product of their middle years. None of this was just in a history book for them. They knew a few things about this place, what it took from you, what it stood to lose.

"They'll understand, though," Klaus shouted at his swimming guest. "You have to trust the audience. It will hurt but they'll understand."

"Whatever you say, boss," Artie shouted over the intermittent splash. "If you ask me though, this Brackett's a grade-A son-of-a-bitch and the boob-tubers are going to salute the fucking flag when he's dead."

Los Angeles Times

June 8, 1989

PAINTER'S ATTACK COLORED BY ABORTION VIEWS

by HAROLD R. ROSE

Diane "Di" Stiegl, renowned post-modernist known for her large political paintings, was leaving her condo building for the grocery store on Wednesday morning when a man entered the lobby in an unseasonable coat, met eyes with her, and then produced a knife. "I thought he would kill me," she said from the L.A. County hospital. "I think he would have."

The man, Benjamin Richard Hightower (42) of Kissimmee, Fla., had traveled across the country with just that purpose in mind. Police discovered a 33-page manifesto in his Buick LeSabre, parked one block away from Stiegl's residence, in which he complained at length about the feminist artist's work, her support for AIDS patients, and her views on abortion. Stiegl suffered multiple slashes to her arms and hands as well as a single stab wound to her left shoulder before her husband, filmmaker Michael French, fought off the attacker. Hightower was then seized with the help of a deliveryman just outside the condo building and the police were called. Had Stiegl been alone, police believe the attack could have taken her life.

Prosecutors are currently weighing attempted-murder charges based on the plans outlined in Mr. Hightower's hand-written manifesto.

Stiegl became a conservative lightning rod in early 1989 when her show, "A Woman's Body: Landscapes and Portraits," opened at the San Francisco Museum of Modern Art. Partially funded by state and federal arts money, the show featured a series of photorealist paintings of abortion clinics and large close-up portraits of religious and political leaders known for their anti-abortion rhetoric. In an interview for the San Francisco Chronicle she said of the paintings, "Women are the targets of right-wing activism that masks as caring for children but is really about controlling a woman's body and her economic and physical freedom as a citizen. These people pretend to care about abortion, or maybe they've been whipped up to care by people who know what they're really after. But it's all about putting women back in the kitchen, waiting for their man to come in the door at dinnertime."

"'These people,'" Congressman Nick Vasilli (R - NJ) responded in the same SF Chronicle story, "don't appreciate having their tax dollars used to popularize baby-killing and to make fun of those who will fight for the lives of unborn children."

The article in question was found by police in Mr. Hightower's vehicle, with heavy underlines and circles around key quotes. "Mr. Hightower appears to be an anti-abortion activist," said Det. Patrick Daley of the Los Angeles Police Department. "But we haven't yet determined an exact motive or why Ms. Stiegl was the target of this action."

Congressman Vasilli declined to comment for this story.

Stiegl's work has often been controversial. Early in her career she produced a series of paintings depicting the final days of gay men dying of what would come to be called AIDS. These works were greeted with complicated responses. Some found their political nature contrary to the direction of art at the time, while others disagreed with the elegiac, even mythic proportion given gay men at a time when homosexuality was still deemed by many an unacceptable lifestyle. Later, as a movement grew to represent victims of AIDS and HIV, as well as gays and lesbians at large, criticism focused on the fact that Ms. Stiegl, a heterosexual woman, was using gay lives to build recognition and income, reaped from private moments of suffering and political oppression. Her later work has addressed many of these concerns. In 1986, in her first West Coast solo show, she sold work already deeded to the Gay Men's Health Alliance, and these paintings showed a broadening of her subject material to general women's topics, racism, and what she called "the flimsy promises of suburbia." Still in her early thirties, Stiegl's work is some of the most valuable among her contemporaries. At her last opening, "Cold Alley," a photorealist oil painting of a darkly-lit residential hallway with a man moving toward the spectator with his armed raised, a scene of spousal abuse rarely depicted in fine art, sold for over $400,000. Secondary sales of her works have brought in million-dollar and even two-million-dollar bids.

The attack on Stiegl comes at a time of increasing threat to abortion clinics and physicians who provide abortion services, according to a spokesperson for NARAL. Since 1982, several clinics have been bombed, set afire, or invaded by force, sometimes causing serious injury to those inside. Mr. French, Ms. Stiegl's husband, said that Mr. Hightower specifically called his wife "the babykiller" as he wielded his knife. "We believe Di was targeted because of her political views. This was an act of terrorism meant to silence an important voice in women's rights today."

An attorney for Mr. Hightower claims that his client was suffering a recent job loss and mental breakdown and that the attack was completely random. Late yesterday evening in a press conference, Det. Daley reiterated that police are "looking into everything. But we're not in the business of telling the accused what they can and can't believe about politics."

DIANE

1990

FOR A WHILE, she couldn't paint. Couldn't really do anything. She hated leaving the house by the front entryway because that was where it had happened, where that man had been waiting for her. She stayed in bed, had the television brought into the room with her, and watched hours of soap operas and old reruns, shutting it off only when Michael returned in the evenings.

When she went to her studio, finally, a couple of months after it had happened, she'd had to go out the back way, through the heavy metal door that opened onto a smelly alleyway shared with a Chinese restaurant and a bakery that specialized in decorative cakes. Her stomach turned. That day the air had been warm and thick with old grease.

At the studio she stared at the canvas she'd left unfinished, the sketch of a televangelist stage, two women with tall hair and a man holding a limp Bible. She could see the television influence, understood it now: she and Michael had only purchased the set earlier that year, to watch the evening news and Carson, a way to wind down. She'd nearly forgotten that she had envisioned a series of TV scenes, slightly out of focus, the colors garish. She had already completed a large "Study of Brackett," her grandfather's famous character frozen in that horrible scene where he kills an innocent Black woman in her home, part of a robbery gone wrong. She'd meant the image as a criticism of all the things Brackett and Dirty Harry and Ronald

Reagan stood for, but after the attack the idea no longer gelled in her mind. It had been Michael's idea to give that one to Track, still living out in Palm Springs, a hardcore Reaganite these days, though he'd said last time she saw him that he wasn't all that keen on Bush. Last year he'd sent her a Christmas card with his two kids and new wife posed outside their latest home. She'd written back to say that she would be sending him a painting or two as a housewarming gift. She hadn't gotten around to it, but an image of her grandfather at his apotheosis couldn't miss.

Ideas interested her: concepts, little sketches, talking through her plans with Michael. But the physical act of painting felt impossible, as if a connection between muscle and mind had been severed. In reality the knife had only left her with minor injuries. Scars on her forearms and one hand and both elbows; a single three-inch-deep puncture in the meat of her shoulder. She had been lucky. The knife was short and not made for killing, the sort of thing a handyman would open to get into a cardboard box. She'd lost blood and required stitches. A single visit to a physical rehab specialist. But she was depressed. Or at least that was Michael's determination. "You've had a shock," he said the day she returned from the studio without painting a single stroke. "It makes sense. And your mind is full of fearful thoughts. That leads to seeing darkness and danger everywhere, blaming yourself. I've been there."

He had been there, of course. About a year after she left New York, he'd OD'd, gone to the hospital, been through the other end of cleaning up that she hadn't had to see—the forced end of it, with criminal charges looming if he fell back off the wagon. Things Nina hadn't told Diane about, had shielded her from. He went to AA and NA, met weekly with a shrink. Diane had skipped all those steps. Not because she was stronger than him. Coming through clean from either direction was a dispiriting nightmare that only ended gradually and left her, at least, feeling foolish and embarrassed for ever having been addicted in the first place.

WHEN SHE WAS being most honest with herself, she knew that she had felt directionless as an artist for some time, even before that morning in June. But she had ignored the sensation, treating it like a debt no one was yet harassing her to collect. The whole last decade felt to her like a slow loss of grip. Reagan and Bush had turned time into this circular arrangement where the present never quite existed, only a nostalgic past held out before the nation as its true and glittering future. To Diane and people like her, the only reaction had been to play along, to create something new by putting old things together, to operate more as a nightclub DJ than a tried-and-true musician. Academics had waxed poetic about the "postmodernity" of all this, and at gallery shows, she'd nodded along to the armchair critics and increasingly wealthy collectors when they quoted or misquoted those academics' work. Somehow, without knowing it, Diane had become the poster girl for a whole movement she didn't necessarily follow. For last year's London show, Annie's copy in the gallery booklet had claimed, without any controversy, that "Di Stiegl is the central and most daring of a new American synthesis," before pointing to *Orfeo 22* as a perfect example, with its Rauschenberg-like print of the Last Supper in the bottom-right corner, where Diane had added images of Mr. T and Pee-wee Herman. She thought of that painting—currently hanging in the San Francisco MOMA—with shame: she'd been chasing someone else's tail there, no longer thinking on her own. But what was "thinking on her own?" Maybe it was just this. Pacing around her studio as the afternoon burned down.

What she wanted more than anything was for Phil to be here, reading a book, listening to her, playing records, guiding her to herself without any instructions the way he had all those years before. Alive. What would he think of her now? A week after returning from the hospital, she'd dug out the old army jacket he'd bought for her at that secondhand store, the EE CUMMINGS nearly faded, the worn fabric musty. What connection had she ever had to E. E. Cummings? It didn't matter. Now she wore it every day.

———

A FEW MONTHS after the attack, when she had settled into her routine of not actually painting in the studio, Nina came out to visit. Walking the La Brea Tar Pits (which she just had to see "after the cartoons") while Michael was at a video shoot, she told Diane, "You two really ought to leave. Michael's scared for you. He'll never tell you. He'll wait for you to do something."

"Where would we go?" Diane asked, not defensive but genuinely unsure. The whole country seemed about the same: steadily headed for a violent Bible camp just over the horizon. And New York seemed impossible. They'd had to put that place behind them. "His work is here," she said. "I can't uproot Michael."

Nina smiled, though her eyes, even through sunglasses, betrayed her weariness. "Like I said. He'll never tell you. He's got this whole hang-up about disappointing you again."

"I wasn't disappointed."

"Okay?" Nina said in a tone that meant, *yeah right.* "You know, he can do the work he really loves anywhere. Those music videos don't matter to him."

Diane had noticed a man in a short black tie and no sports coat eyeing her. Her heart thumped. She pulled Nina a little closer to the mastodons. Nina had finished college, was talking about going to graduate school in literature. She seemed more attuned to reality than Diane had ever been.

"Did you see him?" Diane said when they were at a distance. "The man with the tie?"

Nina looked around. "No." And then, with a serious expression, "Di, you okay?"

Her heart rate was out of control. She had to remind herself to breathe. "I'm not out much. Since the—"

"I can understand that. Hey, that's why I'm here." They walked a little farther. "If you want to know the truth, Mickey's always on about the cops here. He had a friend roughed up because they said he looked like a suspect."

She'd heard about that: a guy named Bill from his AA meetings.

That event had kept Michael awake for two nights in a row. But he'd never said he wanted to leave over it. "The cops here," Diane said vaguely.

"Uh-huh?" said Nina. And when it was clear Diane had nothing more to add, "Besides, I don't think he likes all this sunshine."

"You're giving me the hard sell," Diane said, trying to laugh off her recent panic. "You know I'm really a Californian, right?"

Nina could see through her. "Just ask him. You two can go anywhere."

_____

ANNIE CALLED DIANE the following Monday morning on her studio phone to say she had something amazing to tell her about a film of her grandfather's, the last silent, that one about Hansel and Gretel. That afternoon, the painting started again, and when it did, Diane did no preliminary drawing. For the first time in her life she just began putting paint to canvas, playing around with color and tone, creating abstract forms with no connection to reality. As she painted these she knew that she would never show them. They weren't "Di Stiegls," but they also weren't very good. This didn't trouble her. When Annie came to the studio the next night, Diane hid them in a corner, covered by a blanket, and began blotching paint on the televangelist canvas. "I remember you telling me about this one," Annie said. "What else have you been up to?"

Annie was her exclusive dealer now, a mutually beneficial arrangement since '87, when she had succeeded in broadening the George West Galleries from Impressionism and Abstraction into all forms of contemporary art. The same year one of Diane's paintings sold for a million dollars in the secondary market—not a penny coming to her. The same year Diane realized that her labor had become a commodity for the super-rich. It was also around the time Michael had reappeared, steadying her, keeping her on track to do her work anyway.

"I've been moving slowly," Diane said.

"Understandable," said Annie. She was dressed in a gray pantsuit with big shoulders, her hair done up and curled, looking like a movie star playing a professional woman, a blond Sally Field navigating office life. "I've been dying to see the television paintings, you know."

Diane didn't have the heart to tell her that these two were it, one finished and one barely started. "I'm working every day now," she said, though it was certainly bending the truth. "I'll have more of a sense of things in the spring."

Annie hopped up into the windowsill and smiled. "So I met a lawyer for the Schlossberg Foundation, Alex McAllister. He's a collector. Old paintings. Nothing contemporary. But he says the Foundation has a copy of *Hans & Greta* in storage. Wanted to transfer to video with the rest of their library. They've got a UCLA scholar piecing it together from notes in their archives. Your name came up. What do you think of recording a little introduction?"

"I've never seen it."

"Nobody has. Not even Alex. But you know his films and, you know, you've got this personal connection."

Truthfully, Diane was excited to see the film. All her grandfather's other movies—including *The Bachelor's Wife*, which Diane still had the stolen reel from, despite having no projector—had long been available. They were of interest to colleges and libraries and a few obsessive collectors, and cost about a hundred dollars per videocassette. Michael had surprised her with a newly upgraded set of the tapes, complete with introductions by Charlton Heston, for her birthday last year, replacing the fuzzy ones Mrs. Harlan had sent her. They spent a weekend watching them. She'd developed a deep connection to their shadowy, expressionistic sets, the erotic obsessiveness of the characters, the overwhelming beauty of Kay Stone. He really was an incredible filmmaker. Since the attack, she would often play parts of the videotapes between shows, sometimes only ten minutes at a time, often for an hour or more. They became a place to return to, a world unlike her own. Annie knew all this. But she knew, as well, that Diane didn't like interviews, didn't like being on video, didn't like having a public face at all. "Especially since last summer," Diane said. "I don't want these people to even know who I am."

"Di, that was one crazy dude. And he's in jail. We're talking five minutes in front of a camera reading cue cards."

In September she'd skipped George West's funeral, even though his gallery represented her, even though he was her grandfather's cousin, a legend in the West Coast art scene, even though Annie—as the old man's right hand—delivered the eulogy. She had felt guilty ever since, though really at that time there was no leaving the house. "I'll think about it."

"None of these wackos are even going to see it," Annie said. "And Alex wants to work up an event to screen it. Movie stars. Big Hollywood money. At, like, Grauman's or something."

"Sounds like more than five minutes," Diane said. She'd been listening to a Philip Glass CD before Annie arrived and now, with the sound low, it seemed that someone was crouched in a corner whispering the same word again and again. "I just don't feel comfortable," she said. "I'm not exactly afraid, but I just feel on-edge. You know?"

Annie slid off the windowsill, her flats slapping the concrete floor. "This is legacy stuff, Di. And a lot of potential art buyers. You'll be safe. Everyone you love will be there. Plus security. Let's do this."

———

WITH HER GRANDFATHER in mind, she brought the Brackett painting back out, and soon after started another, this time of Brackett opening that mysterious door in the drain tunnel, where the bearded man sat, seemingly waiting for him, reading a newspaper as Brackett reached for his pistol. She painted this one in the panel style, a diptych, the door opening on one side of a thick black line, the gun pointed at the bearded man's head on the other. Throughout she maintained the hazy, television-grade focus, the near-pointillism of the pixels. From this she moved on to stills from her grandfather's old silent films, including the giant close-up of Kay Stone in tears in *Under a Cherokee Moon*, and by June she ordered from a catalogue one of his Mexican films, *Tijuana Tornado*. It was an awful specimen, not at all redeeming, and she couldn't understand a word. But she painted the interior of an old church where a gunslinger respectfully awaited the end of a wedding before killing the groom.

Productive weeks passed. At some point in all of this she told Annie she would do the introduction for *Hans & Greta*. "You'll have to forgive me," Annie said. "I already told Alex you'd do it. I knew you'd come around."

Sometimes Annie scared her these days. She'd become cutthroat, presumptuous, a flitting social butterfly. But it must come with the job, and these qualities were in the service of Diane's career, her name, her place in the art world. "Okay," she said.

———

MICHAEL, OF COURSE, was over the moon about the idea. He'd been trying to get her in front of the camera for one of his short films for a while, really ever since he came out to L.A. When he'd moved here he was living with Marie, a perfectly nice person, a person Diane had dinner with three separate times, a person she told him to his face was perfect for him, even if saying such things had made her want to stab out her own eyes. She hadn't thought she wanted back with Michael. Had thought, in fact, that they'd been a wreck for each other, a bad turn. But when she saw him again that summer in '87, he was a new man, clean and fattened a little, incredibly sharp of mind. They were, she came to understand, adults. And when they'd first been together they were still hanging on to childhood.

She had slept with him within a month of his arrival in Los Angeles. They'd gone for a late breakfast, a "brunch," as the yuppies were calling it, and alone together for the first time since all they'd been through, she couldn't keep her eyes away from his. She was reminded of that first early morning in New York, what had amounted to their first date. They confessed everything: all their doubts, the terror of cleaning up, the lives they'd led since. Time had already begun to speed up. No longer was a week equal to something like a year. Getting older apparently meant feeling always like the days were running out from beneath you. They talked and talked until they couldn't, and when they left the restaurant, in the broad pre-noon daylight, Michael was gripping her upper arm, tight, like they were in on something together. "Let's go somewhere," she'd said. "I'm not ready to go home."

"A drink?" he'd said. "No, it's too early for that. You said you had a studio around here?"

They went there, to the third floor of what had once been a warehouse on the dead far end of Sunset, and when she pretended to be showing him some painting she lost patience with the ruse and turned to him and brought his face down to hers and then pulled up his shirt and discovered the same soft, flat belly and the same ribs and the same patch of Brillo hair on his chest, and he slung the shirt across the wide, narrow-windowed room and grabbed her up under the arms and they sank together to the floor, cold and hard but in the end leaving a red mark on her buttocks as if it were carpet. After, when they were on the floor staring up at the high gray ceiling, noontime, they said they wouldn't do it again. But they did, as they both knew they would the first time.

He tried to keep the relationship with Marie going, but it soon fell apart. Diane, like someone out of a trashy novel, had simply ignored all of that, sensing the natural course of events would be a breakup, some weeks or months of playing the villain before Michael was hers again. It all happened much more swiftly than she'd imagined. Within a month of that morning at the studio, he was moving in, piling his video equipment on her small, round dinner table. "I'll move that later," he said. "I swear."

The next year they were married: a weekend Las Vegas trip, an Elvis impersonator in a roadside church, Annie as maid of honor and her girlfriend Suzanne, dressed in a bosomy tuxedo, the best man.

Back in Los Angeles they fell right into a groove, the professional couple, the artists, talking endlessly about their work, standing up for each other, giving advice, losing sleep when it was necessary. They were each other's perfect judges and critics. In short order, Michael was considered one of the leading voices in video art, championed by none other than Barbara London, the most important curator in the field. His pieces were being purchased by museums. He'd even had a meeting with a film studio about making a feature.

In that same stretch of time, she had made peace with Percy and Antonia, made real connections with them. She talked with her father on the phone nearly every week; he and Cindy had started working on a book about Klaus von Stiegl. Her mother wrote her letters and once, in the summer of '89, brought her other family out to Disneyland. Mrs. Harlan visited regularly. She and Diane met for shopping and an early dinner once a month. Before that man with the knife, everything had come into alignment. But Diane only saw it as such after the fact. Looking back, those days glowed in an endless summer. At the time, she'd been too busy to notice.

THE MORNING OF the *Hans & Greta* screening she was sick for a third day in a row. She called Lily for advice—or rather, not advice, just someone far away she could tell this to. "You're going to have to get the test," Lily said. "You're putting it off because you think it will stay put off."

"I never wanted to be a mother," Diane said. "I never thought about it."

"The first thing is to find out if it's happening. Bodies are fucked up. This could be just a scare that doesn't amount to anything."

"A scare," Diane said. "That's for sure."

"You know what I mean. But ignoring it won't make the whole thing go away."

"I know," Diane said. Really, it seemed like a metaphor for her whole life. "I know."

"Go on, then. You got a pharmacy around there?"

Diane thought of the local place, the man with the mustache and glasses behind the elevated counter. "I couldn't go in there."

"Then drive around. But get it while you're at the studio and take it there. Michael doesn't even have to know."

"Why shouldn't Michael know?"

Lily sighed. "Gimme a break, Di. You going to get the test?"

She screwed up her courage to call a cab, put on a big coat, a hat, sunglasses, like she was in disguise. It was a sunny, warm day. She'd looked up a Thrifty Drug ten blocks away, a place she wouldn't usually go into, and when they arrived, she asked the cabbie to stay at the curb, "And keep an eye out, please."

The cabbie looked sleepily into the rearview. "For what?"

"Anything," she said. "Suspicious-looking men."

He nodded, smiling only enough to communicate that he was on board.

When she set the box down on the counter she noticed the ridiculous model hands holding one of the tests: perfectly moisturized, almost gleaming, ending with pointed pink nails. Her own nails were necessarily short, made for physical work, stained thick with a dozen paint colors. And she hadn't even begun painting for the day—

"Find everything you need?" asked the dark-haired, over-tall clerk, dressed, somewhat comically, in the same white smock a pharmacist would wear. Maybe she was a pharmacist. Did they work in shifts, going up the little stairs and then back down again to man a register?

Diane grabbed a Reese's Cup from the rack under the counter. "This too."

The clerk looked from one item to the other before meeting Diane's eyes, almost a moment of camaraderie. Then she announced the total and said, "Bag?"

"I'll put them in my purse," Diane said, and did so.

When she returned to the studio she found a manila package propped against the door. "Di," Annie had written in pen on the top. "Here's the film on VHS. Still grainy and no sound. XO."

Annie. Inside was just a black tape with nothing written on the rectangular sticker at its center, a copy someone had put little thought or personality into, surely handed to Annie that morning or last night, and if Diane had been here she would have seen her, likely would have spilled the beans that she thought she might be pregnant, and then the mess and fear of this day would have been mitigated just a little but also invaded, by a friend, surely, but invaded nonetheless. For the first time since June, she was glad to be alone. This was between her and EPT, and then it was between her and Michael. That is, if there was anything to tell Michael.

She read the instructions for the test three times, her mind trying its best to focus on other things—such as the stupidity of her agreeing to introduce her grandfather's film on the same day she would get a VHS copy of it to watch on her studio television. When she left the test on the bathroom counter, she went first to the window, thinking she could wait out the result in a pensive silence. This proved immediately impossible, so she loaded the tape into the VCR and hit Play. It started without a title card, just the image of a picturesque old European city on the banks of a river, the corners faded black like an old photograph, a perfect circle.

Back in the early days, what Michael called their "first marriage," the idea of their having kids had been completely shut down. Michael had turned thirty-two last week, and she was only a year behind. Their careers were exactly that—careers. He'd made music videos with metal and rap and pop groups up and down the charts. His personal work was getting attention from more and more gallerists. He was working on turning Clay Cassius into a TV pilot for that new Fox channel. And even the attack had—according to Annie—made Diane's significance rise among collectors. Never mind the horror of such an idea. If ever there could be a time for this to happen, it was now. But who thought like this? As if life were a series of propositions rather than a tumbling wheel no one could control?

And still she was afraid. She couldn't tell for sure if this was part of the natural fear of motherhood, of everything that was about to

come at her, or if it was rooted in what happened in the entryway
of their building. Or, as she thought with a new kind of terror when
the test showed its plus sign in her studio bathroom, if she was afraid
of what Michael would say. What if he didn't want to go through
with it? And what if she did? What if they both did?

On the screen, a young man and woman—George West and Kay
Stone—walked hand-in-hand into a forest more unreal than any
dream. The trees were shadows trimmed with blinding light. Birds
swooped in and out of the frame in massive groups, schools of aerial
fish. A single home appeared to grow out of the moss and rotting
leaves before them. Without speaking, the pair approached it, touched
the impossible softness of its fleshy walls. A breeze caught their hair;
their eyes met. Something inexplicable was happening, something
Diane couldn't quite follow. But her own eyes had wandered to the
canvas stretched on a frame across the room. Empty. Waiting. Her
chest felt light, the lightest it had felt since the attack. And she crossed
the room, the film still playing, so that she could paint.

The New York Times Book Review

October 6th, 1998

THE HOLLYWOOD REBEL HAS NO CLOTHES

by JESS ST. ANNE

A SILENT LEGACY: THE FIRE AND FAILURES OF KLAUS VON STIEGL
by Cindy Miller-Stiegl, with Percy Stiegl
Scribner, $20.99

As an undergraduate at the University of Virginia in the late eighties, I signed up for a course in the English program that purported to elucidate "The Literature of Native Americans." I must have been a sophomore—used to the challenges and structures of college and not yet ready to leave for that fiction out on the horizon we used to call "real life." The instructor was a recent PhD graduate: bumbling, limp-haired, always reminding us that he wasn't actually qualified to teach the course. He'd taken over last-minute, been given little guidance, and would be learning along with us. His charm and excitability in the classroom won us over anyway, and I think they would have gotten him through the semester had he not, in the week after midterms, pushed the TV/VCR cart into the room and put on

a film, "Under a Cherokee Moon," directed by the silent-film auteur Klaus von Stiegl.

I remember that around the five- or ten-minute point in our viewing, some of my fellow students began quietly tittering. I gave the guy sitting next to me a quizzical look. "They're all white," he'd said, grinning like he'd just made the team. And when I looked back at the fuzzy image on the screen, I realized he was right. The entire cast was made up of white actors in a sort of redface, and by his alarmed and nervous behavior, it was clear our instructor either didn't know or hadn't considered why that would matter until just at that moment.

That silent movie, as well as the other three feature films von Stiegl made in Hollywood before sound changed everything, is explored with both historic precision and literary art in "A Silent Legacy," written by the poet Cindy Miller-Stiegl with the help of her husband, the filmmaker's only son. Rich with behind-the-scenes detail and private family secrets, the book straddles the line between film and television history and tell-all biography, giving both a surprisingly literary sensibility. Much of what we learn is entirely new, even to those who study film, and a good portion of that material will likely change the way movie lovers regard this legendary figure—the sort of man whose name and style one knows better than their actual works. Because, after all, who really watches silent cinema?

As Miller-Stiegl reminds us, at the height of von Stiegl's career in film, practically everyone watched silent cinema, and invested what they saw with a magic that helped to define Hollywood, and America, for the world. "Nobody missed sound, nobody talked about sound, nobody complained as they left the theater about not hearing any sound," Miller-Stiegl writes. "To think clearly about the era one has to imagine a world in which cinema had always been a visual art: moving pictures." And it was in this particular art form that von Stiegl excelled. His four films of the mid-to-late 1920s have come to be seen as major works riding the aesthetic crest of silent cinema,

just before the crash. For quite some time, "Cherokee Moon" was thought to be the last of these to have survived, influencing the work of Welles, Ford, and Hitchcock. But in the late eighties, restoration began on what would be seen as his finest film, the visual masterpiece "Hans & Greta," produced independently in 1928 at a short-lived studio in Palm Springs.

As far as books on nearly-forgotten directors are concerned, this one is a marvel. We see the young immigrant von Stiegl, still using his birth name of Klaus Aaronsohn, falling in love with cinema while living with his pieceworker parents in a Lower East Side tenement, stepping into a new life when he's adopted by his rich uncle, then inventing another self to erase his less-than-aristocratic past. (How strange, in our time, to read of a great Jewish artist who felt the need to so heavily mask his identity as to actually construct a fictional character, complete with a faked résumé of work in a German film studio. That he and Hollywood itself never bothered to unpack this particular item of baggage—though it sat right before them, unavoidable—gives parts of his story a surreal quality.) Miller-Stiegl is especially evocative with the details of tenement life, and harrowing in her description of the fateful afternoon a fire would take the lives of von Stiegl's parents, a tragedy that would haunt and motivate the young man who would, by the shockingly tender age of 22, appear for work at a New York movie studio in the drag of a German film director and promptly make his first masterpiece, "The Bachelor's Wife," which would bring tragic stardom to its female lead, the inimitable Kay Stone.

Maybe we're used to men in power preying on women, especially if we can place their behavior in history; maybe, in our present, as we collectively shrug off the nation's chief executive engaging in an affair with a staffer, these issues seem in some way quaint. But von Stiegl's treatment of Stone is more alarming than the classic "casting couch," and—at least for a number of women—the part of the narrative which will likely damage the filmmaker's reputation. The book shares for the first time very shocking details of the actress being tossed aside after a years-long romance with the director when their connection became inconvenient, as well as a close discussion of her eventual suicide, which the authors argue was caused by von Stiegl's cold and retaliatory actions in the years after he was a Hollywood pariah.

Peopled with characters almost too big to believe, from MGM executives and a silent-film-star-turned-art-dealer (whose gallery represents Di Stiegl, Klaus's granddaughter), the book is comparable to Trollope and Tolstoy in scope and scandal and literary grandeur. There is a wealthy heiress who dies with his secrets. There are years in Mexico making relatively lazy and forgotten Spanish-language films before von Stiegl appears, out of left field, in early television production at CBS, directing weekly sitcoms, variety shows, and golden-age dramas. Fans of the classic TV series "Brackett" will be especially interested in these chapters on von Stiegl's "comeback" period, fostered by an independent production company and yet another ruined career for an actor who had tied his fate to von Stiegl's rebel schtick. And forgotten in between the bookends of his career: naming names before HUAC and causing the ruin of a promising young writer.

Still, in spite of all the bad news, one is left with a cautionary and somehow inspiring tale of an unfettered artist often creating at the very top of his field, as well as a stronger belief in the visual power of cinema. Writing about von Stiegl's second film, "Heartbreak City," Miller-Stiegl tells us, "He had effectively hijacked production from the most powerful men in Hollywood. Instead of turning in simply a well-made version of a program picture, what he gave them was a series of evocative paintings where human actors happened to find themselves, a kind of dream, a world the viewer disappears into and doesn't want to leave." It is a reminder, too, that the family's other great painter, Di Stiegl, has spent the last two decades creating a "kind of dream"—one which turns a critical eye on this country's moral failings, its fraying social fabric—and that von Stiegl's cinema, like a mirror image, often celebrated the dark and individualistic forces which beat in its heart.

Jess St. Anne is the author of the novel "Betrothings" (Little, Brown) as well as the forthcoming memoir "My Cincinnati."

KLAUS
1971

H E HAD BEEN drifting off to sleep with a book in his hands when the phone rang. The nurse, Arnetta, answered. Klaus sat up on a stack of pillows and held his ear toward the open doorway to listen when he heard her say something about Mr. von Stiegl being on bed rest. "What do you mean you're his son? He never mentioned a son." And then, as a great weight settled on his shoulders, "Yes, yes, it's quite serious. Cancer. Started in the stomach and spread to the intestines. Yes, sir. Yes it's quite bad. He's sleeping now, or I would get him."

A minute later, Arnetta came to the doorway, crossed her arms, and shook her head in disappointment. Klaus tried to appear ignorant and sleepy, deaf to whatever had just happened in the kitchen. But clearly this wasn't working. So he said, "Percy?"

"He's on his way," she said to his fake-closed eyes. "Your *son* said he's leaving tonight."

———

THE LAUGHABLE PART of it all was that Klaus was expected to pretend Percy had driven halfway across the country to take care of him, as if he hadn't spent the last year or more drifting like some Steinbeck character, that poor girl in tow, taking jobs for weeks at a time before breaking a lease and appearing in another state, always sending a letter upon arrival, blathering about some new prospect, asking for a little money to help get them settled. Coming here, to Palm Springs, had clearly been like the landing of a vulture: his wings were tired and death hung in the air.

———

THE NEXT DAY, Frank Harlan's estranged wife came to check on Klaus—a regular occurrence these last few years, the two of them beached here so many miles from the sea after *Brackett*. If Percy wanted to know where his family's dear money ran off to, well, some of it, a good pile one could say, had made it by way of personal check over to Mrs. Tessa Harlan's bank account. What could Klaus do after her husband walked out on her for a teenage script-girl, after Frank had made a circus of seeing in the mirror one day that he was getting old? Klaus had cautioned the man against the affair, had sung the praises of monogamy and the institution of marriage— but the times were the times. Frank Harlan used the leg up Klaus had given him to embrace the sexual revolution, drop acid, and tank what was left of his career. Showing up soused for an audition with John Frankenheimer, backing out of a multi-episode guest spot on *Gunsmoke*, outright turning down a role the kid Bogdanovich had requested him for. And drinking like another Prohibition was looming around the corner.

In that fool's destructive wake remained poor Tessa Harlan and their kid, Track, beggars at the doorstep of Frank's business partner. Klaus couldn't turn them down. He'd covered their back bills, paid off her Oldsmobile, floated them money to get by month-to-month, offered without her asking to pay for the kid's school clothes and a little summer vacation for the two of them and even Tessa's college expenses. He'd got them through the worst of it and put a little money in savings as she remade her life, becoming a schoolteacher even as Frank ran aground and threatened lawsuits and claimed that he was writing the tell-all biography of the century, "one that'll burn Hollywood to the ground."

Klaus and Frank's real estate venture—always operating only

by the strength of Scotch tape and bubble gum—had gone from a healthy moneymaking scheme between two upstanding citizens to an open shopfront for the postal service. The only thing it produced was stamped envelopes moving from one lawyer's office to another. Frank had grown paranoid after *Brackett* failed to deliver on the movie stardom Klaus had promised. He wouldn't speak to Klaus, made erratic decisions, dragged his feet on anything that could make the company money. Klaus had ceded any control, the company spiraling into debt. "I don't care what happens with the real estate," he'd told George, to his cousin's great consternation. "Not if it means dealing with that lunatic."

"You should have let me look at the books," George said. "You never understood business."

"Chalk it up to a loss," Klaus said. "It's too late to matter."

Before Tessa and her son arrived, Arnetta had helped Klaus into a decent-looking shirt and cardigan, his lower half still in pajama pants, covered by a blanket. "She heard from around the bend," Arnetta told him. "The prognosis. Near everyone in town's heard, I guess."

The prognosis had been Arnetta's term, a doctorly and final summation, announced in person last week in this very room by Dr. Weintraub. Klaus, in a moment of despondency, had called Artie and told him everything. The cancer had spread to the liver, the gall bladder, and a whole new region of his intestines. "Tell the old gang for me," he'd told Artie. "Drop a line to Clumsky over at *Variety*."

And now Tessa Harlan was here, sweeping into the room, her downcast son, freckled and floppy-haired, right at her elbow. "My God, Klaus I only heard today at lunch. There I am in the cafeteria playing monitor and who but Jessie Martin blurted it out and I didn't want to believe it at all. Is there nothing to be done? Tell me it's a rumor. A vicious rumor."

"I've known a while," he said. "One knows these things before the doctors. And then I'll be with Olive. I don't really believe in such things. The soul. Afterlife. But I do believe I'll be with Olive."

There had followed a long evening of conversation and television and Tessa and Track eating dinner with Arnetta as Klaus told them again and again he didn't have an appetite. Later, when the mood had shifted to more positive commentary (Elizabeth Taylor this, Nixon's campaign that), he had mentioned offhand that his son had also gotten word, that he was en route, driving or at least driving soon to Palm Springs, his daughter along for the ride. "He's a lonely man," he told Tessa. "A little peripatetic, a very unsettled man. But it would mean the world if you could help welcome them. Him and Diane. A wonderful girl. She drew those fine pictures on the refrigerator of that band you enjoy."

"The Monkees?" she said. "Track used to love them. He's only into Miles Davis now."

To this Track gazed at the ceiling as if awaiting celestial deliverance. "John Coltrane, Mom. That or Ornette Coleman."

"Yes," she said, laughing an honest, dry laugh. "The crazy horn music. How could I forget? Anyway we'll look forward to meeting them. To think: another artist in the family."

IT WOULD BE two more days before the yapping dog announced Percy and Diane's arrival on the front porch, and Arnetta sailed from the bedroom to get the door. Walter Cronkite shuffled papers and looked jovial onscreen as he moved from Vietnam to a story about the women's tennis player Billie Jean King. Klaus wanted to disappear. *Take me up*, he thought. *Send me into the goddamn light.*

Alas, no. Klaus heard the low, concerned-in-quotation-marks voice of Percy, the whispering of Diane, the sniffing and jangling of the dog—who would of course find him first, bounding onto the bed and licking at his hands and neck before the remaining members of Klaus's crinkled family appeared as a long and short silhouette in the doorway, calling out the name Peanut Pattie. The girl ran forth, tall and lanky, bigger than Klaus had imagined her. "Peanut Pattie," she said again. "Get down. Get down. Bad dog."

When Percy approached, Klaus felt the instinctive need to scooch up on his pillows. "Dad," the boy said. "Dad, how are you feeling? Sorry about the dog. We got here as soon as we could."

It wasn't that he didn't love his son. He did. But in the years since Olive's death, the boy's only interest in his widowed father had to do with the money he believed himself to be owed. "You've taken all Mom's money to punish me," he'd said on the phone last year. "Because you hate Antonia."

"I don't hate anyone, and neither did your mother. But the woman needs help. Son, she needs to go to a hospital."

That's when another voice spoke on the line: Antonia's. She had been listening on another phone, in another room. "You horrible old man," she'd said. "You greedy, horrible, old man."

Klaus, chilled to the bone with terror and guilt, had slammed down the receiver. What should he have done? Stayed on the line for them both to go after him? He'd wanted that day to go see his lawyer, Paul Garland, and arrange to have Olive's remaining fortune split down the middle, half to Percy and his family, and to never speak to them again. He'd gone so far as to make an appointment and dress himself in suit and tie. But as he passed the old family photos on the hallway wall, his rage got the better of him. He would do nothing of the sort. The best the boy would get from him would be the monthly check.

He'd thought for a long while that they wouldn't speak again, that he would go on writing the checks with no response in return, no news of Diane's schoolwork or drawings. But then Percy had called to say that he and his wife had split, that he and Diane were moving—and now here was this man, this boy, sauntering into Klaus's bedroom to retrieve an overexcited dog, rambling about traffic and what is there to eat because Diane is hungry and gee, Dad, you don't look all that bad just a little thin, a little tired, are you tired, do you want us to get out of your way?

THE GIRL HAD grown. Deedee. That's what Percy insisted on calling her still, though she confided to Klaus that she hated the nickname. "Diane, then," he said, moved now to the dining table, one hand on the metal cane he'd come to rely upon these last months. "Tell me, Diane. Is that the dog your daddy promised you last time you were here?"

She scrunched her face. "Peanut Pattie? How do you know that?"

The dog, curled at their feet under the table, perked up its ears.

"You told me," Klaus said. "You said he promised you a dog when you got home."

Diane stroked a bare toe against the dog's haunches, apparently an acceptable form of affection. Why the girl was barefoot and what kept her from putting her shoes on, even after Arnetta had brought them to her, Klaus settled up to the vague hippie lifestyle he'd come to imagine as Percy and Antonia's in Chicago. About the time of that awful phone call, a Christmas card had arrived with a family picture inside: the woman's hair had grown as long as an Indian's. Not only that, but she wore large-framed glasses with tinted lenses. A sickle moon hung from her neck by what looked like a leather shoestring. "I don't remember," she said. "I only remember the funeral and going to eat egg rolls after. Mom let me get two orders of egg rolls."

"Sometimes we deserve a little extra," he said, "just to remember the day. Did you love your grandma?"

And though he'd expected a simple, perhaps performative yes, she said, "No, I never knew her. And she hurt Dad's feelings."

He had to stare at the opposite wall a minute, swallowing, before he could say, "That's too bad, because she loved you."

Diane narrowed her eyes at him, sizing him up. "We saw your show on TV last week. The one about the detective? It was sort of crazy."

"That's what they said about it. You get used to that sort of thing. If you make things for a living, total strangers will show up in your life to tell you how you did it wrong."

She looked at the floor. "I liked it."

"I'm glad," he said. "But I didn't mean you, my dear. Critics. Men on the street. They'll pop their heads up to tell you how you should have done this or that. Not to mention whoever is paying for it—whoever thinks they're your boss. In America, art is always paid for by somebody and griped about by somebody else. Occasionally something breaks through, people see it, people like it, their lives are changed by an infinitesimal degree. If you're lucky other people remember that it ever happened. And if you're really lucky you can make a living looking at all this and making some sense of it and communicating it to others."

He'd thought for a moment that he'd gone on too long, that he'd rambled in the way he could to Orson or John and that Bogdanovich kid who'd made good in the years since writing a book about him. But then Diane raised her eyes from the floor and said, "We just have to keep at it, right?"

"Exactly right."

For years, Percy and Antonia had been sending him envelopes full of the girl's drawings. First these were in crayon and over time they were in pencil and finally ink. Her skill had developed quickly. The subjects she attempted quite often were characters and scenes from *Hans & Greta*, built entirely from her imagination, from the limited information she'd learned from him years ago when Antonia had brought up the film. He was an unsentimental man. He had looked at these images, registered their quality, accepted them as a sign of love or respect. Then he had added them, sometimes five or six at a time, to the growing pile out in the studio. What kind of man was he to do this? The drawings should have papered his walls. He should be surrounded by them at this very moment.

A pain shot through his gut, burning in the upper-left just under his ribs and then emanating outward like a radar ring. He would need to stand up. He would need to go to the bathroom. His doctor had told him that this is what is meant by the old saying "It only hurts to laugh." The body is a rebellion. He was, at every step these days, being overthrown.

"I'll be right back, young lady," he said, pushing himself up onto the cane.

When he returned, she was out walking the dog. Percy waited for him at the table. "Dad, are you feeling okay?" he asked again. And when, because there was nothing else to do, Klaus nodded, his prodigal son added, "I thought we could talk."

He hadn't told Percy yet that he'd given most everything to George and Marjorie, that he'd sent another hefty contribution to the Schlossberg Foundation for Motion Picture Arts, that he'd set aside an inheritance for Diane so that she could begin adulthood without any worries. He hadn't told him about all the money Olive had been happy to spend on the television production company. And he'd said nothing about how Frank Harlan had gambled half the value of their real estate company on a failed strip mall in San Bernardino. Going into business with an actor had likely been the worst decision of Klaus's career.

"I don't have any money," Klaus said before he dropped into the chair next to his son. "Not the money you think. I've got my nurse, Arnetta, to consider. And hospital bills. And—"

"That's not what I wanted to talk about," Percy said. "Jeez, Dad. I want to know how you're doing. What we can do to improve things. You know? They're saying that a vegetarian diet—"

"Who is saying?"

Percy met his eyes like they were squaring up for a fight. "Antonia, for one. People who care about nutrition. It's supposed to clear the bowels. And the nutrients bring about better health than all this meat and gelatin and pasta you're eating."

"The gelatin is prescribed by my doctor," Klaus said. "I wish I was eating meat and pasta. You didn't tell me you were still in contact with that woman."

"My wife?"

"Ex-wife, I'd thought."

"We're separated," Percy said. "A trial separation. And you don't need to say anything about this subject to Deedee."

"Young man, I don't know what a 'trial separation' even means."

"It means—"

"I know what it *means*," Klaus said. A directionless anger welled up from the pain in his stomach. "I'm not really that stupid, you know. I've been meaning to ask you about that competitive checkers tournament of yours. And about Sally. Do you ever hear from her? The girl you knocked up in school."

Percy looked offended, his arms crossed tight on his chest, his brows furrowed. "What are you talking about?"

"You lied to me about that girl, didn't you? About her medical bills? Her procedure? Just like you lied to your mother again and again and again." Klaus pointed at the photographs of Olive arrayed on top of the console television. "She always knew when you were lying to her, you know, always for money."

Percy, to his surprise, was in tears, wiping furiously at his eyes with the sleeve of his shirt. Klaus couldn't bring himself to continue. Why had he come at him like this? To what purpose?

His son took a deep, choking breath. "We're here to help," he managed. "You, you can't go, go through this alone."

Go through what? Klaus wanted to say. *Who is alone?* But his defenses were down. Some part of him understood the war was over. "I've got an appointment Thursday," he said. "If you could drive. And if you and Diane could do your own cooking? I don't want to put that on Arnetta. She does enough around here already."

Percy wiped at his nose. "I can do that, Dad."

"I'm very tired," said Klaus. "All the time. This has been a lot. I need to lie down."

A WEEK INTO this visit, Percy returned from the grocery store with the welcome news that he'd met Mrs. Harlan and determined himself enamored by her. "You understand that I'm still in business with Frank?" Klaus said with an irony his son would never understand. "That there are a hundred widows and divorcees between Palm Desert and San Berdoo without the name Harlan attached to them?"

"She's ravishing," Percy said. "And so clever. So intelligent. We had a whole conversation about Gore Vidal at the deli counter."

"That must have been very exciting," said Klaus. "Can I send you back to the store to talk about Mark Twain over the tomatoes?"

Percy feigned amusement, then narrowed his eyes. "We're getting coffee tomorrow. She's a schoolteacher. Thinks very highly of you, I might add."

"I would hope so," said Klaus. And seeing his son in this light state, he thought with guilt of that confrontation about the past. He should clear the air; he should say something. *I'm sorry all this has come between us. I remember you still as that child who looked up to me. I'll forgive you anything if we could only talk to one another like adults.*

But Percy had walked down the hall.

He was forgetting things, losing days. Time moved differently now. The dog—Peanut Pattie—came to him night and day, his closest comrade as the edges of his sight darkened and then filled in with other spaces, other years. He listened hard for the sound of Olive's voice. Petting the dog, he thought for a moment that she was speaking from another room. Then Arnetta sidled by the door complaining about an episode of *Green Acres*. "You okay, Mr. Stiegl?" she asked. And he'd gone on petting Peanut Pattie, staring back at Arnetta without the comfort to form words.

George came to visit. They talked but Klaus remembered none of the words they exchanged, only the sudden appearance of that little dog, of Diane coming after it. Then at some point his cousin

was gone, and yet again he felt as if he'd failed to say something he
needed to say. The foggy quality of his days and nights told him that
he needed now to say everything he'd ever needed to say. But with
this sensation came an equal and opposite force of dull silence.

He tried to concentrate his memory on those heady days before
George's accident, when the studio was operational, his rebel studio,
the months of full artistic freedom, everyone around him enamored
by his vision, his genius—that's what they'd called him then: MGM's
other boy genius, the young man who would drag cinema into the
1930s with the artistic quality of the Old Masters, a foundational figure nearly as important as Griffith and Chaplin, yes, that's what he'd
heard, the sort of thing the young film students said of him now. Had
things been like this on the set of *Brackett*? That last year? Not exactly. The cast and crew were there for paychecks, following orders,
only a few of them at any time swept up in the full obsession of what
Klaus had been trying to do. But it had been done. He'd made what
he'd set out to make.

"Dad?" Percy said from the doorway, leaned in silhouette against
the jamb. "We're back from dinner."

The girl crossed behind him, clicking her tongue to call Peanut
Pattie from the room.

"You were at dinner?"

"I told you," Percy said in that apologetic, talking-to-an-invalid
voice he'd begun using when addressing his father. "Dinner out with
Tessa? We had a good time. Deedee was a little rude but we talked
it out."

A flash of memory intruded on the scene: Percy as a gangly teen,
in Mexico, his mother laughing at a joke the boy had read from a
book. They had been happy there at times.

"I want her to see the watercolors," Klaus said.

Percy looked confused. "What?"

"The ones of your mother on the beach in Mexico. Remember?"

"Sure, Dad." Percy shoved himself off the jamb and stood in
the center of the over-bright doorway, a black figure with shaggy

sideburns and wispy hair. "We'll do that tomorrow. I wanted to tell you about Tessa. She's really great, Dad."

"It's okay," Klaus said. But he knew that he was losing the thread again. "I need to get hers too. I'll get them. The drawings. I'll do it."

"Time for bed, Dad," Percy said. "G'night."

When Klaus's eyes next fluttered open, Percy was gone.

HE DREAMED OF the Lower East Side again, of Mother and Father, the dank smell of laundry and garlic and horse dung and cabbage, the sound of fiddle music and stamping feet, of the piano playing at the Owl-Eye Dancehall, converted every Sunday night to a rudimentary picture palace, those flickering old reels blazed against a white sheet on the wall, the proprietor's wife not only hammering the piano keys but reading aloud the words on every intertitle, as if the audience couldn't read at all. There had been cold and cigar smoke and Irish and Italians and Jews from every part of Europe and the creaking stairs up Romanov's building to the third floor and all those glowing white angel wings of fabric that Mother and Father worked from morning until night and again in the morning and again until night and then it had all been swept away in his absence, his only true loves in life then, Mama and Papa, his whole world, choked and burned and gone. The smoke billowing, the deed not yet done, he went running—in the dream—toward the building, only to find that the toe of his shoe hooked the lip of a jagged crack, sending him flat on the sidewalk, again and again, running and tripping and falling, his whole body thrusting and flying and smacking down on concrete, once and twice and three times or more.

Then he woke.

It must have been morning. Or later. Bright desert light glowed around the thick, dark curtains at every side. In the living room, the television played. He could hear the coffee machine gurgling, Percy whistling the show tune "I Cain't Say No." A scent of eggs and bacon, but lingering, already spent, like breakfast had passed into the digestive tract of his guests a couple of hours ago.

He had run from that tenement life, its poverty, its desperation, run from the horror of that unspeakable loss, and only now could he see that for a time he became no one at all: a boy and then a young man who was nothing more than an empty pitcher. He had filled himself later with the gentile obsessions with class and comfort, with his cousin's interest in "culture," with the desires surfaced in Klaus by all those Weimar Berlin nightclubs, the freedom and reinvention they promised, and finally he had filled himself with "von Stiegl," with the life of a twentieth-century prince, sunbathing and dallying nearly to the end of life. Now here he was, longing for Mother and Father, for the stench of cabbage and horse dung, for the piles of white piecework and laundry on the boil and Romanov's voice bellowing up the stairs. He had been that boy.

Thoughts of childhood led him back to Diane. The poor girl. Dragged around by her father at this age. A mother beset by madness. The girl had talent and also a certain quality to her personality that would help her weather a shaky life. Something of her grandfather. Perhaps he was being sentimental after all. He couldn't say. But he pictured the drawings Percy had been sending over the years, especially those of *Hans & Greta*, a film she'd never seen, that no one had seen, a film she'd only heard about secondhand after Olive's funeral. He saw himself arranging those drawings on the wall and holding forth with the story of that film, showing it to them as if it were projected on a screen before them.

Klaus found that he had the strength to push himself up on his elbows, to slide his legs free of the covers. And then, with a grunt of force, to stand. He walked shakily from the bed to Olive's old dresser. He'd wet himself in the night. It didn't matter. Atop the dresser, folded neatly by the fastidious Arnetta, his robe waited for him. He hooked a finger on its collar, slung the thing over his shoulders, wrestled his arms into the sleeves. Then he tied the cotton belt loosely around his slimming belly. He was, to his surprise, relatively smooth on his feet. Only a little of the sea legs he'd grown used to keeping him bed-bound the last several weeks.

He paced back and forth. To his dresser and back to Olive's. Perhaps he was on a comeback. He felt sprightly. Strong. He would go to the scrim of Lüneberg, see it one more time, and then he would retrieve Diane's drawings, bringing them back and calling Percy and Diane and Arnetta in for the show. He would ask Arnetta for the tin of thumbtacks and put all of Diane's pictures of *Hans & Greta* on the wall and then he would lie down and look at the pictures and all of it would come back to him. He'd never seen the film. MGM had taken the reels. Schlossberg may have held on to negatives. But it had never been pieced together, never edited; in a very real sense he'd never completed it. Now he could. Yes, that's right. Now he could do just that. Lying on his back, with the songs of Fauré playing from the hi-fi, he would sew together his story, the film alive in a single moment, time compressed and stretched and folded over itself, like a grand painting, like one of those old Christian images where the same saint is conversing with God here, glowing with inspiration there, performing a miracle over here, and beheaded over there. The all-at-once-ness. That's what he would see. He would describe to them—to everyone assembled in that grand denouement, that if one looked closely one could also see *Brackett*, could see the full vision of all he'd had to say in this life. They would see that he had traded all this loneliness in a fair exchange for something greater than everyday life, for something like illumination. But he needed her pictures.

He was out in the living room. On the television, one of Arnetta's soap operas. But he didn't see her. From the kitchen, Percy's whistling stopped. "Dad?" he said. "That you?"

Klaus didn't have time to answer. He was at the door, turning the knob, pulling it open. Out in the blinding-bright glare of day, he flung a hand up to his brow. Here was Arnetta, watering the raised bed of flowers, always going the extra mile, she'd been such a saint, and though her mouth opened wide and words seemed to come from her, he didn't bother listening. Only as he passed the back fender of

Percy's dust-brown car did her voice register: yelling, but muffled, a woman shouting into the feathered stuffing of a pillow. "Mr. Stiegl," she was saying, "what are you doing out of bed?"

He didn't look back. Into the fine, dry air he said, "I'll be back in a minute."

Her voice again came to him like a distant and muffled terror: "But Mr. Stiegl!"

Then he was in the loose and clumpy sand. The two-acre rectangle he'd never sold, surrounded now by shimmering pools, gray patios, modern homes of glass and formed concrete, his old film studio in a bramble of desert, still blinding and squinting, still capable of bringing his eyes to tears. The damp of his crotch felt dank and chafing in the sunny heat. At the fence he turned the padlock left and right and left, 32 and 77 and 27. Leaving this open behind him, he made for the wide double doors of the studio. There, too, on the padlock he notched the numbers around, 32-77-27, and dropped both of the locks in the sand before pushing with all his might the left-hand door along its wheeled track above. *Clackety-clackety-clackety-clack*: the world's slowest and smallest train.

Only inside did he remember that he hadn't grabbed a flashlight. Well, never mind; an oil lamp hung on a hook near the door. It was a decorative thing Olive had bought years ago and Klaus had put out here when the flywheel had rusted and the roof no longer opened. A box of matches sat on a table nearby. He took down the lamp and slid open the matchbox. *Fflitt. Fff-lit.* Alive, the flame, a bright-orange leap into the air. When he brought the match down to meet the oil lamp it leapt again.

What happened next couldn't really be happening. He was dreaming. The flame had missed the lamp entirely and caught the edge of one of Diane's drawings, the orange and red and white spreading with a rapidity that made no sense at all. Then the flames rose. A half and then a full dozen, flinging and growing and spiraling up like little upside-down tornadoes, and as Klaus backed away, trying to draw a full breath so that he could figure out how to react, the flames rediscovered their original purpose, swept up the lamp's glass-and-tin skeleton, flickered black and wild for a single impossible second. Then a *whoomp*—the sucking preparation to exhale, to explode, to throw Klaus onto his back several feet away, screaming now, yowling for his son and for Arnetta and for Olive, the flames eating his robe in a single bite, leaving him rolling on the dusty, hard floor, a man in tatters, singed and partially burning, slapping at the wet-boiling heat of his groin and ass, a tragic and stupid figure, crying and writhing and kicking at the floor, his head banged and banged like he was trying to crack it open. When Percy appeared above him, shouting and slapping at the remnant flames, Klaus couldn't stay alive. His embarrassment was too great. He chose to die, to have it done, to disappear.

But Percy wouldn't let him. He had him up on his feet, no longer burning, a shoulder tucked painfully under Klaus's armpit. "Dad, we're going. Okay. Back to the house. We'll call an ambulance."

Klaus thought again of saying something meaningful. "I'm tired," he said instead. "It hurts."

And Percy shouted as he slipped again to the ground, "Dad, Dad!"

CAHIERS DU CINÉMA

August, 1961

INTERVIEW WITH KLAUS VON STIEGL

by ANDRÉ GUILLARD

TRANS. LUCY SMITHFIELD-BOYCE

One of the great auteurs of early Hollywood cinema, Klaus von Stiegl's career can be roughly grouped into three distinct phases: his silent period of expressionist masterpieces which culminates in the lost film *Hans & Greta*, a spotty period in the 1940s when he returned to filmmaking as a director for Mexico's CLASA studio, and then to his current period in television which began with live theatrical productions and has moved through comedy and drama series and, two years ago, the creation of an independent production company. I met the great von Stiegl at the Los Angeles office of his TV production company, a small room with a desk and two chairs which shares a hallway with talent agents and songwriters, the plinking sound of a piano in the distance. He is a small man who somehow seems larger than life. His swept-back hair, his monocle, his pointed beard, his almost dandyish sartorial excellence: he seems very much like a man who has stepped out of an old novel. He speaks with a carefully paced German accent, his eyes glowing at times while at other times quite hard, and one gets the sense that any conversation with this monumental figure of American film boils down to a confrontation about something much more significant than even the art of cinema—as if to talk at all were a form of wrestling.

André Guillard: You are comfortable? Ready to begin?

Klaus von Stiegl: I have no complaints. Scratch that. I would like to complain about the traffic outside. I arrived late. To my own office. There is insistent honking. We're on the second floor and there is the sound of insistent honking. I believe your readers should know that.

AG: It is an important detail. Perhaps we should start there. You are a director known for careful visual detail. I recall reading somewhere that crews on your *CBS Sunday Theatre Program*—those which you directed—had to be in studio a full day earlier than other shoots in order to arrange all the details for the shots you wanted?

KS: I directed eighteen live shows for CBS during that program's two-year run. We did only contemporary work. Television screens were very small at that time. The idea usually was to shoot everything in close-up so everyone at home could see the faces the actors were making, could tell one character from another. But that's counter to visual art, which is my field. I wanted to make pictures worth looking at. So we built sets, we moved the camera, we shaped a kind of visual dynamic. You've got to remember that these were live performances. When we started rolling, we were beaming right out to the viewer. I didn't want mistakes.

AG: Hitchcock has joked that actors are like cattle. In other words, that they are only another part of the visual scenery. Is that what you're getting at?

KS: To a degree. I think Mr. Hitchcock is playing up the severity of the situation. Anyone who has been behind the camera knows that film is not about actors but about how pictures tell a story.

AG: Would you say that cinema is a universal language, then? Pictorial at its purest form?

KS: Nothing is universal.

AG: Well, that's interesting. I would say that some visuals are universal in nature. *King Kong*, for instance. The Odessa Steps sequence in *Battleship Potemkin*. *The Cabinet of Dr. Caligari*—which I know you love?

KS: The notion is ludicrous. A hundred years from now, if nuclear war hasn't decimated us entirely, an audience may laugh at *Caligari* and *King Kong*. They probably laugh now.

AG: But the aesthetic qualities—

KS: No, no. We can't know that. As individuals we must act to the best of our knowledge and imagination, to the best of our skill level. We make what we can, in the culture we live in. If that thing is an expression of ourselves, our true nature, and if it speaks in conversation with the works which speak to us—in other words if it resides in that place where art is made—then it is good. But it may not remain good. It may not even remain art.

AG: Do you feel like cinema, or television where you work now, are fields for such an individual? Your career seems like a testament to how an industry that values the team or corporate effort can silence the individual artist.

KS: I would disagree.

AG: That is a surprising response. What do you mean?

KS: That work is done in opposition. True work. The artist tries this, then that, always going in at a new angle, always resisted by those who would rather he do something else. "Why isn't this the thing I wanted it to be?" That is the audience question, the critic's question. But the artist says only that "it is." So it is about struggle. Pushing against. Does this art form require the employment of actors and writers and technicians and producers and truck drivers to deliver film and projectionists to reel that film onto the machine? Yes. Your magazine often discusses the concept of the director as "auteur." I would say that this term is too weak for what it tries to encompass. There are artists in this field—even in television—who are working just as hard as Van Gogh and his silly ear to get their vision onscreen.

AG: I worry that I have led you into a misunderstanding of my intentions. Let's talk about *Hans & Greta.* That to me seems like an example of the studio clearly taking away the self-expression of the individual. Would you agree?

KS: I would not.

AG: You would disagree, then?

KS: You must understand that the picture was nearly finished. When the reels were taken from me, when they were "reclaimed" by MGM, we had very little to add. The material had all been set to film. I could have used a week of post-production. That's all.

AG: So it doesn't matter that an audience couldn't see it?

KS: I had never yet had so much control of my work before *Hans & Greta*. At every step I was in charge, at every decision. It went directly from my mind to the film—just the way a novelist does his work. I am satisfied with the experience.

AG: And so audience doesn't matter at all?

KS: Audience matters after the fact, but only in a small way. Imagine that you have spent your weekend painting your living room. In the process of that work you lost yourself in the making, in seeing out your vision: "This room will be yellow now." By the end of your work you are satisfied with that work, with the yellow room you have created through your labor. Maybe some friends come over to play cards the following weekend. Maybe one person says they like the new paint job. But maybe nobody does. Maybe it goes unremarked. Maybe—and follow me here—your dearest friend looks at that yellow wall and laughs out loud. To him it is disgusting, a spilled jar of mustard. He tells you so. Does it change your experience of the work, of your vision? Should you regret what you've done?

AG: Do you plan a great deal ahead of time? Do you start with a clear sense of what you want to see onscreen?

KS: Let's take my most recent production as an example. You may not know that I have created an independent production company, like Desilu but obviously much smaller. I have had a mutually beneficial relationship with CBS for a decade now, and so I had a deal with them, an order for these last two productions, both feature-length but made for television: *A Christmas Miracle in Brooklyn* and this more recent one, *Killer on the Road*. For this one, for *Killer*, I certainly had a plan. I worked closely with our screenwriter, Hugh Littlefield, before we even moved to the casting stage. By the point I was scouting locations and drafting storyboards, everything else was in place, and it all becomes clockwork. I shoot only a little more than I need and already know, before editing, what I will use for the final product. You see, I am my own producer now—I've come to appreciate what the producer does—and I have always been involved in editing, always in the room, even when editors and producers didn't want me there. Anyway, I would say that unpredictability is to be avoided.

AG: *Bachelor's Wife* is one of your masterpieces, undisputedly. From what I understand, the film sent shockwaves through Hollywood. Were you concerned at all that you would be defined as a homosexual filmmaker?

KS: Not at all. The book was rather famous for a short time.

AG: Well, it must have been shocking to American audiences? The lead character is a homosexual. Had that been done onscreen?

KS: Americans were shocked when Edison had a husband and wife kiss in a nickelodeon film at the turn of the century. There is no end to what will send my countrymen into gasps and pearl-clutching. But no, I don't believe the people who saw the film at the time found it all that troubling. There was a kind of opening in the culture at the time. This when the Klan was on the march and a great deal of air was taken up by the subject of public morality, but at the same time there was an opening, an interest in experimentation, in desire, in Freud, in being more continental about things.

AG: Would it be right to say that the studios have an interest in the 'bottom line' while the artist, the filmmaker, is interested in something else?

KS: That goes without saying. But I am a capitalist. That is the economic system I feel works best for society. Art is not part of the market. Art lives in the tension between the marketplace and the artist. On the one hand you have the expectations of consumers—an audience, all their biases and apprehensions and need to feel comfortable. On the other you have the absolute individual. Creating something new that states his values, his vision of how this reality functions, what makes it pleasing or

not pleasing. I believe our natural state is to all be artists. To live among
one another, creating, making, feeling as if—in every moment of our
lives—we matter. For me, in this time, it is capitalism that allows that
freedom. I make, and by making I show to others that making is our way,
the human way, that being invested in what you're doing—laying bricks,
fixing a car, painting a painting—that this is what we are here for and
almost nothing else. That is the job.

AG: It sounds like you're saying everyday labor is equal to art.

KS: I'm saying that it should be. That the artistic experience—that of
observing and making, of being invested with one's imagination—is
natural.

AG: I was recently at a Paris screening of *El Corazón Atribulado*, from
your time with the CLASA studio in Mexico. I was surprised by how
much it looked like a von Stiegl picture. The use of doorways and shadows, the doubling of characters, the idiosyncratic close-ups on objects,
the free-flowing camerawork: all those signature von Stiegl touches. How
do you feel about that phase of your career?

KS: I am happy with some of those films. *The Troubled Heart* was quite
good, I believe. It was rewarding to work with talents such as Ignacio
Pérez and Sylvia Moreno. The film was also quite well received. I believe it played in the States, at least in New York and Chicago and Los
Angeles. I made a dozen or so pictures when we lived there, just outside
of Puerto Vallarta. Film production was comical and sometimes infuri-
ating. I couldn't speak Spanish and almost no one understood me at any
time, but there is a kind of joy in that unchecked chaos. I wasn't welcome in Hollywood at the time and needed something to do. Yes, when I
could, of course, I put my signature to the work. But often I didn't.

AG: And what about television? We've touched on it a bit, but it strikes
me that I don't know of other great filmmakers who have moved into the
medium of television. What have you learned there?

KS: First that it's a screenwriter's medium. That was a tough lesson. But
I learned quickly, as I mentioned before, to bring the role of the director
to bear on it, to focus on the visual aspect. I guess I learned those things

and also how to work quickly, how to get actors to do what needs to be done when they don't have all the time in the world to prepare a character, let alone memorize their lines. I enjoyed working with actors in New York as well—before we opened the studio in L.A. Many of them are getting their start onstage, then television, and finally going to Hollywood very prepared, very serious. Nothing like that machine Hollywood used to be, scouting and training talent. But my work—however uncelebrated at the moment, this television work—is getting to many more people than any of my films. That is interesting. Like I said before, the work is in the doing. But it is interesting, when I step back, to know that perhaps millions of people will have tuned in for *Christmas Miracle*, for instance, this thing we taped in September in Los Angeles, in a sound stage rented from Metro-Goldwyn-Mayer—my long-ago employer.

AG: Would you say that your television career has been a "comeback"?

KS: Having come back from what? Honestly, it was a new form. It shares quality with the cinema, but in a way, I wonder if I had fallen out of love with cinema during the long years between my time with MGM and my early work at CBS. I can remember feeling bored, rather useless. The first time I was in a television studio, I felt something return. That drive, that sense of invention, of necessity.

AG: That's interesting. Does this mean you have no plans to return to cinema?

KS: I'm at work on a new series called *Brackett*. It's a von Stiegl production, entirely my own, a sort of crime series with a detective in the lead role, played by my dear friend Frank Harlan, who starred in *Killer on the Road*. My goal is to make the series at the highest quality level possible, as if it *were* cinema, or what television can do that cinema cannot.

TOBEY

2024

TRACK SWUNG. THE ball arced high over the rolling grass and then seemed to fall in slow-motion before hitting the earth, bouncing, and finally rolling rapidly in the direction of the green. "Fuck yeah," he said. "See what I was telling you about the knees?" He displayed it again: a little dip and then a slight turn in the direction of his swing. "See?"

"Yeah," said Tobey. "It's good."

Track pointed at the ground where moments before a tee and ball had been resting. "Go ahead."

Tobey looked around. There wasn't a single thing on Earth he wanted to do less than learn how to play golf. "Okay," he said, and took the proffered club. "Where do I get one of those tees?"

Track pulled one from his pocket and then dropped it into Tobey's outstretched hand. "Stick it right there, in front of your toes."

Tobey did this, finding the dirt surprisingly soft, and set the ball on its cup. As soon as he squared to the tee, Track started in with more coaching: straighten your shoulders, no don't hunch over, now bend the knees like I said, put your hands like this, et cetera. "Okay," Tobey said, repeatedly, and then began swinging the club up high and down low, taking aim, just like he'd seen on television. Or no, like he'd seen on a video game. Rory McIlroy PGA Tour. Who the fuck was Rory McIlroy? How is it that Tobey could remember that guy's name but couldn't remember his own Apple ID password to save his life? "Okay, okay," he repeated, making little corrections with each bit of fatherly instruction, swinging the club back a little higher each time. Finally, without any real sense that he was about to do it, he swung through, the club whistling the air, his arms circling all the way back like Track had shown him, his eyes following through as well. A perfect swing.

On the tee, the ball sat untouched, a shining white orb.

"Ha," he said. "Look at that."

"No biggie," Track said. "Try again."

"I get to try again?"

"It's a swing against you but it's okay. We won't even count it."

He squared up again. "That's mighty fine of you, Pops, but we don't have to wait around on my part. It's your game."

"Pops?" Track said. "That's a grandpa name. Do I look like your grandpa?"

"You look like somebody's—"

"All right, all right. Eye on the ball."

It was like that for nine holes, probably the longest game of golf in human history. For some reason Track kept forgiving Tobey's bad swings, letting him pick up the ball and drop it at an easier spot, and on the eight hole he snatched Tobey's ball from the green, walked it to the hole, and dropped it in so they could move along.

That little bit of corner-cutting reminded Tobey about the NFT money-laundering thing. So he finally got around to asking about it. When Track ignored the basic question, he said, "Dad, they're saying you took money from drug dealers and some dude from Iran. Like, shouldn't you give us an explanation?"

Track shot him a hateful look as he adjusted his stance over the tee. "Us?"

"Your kids."

Track's face pinched up like the words gave off a bad odor. "Where'd you even hear that garbage?"

"The news," Tobey said. "*L.A. Times*, I think."

"Liberal bullshit, T. They see a successful guy making investments in something new, something disruptive, and they decide there's something bad going on there. When you're me you get used to this sort of thing." He swung. The ball shot high in the air, dropped, bounced. "Should have heard what those same bums had to say about me when you got in trouble at school."

"So it's not real? You're not, like, being investigated or anything?"

Track started for the cart, as if Tobey weren't playing at all. "There's always some investigation. That's what I'm saying. Elite know-nothings who want every minute of our lives regulated. This is how they do it. Sue, investigate, write up BS stories like the one you ran into. Gotta let it roll off your back."

"I was surprised you even knew what an NFT was. I was telling Susan—"

"Susan? Your sister Susan? Is this who's putting this stuff in your head?"

For some reason Tobey felt like coming to his half-sister's defense, or at least deflecting his father's ire from her. "No, I just read it on the interwebs."

In the cart, with the prospect of Tobey's swing set aside, Track changed the subject. "So what is it you plan to do next, job-wise?"

Here was the real purpose of this golf game. Track wanted to know about Tobey's future, what he planned to do now that his town was ashes, how he would use this, er, minor tragedy (his words) to jump-start (his again) the next stage in his life. "It took your brother some time to find his calling. Hell, I don't like his calling. Writing emails for that sugar daddy. But he was looking. I'm worried you're not looking."

Tobey felt annoyed. Track had backed right into real estate, starting with *Brackett*'s company and *Brackett*'s money and even Brackett's face. What kind of looking was it for him to sop up Grandpa's fame and squeeze it out for more money? "First of all," he said. "I had a thing I wanted to do and it didn't fit all this market garbage."

"That communist summer camp?"

"Yes, that communist summer camp. But you know that's not what it is. You're just trying to get a rise out of me."

Track shut off the cart. They were at the top of a gumdrop hill with a series of smaller mounds toothing down to an amoeba-shaped green. Out from under the cart's shade the world was a numbing blaze. "That didn't work," he said, hefting the club bag. "They don't want you. So now what do you want out of life?"

He sounded like Mr. Mercado, only a shitty version of him. "I'll work it out," Tobey said.

———————

IN THE MOST forgiving reading of events, the whole trip to the golf course had been an advertisement. A straight-up marketing campaign to get Tobey to move back to Palm Springs permanently and take a job managing Track's friend's car wash. But Track only brought it up on the drive home. "The last guy walked out," he said. "Hugh's been driving across town to cover for him. You could start Monday."

Tobey's first reaction was to say he didn't think car washes needed managers. You just swiped a card or maybe dropped in some quarters. What was there to do? But Track explained it was actually more of a speedy detail shop, the sort of place where the client sits in an air-conditioned waiting room as half a dozen employees attack their car at once, cleaning it inside and out in less than fifteen minutes. "Cool," Tobey said. "Yeah, I'm not doing that."

"For a while," Track said. "It wouldn't kill you. You know, son, you've got to take things when they come at you. That's what life is about: taking. Don't believe all that woke garbage about helping each other out. It's dog-eat-dog and it always has been. One day you get a job offer at a car wash, the next you're running your own chain. Then who knows. Can you say yes to an actual job or do you want to wait for AOC to bail you out?"

Tobey let the AOC bait float by. "Sure," he said, knowing the only thing to do was say yes. "I'll try it out."

Track drummed his hands on the steering wheel of his Porsche. "Hugh's going to love this," he said. "He asked for you by name. He said, 'How about Tobey? He's not doing anything.'"

Yeah, yeah. Tobey wasn't doing anything except removing three paintings from their frames and rolling them up and stuffing them into his car later that evening and driving south to meet James and wait for the half million in Bitcoin to appear in his account before helping his brother move them into a rented van. Anytime he actually thought about it, his stomach knotted up, his mouth went dry. Was he really doing this? In Stockton, when he'd dreamed this up, it seemed simple. Track didn't give a shit about the paintings (one of them was half-hidden by the headboard in the master bedroom) and wouldn't miss them, only what they stood for, their potential in the marketplace. Of course, he would be pissed, maybe even hurt, certainly disappointed—that is, if he could actually be more disappointed with Tobey—and doing this meant that Tobey could never return, not to Palm Springs and not to his father.

Well, thinking along those lines actually made it all seem less insane. To run off, to change his name, to break free of the gravitational pull of the Harlan family. All that stuff went to the heart of Tobey's identity. Hell, he'd daydreamed of hitching out of Palm Springs and becoming someone else all the way back in junior high.

But setting aside all the Freudian psychodrama, the plan was most definitely insane. Rolling up paintings? Meeting his brother in a parking lot? Bitcoin? Tobey didn't have the foggiest notion what Bitcoin actually was, let alone what to do with it. What was the exchange rate? How did a person even use it? Would he have to add glowing red eyes to his social accounts? He'd made a concerted effort not to google this stuff because if he knew anything from crime shows it was that your search history is the first thing anyone looks at. So he'd decided he would ask James when they met. And if things seemed too shady there (could it get any more shady? the parking lot of the Escondido Walmart?) he would back out, drive south, and rehang the paintings, making it all look untouched before Track and Judith even got home from their trip.

"—T?" Track was saying. "You in there?"

They were just a couple blocks from home. "Uh-huh," Tobey said. "Sorry."

"I was just talking about these woke professors with their critical *racist* theory."

"Yeah," Tobey said without inflection. He knew a trap when he heard one.

When they pulled into the drive, Judith came out the glass storm door in sunglasses, her handbag and iPad under one arm, the other dragging a massive green suitcase. She wore a consciously casual outfit: flip-flops, tan shorts, New England Patriots T-shirt. "You're late," she announced. "Why didn't you answer any of my texts?"

"Oh, hold your horses." Then after a quick trip to the bathroom and to change his shoes and shirt, Track was back behind the wheel, waving at Tobey on the porch, all four of the dogs whimpering and grumbling.

Tobey watched the SUV back out of the drive and start down the street. Only at the last moment, just as her face disappeared from his view, did Judith look up from her phone and meet Tobey's gaze, her eyes popped open, almost protruding, as if in a state of terror.

He stood on the porch for at least a minute after he could no longer see them, thinking that surely they would have forgotten something, would have to return. Then he remembered Gray.

––––––––

AT THE DOOR to the garage, three of the dogs sat panting at Gray's scent. "Fuck off," Tobey said. And when that didn't work, "Out. Go."

They met him halfway by standing up and glaring at him like an intruder.

"You want a treat?" he said, and like that, they all sat with their ears back, eyes wide. "Okay. Fuck off."

In the garage he pulled the bell-tipped string and looked up to see Gray seated at eye level on top of a cardboard file box labeled in black marker, "Purchases 2018–2022." There were actually dozens of these file boxes, stacked shoulder-high in places. He spotted one next to the tool drawers labeled with only the name "Stiegl." As in Di Stiegl? Her whole family? Grandpa had some business with the guy who'd made *Brackett*, once Tobey's favorite old show. He pulled off the lid and looked inside. Letters, private correspondence, clippings, handwritten fax cover pages with dates from the '90s. He set the lid back in place.

He felt a shiver of doubt about Dad's business again. Serious paperwork out in the garage? With nothing but that aluminum automatic door between it and the outside world? Sheesh. But he didn't want to know any more than that, didn't even—as enticing as it looked—want to dig any further into that Stiegl file box. He lifted down the cat, who seemed fine until the last minute, just as he was about to set her on the concrete floor, when her whole body torqued and her back claws dug into his forearm again, using it as a base to launch into the distant corner, where a table saw stood in front of a John Coltrane subway poster. Tobey looked down at the new rips in his flesh just as the red beads of blood appeared. He cursed, sighed, and then checked the food and water bowls.

Back in the kitchen he washed both his arms with soap. The older scrapes were all scar tissue now, thin lines that crisscrossed and ended in blackened gouges. Maybe Judith was right. Maybe he'd get an infection. Or had it been Mr. Mercado who said that first? Anyway he could. His left arm, down near the elbow, felt abnormally hot. Did he have a fever? Who could tell. It wasn't even lunchtime and he was about to rob his own father.

"You've got to make something to be worth anything," Track liked to say. "Tobey, you've got to *create* if you want to get anywhere in this life." But create what? A housing addition? A strip mall? When Tobey was younger, he'd thought of himself as creative, that maybe one day he would discover a latent talent and run with it, finding himself and his purpose at last. He wouldn't make movies or paintings like his grandfather or Di Stiegl. But maybe he would be a poet, drafting clever little turns of phrase that spoke to the heart of various matters. Then again, the closest he'd ever gotten to poetry had been that Robert Frost collection his real mom had sent him for high school graduation, *The Road Less Traveled* dog-eared as if she were trying to define for him the meaning of the word "cliché." And did anyone actually create anything anymore? Weren't we past all that to just pure consumption? Everyone knew that not a single new thing had happened in Tobey's lifetime. Instead all things that had ever happened were available right now, to watch and listen to and read again, to revamp or remake, to meme into meaninglessness. The very idea of "new" seemed suspiciously like marketing language. New wasn't getting rid of cabs but making everyone a cabbie, after all. New was a mashup flavor of potato chips you passed over for the classic salt-and-vinegar. New was electing reality-show-hosts for president. Create? It was just Track Harlan's word for the grind.

"Fuck," he said. Hearing his own voice in the house seemed to help. He hunted for a towel. The first drawer was stuffed with mail: bills, some of them with red labels and exclamation points. In the drawer beneath he found a fine set of chef's towels, absorbent and pinstriped.

Now, with his arms dry, with Judith's antibiotic cream applied, he called James. "Is this real? Are you guys just fucking with me?"

"Who is this?" said James, and laughed. "We're going to that game for sure. Wouldn't miss it. You're still down?"

Tobey met eyes with one of the dogs: sleepy, only half-interested.

"Yeah," he said, but he didn't know for sure why he was saying it. "I'm down."

James told him where they would meet to go to the basketball game—a ruse so silly Tobey couldn't imagine who it was meant to fool, what sort of spy would find it believable. But he'd agreed, yeah, a basketball game in Escondido, sure, his brother was flying into San Diego in the morning, absolutely, the Walmart on Grand Ave., definitely, between eight o'clock and nine. Then he'd sent a link by text, which prompted Tobey to download an app called TimeGreen, created by Osip and not yet public, which he could find nothing about online—the single thing he'd searched in spite of the trail it would leave. That's when he'd really gone in too far to back out. Because that app shot him over to a legit-looking banking site, where an account had already been started with his name and information, and where a single "deposit" of one Bitcoin stared back at him. He'd again troubled over his own ignorance: "What is this thing? What am I supposed to do with it? Why can't we just do regular money?"

"In due time," James said. "Now, get moving."

Off the phone, Tobey googled the Bitcoin's value. Seventy-something thousand dollars.

He went out to his car, dropped into the passenger seat, and dug out his pipe and lighter. He left the door open. Dad's nearest neighbor, in another grand McMansion of Spanish-themed postmodernism, was more than a city block away. Tobey pushed back his seat, hung his head out sideways so he could look up at the sky as he smoked. All he'd ever wanted was a chance to figure himself out, to do something creative with his time, to feel connected to something. But so far everything had been a race: grades in high school, life-and-death choices at college, nearly a decade of slipping further from any sort of job that mattered to anyone, all while still having to pay the rent. It seemed a world set against him, or really anybody. A world designed to chew you up. And he'd had all the advantages, as they say.

Oof. He was either going to take these paintings or drive off a cliff. Ha! No, he was taking the paintings. A victimless crime. All Tobey was doing was moving some objects back into the market, applying them to the natural chain of exchange; you could almost say that he was giving them meaning by accepting a price and approving a value. Just like Track preached. If anything, he was doing the world a favor, doing Di Stiegl a favor, doing a favor for Professor Heinen, his environmental studies teacher from years ago, fulfilling some credit Tobey had needed to graduate. He pictured himself standing in the doorway of Professor Heinen's office, extending a hand, and Professor Heinen shaking it, "Why, Tobey! What a gift you gave us all by uncovering those lost Stiegls. I really should have given you an A on that stupid fucking paper."

He stood from the car: noon, squinting. He didn't have a lot of time to waste.

Inside, he found his phone on the dining table, the blue "missed call" banner still glowing on its screen. Sophie, he thought hopefully. But no. James. He played the message on speakerphone as he ducked under the sink for a pair of the throwaway plastic gloves Judith had bought back when Covid first started up.

"Just landed," is all his brother said. "Call me back."

First Tobey set to work. There would be no getting the frames into the car, so he had to remove each of the canvases and roll them up, being careful not to squash or wrinkle them once they were in the car. He started with the portrait of Grandpa as Brackett. Grandpa had already been old when Tobey was a child, old and senile, literally losing his mind in an assisted-living place across town. He never forgot Tobey's name or anything, but he'd done a lot of riffing, going into old Hollywood stories, a handshake deal to be in Orson Welles's next picture, something he thought was still going to happen one day soon, even though by then it was the '90s, Tobey starting grade school.

Tobey didn't watch *Brackett* until he was a teenager, a few years after Grandpa died, though it had seemed familiar. Maybe it had been this painting, or maybe he'd seen clips. By the time the fourth season was released on disc, Tobey had his little blog, Tobey's Couch Potatoes. Sixteen and going on about *Arrested Development* like it was James Joyce. Although he had posted something about *The Apprentice* that he wouldn't mind taking another look at now — something about a failed TV personality playing a successful businessman, something about the country losing its mind. Huh. How had he ever let his father convince him to go into PR instead of the arts? PR was James's bag, clearly. Let the younger son use a little critical theory! Let him write papers about TikTok videos!

With all the staples pulled, he set the frame facedown on the carpet and began unfolding the canvas from the back. For some reason it was this part of the action that drew the dogs back into the living room, the four of them seated attentively on the sofa, looking like they knew he was up to something criminal. He rolled up the canvas, this one about four feet by two and a half, set it on the dining table, and then took the frame into the backyard to break it up for transport. He couldn't leave anything. Couldn't even leave his fingerprints. At least, not around where the paintings would go missing.

With the back door still open, he called the dogs to go outside, and they dashed past him in a cavalcade of squeals and scratching nails. Back inside, with one down, he called his brother back, leaving the phone on speaker as he went to the master bedroom for the next painting, one of the two big ones, ten feet across and five feet high.

James answered after one ring. "You on the road yet?"

"Still getting ready."

"Man, you better move." By the noise on the line it was clear James was already on the highway. "So on the news they said that town of yours is fully wiped out."

"That's right," Tobey said. "Total apocalypse."

"And Dad took you golfing after?"

Tobey lifted one of the Dream of Fire paintings off the wall, realizing only when its wire pranged loose from the hook that the thing was very, very heavy. The far corner nearly hit the floor. "If you mean did he play golf while I tried not to leave my physical body out of boredom, then yes."

"Shitty," his brother said.

Tobey got to why he was calling. "You sure about all of this?"

"Yeah. Totally. You know me. I roll hard, motherfucker."

"I mean it's sort of crazy," Tobey said. "Like, maybe a really bad idea."

"No," James said with a little too much force. "I mean, fuck, man. This is going to be too easy. And you're golden. Totally safe. Besides, it was your idea, numbnuts."

Yes, in a way it was. Hard to believe that, given that the machinery had been put in place so quickly. "Does he, like, do this sort of thing all the time?"

There was a pause on the end of the line and then James said, "Who?"

"Osip?" Tobey said.

"Osip?" He laughed. "He does what he does. The man's a fucking legend."

Tobey had the picture facedown on the carpet. He began pulling out staples. Underneath one corner of folded canvas was a piece of paper, folded in half. Written in faded pencil: *To my oldest friend and nearly my brother. We've drifted apart but I hope that these bring us together again. XO, Di*

Tobey stuffed the note in his pocket. "Dad's going to flip his lid."

"Fuck that," James said. "Let him. All you gotta do is be real with them. Like, 'I went to a basketball game with my brother in Escondido.' Just be sure nobody sees you load them in the car. Pull in the garage."

Oh. He hadn't thought of that. He'd have to move Gray.

"So we'll tell Dad and Judith," Tobey said, "That I've developed a sudden interest in Escondido high school basketball? And you have too?"

"Well, yeah. And the cops and insurance investigators."

"Insurance investigators? Fucking cops?" One of the dogs wandered in, hopped on the bed, and stared glumly at Tobey's labor. "What the fuck, man?"

"It's nothing. And it doesn't matter if you're nervous. They'll expect that from a guy who's just been robbed. Just remember you were in Escondido with your brother."

"Right," Tobey said, but this fact didn't make him any less anxious. It was all getting out of hand very quickly. "Is it too late to call this thing off? I mean, nothing's happened yet."

His brother was quiet on the line for a moment. "Everything's happened," he said. "It's definitely too fucking late, dude. All the wheels are turning. All you gotta do is meet me in Escondido. Like the song."

"Is that a song?"

"It should be. Anyway you won't be a suspect. You'll have an alibi and no motivation. And they won't know anything about your TimeGreen account. That shit is what the fucking cartels use."

Tobey had the canvas loose all around. He folded down the corners on one end and levered the frame out as he stood up, making a quiet scratch noise that pricked up the dog's ears. "See a lot of those words aren't confidence-builders, James. 'Alibi,' 'suspect,' 'cartels.' Fuck, man."

James laughed. The sound—sharp, brief, somehow a touch angry no matter the circumstances—had scared Tobey when he was a kid. It scared him again now. "Would Osip let you get in trouble? Think about who you're talking about, here."

Tobey didn't really like thinking about Osip Yander. The man seemed creepy, out only for himself, altogether too powerful. Track had called Osip his brother's "sugar daddy" when they were on the golf course that morning. But Tobey would never repeat such a thing, even if James pissed him off.

Wait. How had James known about the golf game with Track?

"Tobe?" his brother said. "You still there?"

Tobey was thinking about Harlan NextGen, about everything Susan had said. He was thinking about those bills and letters in the drawer. He was thinking about that box in the garage labeled "Stiegl." All those boxes in the garage.

"Yeah," Tobey said. "I'm here."

"There's nothing to fear with Osip. He'll have your back."

Tobey was finding it hard to concentrate. "Why's he want these paintings so bad?"

"Are you kidding? With the value of Di Stiegl's other paintings, I mean, he's estimating what he can get on the market later on. You know, when it's safe to sell. In between he's got them stored and ready, just building up value, and—"

"Yeah, I get it," Tobey said. "Hey, I'm rolling a canvas now and have one more to get. I'll see you tonight."

"Rad," his brother said.

———

HE DESPERATELY NEEDED advice. He thought of texting Sophie. She had known him so well and he'd thought he'd known her. Wouldn't she be able to tell him what to do? It didn't matter. She wouldn't respond. What about Mom? She would tell him to put everything back on the walls and get on a plane and go to her. That wasn't what he wanted to hear. Maybe he should call Susan. She would at least understand something of what their father had been up to, maybe be able to calm Tobey's nerves and talk him out of all this. Maybe she could explain to him what the hell an NFT was and how Track got involved in them and why he'd needed to in the first place and what had happened to all the money the houses and property were supposed to be worth and not just tell him "I told you so" but he knew for sure that she'd say "I told you so" or at least mean it in every word and he wouldn't be able to blame her because, yeah, sure, she had told him so, and so he was alone. The stupid and myriad and glowering message of his life: Tobey Harlan was alone.

In the kitchen he opened the top drawer and pulled out each of the bills. They really were back payments, impending foreclosures, notifications from law offices, a lengthy document from the district attorney of Riverside County requesting documents related to an "ongoing investigation."

He sat down at the table. One of the dogs stood by him, giving him a sympathetic look. Tobey scratched the dog behind the ears, under the chin, between the shoulders. He thought of the paperwork out in the garage, and of how Track had to run a credit card at the golf club instead of just using his membership—he'd thought at the time that it seemed like he didn't have a membership, that it had been revoked. The way the man at the front desk had whispered with Track and seemed to give in to something. Tobey had read the event backwards, as if the club had made a mistake. That's probably what Dad wanted him to see. If his father needed money, he could sell the paintings and clear some of these debts. You could believe that they were too sentimental to him – or you could also believe that selling them would tell everyone in Palm Springs that Track Harlan had hit rock bottom.

Tobey wasn't stealing the paintings; he was making them *look* stolen.

How had James known Track had taken Tobey golfing? For years it had been a point of pride for James that he didn't talk to their father. That Tobey was a sucker for even keeping up with him. Now the fact of Harlan NextGen being a father-and-son company seemed more than self-evident. And worse: Tobey was the patsy. The one person who wouldn't know what was happening, the resident pothead, visiting because of a natural disaster, off to see his brother the night it "happens," still getting a payoff he thinks he earned on his own criminal enterprise. What better way to keep any questions from being asked? The patsy thinks he's the one who came up with the idea. He has no reason to know anyone else is involved.

And then Osip Yander would pay Track a reasonable price for works the insurance company would cover as well—creating two streams of profit—and Tobey would get his minuscule slice for having the courage and backstabbery to load the paintings into his car and drive them to Escondido. They go into storage, then come out a few decades later, when the principal owners have passed away. JESUS.

It was too crazy. His brain was fried. Too much weed, not enough sleep, the whole vast apocalypse out the window.

He went out to the garage, pulled the "Stiegl" box, and carried it into the dining room. On the table, he lifted its dusty lid. Inside were personal letters, someone's diary, hundreds of pages of Xerox copies, and between stacks of these, those old fax-machine cover letters with dates from the 1990s. They were all from Dad and addressed to someone named Cindy Miller-Stiegl, a person Tobey had never heard of. In thick black marker, dad had written little messages like "Here's the first six letters from Pomeroy" and "You'll find this part of the diary really useful" and "This one is the coup-de-grâce." At the back, typewritten pages of something titled *The Real Brackett: A Memoir*, by Frank Harlan, read like the endless rambles of a drunken Kerouac. "You'll love this part," claimed the fax page for that stuff.

Just what in the fuck was all this shit?

He piled everything back in the box and left it on the table. Then he returned to the master bedroom, to the closet, to the metal safe up on the sweater shelf. He set this on the bed. In the top drawer of their dresser, he found the tiny key. Nothing around here had changed since high school. He opened the flimsy little safe, dug past old paperwork, birth certificates, letters, and there, at the very bottom, found an envelope with sharp, clean edges, the words "George West Fine Art Appraisal" printed in black cursive letters across its center, the name Franklin Brown, Supervising Appraiser.

He didn't need to open it; opening it was overkill. But he did it anyway.

———

HE CALLED MR. Mercado after all. He wasn't even sure why. The car was already loaded. Gray was in the front floorboard in one of the secret filing boxes, holes cut in the top. Everything, as James had put it, was already happening.

"We're at Target," Mr. Mercado said, loudly, as if he were in a nightclub rather than a big-box store. "Getting a few things. I found an extended-stay place across town. We're going to Tinsley tomorrow. You?"

"Uh, yeah, soon." Tobey couldn't actually think of what to ask, what he wanted to get out of the old man. "I'm actually thinking about where to stay. Do you want to split a place or something? At least to start out?"

On the other end, a long silence. Then, whispered, "It's that young man who gave me a ride. Tony."

Tony?

"Listen, Tony," Mr. Mercado said. "I'm staying in Stockton awhile. My daughter and I buried the hatchet, you know? And I love seeing my grandchildren."

"Of course. Yeah. No problem at all. Just a passing thought."

"Good," said Mr. Mercado. "You know, I think we're heading into a golden age, me and her. Really close. So I want to thank you."

Tobey was standing on the bright cement driveway, squinting, feeling even more alone than he had only a few minutes ago. "Can I ask you some advice?"

"Sure thing."

"There's a thing I care about. It's my grandpa's. Well, a picture of him. My dad wants to sell it. Should I take it? Like, should I break the rules? Should I steal it?"

"A picture?"

"Yeah, a picture."

In the background, Mr. Mercado's daughter was talking, telling her father to meet her in electronics. "Okay," he said to her. "One minute. Tony?"

"Tobey."

"Tobey! Oh God! How rude is that, my friend? What an idiot I am." He chuckled. Tobey could see his ragged beard, his ponytail. Somehow he'd thought this total stranger would be a sort of replacement, an extra father. Complete nonsense. "You ever hear that Dylan song 'Idiot Wind'?"

"Not sure," said Tobey.

"One of his best. Wind blowing right through my head, buddy."

"Yeah, I don't think I know it."

Mr. Mercado coughed. "After what we've been through? If this picture matters to you, I'd take it. Do you even have any pictures?"

He thought of Sophie, the apartment, Gray napping in the sunlight. "Just what's on my phone."

"Then yeah, family's what matters most. You can build a new home around that picture, huh?"

"Yeah," Tobey said. "You're right."

THE TRIP TO Escondido had been a blur: mountains, desert, asphalt. The only thing keeping him in the moment had been the near-constant meowing of Gray, whom Tobey intermittently hushed by singing the words to "Beds Are Burning," which he'd heard in a gas station when they first left town. He'd pocketed the envelope with the art appraisal before pouring out several bowls of dog food, lifting the toilet lids for water, and unlatching the doggie door into the backyard. The two-hour drive had been without real music, without the news, just Gray, complaining, whining, a perfect soundtrack to Tobey's boiling-over mind, an echo of his own sinking terror.

Now he sat in the Walmart parking lot, waiting for his brother to show. He texted Sophie again, asking if she'd heard about Tinsley, if there was any chance the folks at Two Bears would let him in as a kind of refugee. He didn't expect an answer.

He was just beginning to feel sorry for himself again when a big white-and-silver SUV pulled up beside him, James at the wheel. Rangy, shaven-headed, as thin—Track would say—as kindling, Tobey's half-brother looked completely untroubled by what they were doing here. He hopped out of the car and came around to Tobey's door. "Jesus, that a cat in there? What a racket."

"I'm keeping the one of grandpa," Tobey said.

James's face went slack. His chin tucked into his sweatshirt. "What?"

"I took them," Tobey said. "Right now they're mine. I decided I don't want to sell the one with grandpa. That one I'm keeping."

"But there's a deal," James said. "Osip gets all three—"

"He can pay me one-third less. Or wait. That one's smaller. I'll take four hundred thousand for the two big ones."

"Man, quit fucking around," James said. "You're fucking this whole thing up."

One aisle over, a Latino family pushed a cart full of blue plastic bags to their car. The youngest child ran ahead, tapping on the trunk. The parents stared at the two Harlan sons.

"Do you need to call Osip or do you need to call Dad?" Tobey said. "Either way, I'm leaving with the painting of Grandpa."

James laughed that laugh of his. "You're talking out of your ass," he said. "You sound crazy, you know that? Take the fucking painting. Osip will go along with it. But you're being stupid. Where are you going to hide it when you go back? The cops will come, the insurance."

"I'm not going back, stupid."

"But that's—" James paced back and forth between the cars, clawing at his hairless head. "That's— That's fucking crazy. The whole thing comes apart if you do that."

"Dad's part of it, right? You guys called him yesterday?"

James's cheeks flexed, all bone and tendon, and that said everything that needed to be said. "You're royally fucking up here, brother. You're making this a lot more complicated than it needs to be."

Tobey shrugged. He opened the car door. Clicked the hatchback unlocked. "I don't care. Osip pays me, takes the two big ones, never hears from me again. Anything else and I call the police."

"Oh, you're a real tough motherfucker now? Fucking Robert fucking De Niro?"

"I didn't say that. All I said was I'm taking Grandpa's painting."

James stood next to him, wincing, gritting his teeth. From inside the car, Gray let out a long, low howl. "Fuck it," said James, finally. "Gimme the paintings and get the fuck out of here. Wait. Take this too. If you change your mind and need something to show you weren't home."

He handed him a torn ticket. Tonight's home game between Escondido High and San Pasqual. What an incredibly dumb alibi.

"Okay," Tobey said. He stood at the back of the car, watching his half-brother load the two paintings into the SUV. "When do I check TimeGreen?"

James rolled his eyes, sighed. The Latino family had loaded up their car, seeming to have forgotten they were there at all. Tobey realized he hadn't eaten anything in quite a long time. "Look in an hour," James said. "Two, tops. But don't flip out if it's a little later. Remember, I've got to smooth this whole shitshow out with a guy who doesn't usually get dicked around by fucking losers."

"Two hours," Tobey said. Then he reached for his door handle. "Don't follow me."

James smiled. "Fuck you, man."

————

HE DROVE ONWARD, skirting the north side of Los Angeles, and then joined the 5, straight up the spine of California. Hours fell behind him. At Lost Hills he stopped for gas at the ARCO station. The place had a desolate, middle-of-nowhere feeling: just a bunch of gas stations with a Denny's across the street. The actual town seemed to be farther in the distance, maybe a mile up the road. How had it come by such a name? There wasn't a hill in sight. Tobey wasn't sure if he'd ever seen anywhere so flat. So endless. He checked the TimeGreen app. Nothing had changed.

He put it out of mind. He had to keep driving. He figured at least getting into Oregon would be enough: over the state line. That was pretty damn far away. He could get up there, buy an RV and go off-grid, live in the forest, disappear from modern life. That was nothing special in the Northwest. Just another guy checking out of the system. He would finally start a garden of his own, maybe a farm.

If everything James and Dad and Osip Yander had planned worked as it was supposed to, he wouldn't have to go into hiding at all, he could end up with Mom in Wichita or Susan in Virginia.

An hour later he checked the app again, this time while still speeding up the highway. He kept fumbling the screen, looking back and away. As a truck passed, he let the phone go back to sleep again so that he had to type in his passcode to reopen. And when he looked then, to his surprise, it was there. Not just four hundred thousand but the entire half million. At least, that's how the app counted the value of the Bitcoins. However it was presented, it was more money than he'd ever imagined. He screamed a long vowel sound that never settled into the shape of a word. Gray made a worried noise in her box.

He understood now that every action in his life had been about getting here, to this moment. Like a clock, like a perfect machine, he'd taken all the correct turns. Everything had been a test; nothing had stopped him. Not just the incineration of Tinsley but all that had been in his way, all that had nearly crushed him: college and prison and dead-end jobs and a shitty family and Two Bears and Sophie and even some fucking tech dildo enhancing his little art collection. Tobey had made it. He'd thought for so long that he needed to find some kind of community or family to be happy, but really what he'd always needed was to be left alone, to take charge of his own life, to be responsible for his own actions. In a way, maybe Track was right about a few things. Now Tobey had left all his ties behind and would become someone unfettered and without history, a nameless man treading the frontier, a blazing and wild figure people would regard with their mouths agape. The Toyota flew into the dark, into something never before seen, into all that Tobey could ever be.

Free, free, an American at last.

ACKNOWLEDGMENTS

This novel went through several drafts as it closed in on its final shape and scope. In order to get to this stage, I am indebted to my early readers, including Ye Chun, Matt Modica, and Asako Serizawa. This book would be an outright mess without their insights, feedback, and friendship.

There is a wider group of folks who provided moral support during the writing of the book and believed in my work when I had doubts. Here I would like to thank Laura Warrell, Hernan Diaz, Nicola Barker, Rachel Beanland, Jon Pineda, Matt Bell, Yatika Starr Fields, Jason Christian, Shannon O'Neill, Tom Batten, Boris Dralyuk, and Kelli Jo Ford.

I would like to thank the Eastern Frontier Society for giving me space and time to work on part of this project way back in 2014, and Geoff Shandler for believing in me enough to publish my first book a few years later at Custom House.

This novel would not exist in any form without my incredible agent, Chad Luibl, who is the best cheerleader and psychoanalyst, friend and straight-talker, as well as one of the sharpest readers around. I also want to thank Maya Horn at Mariner Books, Roma Panganiban at J&N, and my genius copyeditor, Rachelle Mandik, all of whom helped get this book to the finish line.

But I would especially like to thank Kate Nintzel, the greatest of all editors, who has shepherded this book from its early stages, challenged me to discover its full potential, responded to my shifting ideas with great patience, and always knew what I was after with every single word. I can only give my infinite gratitude for your brilliance and openness to this book.

And to Crystal for all the years.

ABOUT THE AUTHOR

TK